THE BOOK OF AIR AND SHADOWS

As the ghost writer for a series of thrillers, Michael Gruber found happiness in writing but frustration in keeping his identity secret. Born October 1, 1940 in Brooklyn, Michael now lives in Seattle, WA. He attended Columbia University and received his Ph.D. in biology from the University of Miami. He has worked as a cook, a marine biologist, a speech writer, a policy advisor for the Jimmy Carter White House, and a bureaucrat for the EPA before becoming a novelist.

Visit www.AuthorTracker.co.uk for exclusive updates on Michael Gruber.

Also by Michael Gruber

Night of the Jaguar
Valley of Bones
The Tropic of Night

The Witch's Boy

THE Book of Air AND Shadows

MICHAEL GRUBER

HARPER

This novel is entirely a work of fiction.
The names, characters and incidents portrayed in it are the work of the author's imagination. Any resemblance to actual persons, living or dead, events or localities is entirely coincidental.

Harper
An imprint of HarperCollins*Publishers*
77–85 Fulham Palace Road,
Hammersmith, London W6 8JB

www.harpercollins.co.uk

This paperback edition 2007

2

First published in the USA by
HarperCollins Publishers 2007

ISBN-13: 978-0-00-725190-2

Set in Sabon by Palimpsest Book Production Limited,
Grangemouth, Stirlingshire

Printed and bound in Great Britain by
Clays Ltd, St Ives plc

For E.W.N.

Our Revels now are ended: These our actors
(As I foretold you) were all Spirits, and
Are melted into Ayre, into thin Ayre,
And like the baselesse fabricke of this vision
The Clowd-capt Towres, the gorgeous Pallaces,
The solmne Temples, the great Globe it selfe,
Yea, all which it inherit, shall dissolve,
And like this insubstantial Pageant faded
Leave not a racke behinde: we are such stuffe
As dreames are made on; and our little life
Is rounded with a sleepe . . .

– William Shakespeare,
The Tempest, act IV, scene i,
The First Folio, 1623

Acknowledgment

The author would like to thank Thomas D. Selz, Esq., of Frankfurt Kurnit Klein & Selz for his help explaining the mysteries of intellectual property law and for the view from his office, other than which he has not a thing in common with the intellectual property lawyer depicted in this novel.

THE BOOK OF AIR AND SHADOWS

1

Tap-tapping the keys and out come the words on this little screen, and who will read them I hardly know. I could be dead by the time anyone actually sees this, as dead as, say, Tolstoy. Or Shakespeare. Does it matter, when you read, if the person who wrote still lives? It sort of does, I think. If you read something by a living writer, you could, at least in theory, dash off a letter, establish a relationship maybe. I think a lot of readers feel this way. Some readers write to fictional characters as well, which is a little spookier.

But clearly I am not dead yet, although this could change at any moment, one reason why I'm writing this down. It's a fact of writing that the writer never knows the fate of the text he's grinding out, paper being good for so many uses other than displaying words in ordered array, nor are the tiny electromagnetic charges I am creating on this laptop machine immune to the insults of time. Bracegirdle is definitely dead, having succumbed to wounds received at the Battle of Edgehill in the English Civil War, sometime in late October of 1642. We think. But dead nevertheless, although before dying he composed the fifty-two-page manuscript that has more or less screwed up my life, or killed me, I don't know which yet. Or maybe the little professor was more to blame, Andrew Bulstrode, because he dropped the thing in my lap and then got himself murdered, or I could blame Mickey Haas, my old college roomie, who turned Bulstrode on to me. Mickey's still alive as far as I know, or the girl, the woman I should say, she has to carry some freight for this, because I seriously doubt I would have plunged as I did if I had not spied her long white neck rising from her collar there in the Brooke Russell Astor Reading Room of the New York Public Library, and wanted to kiss it so much it made my jaw hurt.

And Albert Crosetti and his unusual mom and his even more remarkable girlfriend, Carolyn, if girlfriend she is, all discoverers, and explicators, and decipherers, of Bracegirdle, my nemesis, without whom . . .

I don't forget the actual villains, but I can't really *blame* them. Villains are just there, like rust, dull and almost chemical in the stupid simplicity of their greed or pride. Remarkable how easy it is to avoid these, how often we fail to do so. Not to mention Mary, Queen of Scots (speaking of stupid), one more conspiracy added to her score, even if all she did in this case was to exist. Naturally, I blame my dad, the old crook. And why not? I blame him for everything else.

I see I am not doing this right. Okay, regain focus, at least array the facts, and begin by identifying the writer, me, Jake Mishkin, by profession an intellectual property lawyer. I believe that some gangsters may in the near future attempt to kill me. Although there is a kind of lawyer who can reasonably expect a certain level of physical danger as part of the employment picture, I am not that kind of lawyer – by design, actually. In my youth, I was familiar enough with such lawyers; a few of them, I have reason to believe, actually did get whacked, and so when I chose my field of law I made sure it was one in which the ordinary participants did not routinely pack heat. IP law has its share of violent lunatics (perhaps more than its share), but when they scream obscenities and threaten to kill you and your client, they are, almost all the time, speaking figuratively.

Even then, much of this venom is directed at litigators, and I am not a litigator. I don't have the personality for it, being a large peaceful person who believes that nearly all lawsuits, especially those involving intellectual property, are stupid, often grotesquely so, and that the underlying issues in virtually all of them could be solved by reasonable people in twenty minutes of conversation. This is not the mindset of a successful litigator. Ed Geller, our senior partner, is a litigator: he is a pugnacious, aggressive, flamboyant, obnoxious little man, a being who might have served as the template for any nasty lawyer joke, yet to my certain knowledge, Ed (an individual for whom I have, by the way, the utmost professional respect) has never heard the snap of a bullet fired at him with bad intent, or tussled with thugs bent on robbery, both of which are now part of my life experience.

I should say that IP law is divided broadly into industrial, which covers trademarks and patents, and probably software fits in this class too, and copyright, which covers all the arts of humanity – music, writing, films, images of all kinds, Mickey Mouse, etc., and I will record here the instinctive punch of the special key on my machine that adds the sacred (c) to the little rodent's name, and which I have just gone back and removed, because this is a new me writing this whatever it is. My firm, Geller Linz Grossbart & Mishkin, is a copyright house, and although each of the partners handles the full spectrum of copyright work, you could make a case that each of us has a different specialty. Marty Linz does TV and movies, Shelly Grossbart does music, Ed Geller is, as I said, our litigation chief. And I handle the literary business, which means I spend a good deal of time with writers, enough to realize that I am not and will never be one of their number. Quite a few of my clients have told me, often with a patronizing tone, that within every lawyer is a strangled poet, attributing the quotation to a variety of different authors. I don't really mind this sort of thing, since all these people are as helpless as kittens in the real, as opposed to the imaginary, universe. I can do cutting irony too, when I choose, which is not that often because, in all honesty, I admire the hell out of them. I mean, just making up a story out of your head and writing it so that someone else, a complete stranger, can read it and understand it and have real feelings about fictitious persons! Were you ever so unfortunate as to have a seat on a packed-tight plane or train where you were stuck in front of a couple of jerks exchanging anecdotes? You want to cut your throat out of sheer boredom, right? Or kill them. My point is, at the risk of repeating myself, it's damn hard to tell a coherent story. One client of mine told me that in order to write a story you start with everything that ever happened to anyone and carve away the parts that don't fit. This was a joke, however. Although I seem to be doing something like it now.

Perhaps, though, I am being too diffident. The legal profession is not without its creative side. We do a lot of writing, nearly all of it of interest only to other lawyers, but still there is the business of telling a story, setting a scene, laying out the facts and assumptions behind one's case. Young Charles Dickens started out as a court reporter, and scholars believe that this experience formed the sense of the human drama evident in his novels. Besides which, those novels are nearly all about crimes, mainly of the white-collar type. Mickey Haas is my source for that factoid, and he should know, as he is a professor of English literature at Columbia. And he is also the beginning of this story.

How much do you need to know about Mickey? Well, first of all you know something, because only a certain type of mature man allows himself to be called by a schoolboy diminutive nickname. I don't believe that 'Jake' is a nickname of the same type at all. He is certainly my oldest friend, but he is not entirely a serious person. Perhaps if he were a more serious person he would have shined the little professor on, and this business would not have occurred. Fittingly, therefore, I have ended up at Mickey's house, a cabin on Lake Henry deep in Adirondack State Park, where I am currently in . . . I suppose I am hiding out, but I can hardly bring myself to use such a dramatic term. In seclusion, let us say. Armed seclusion, let us say.

I have known Mickey (or Melville C. Haas, as it appears on the spines of his many books) since my youth, starting from our sophomore year at Columbia, when I answered an ad asking for a roommate to share a fourth-floor walk-up on 113th Street off Amsterdam Avenue. It is typical of Mickey that the ad was posted in the window of a Chinese laundry on Amsterdam rather than at the student union or with the university housing office. When I asked him later why he'd done that, he replied that he wished to solicit roommates from the subpopulation that wore professionally cleaned and ironed shirts. Oddly enough I was not really of that population; I owned a single dress shirt, a white-on-white De Pinna discarded by my father, and had gone into the little shop to have it pressed for a job interview.

At the time I was living in a greasy single-room-occupancy building, having recently run away from home. I was eighteen and grindingly poor, and the SRO was charging me fifteen bucks a day, kitchen and bath down the hall. Both of these rooms stank, in different but equally unpleasant ways, nor was the stench contained within either. So I was a little desperate, and it was a nice apartment, a two-bedroom with a partial view of the cathedral, and while dark in the manner of such long-hall uptown apartments, it was reasonably clean, and Mickey seemed a decent enough guy. I had seen him on campus before this, for he was a noticeable fellow: big, nearly as big as me, red-haired, with the pendulous lip and the protuberant, hooded blue eyes of one of the lesser Habsburgs. He wore tweed jackets and flannel pants and, in cold weather, an enveloping genuine Royal Navy duffel coat in camel, and he spoke in the precise, charmingly hesitant, anglophiliac accents we heard from those of Columbia's famous English lit professors who were unfortunate enough to have been born in the USA.

Despite these affectations, Mickey was, like most of New York's sophisticates and unlike me, a hick. He came from – I can't for the life of me recall the name of the place. Not Peoria, but like that. Kenosha. Ashtabula. Moline, maybe. One of those midsize midwestern industrial cities. Anyway, as he told me at that first interview, he was 'the scion of a small business empire' that made industrial fasteners. I recall asking him what those might be and he laughed and said he had no idea, but he always imagined an immense zipper the size of a freight train. It was the great-grandfather who'd made the money, and Mickey's dad and uncles just sat on the board and played golf a lot and were pillars of the community. Apparently there are thousands of such families across this nation, descendants of people who made their pile before taxes and globalization and hung on to it through safe investments and a horror of extravagance.

And then, inevitably, the talk got around to me, and inspired by his frankness, and sensing that he wished for some urban exoticism in his roommate, I told him that I was the scion of Isaac Mishkin, known to federal investigators and organized criminals from here to Vegas as Izzy the Book, or sometimes Izzy Numbers, a certified public accountant and a bookkeeper to the mob. To which his response was the familiar 'I didn't know there were Jewish gangsters,' and I explained about Murder Inc., Louie Lepke, Kid Reles, and Meyer Lansky, this last person being Dad's instructor and patron. That was, I believe, the first time I used my family history as a conversational gambit, and marked the end of the kind of shame I had writhed under all through high school. Why could I reveal all to Mickey? Because it was obvious that he had no idea what any of it meant, and regarded it as mere color, as if I'd been born in the circus or in a gypsy caravan. And there was, of course, yet more.

So you're Jewish? The natural query from Mickey here; I could tell he was surprised when I said no, actually, I'm not.

Now I hear the sound of a boat's motor out on the lake, a distant humming. It's the middle of the night. No one fishes at night. Or do they? I am not a fisherman myself. Perhaps there are fish that bite in the dark, like mosquitoes, perhaps night fishing is like ice fishing, an unlikely sport but widely practiced by self-torturing fanatics. Or perhaps it's them.

Back again. I went out on the deck clutching my weapon and listened, but I heard nothing. It must have been some automatic motor switching on in one of the other cabins. There are several dozen here, widely spaced, apparently deserted now, in the interval between the summer and the skiing season, and sound, I know, can travel amazing distances across the water, especially on so calm a night. I had a flashlight too, and I was so moronic as to turn it on, making myself a perfect target for anyone who might be lurking out there. Although they would not want to just shoot me, oh no, it would not be anything so easy. The sky was heavily overcast, and before I realized the foolishness of the action, I was startled to observe how the blackness over the lake utterly consumed the thin beam. I found this oppressive, depressing: the feeble beam lost in vast darkness. Oh, a little memento mori here? Or merely a reminder of the extremity of my current isolation.

Reading this over, I see I am still entangled in the distant past; this account will be another *Tristram Shandy* if I'm not careful, never getting to the fucking point.

To resume, however: on that particular afternoon, I fed Mickey Haas's exoticism jones with a little more of my personal history. No, as a matter of fact, I wasn't Jewish (here a sidebar on the matrilineal-descent rule) because my mother was a Catholic, and in those days, if a Catholic married a non, they were excommunicated unless they made their peace with the Church, the main part of which was swearing to raise the kids in the faith and we all were, me and my older brother, Paul, and my sister, the youngest, Miriam, the whole nine yards: baptism, catechism class, First Communion, altar service for us boys. And, naturally, lapsing, except for Paul, although Paul lapsed like a bastard, until he unlapsed and got his Vocation.

And the cherry on top? Okay, another flashback, and I believe I have time, because I suddenly realized that they would not be so foolish as to try to cross Lake Henry in this darkness, and why should they? So I have all night, I suppose. Anyway, here's my dad, eighteen years old, a Brooklyn wiseguy in training, a budding bookmaker of sports bets. Unfortunately for Dad's career, it was 1944 and he got drafted. Of course, he went to the dons on it, but they said he'd have to go unless he wanted a guy to run an ice pick into his ears, pop his drums, they'd be glad to help out there. He declined.

So a year or so later, Dad finds himself attached to Third Army headquarters as a cipher clerk, a good job for a nice Jewish boy, clean indoor work, never heard a shot fired in anger; besides it's March 1945 by now, and for the American forces in Europe, the fun part of World War II is just beginning. The Wehrmacht had essentially stopped fighting in the west and its legions were drifting docilely into the POW cages. The American soldiery soon discovered that anything could be had in exchange for American cigarettes – antiques, heirlooms, girls, unlimited amounts of intoxicants – and Dad was not slow in understanding that here was a once-in-a-lifetime opportunity to accumulate capital.

He was stationed in Ulm, where his official duties – coding messages for transmission – were not onerous. His real job was running a black market operation, moving fuel and food from army stores to the hungry civilian economy. He had no trouble setting up an organization, for Germany at the time was well supplied with underemployed thugs. These fellows had simply shed the handsome Nazi regalia they'd worn for twelve years and were open to opportunities in free-market, rather than state-sponsored, gangsterism. Dad was able to help with de-Nazification certificates, of course, and also used his accountancy genius to cover up the pilferage. He had no compunction about using the former Gestapo in his business. I think it tickled him to see these guys meekly taking orders from a Jew, and from time to time he'd covertly feed one of them to the authorities or, worse, to the Jewish revenge underground that was active at the time. It kept the others in line.

Although officially lodged in the Third Army headquarters – company barracks, Dad spent most of his time in a suite he maintained in the Kaiserhof Hotel in Ulm. Now, it is one of my father's eccentricities that he never enters a place of public accommodation through the main, or normal, entrance, but only through the service areas. I think he got this tic from the mobsters of the '40s, whose habit this also was, when visiting, say, the Copa or El Morocco. It may have had something to do with security, or maybe they did it just because they could; who was going to stop them? In any case, one night in the winter of 1946, returning from a nightclub and approaching the Kaiserhof via its kitchen entrance, he found my mother among the urchins and old ladies rooting through the garbage cans set out there. He ignored them, as he usually did, and they ignored him, except for one who, lifting her head from the filth, said, 'Give me cigarette, Joe.'

He looked, and there – only partially disguised by dirt and the soiled rag she wore around her head – was that face. I've seen photographs taken around then and it's quite amazing – she looks just like a younger Carole Lombard, blond and ridiculously exquisite. She was just a week past her seventeenth birthday. Of course he gave her cigarettes, of course he invited her up to his suite, for a bath, some nylons, a change of clothes. He was gaping. How had this creature survived unclaimed in 1945 Germany? Somewhat later, when she was clean and shiny, and draped in a pink silk robe, and he attempted the usual quid pro, he found out why. She had a pistol and she pointed it at him in a determined manner, and told him that war or no war, she was a good girl, the daughter of an officer, that she had shot three men before this and would shoot him too if he attempted to force her virtue. Dad was astounded, he was charmed, he was fascinated. This was, after all, an era when you could fuck a countess for a pound of sugar; that she could have successfully defended her body against a mass of wandering DPs and escaped prisoners, plus the dregs of one defeated army, plus the forces of three victorious ones, indicated a more than ordinary supply of moxie. One of Dad's words, *moxie*. According to him, my sister has all of it in our generation, me and my brother are moxie-deficient.

So, faced by the pistol, he relaxed, they had a drink and a smoke, and they exchanged life stories like the teenagers they were. Her name was Ermentrude Stieff. Her parents were dead, her father, the officer, had died in the summer of '44, and her mother had been killed by a stray bomb in the war's final weeks. This was in Regensburg. After that she'd wandered through the chaos of the Reich's final days, dragging the little suitcase she had stashed in her locker at the hospital. People did such prudent things in those days, so if what happened to her ever happened one would not be an utterly destitute refugee. Sometimes she traveled with groups of fleeing civilians, and here she had two means of establishing friendly relations, depending on the nature of the group. One of these items was a yellow star of the kind the Nazis made the Jews wear. The other was a narrow strip of black cloth with the words DAS REICH embroidered on it, which was designed to go around the lower left sleeve of the uniform worn by the soldiers of the Second SS-Panzer Division. She never told Dad where she got the yellow star, but she got the SS unit marker from Hauptsturmführer-SS Helmut Stieff, her father, fallen for the Fatherland in Normandy and, as a matter of fact, eventually buried in that Bitburg cemetery that got President Reagan briefly into trouble some years ago.

This tale says something about the deviousness of both my parents, and about my own character as well, I think, in that I chose to, in a manner of speaking, dine out on it to amuse or impress Mickey Haas that afternoon on 113th Street. It's the sort of thing many people would want to keep quiet about. My mother, by the way, denied the cute meeting entirely. She claimed she met Dad at a dance and thought that he was a gentleman. She never scrabbled through garbage cans, or shot anyone. She acknowledged that her father was indeed an SS officer, but she was careful to point out to us children the difference between the Waffen and the Allgemein, or general, SS, the people responsible for the camps. The Waffen-SS were brave soldiers fighting the horrible commie Russians.

Rambling. Basically who gives a shit at this juncture? I suppose the only lasting point is that truth was ever flexible in the hands of my parents. Not only was the far past in play, but they also often disagreed violently about events of the previous evening. This bred in me an early cynicism about historical fact, which makes my present situation, as a martyr, in a way, to different versions of four-hundred-year-old events, not a little ironic.

In any case, now we have to flash forward twenty or so years. As I've said, I became an intellectual prop lawyer, and Mickey has managed to stay within, nearly, a stone's throw of where we first met, for he is a professor of English literature at Columbia College. Mickey apparently draws a great deal of water in lit-crit circles. He was president of the Modern Language Association a few years back, which I gather is a big deal, and he seems to be respected with varying degrees of grudgingness by most of the interpretive fiefs into which the literary critical world seems nowadays to be divided. His field of study is William Shakespeare's plays, which is how he came to know Bulstrode. Professor B. was a visiting scholar at Columbia, also a Shakespeare expert, from the University of Oxford. One day, it seems, Bulstrode comes up to Mickey and says, 'I say, old bean, you wouldn't happen to know an intellectual property lawyer, would you?' and Mickey comes back with, 'As a matter of fact, I do.' Or something like that.

Let me recall the day. It was October 11, a Wednesday, the weather a little chilly, so that you knew the summer was over for sure, and there was a threat of rain in the air. People were in raincoats, as was I. I can see my raincoat, a tan Aquascutum, hanging on a coat-stand in the corner of my office, which is smallish for a partner's office, but comfortable enough. Our building is on Madison in the low Fifties, and through my window I can see one of the monitory spires of St Patrick's Cathedral, this view being nearly my sole connection to the religion of my youth. My office is furnished in an unpretentious, vaguely modern manner reminiscent of Jean-Luc Picard's ready room on the starship *Enterprise*. I have my diplomas and licenses up on the wall, together with three chrome-framed photographs: one is a professional portrait of my two kids as they looked a few years ago, and another is of me and my son Niko in which I am running alongside him as he learns how to ride a two-wheeler, a quite good shot taken by his mother. The only object in the room that one might consider unusual is the third photograph, which shows a large, crop-haired young man in red-white-and-blue weight-lifting togs holding high a heavy barbell. The barbell is so heavy that it bends slightly at each end, for this athlete is in the 1921/2 lb+ class, the heaviest, and he is lifting over five hundred pounds. Five hundred thirty-two, to be precise. This person is me, and the photo was shot at the Mexico City games in 1968, where I was part of the U.S. Olympic team. This was more weight than I had ever lifted in the clean-and-jerk and would have got me the bronze medal, but I messed up on the snatch, and Joe Dube took it. I have kept up training since then, at a lower level, of course, but I can still yank somewhat more than a quarter of a ton over my head.

A perfectly useless skill, which is why I like it, why I took it up. I started at ten with a set of homemade weights and lifted all through high school and college. At present I'm a hair over six feet two and I weigh two-fifty, more or less, eighteen-inch neck, fifty-two chest, and the rest to match. Many people take me for a fat person, which I certainly am not. Since the coming of Arnold, people tend to confuse the use of weights to sculpt the body with competitive weight lifting. They are completely different enterprises. Weight lifters almost never have cute or pretty bodies, which are in any case more to do with the absence of subcutaneous fat than with strength. Any serious heavy-class weight lifter could break Mr Universe over his knee. Only potentially, of course: I have found it to be the case that large, strong people are mild of temperament unless they are into steroids, which is more and more common nowadays, I fear. I remain non-steroidally mild, however.

I see I have drifted yet again. I was just trying to set myself in my office on the relevant day, which was quite an ordinary one, the morning spent at a meeting about Chinese T-shirt piracy of a rock album image, an increasing part of the normal practice of IP law. Quiet meetings, billable hours, the marshaling of expertise, and the delicate suggestion that lawsuits in this business are largely a waste of time, for Chinese piracy of rock album cover images is an unavoidable cost of doing business in our fallen world. I returned to my own office after this meeting – it was about twenty minutes to twelve and I was already looking forward to lunch – but as I passed my secretary's desk she hailed me. My secretary is Ms Olivia Maldonado, a young woman both decorative and competent. Many in the office lust after her, as do I, but it is an iron rule here at Geller Linz Grossbart & Mishkin that we don't screw around with the staff, a rule I entirely support. It was nearly the sole instance of my forbearance in that department, and I was stupidly proud of it.

I recall she was wearing an outfit I particularly liked, a gray skirt, somewhat clingy, and a dusky rose cardigan sweater with the top two buttons open. Pearl buttons. Her shiny dark hair was wound up on her head and clasped with an amber comb, exposing a small brown beauty mark on the base of her neck, and she had the scent of iris faintly about her.

There was a man waiting to see me, I learned; he had no appointment, could I squeeze him in? A Mr Bulstrode. Walk-ins are rare in our business – it's not as if we're upstairs from the bail bondsman – and I was intrigued.

I went into my office and sat behind my desk and shortly Ms M. showed the fellow in, man with a briefcase. Bulstrode had dressed his portly form in a brownish three-piece suit of well-worn tweeds and wore tortoiseshell spectacles on his little marshmallow of a nose. Worn Burberry draped over arm, good oxblood shoes on his feet and a paisley square in the breast pocket; thin snuff-colored hair moderately long and combed across the scalp, a little vanity there. His face was flushed, up from the neck and across the cheeks. He blinked colorless lashes at me as we shook hands (soft, dampish). I thought 'professor' and I was correct: he introduced himself as Andrew Bulstrode, a professor indeed, late of Oxford in the U.K. and visiting at Columbia. Professor Haas good enough to give me your name . . .

I sat him and after the usual chat asked what I could do for him. He said he wanted some IP advice. I said he'd come to the right place. Asked if he could put me a hypothetical. I don't like hypotheticals because when the client talks in hypotheticals it usually means he's not going to be frank about the real. But I gave him the nod. Suppose, he said, that I discovered a manuscript of a literary work, a lost literary work. Who would own the rights to it? I said, that would depend. Author dead? Yes. Before or after 1933? Before. Heirs or assigns? None. I told him that under the U.S. Copyright Revision Act of 1978, unpublished manuscripts created before January 1, 1978, by authors who died before 1933, became part of the public domain on January 1, 2003. His face fell a little at that, from which I gathered that he had wanted a different answer, such as that what he had discovered might be copyrightable. He asked whether by chance I knew the relevant law obtaining in the United Kingdom, and I was happy to answer that I did, for our firm does a good deal of consultation back and forth across the gray Atlantic. I told him that the U.K. was friendlier to creators than the U.S., to wit: that the author had indefinite common law copyright to unpublished work, and if published or performed, the copyright ran fifty years from first publication or performance. The author being dead in our case, I continued, the copyright would run fifty years from the calendar year in which the provision of the Copyright Act of 1988 came into force, i.e., fifty years from January 1, 1990.

Here he nodded and asked about ownership – who held the copyright in an unpublished manuscript of a deceased author? I explained that under British law, unless ownership was established by testamentary evidence, such copyright reverted, under U.K. intestacy law, to the Crown. I love saying that, by the way, *the Crown*; the image of Elizabeth II R rubbing her hands in glee as the lucre pours in, corgis yapping around the piles of bright guineas.

He didn't like this part either. Surely not, he said. Whatever happened to finders keepers? What about possession being nine-tenths of the law?

To which I answered that these saws were true enough, but also that should he publish or perform such a work he should be prepared to have the Crown come after him, and if he published or performed in the U.S., he might have a hard time defending his copyright from outright piracy; and now would he care to leave the hypothetical and tell me what was going on?

I said this in a manner that suggested I was about to wish him good day were he not prepared to be more forthcoming. He considered the request for some time in silence, and I observed that sweat beads had accumulated on his forehead and upper lip, although it was cool in my office. At the time I thought he might be ill. It did not occur to me that he was badly frightened.

I have been in this business long enough to tell when a client is being frank and when not, and Professor Bulstrode was clearly in the latter class. He said he had come into possession (that's a phrase that always raises my hackles) of documentary evidence, a manuscript from the seventeenth century, a personal letter from a man named Richard Bracegirdle to his wife. He thought this manuscript was genuine, and that it revealed the existence of a certain literary Work, of enormous potential import to scholarship, the existence of which had never been suspected. This manuscript alone was enough to launch a field of study, but to have The Work itself . . .

When he said The Work, I heard the capital letters and so I include them here.

What is The Work? I asked.

Here he demurred, asking instead about the protocols of confidentiality between lawyer and client. I explained that our normal retainer was twenty-five hundred dollars and that once his check was in my hands no power on earth could extract the substance of any conversation the two of us might have, save only an admission that he was about to commit a felony. With that, he drew out a leather-covered checkbook, wrote out the check, and handed it over. Then he asked me if we had a safe on the premises. I said we had locked, armored, fireproof files. Not good enough. I said we had an arrangement with the Citibank downstairs, a large safe-deposit box. He opened his briefcase and handed me a heavily taped manila envelope. Would I secure this for him, temporarily?

There's that engine noise again.

THE BRACEGIRDLE LETTER (1)

Banbury 25th Octobr. Ann. Dom. 1642

My dear goode wife may the blessinges of almighty God be upon you & oure sonne. Well Nan I am killed as you fortolde & I bid you have a care with youre foretellinges lest they take you up for a witch, for I am shot threw the tripes with a balle it is lodged in my spine or so saith the chirurgeon here; his name is Tolson & a trew Christian man: Tom Cromer my matrosse you will recall hym a goode loyal boye though he ran in the fight did return & find mee among the fallen & found a horse & brought mee here to Banbury-towne. Mr Tolson is lodging me for 2d per daye all founde a good price in these tymes but he sayes my case is such as I will never pay so much as a shillinge & so I write my laste before I am taken uppe to heavene as I hope or (what is more lykley) put down in the fierie pitte as I am sure by my lyfe I am not one of the Electe. But it is in Gods handes & I caste myselfe uppon his mercy.

This was the waye of it. You knowe we marched out late in sommer from London in the artillerie park of my Lord Essex his army when the King refused the rights of Parliament & made to bring his power gainst his owne people to crush theyre liberties. At Northhampton we hearde that the King wase at

Worcester & on the road south so we hastened in a craweling waye to place oure armes between him & London. We failed this through want of speede & our force was spread out across the lande: yet hearing the King was to attack Banbury we rallyed us & gathered north of there near Kineton towne & there the King turned & met us.

Now you know Nan that Warre is like the game children play with paper, stone & fyre as: paper covereth stone, stone crusheth fyre, &c: & the figure I intend is this – horse can capture gonnes, for wee may fyre one volley but then they are upon us before we can shoote again. Foot can defeat horse, for the horsemen will not dare the wall of pike, so your foot must guard the gonnes in batterie: the gonnes can smash the pike battalions of the enemie into disarray, so the horse can get at 'em. Thus the generals art is to make all work together. So wee had set up our batterie & made good practice that morning having more gonnes than the royales did & had a shotte at the Kinges partie but not the range which wase too bad but could see him beneath the royal banner & Prince Rupert and otheres of his trayne. Wee were guarded afront by Sir Nicholas Byrons troop being the last on the left flanke of oure force oure flanke resting upon a hedge and som woods.

Then the Kinges horse attacked on oure right & wee could see the smoakes & banneres flying & what happened but oure right being pressed back, oure left shifted thereto, a thinge most common in battel & the wyse guard against it. But these fellowes were scarce skilled in warre & soe they moved & soe our left flanke came loose from the hedges & hung in aire. Now Nan twere never good practice to trail a flanke before Rupert of the Rhine. You well know I have sayde that they are noddles in the mayne who serve the King but they are cavaliers for all that & the one thynge they can doe is charge with sword and pistol: soe with a greate crie they did. They struck us hard & rolled up oure foote like drapers linen & then they were upon the gonnes. I snatched up a partizan & made to defend my piece (for though the gonnes fly no colours and hath not honour so tis sayde, yet I would be shamed to see my pieces lightly taken) but a cavalier stod off & shot his carbine at me & I fell & lay there all the day, not beeing able to feele or move my legges until young Tom found me when dusk wase nigh, & carreyed mee to where I now am to die. I know not even now who won the daye.

Soe now I write you being the laste thynge on earth I doe & I thinke me that though God did not call mee to stande among the greate still I am a man not a clod & my story bears telling if onlie to holpe in the breding of my sonne: who needs muste rise to manhoode lacking what ever poore model I might have supply'd.

2

On the evening of the little fire, the revelatory fire that changed his life, Albert Crosetti was working in the basement as usual, and so was the first one to detect it. He was there because Sidney Glaser Rare Books kept its computer in the basement. Mr Glaser did not like the devices and resented that they were now essential to earning a living in the book trade. He preferred to proffer his treasures by hand, in a well-lit, paneled, carpeted room like the showroom in his shop. But some years ago, when in the market for a bookshop clerk, he had accepted the current reality and enquired of all candidates whether they knew enough about computers to set up and maintain a Web-based catalog, and he had hired the first nonsmoking person answering in the affirmative. This was Albert Crosetti, then age twenty-four. Crosetti came from Queens, and still lived there in a brick bungalow in Ozone Park, with his mother. She was a retired research librarian and widow, with whom he enjoyed a relationship minimally fraught with Freudian katzenjammer. Crosetti wished someday to make films and was saving up money to go to the famous film school at New York

University. He was a graduate of Queens College and had started working for Glaser within a month of receiving his diploma. He liked his job; the hours were regular, the pay fair, and while Glaser could be something of a nut when it came to antique books, the old man knew he had a good thing in Crosetti and let him handle the mail-order business and its electronic impedimenta almost without supervision.

His workspace consisted of a tiny alcove whose walls were shelves and glass cabinets and crates, all packed with books. Here he updated the online catalog, working from lists drawn by Mr Glaser's fountain pen in the beautiful penmanship of bygone days. He also kept the inventory current and accessed the various systems whereby requests for items were transmitted from bibliophiles around the world, printing these off for the proprietor's later attention. Beyond that, his duties included unpacking and shipping books and other factotum work associated with the trade. He rarely ventured upstairs to the showroom, where quiet, well-dressed people handled old volumes with the care and tenderness due newborn babes.

The only unpleasant aspect of this work was the smell, compounded of old books, mice, the poisons laid to keep these at bay, drains, heated paint, and beneath all – an olfactory bass note – the stink of frying grease. This last came from next door, an establishment called the Aegean, a joint typical of midtown New York, purveying Danish pastries, toast, eggs, and weak coffee in the morning, and sandwiches, fried substances, and fizzy drinks for a couple of hours around noon. It was somewhat past that hour just now, on a fine July day, and Crosetti was wondering whether he should stop tweaking the Web site and take a lunch break or just phone and have the kid bring over a sandwich.

Or he could skip lunch. He often thought that he was probably taking in from the Aegean sufficient calories through his lungs, mainly fat. Crosetti was not an exerciser, and he enjoyed his mother's cooking: a bit of a spare tire hung around his waist, a face more jowly than he liked stared back at him from the mirror when he shaved. He considered asking the upstairs clerk to join him, assuming that Carolyn Rolly lived upon substances grosser than air scented by old books. She occasionally ate with Glaser, he knew; they would close up the upstairs and go out, leaving Crosetti laboring below. He allowed this fantasy a brief bubble of life, then shrugged it away. Rolly was a book person, and he was, at bottom, not, even though he had learned a good deal about the book business (prices and conditions and so on) as part of his work with the computer. She was not a beauty by the prevailing standards of meat magazines or movies, being tall enough but somewhat more solidly built than was the current fashion. Crosetti had read somewhere about women who looked better out of clothes than in them, and he thought Rolly was one of these. Clothed, certainly, she was undistinguished: she wore black like everyone else.

But there was something about her that drew the eye. The shiny, smooth dark hair hung neck length, held away from her face with a silver clasp. The nose was sharp and seemed to have more than the usual number of component bones making odd little corrugations all over it. Her lips were unfashionably thin and pale, and when she spoke you could see that her teeth were odd too, the incisors especially long and dangerous looking. Her eyes were ridiculously blue, like (duh!) the sky in summer with, he thought, unnaturally tiny pupils. If not a book person, Crosetti was still a reader, his tastes in novels running largely to fantasy and science fiction, and sometimes he entertained the notion that Ms Rolly was a vampire: it would explain the dark clothes, the physical presence, those teeth – although a vampire who came out in the day.

Perhaps he would invite her to lunch and ask her. It would be a conversation starter; he could not imagine what else they might have to talk about. She had been working for the shop when Crosetti started there, and over the course of several years they had yet to share more than a few formal sentences at a time. She came to work on a bicycle, which suggested that she lived more or less in the neighborhood. The neighborhood being Murray Hill, this meant she had money, because one could not afford to live locally on what Glaser paid. In Crosetti's experience, young, attractive, and wealthy Manhattan women did not yearn for semihefty Italian guys who lived with their mothers in Queens. Rolly might be an exception, though; one never could tell . . .

Crosetti was working on a particularly tricky bit of hypertext markup language at the same time as he was thinking these amusing thoughts. He was thinking about Rolly's eyes, the element of the electric in her glance that made him wish for more eye contact than he ordinarily got. His mind was so thoroughly occupied with those eyes and the computer work that it took a good while before he noticed that the frying smell had waxed unusually strong, was more than a mere odor, was actual smoke. He rose, coughing a little now, and made his way to the back of the basement so that he faced the party wall that divided the bookshop basement from that of the restaurant. The smoke was thicker here, he could actually see the sooty tendrils creeping from cracks in the old brick. And the wall was warm under his hand when he touched it.

Quickly he clattered up the wooden stairs to the shop proper – deserted, and the sign with its paper BACK-AT clock hung in the door, for it was lunchtime, and Glaser had obviously taken his protégée for a bite. He went out to the street, where he discovered a small crowd milling around the entrance to the Aegean, from the door of which issued plumes of greasy gray smoke. Crosetti asked one of the crowd what was going on. Some kind of fire, the man said, in the kitchen. Now he heard sirens. A police car rolled up and the officers started to clear people away. Crosetti darted back into the shop and down the stairs again. The smoke had become dense, choking, bearing a nauseating tang of ancient grease. Crosetti pulled his backup CD from the computer and then ran upstairs, directly to the locked case where the most valuable items were kept. Glaser had the key, of course, and after a brief hesitation Crosetti kicked in the glass. The first thing he grabbed was the McKenney and Hall *History of the Indian Tribes of North America*, in three folio volumes, the prize of the establishment. Out of the case, onto a table. On top of that the three-volume *Pride and Prejudice* first edition, and then the *Leaves of Grass*, another prime first, giving him a short stack worth a quarter of a million retail. He picked these up, made for the door, halted, and uttered a despairing curse as he recalled that the new Churchill *Voyages* was still downstairs. He hung there in an agony of indecision – rescue these in hand or go down for the *Voyages*?

No, he had to go down again. He put the books back on the table, but as he reached the head of the basement stairs, a heavy hand grabbed the back of his jacket and demanded to know where the fuck he thought he was going. It was a big fireman in a smoke mask, who was apparently also not a book person, although he did let Crosetti come out with the three precious titles from the case. The young clerk was standing on the sidewalk outside the security line the cops had established, gasping, filthy, clutching these to his breast when Glaser and Rolly arrived. Glaser took in what his clerk was holding and asked, 'What about the Dickens?'

He meant the 1902 edition with extra watercolor illustrations by Kyd and Green. Sixty volumes. Crosetti said he was sorry. Glaser tried to push past a pair of cops, who stopped him, grabbed him, yelled angry words, which Glaser returned.

Looking up at Crosetti, Rolly asked, 'Did you manage to get the Churchill out of the basement?'

'No. I was going to, but they wouldn't let me.' He explained about the big fireman.

She sniffed the air. 'Everything in there is going to smell like bad French fries. But you saved the *Indian Tribes* at least.'

'And Jane and Walt.'

'Yes, them too. Sidney doesn't think you know anything about books.'

'Just what they cost,' he said.

'Yes. Tell me, if that firefighter hadn't shown up, would you have dashed into the flames to save the *Voyages*?'

'There weren't any flames,' he said modestly, 'or hardly any.' She gave him the first smile that ever she gave him, the toothed grin of a young wolf.

The next day they took stock and discovered that, aside from some smoke damage, and the smell, the showroom and its contents were unharmed. It turned out that in the kitchen of the restaurant next door was a hole in the floor, and into this hole over the years the cooks had poured odd lots of grease when the main grease barrel was full or when they were too pressed or lazy to carry the stuff to where it belonged. This had pooled down in the basement, between the walls, and somehow ignited. The firefighters had smashed through the party wall in their efforts to halt the burning, and as a result much of what had occupied the bookstore's basement was wrecked by heat, collapsed brickwork, or water. The packing case containing the six volumes of Awnsham and John Churchill's *Collection of Voyages and Travels* (1732 edition) had unfortunately taken the brunt of the wall's collapse. These volumes now lay upon a worktable amid the ruins, around which table stood Mr Glaser, Crosetti, and Rolly, like cops examining a murder victim, or rather the two young people were like cops – Mr Glaser was like the victim's mom. Tenderly he ran his fingers over the crushed, soaked, and blackened full-calf cover of volume one.

'I don't know,' he said in a little creaky voice, 'I don't know if it's even worth the effort. What a colossal loss!'

'Wasn't it insured?' asked Crosetti. They both stared at him in distaste.

'Of course it was insured,' Glaser replied tartly. 'That's hardly the point. This is probably the finest set of the Churchill 1732 in the world. Or was. It was in the library of one of the minor Godolphins, probably untouched and unread from the time it was delivered until the library was broken up at the death of the last heir in 1965. Then it belonged to a Spanish industrialist for nearly forty years and then I purchased it at auction last month. It was perfect, not a trace of wear or foxing or . . . oh, well. Impossible to recover. They'll have to be broken for the maps and illustrations.'

'Oh, no!' exclaimed Rolly. 'Surely they can be restored.'

Glaser peered at her over his thick half-glasses. 'No, it simply doesn't make economic sense, when you calculate what restoration would cost and what we might realize from a rebound and doctored set.' He paused, cleared his throat:

'No, we'll have to break them, I'm afraid.' This in the tone of an oncologist saying 'stage four melanoma.'

Glaser issued an immense sigh and waved his hands weakly, as if chasing gnats.

'Caro, I'll leave it in your hands; do it quickly before the mold starts.' He shuffled away to his private office.

'He wants you to break the volumes?' Crosetti asked.

'It's not a complex task. But we have to dry the set out,' she replied, a distracted look on her face. 'Look, the fact is I'm going to need some help.' She seemed to notice him again, and an appealing expression came to her face, a look he rather liked. He mimed searching for someone behind him and said, 'Oh, not me! Man, I failed finger painting. I never once colored completely inside the lines.'

'No, this involves handling paper towels. The drying operation has to go on all day and night, maybe for days.'

'What about our jobs?'

She gestured broadly to the environs. 'This place'll be closed for a month while they fix it up, and you can run the mail-order operation from any computer, can't you?'

'I guess. Where are you going to work out of?'

'My place. I have a good deal of space. Let's go.' She hoisted two of the folio volumes onto her hip.

'You mean now?'

'Of course. You heard what Glaser said: the faster we begin, the less damage from the damp. Get the rest of them. We'll wrap them in paper for the trip.'

'Where do you live?' he asked, lifting the ruined volumes up against his chest.

'In Red Hook.' She was already at the shipping desk, stripping brown paper from a large roll.

'You come from Red Hook on a bicycle?' Crosetti had never been to Red Hook, a region on the southeastern coast of Brooklyn behind what used to be the Brooklyn docks. There are no subway stops in Red Hook, because until the shipping industry moved to New Jersey, everyone in the area worked longshore jobs and walked to work, nor was there any reason for outsiders to go there, unless they wanted their heads busted.

'No, of course not,' she replied as she wrapped volume six. 'I bike over to the river and take the water taxi from the Thirty-fourth Street pier.'

'I thought that was real expensive.'

'It is, but my rent is cheap. You should put those in plastic.' Crosetti looked at the book he was holding. It had oozed a sooty liquor down the front of his tan trousers. For the first time he regretted not dressing entirely in black, like so many of his hipper peers; or like Carolyn. She excused herself and went upstairs, leaving him to wrap the rest of the volumes.

When this had been done, the two of them took off east, with their burden stuffed into the wire panniers of Rolly's bike, a heavy, worn vehicle of the type favored by food delivery personnel or, some years ago, by the Vietcong. His few attempts to make conversation being greeted by short answers, he fell silent; we're not on a date, bub, seemed to be the message. On the other hand, it was a fairly pleasant day, in the low eighties, the humidity somewhat less than tropical, and being paid to stroll across town with even a silent Carolyn Rolly beat the hell out of doing inventory in a grease-smelling basement. Crosetti looked hopefully ahead to what might occur in the woman's apartment.

Crosetti had never been on a water taxi. He found traveling on one greatly superior to a subway journey. Rolly secured her bike to the rails at the front of the craft and stood by it, and he stood by her, with his hand on the same rail. The other people on the boat seemed to be tourists.

'Are you all right?' Rolly asked him as they bounced down the middle of the East River.

'Of course. I'm an old sailor. I spent half my life when I was a kid out on Sheepshead Bay fishing in crummy little rental boats. Would you like me to hold you out over the prow like Kate Winslet on the *Titanic*?'

She gave him one of her formal deadpan looks and turned forward again. Definitely not a date.

Carolyn Rolly lived on the second floor of a Civil War-era warehouse made of blackened brick, on the corner of Van Brunt and Coffey streets. Crosetti held the folios while she hauled her bicycle up the dark, splintery stairs. There was a heavy smell in the air he could not identify, sweetish and chemical at the same time. The door to her apartment was thick wood strapped with iron, painted battleship gray.

Inside was a loft, and not the kind millionaires move into in SoHo. It was a room around sixty by thirty feet in area, with dark-stained wood-planked floors, from which there rose at intervals cast iron columns reaching to the gray stamped-tin ceiling high above. The walls were red brick, edged roughly with crumbling, filthy mortar. The room was oriented east-west, and light flooded in from tall dirty windows on either end, some of whose panes had been replaced by squares of plywood or grayish, tattered plastic sheeting.

Rolly leaned her bike against a wall by the door, walked toward the window, and placed one of the folio packages on a long table. Crosetti followed, looking about curiously for some door or hallway that led to the living quarters. Rolly was already unwrapping a book. Coming closer, Crosetti observed that the table was handmade, its top composed of many short boards laminated edge-on and sanded to a satiny finish. The six stout legs were constructed of what looked like yellow fiberglass. He placed the rest of the books down on it. It felt as solid as a marble plinth and had the simple elegance of the sort of thing you saw in the design showrooms.

She unwrapped the folios and lined them up on the table. Even he could see that two of the volumes had sustained irreparable damage to their covers.

'Nice place,' Crosetti said, when it became clear that Rolly was not about to start a conversation, or offer tea or a beer. No response. Her head was bent down over the ravaged cover of volume one.

'What's that smell?' he asked.

'Mainly malt. There was a brewery here for about a century and then they stored chemicals.'

'Mind if I look around?'

Rolly answered this with 'There's a big package of paper towels on those shelves on the south wall. Bring it over here.'

Crosetti took his time and made a slow circuit around the huge room. In one corner he found stacks of wooden pallets, dozens of them, and also stacks of boards resulting from their disassembly. The south wall was almost entirely occupied with shelving and cabinets constructed from this wood, sanded smooth, stained, and varnished. The shelving was packed with books, all hard-covered, most with dust jackets, some with plastic covers. He looked in vain for any personal items, framed photos, souvenirs.

The work surfaces in the kitchen (which consisted of a double hot plate, a tiny microwave oven, and a small, chipped porcelain sink) were made of the same edge-on, tightly laminated planking as the big worktable, but coated thickly with amber-colored resin. Along the east wall he found a pallet of pallets, with a futon neatly rolled up on it and a table made from a cable spool and two of the sort of chairs one finds on trash heaps, all competently restored and painted cream. A chair for her and one for a visitor? Spoke to a social life and he wondered who. In the southeast corner an enclosure had been built, also out of pallet wood, within which he assumed was her toilet. Against this leaned a large battered wardrobe, hidden from the rest of the room by a folding screen of laquered wood and decoupaged paper. Interesting: she lived alone but had rigged a privacy screen. Spoke to sexual activity.

He was about to take a peek behind this screen when Rolly called out testily. He found the six-pack of paper towels and rejoined her. Between every ten pages in the damp volumes a pair of paper towels had to be interleaved, and these towels had to be changed every hour. While they dried, the wet volumes were laid flat on the worktable and weighted down with cloth-covered steel plates to prevent swelling.

'What I don't get,' said Crosetti when the books were all interleaved and weighted, 'is why you're drying the whole of the set if you're just going to break them for the maps and illustrations. Why not just pull the good stuff and junk the rest?'

'Because it's the right way to do it,' said Rolly after a brief hesitation. 'The plates would curl if you pulled them wet.'

'I see,' he said, not seeing at all, seeing the young woman in an entirely new and not very attractive light. He sat on a stool and studied her profile. 'So . . . this is kind of interesting,' he said. 'Watching books dry. I don't think I ever did it before. Maybe you could point out the highlights, so I don't miss anything.'

He grinned at her and was rewarded with a tiny azure spark in her eyes, while her mouth assumed the set of one trying not to smile. 'You're welcome to read a book while you wait,' she said. 'I have a good many of them.'

'Alternatively, we could converse. I could tell you all my hopes and dreams and you could tell me yours, and the hours would fly past, and we could get to know each other.'

'Go ahead,' she replied after a brief pause, uninvitingly.

'No, ladies first. You look like you've had a lot more interesting life than I have.'

A shocked expression appeared on her face. She gaped, then snorted, then blushed. 'Sorry,' she said. 'Oh, God! That is so opposite from the case. Why would you imagine that? That I have an interesting life?'

'Oh, this place, for one thing. You live in a warehouse in Red Hook . . .'

'It's a loft. Thousands of people in the city live in lofts.'

'No, they live in apartments in loft buildings. And usually they have furniture they bought in stores, not made out of pallets. Are you even legal here?'

'The landlord doesn't mind.'

'Assuming he knows. Also you're a bookbinder. Unusual, wouldn't you say? How did you get into it?'

'And how about *your* hopes and dreams?'

'And, see? You're secretive too. There's nothing more interesting than that. Okay. Here's the whole deal. I'm twenty-eight and I live with my mom in Queens, Ozone Park. I'm saving money so I can go to film school, which at the rate I put it away will be a month after my fifty-second birthday. I should take out a loan, but I'm scared of getting into debt.'

'How much do you have saved?'

'About three and a half grand.'

'I have more than that.'

'I bet. Glaser probably pays you more than he pays me, you get commissions on sales, you live in Red Hook, and you own two outfits, what you're wearing now and the one with the collar. What are you saving for?'

'I want to go to Gelsenkirchen in Germany and take an apprenticeship at the Buchbinderei Klein.' When he didn't react, she added, 'Obviously, you've never heard of it.'

'Of course I have. Buch-whatever Klein. It's like the Harvard of the bookbinding world. But I thought you already knew all about it. You have all the gear . . .' He gestured to the racks of tools laid out on the worktable, the cutting press and plow, whetstones, knives, leather pillows, and paste pots. It all looked very eighteenth century; Crosetti imagined that the Churchill *Voyages* had been bound with tools quite like these.

'I barely know anything,' she protested.

'Really.'

'I mean compared with what you have to know to make a book from scratch. I can do *repairs*. It's like . . . it's like the difference between being able to repair a cracked Ming porcelain vase and *making* one out of clay and glazes.'

'Uh-huh. And while we're sharing confidences like this, getting cozy and all, why don't you tell me what you're going to do with the Churchill when you've got it doctored?'

'What? I'm not doctoring them. I'm going to break them.'

Red splotches appeared on her cheeks and her eyes darted – picture: girl caught in lie.

'No,' he said confidently. 'If you were going to break them you would have just airfreighted them to Andover and had them vacuum dried. No muss, no fuss. You get them back dry and clean and snip snip. You look surprised. I'm not what you'd call a book guy but I'm not stupid either. So what are you going to do with the doctored books?'

'Sell them,' she said, looking down at the sodden volumes.

'As doctored?'

'No. Everyone knows we own an extremely fine set. There are private clients who like discretion. They have funny money they want to stash in collectibles. Glaser does it all the time. Look, he's going to declare these a total loss to the insurance company, and show them the invoices for the broken-out items. They'll come to, I don't know, not more than twenty-five hundred, and the insurance company will pay him the difference between that and what he paid for the set, figure around twenty thousand dollars.'

'Which is approximately the amount you're planning to divert to your own pocket when you sell to your shady character. Isn't there a word for that? Begins with an *s* . . . ?'

'It's not . . . it's *nothing* like stealing. He told me to break the books. As far as Glaser's concerned, the set no longer exists. He's made whole by the insurance company and I'm profiting from my own skill. It's no different from making things out of pallets that're being thrown away.'

'Um, no, actually it's not the same thing at all, but that's my Jesuit high school education talking. See, you *are* an interesting person. Devious is interesting. How are you going to produce the invoices for the illustrations, since you're not really breaking the books?'

She shrugged. 'Sidney never bothers with broken items. It depresses him. He calls it vulture food.'

'Not answering the question. But I figure you're going to sell the set for twenty-two K, give Sidney a couple of grand, let him collect from the insurance, meanwhile phonying up the accounting system with fake invoices. You're simultaneously screwing the insurance company, Glaser, your shady client, and the tax people. That's quite a plan.'

'You're going to rat me out!' Crosetti had heard of blazing eyes but had never actually seen any outside a movie screen until now. Little blue sparks were whizzing around in there.

'No,' he said, smiling. 'That would be boring. So . . . how're you going to fix the broken covers?'

He saw the relief on her face as she turned away from ethical issues to the moral neutrality of technique.

'Well, I think I can save the leather cover on volume one. The boards are cracked and the spine, but I can strip the leather off of it and replace the boards.'

With that she pulled a thin spatulate tool from a can and started to peel back the marbleized paper that held the leather cover to the boards. She worked carefully, and Crosetti was content to watch her small skillful hands at their task until the kitchen timer she had set previously rang out and he had to change the towels between the drying pages. When he had finished with this, he saw that she had the leather cover loose. Underneath it, between the leather and the cracked pasteboard were damp sheets of paper with closely set lines of handwriting on them. She put these aside and held the leather up to the light from the window, examining it closely.

'What're these papers?' he asked, idly separating the damp sheets. They were covered with writing in rusty black ink on both sides.

'Just padding. They used wastepaper to plump out the covers, and protect the leather from internal abrasion from the boards.'

'What language is this in?'

'English probably. Just some old wastepaper they used.'

'It doesn't look like English. I can read English – unless the guy had really terrible handwriting . . .'

She took the paper from him carefully and peered at it. 'That's funny. It looks like Jacobean secretary hand.'

'Excuse me?'

'I mean I'm not a paleographer, but that hand doesn't look contemporary with the publication of this book. It looks a lot earlier than 1732. Funny.'

'What, someone hid an old manuscript in the binding?'

'No, of course not. Bookbinders used scrap paper to back boards, any kind of scrap, but you'd expect, oh, contemporary proofs or old handbills, not an antique manuscript.'

'Why would they have done that? I mean an old manuscript would've been valuable in its own right, no?'

'Not at all. No one gave a hoot about old paper until much later. Original manuscripts got recycled when they were set in type, pulped, or used to start fires or line baking pans. Only a handful of antiquaries had any idea that preserving artifacts from the past was important, and most people thought *they* were nut cases. That's why practically the only handwriting that survives from the early modern period is in legal or financial records. Literary stuff had no value at all.'

'So it *could* be valuable now. This document.'

'I don't know. It depends on what it is. And who wrote it, of course.' She held it up to the light. 'Oh, I get it now. This sheet was printer's copy. It's got corrections on it in lead pencil. Interesting – so it became a book, probably printed by whoever did the Churchill books for John Walthoe.' She unweighted and opened the first volume and examined the imprint. 'Peter Deane. We might as well change the blotters now.'

After this was done, Crosetti asked, 'Aren't you curious to know what book it was the manuscript for? What if the rest of the backing is from the same book? What if it's someone famous, like, I don't know, Donne or Milton or Defoe? A holographic manuscript from someone like that'd be worth a pile, no?'

'It's probably the musings of an obscure clergyman. Commentaries on the Epistles.'

'But we don't know that. Why don't you open the other covers and see?'

'Because it's more work. I'd have to make them right again. And I don't have a lot of time.'

'We have time now,' he said, 'watching the books dry. Come on, I'd consider it a favor. I'm doing *you* one.'

She gave him a flat blue stare, acknowledging the manipulation, he thought. 'If it'll make you happy,' she said and picked up her little spatula.

An hour later, Crosetti regarded with pleasure what looked like a line of washing hanging from strings he had rigged between the support columns that held up the roof of the loft. They were the damp folio pages that had served as backing in the six volumes, four sheets from each cover, forty-eight pages in all. For reasons that were not entirely clear to him, the discovery of manuscript pages that had not seen the light for over two and a half centuries made him less uneasy about what he knew in his heart was participation in an act of fraud. He had rather shocked himself by how brazenly he had manipulated her into opening the covers to yield this manuscript, and he consequently desired that the papers hold some historical or literary importance. It was with great impatience that he waited for the sheets to be dry enough to handle.

In the meantime, the interleaving had to be changed on the hour. Rolly seemed content to let him do it unsupervised after she determined during the first few changes that he could manage it correctly. The main thing was to make sure not to rush the process by shoving in too many towels or interspersing the blotting medium between groups of fewer than ten leaves. If they did that, she'd explained, the book would swell out of shape and burst its bindings. Around six, Crosetti announced that he was hungry and learned that ramen noodles and take-out containers of varying ages constituted virtually all of her available foodstuffs. He could see why she went so often to lunch with Glaser. Crosetti ran out and braved the mean streets of Red Hook, returning with a couple of bottles of Mondavi red and a large pizza.

'You bought wine,' she said when he came in and placed the bag on the table. 'I never buy wine.'

'But you drink it.'

'Oh, yes. This is very nice of you. Thank you.' Again that little wolf's smile; number two.

Their employer made up the main subject of their table talk, as they otherwise had little in common. Crosetti's interest in books as physical objects was as slender as hers in current films. Besides, he was curious about the old man, and Rolly was willing to supply information when pressed, the more so as the wine took effect. He liked watching her eat: she was ravenous, she ate as if the slices were about to be snatched away, she ate the crusts to the last crumb and licked her fingers while she spun out what she knew. The story was that Glaser had entered the trade from his life as a collector, a common progression. His family made its pile two generations ago in department stores, and he had been raised in the upper bourgeoisie of Manhattan. The Glasers had intellectual pretensions – opera boxes, concert tickets, European tours à la mode, and the rest of it; a large apartment near Central Park had held a substantial library. In the course of time the ancestral emporiums had been absorbed by larger firms, the money not well invested, the inheritance scattered thinly among a too-numerous family. By the late 1970s Sidney Glaser had converted his hobby into his livelihood.

According to Rolly, he was not much of a businessman. Crosetti objected that the shop seemed to be a going concern, with many choice items.

'That's just the problem. He's got no business buying stuff like that McKenney and Hall for a hundred and fifty thousand. That's for Baumann or Sotheby's and the other big boys, and Glaser's not a big boy. He's got the clothes and the air but not the resources. Or the eye. Someone on his level should be picking up thousand-dollar books for two hundred, not hundred-thousand-dollar books for eighty-nine five. And they're going to raise the rent – it already takes nearly half the average monthly profit – I mean paper profit – I doubt he's made a real profit in years. It's an old story in the book business. A rich collector thinks, I buy lots of books, why shouldn't I pay for my hobby out of the profits?'

'Doesn't it work?'

'On occasion. But like I said, you have to know your level, and work up. You can't expect to start selling at the level you operated on as a rich collector, unless you're willing to pour your own money into the business. And then it's not really a business, is it? It's a *more* expensive hobby, with pretensions. Speaking of which, the little New York East Side antiquarian dealer with the paneled shop – it's a complete anachronism. There's no way he can pay that rent and compete with *both* the Internet mail-order dealers and the big-name houses. Glaser's going down. That fire was the best thing that could've happened to him. He'll diddle the insurance companies on a couple of dozen select items, declare total losses, and sell them as fair to good. It'll give him some operating capital again, but it won't last long . . .'

'You think he started the fire?'

'No, he's a book man. He'd never knowingly destroy a book. He was practically crying – you saw it – over that Churchill. But since there *was* a fire, he's not above taking as much advantage of it as he can.'

'Just like you.'

She narrowed her eyes at him. 'Yes, just like me. But at least I have an excuse, since I don't live in an eighteen-room apartment on Park Avenue. I *need* money.' She poured herself more wine, drank a swallow, added, 'And how about you, Crosetti? If those sheets you've got drying turn out to be the holograph of John Locke's preface to Churchill, what'll you do? Take them to Glaser and say, Oh, look what I found, Mr G., something you can sell to the Widener for ten grand, and can I have a pat on the head?'

'It's not Locke, if you're right about it being a Jacobean hand.'

'Oh, now he's literate, is he? I thought you were a computer nerd movie guy.'

'I read book catalogs.'

'Oh, right. But not books. You don't even like books, do you?'

'I like them fine.' He examined her in the waning light and found a belligerent thrust to her jaw he hadn't noticed before this, and a blurred, aggrieved look to her face.

'You're not going to be a nasty drunk, are you, Carolyn?'

'I will if I want to. It's my place.'

'Uh-huh. But I don't have to stay here. My sheets look pretty dry. I could just take them and leave you to change the diapers on your baby every hour all night long.'

And he would have too, except that no sooner were these words out than she burst into tears, horrible, hopeless wails, and, like the decent guy he was, Al Crosetti went around and knelt by her chair and held Rolly while she shook and soaked his shoulder with her tears.

The Bracegirdle Letter (2)

So to begin, asking always the favour of almighty God to keep me stricktlie on the path of truthfullnesse as I have muche of the olde Adam in me as thou knowest & mayhap I have told you som of it before nowe, yet you may forget and, which God foirbid, die before oure lad hath reached the age of understanding, soe it is better wrote down.

My father was named Richard his family the Bracegirdles were from Titchfield in the Weald, & iron-makeres from an earlie tyme. My father being but a youngere sonne was sent prentice to his nuncle John Bracegirdle who wase iron-factor at Leadenhall. Haveinge done with his prenticeshippe he removed to Fish Streete hard by Fenchurch Street & set hymselfe to be a factor in ironworkes. He throve there oweing to his goode connexiones with the Tichfield Bracegirdles & no lesse I thinke for his haveing a goode head for trade. He wase a grave & sober man, of little learning but a ready witte. Aetat 22 he wase converted to the true Christian religion by Gods grace & the sermons of Dr Abernathy of Water Street & thereafter lived a blamelesse lyfe. He was bye & large a generous Christian man & no wretch left his doore unfed if he would heare a little of the Word of God: although he could not stande a papiste. All though he traded in the ordinary pots, kettels firebacks, &c his chiefe werke was in bells &

gonnes. He oft hath sayde that if a man disired to make a greate noyse in the worlde whether in peace or in warre he had best hie hym to Bracegirdles of Fish Street.

My mother wase called Lucinda. Her family were Warwick-bred & of a higher estate than his, being gentry of the place & related to the Lord Arden: but distantly, distantly as my father all ways sayde. Her father Thomas Arden wase attainted traitor the 10th year of our late Quene Elizabeth & lost all: afterward, her mother dieing she, aetat eight yeares, wase taken in by Margaret Brandell an aunt of Cheapside. As a girl my mother was prettey enough yet wase not thought a match for any of worshippe in her native countie for not having a groate & the attainder besydes & wished verey much to leave the auntes home: a verey Godly woman so my mother sayde but kept a leane tabel & stanke. It chanced she bought a fyreback from my father on a day, and twelvemonth after were married in St Giles Cheapside & lyked one another wel enow. She wase not at first of the trew reformed religion but later she came to it: for the man is the heade of the woman as is written in Scripture.

Now after many fervente prayers I wase born on the fifte day of March in the year of Our Lord 1590 for they had by the unknowable judgement of Almightie God lost to fevers three children all infantes yet I wase a lustie babe hale as an ox soe I am told & survived to man's estate through Gods grace. My mother hadde three more children one lived to six the others not past a yeare, leaving me alone to rise to manhoode. At four years I wase put to dame school on our street & learnt my letteres well enow & afterward my father sent me as a scholere to Mr Eddingstone in Deal St where he had hym a scole. It wase my fatheres fancie to breed me up a learned man mayhap a divine but such wase not to bee, for I wase I admit froward & would not learn my Latine far less Greeke: hic haec hoc wase all a muddel to me. Once I asked Mr Eddingstone why it wase, we having englished the Bible we had to learne the tongues of paganes after all but I wase whippt for it & not only that time: & at laste he told my father it would not doe, I wase borne a foole & would remaine so. Then quoth my father what shall we doe with you, why did God send me such a block-heade for a son, can we make a factor of you, pray God at leaste you have a cleare hande. So wase I put to copeying but my hande wase soe crabbed & I made soe many blotts that he wase in dispaire for me. A blacksmythe you shalbe then & earne your bread by the sweat of your browe he sayde a mere blacksmythe for your back is stronge I see and youre handes are all readie black as a smiths with your blottynges: at that my mothere weepeth. She wase ever kinde to me even beyonde the measoure of a woman to a childe, the moreso as my father wase displeazed with mee.

A thinge then happened that changed all, how wondrous is Gods plan for us his creatoures all though we cannot fadom his wayes at the tyme. For we had then a lodger Mr Wenke: from Leiden came he being a nephew of a man that my father did trade with in ironworkes. We laboured chayre by chayre in my fatheres counting-house & one day I saw him doeing workynges with a little pensille & a scrap & I quized him what are you about sir. He sayde look & see. I looked but I could not mayke it out. I will saye now what it was: he was casting sums for our accountes in a fashioun I never saw before, but he kindley instructed me thus: look you we have solde seven & eighty smalle kettels this quarter for 8s. 6d. each & on each profiteth 1s. 2d. What have we gathered in all & what is our gaine? I sayde we must use comptoirs for that, shall I fetch the board? Nay quoth he I can doe it without anie comptoirs & do you watch me as I write & I shall expound upon my methode. Soe he did & I wase amazed so quick did his pensille fly & the grosse & profit all clare & exact. He sayde this is Multiplicatioun by Algorithme a word I never before this moment hearde & he sayde further it is but part of the art Arithmetick lately uzed in the bancks & compting-houses of Hollande & Italy: wold you learn it boy for it shalbe to your verie greate profit? I sayde yea with all my harte.

3

I'm back from a tour of the grounds, nothing visible from any of the windows, and I don't really feel like wandering around out there again in that dark. It occurs to me that I am a perfect target sitting here at my laptop under a table lamp. I'm in the living room, I suppose you could call it, of this house. A lodge, really, built of actual logs in the traditional manner. There is this one large room on the first floor and three bedrooms on the upper floor, which one reaches by a stairway that leads to a kind of railed balcony above me. Then there's a garret-type thing in the roof peak you get to via a drop ladder. The servants used to sleep there, when they had them. The walls are all pickled pine, and there are bookcases built in and a nice stereo system and a fieldstone fireplace that is literally large enough to roast an ox. A small ox. I have a fire going now, made from the good supply of oak, birch, and pine stored in the woodpile outside the kitchen door. Moose heads and racks of deer antlers decorate the base of the balcony, proof that, as Mickey has informed me, the Haas men were mighty hunters back in the day. There's a full kitchen with stone floors and a full array of '50S appliances on the first floor, and a couple of baths. Mickey installed a hot tub on the deck outside, although it's drained now. I got the impression he doesn't use the place much, although when he was a kid the family came up here every summer. It was a rich-family thing to do, apparently. I've been here many times before. When we were both young studs we used to bring girls for romantic weekends.

To resume the story: Professor Bulstrode handed the package over, a thick envelope bound, as I say, in tape. I asked him what was in it, and he said that it was a manuscript dating from 1642. This is the Work? I asked. No, not at all. This was merely the evidence that the Work exists, the Bracegirdle screed. But not valuable in its own right? Not as such – of purely scholarly interest, he said, and here a note of even greater nervousness entered his voice as he pressed upon me the absolute necessity of keeping the information in this package entirely confidential. That was why he was securing it in this way. I assured him that it would be perfectly safe and free from any prying eyes. He appeared to relax at this assurance; I then buzzed for Ms Maldonado and asked her for a standard representation letter and receipt for retainer.

While this was being prepared, I attempted to engage Professor Bulstrode in casual conversation. It did not flow. He kept eyeing the taped manila envelope as if it were a bomb, and it seemed to me that he could hardly wait to put distance between him and its menace. Finally, I asked him if he'd made a copy of the document inside, and he said he had not, for reasons of security, after which he drew from me a solemn assurance that I would make none either. Here I began to lose patience and I told him that I was starting to get a little uncomfortable with this air of secrecy. The point of hiring a lawyer, I said, was that it gave you someone to speak to confidentially, and that it was obvious that he wasn't comfortable doing that, and that this in turn made me uncomfortable representing him. In my experience, I added, people act that way with their counsel when they are trying to pull off something shady. Perhaps it would be best for all concerned if he took back his check, no hard feelings, etc.

At this he broke out into fresh floods of sweat and his face became quite flushed. He assured me that he didn't mean to make a mystery nor, of course, was there anything in the remotest sense illegal or shady about his situation. But in academic affairs involving unique items a certain reticence was usual. He begged my pardon if he'd offended. Here Ms Maldonado popped in and dropped the agreement on my desk. I made no move to pick up the folder. She left. I said that perhaps we'd gotten off on the wrong foot. I wanted him to trust me. He said he did. I asked him to start again: who was Bracegirdle, what was in the envelope, and what was the Work it led to?

So he told his story: He'd come across the manuscript in the course of some research into trends in Renaissance philosophy. The ms. consisted of some twenty-six folio sheets, closely written, dated 1642. Richard Bracegirdle was nobody special, a soldier who died soon after the battle of Edgehill in the English Civil War. Most of the writing was of no interest, but there were indications that Bracegirdle had been hired to move the property of a nobleman named Lord Dunbarton. Both Bracegirdle and Dunbarton were on the Parliamentary side in the war, and Dunbarton's estate was in territory controlled, or about to be controlled, by the Royalists. He feared confiscation of his valuables and muniments and so had engaged Bracegirdle to move them, including the rarest items in the library, to his London house. What happened, however, was that the Royalist forces moved on London, blocking his path. So he buried the treasure and sent Dunbarton a letter informing him where he'd buried the swag.

Buried treasure, said I, noncommittally, and I asked him what this had to do with intellectual property. The library, he said, the library.

I asked him what was in the library, if he knew.

He didn't answer. Instead he asked me if *I* knew what the Leicester Codex was. As a matter of fact I did. One of the growing edges of the IP game is the digitization of books, manuscripts, and artworks, and the assignment and negotiation of the various rights thereto pertaining. Mr William Gates, the software billionaire, is a major player in this field, and IP lawyers tend to keep themselves apprised of his many doings. I told Bulstrode that I knew that some ten years ago Gates had purchased the Leicester Codex, one of Leonardo's notebooks, for thirty million dollars.

At this, Bulstrode blurted out, Dunbarton had a *Shakespeare* manuscript. Can you imagine the value of such a thing? Now all reticence was gone, an odd little light shone in his mild eyes.

Those eyes were starting to positively bulge here, so I nodded amiably and said I supposed it would be worth a great deal, and with these words there struck the first pangs of that leaden claustral feeling I always get in the presence of a maniac. It is sadly not an unfamiliar one, for we IP lawyers are all too well-acquainted with the mad. No showbiz hit, no world-conquering diet book, no moneymaking product of the human imagination ever appears unaccompanied by a gang of shabby pretenders clutching greasy folders stuffed with documentary proof that they thought of it first. And they don't want to hear that no one can copyright an idea, a concept. They don't want to hear that ideas are like water or air or carbon, free for the taking, and the only thing from which loot can be wrenched by copyright is a particular *set* of words, or musical notes, or chemicals. I admit I had not had the Secret Document type before, but here he now was. I recall hoping that the poor bastard's check was good.

So I waited for the florescence of the craziness: an outpouring of hectic enthusiasm about how important the lost manuscript was, what literary secrets it might reveal, its provenance, how close he was to cracking the secret code, but, somewhat to my surprise, he seemed to deflate after his revelation, and I thought that he was regretting having shared so much, and had already started to work me into his paranoia, yet another potential thief of his Precious.

We signed the forms and he left. I had Ms M. zip downstairs and deposit the check and place the package in our safe-deposit box; and then, although I was feeling the belly rumbles of my delayed lunch, I turned to my computer and googled Andrew Bulstrode, and found a good deal more on Dr B. than one might have expected on a simple academic. Five years ago, it appeared, Bulstrode had been a professor of English lit at Oxford, an expert on Shakespearean editions, and he had fallen prey to a man who turned out to be one of the great forgers of modern times. Leonard Hastings Pascoe was a name that even I recognized. His specialty was early printing – incunabula – and manuscripts associated with significant authors, and he was very clever indeed. He claimed to have discovered a new bad quarto of *Hamlet*. A bad quarto is a sort of early literary piracy, in which printers would assemble a play from the memories of actors, and whatever actual scripts they could get hold of, and print it without the permission of the author.

This was apparently a major find, for (according to the googled articles) the publishing history of *Hamlet* is extremely complex. There is a First Quarto (bad) and a Second Quarto (good, or authorized by the author) and the First Folio, which Shakespeare's friends and theatrical-business partners, Heminge and Condell, had assembled after his death, which is essentially the play we now know. The supposed new bad quarto had in it many intriguing differences from the authorized play and suggested a view into Shakespeare's writing process. It was dated 1602, right after *Hamlet* was registered and a year earlier than the First Quarto, raising interesting questions: were the differences mere transcription errors or did they mean that the author had changed his play after it was performed? It was the sort of thing that generates multiple orgasms among the learned. The British Museum was offered first crack by the patriotic Pascoe, and they snapped at it for the asking price, provided that the distinguished expert Andrew Bulstrode vetted it as genuine.

Which he did. Pascoe had used genuine seventeenth-century paper and ox-gall-iron ink of the correct formulation and period (derived by chemical extraction from contemporary documents, to defeat any ink-aging tests) and his type fonts had been meticulously copied from one of the bad quartos in the Folger Library. The museum bought the thing for £850,000. Bulstrode had first dibs on it, of course, and within six months had produced a magisterial work, demonstrating that in his opinion the author had heavily rewritten the great play and that in fact the Pascoe Quarto, so called, was in actuality an important link among the various proto-Hamlets that Shakespeare had used as source texts. Sensation among the dons!

And it might have become part of the critical canon had not L. H. Pascoe delighted in delicious young fellows with smoky eyes and pouting lips, and having such a taste, not promised one of these a trip to Cap d'Antibes, and a new wardrobe with it, and having so promised, not reneged, causing the young fellow, naturally enough, to drop a dime on his patron. The police raided a certain industrial estate in Ealing and found the handpress and the paper and the ink, with the fake *Hamlet* still set up in the forms. This occurred some eighteen months after the sale.

The money from this had apparently been mostly spent on high living of a particularly lubricious kind. The tabloids ate it whole, reserving a special venom for the peccant expert, Bulstrode. Into this mess strode my old pal Mickey Haas, who defended his colleague in the public press as having made an error that any other expert in the world would have made, including Dr Haas himself. He arranged for Bulstrode to occupy a visiting professorship at Columbia in the hope that England might cool down after an interval. And now it seemed someone else had unloaded a document on Bulstrode, which I thought odd, since he was the last person eligible to present any important manuscript to the world, and also the last person to want to. But I had long surrendered any notion that experience was an efficient teacher. I, for example, would still be happily married had I been able to learn from my mistakes.

Or perhaps he had snapped under the strain. Professors go batty too, perhaps more often than other people, although owing to their profession their madness is less often remarked. As a reality check I looked up Lord Dunbarton and, somewhat to my surprise, found he was no figment. Henry Reith (1570–1655), second Baron Dunbarton, was a Puritan grandee. His dad, the first Lord Dunbarton, had won his spurs as one of Henry VIII's ransacking minions, a 'visitor' as they called them, kicking nuns and monks out of their cloisters and making sure that the Protestant Reformation reached every lootable ecclesiastic property in England. He was rewarded with a title and an estate in Warwickshire, Darden Hall. The son was introduced at court late in Elizabeth's reign, won the favor of Lord Burghley, and got into what they then called the 'intelligencer' business, working to catch Jesuits and expose their knavish plots against the queen's and later King James's peace. Under Charles I, he was a staunch Parliamentarian, having, like his father, a keen eye for the winning side, although he seemed also to be a sincere Puritan fanatic, energetically pursuing the recusants of Warwickshire. Darden Hall was occupied by Royalist troops during the brief campaign that ended at the battle of Edgehill. No mention of libraries, of Bracegirdles, of lost Shakespeariana. Now I thought that I should call Mickey Haas, to get the full story on the poor man, and I did, and was informed that Dr Haas was at a conference in Austin and would not be back until the beginning of next week. So I went to lunch.

Here I consult my diary. Ms Maldonado keeps my appointments, of course, and every Monday I get a sheet of paper telling me what I have for the week, but I transfer these appointments to a little leather-bound diary with blue tissue pages that I keep in the breast pocket of my shirt. I am not really what one could call absentminded, but I do get involved in the library sometimes or on the telephone, and unless I glance at this every so often I find that I miss meetings. This is how I knew it was the eleventh of October that I met Dr B., and as I now consult it again, I learn that on the day I met Bulstrode I left work early to pick up Imogen and Nicholas at their school and take them to dinner and a movie. Wednesday evening is my official midweek appointment with my children and I also see them on alternate weekends and for two weeks in the summer.

Imogen, my daughter, is thirteen. She has straw-blond hair and gray eyes and looks so like her mother that she might have been budded from the maternal stem instead of being generated by the usual method. This, by the way, seems to be a peculiarity of our family. The Mishkin genes do not work and play well with others. They either dominate totally or leave the field in a huff. Thus I look exactly like my dad, the Jewish refrigerator carton, while my brother and sister are blondie rails, recruiting posters for the *Hitlerjugend*. My son, Nicholas, aged eleven, is an absurd little Jake. When I was courting Amalie, my sister pointed out to me that she looked exactly like a younger version of our mom. I can't say that I ever saw it, although the coloring and general facial type is similar. German, you could say. When Uncle Paul and Aunt Miri take Imogen out, it is universally assumed that she is their daughter, while when I am with her the average passerby gives us unfriendly looks, as if I were an abducting perve.

As for character, unlike her mother, Imogen is a perfect Narcissus; all others exist but to worship her and if not, watch out! She is an athlete – a swimmer of some talent – and wants to be an actress, an ambition I support, for I consider her unsuited for any other life. I believe she gets this tendency from me. When I was in high school in Brooklyn, a teacher told me that I had a good voice and that I should go out for drama, and I did and got the part of Telegin in *Uncle Vanya*, a small role, but like all Chekhov roles it can be made memorable. I suppose that they no longer do Chekhov in Brooklyn public high schools, but then they did, along with many other cultural activities that are no longer possible in this current age of brass. Telegin is called Waffles in the play because his face is pocked, and mine at sixteen was a mess too. My big line was 'I have forfeited my happiness but I have kept my pride.' Naturally, I fell in love with Gloria Gottleib, who played Sonia and who didn't know I was alive, etc., but the interesting thing was that even after I was offstage and even after we'd done our three performances in the orange-juice-smelling auditorium, I still felt inhabited by Telegin, and this was wonderful to me, that a made-up person created by a man long dead could in a sense displace my own personality.

I should mention here that until I appeared in this thing I had been a miserable figure, too obscure even to be a butt of mockery. It is relatively easy to disappear in a large urban high school, but I had special reasons for becoming one with the tan tiles of the wall. I was a Catholic kid with a Jewish name and a Nazi grandfather in a school where the aristocracy was intellectual and almost entirely Jewish, plus Izzy the Book was not unknown to the tabloids at the time as oft indicted, never convicted. I lived in terror of someone (i.e., Gloria Gottleib) making the connection. On top of this, my brother Paul, two years older, was a thug. He announced this, as thugs did then, with the black leather jacket and the collar up in back and the duck's ass hairdo. Being a nonentity was preferable to being famous as Paulie Mishkin's brother. At some level I knew that I was protected by his ferocious aura from the light bullying that would've been my fate otherwise. Paul insisted that when I got pounded, which was fairly often, the pounder would be him only. The worst fight I ever saw when I was growing up was Paul taking out two guys from a well-known street-fighting gang who had mugged my lunch money on the way to school. He used a brick.

These obsessive images. That's not what I want to write down at all, although perhaps it's significant that after this fight, and Paul's suspension from school as a result, was when I started serious lifting. I resolved not to have to depend on him to stick up for me, and further, I supposed that if I became a moose I could avoid fights. Little did I know.

In any case, after *Uncle Vanya* I made a terrific ass of myself by more or less staying in character perpetually, wearing an antique brocade vest I found in a junk shop, speaking with a slight accent, pretending to have to reach for an English word, mumbling in what I imagined sounded like Russian. I became somewhat more popular, as amusing lunatics sometimes do, and I began to get invitations to high-end parties thrown by the popular Jewish girls. The next play we did was *Romeo and Juliet* and I was Mercutio. The fit with him was much better than with Telegin, for to fill the harmless air with witty nonsense, strike antic poses, and absurdly die seems glorious to the young; nor is it o'er taxing to speak, like this, in rich and flowing iambs, till all about you wish you dead. For the teenaged boy playing Mercutio the hard part is to speak the dirty stuff without cracking up, all that business about pricks in act I, scene iv, for example, may be even harder than doing a convincing job as Romeo. As for Juliet . . . you know, speaking as an IP lawyer, I would say that Shakespeare's famous powers of invention do not show well in the matter of plots. All but two of the plays are ripped off, sometimes blatantly, from prior sources; and it was a good thing for him they didn't have copyright in those days. We go to hear his plays for the language, just as we go to opera for the music; plot is secondary in both, trivial really, but – and contemporaries picked this up as well – there is no one like him for seizing something out of life and putting it on the stage. Such a coup is the end of act II, scene ii. This is the famous balcony scene, and I don't mean the front part that everyone quotes but the depiction of a love-mad child at the end. An adult playing it – Claire Bloom perhaps – can't help but seem absurd, but a sixteen-year-old can make it live, especially if one is in love with the girl, as I was, and I recall very distinctly the moment when, as I watched the divine Miss Gottleib draw out the long goodbye, I thought to myself this is the life for me, this is my destiny, to open my being to genius, to be possessed, to be free of my miserable self.

This was my junior year in high school, a year that marked the beginning of the long twilight of the mob in New York. In that era, before the code of silence collapsed with Mr Valachi, the best way to put a big-shot Italian away was to get him for tax violations, and my dad was therefore right in the crosshairs. As usual, they had him on numerous charges and were putting on the pressure to make him testify against his employers. Had they taken time to consult his family they would not have thus confused him with someone lacking moxie. All during the fall of that year, while we rehearsed *R&J*, Dad was on trial in federal court for the southern district of New York. While we had never been what you could call a happy household, this period was especially grim.

Let me here touch briefly upon the family drama. Izzy and Ermentrude continued as they had begun, at gunpoint (at least metaphorically), although I believe they believed they were in love, this defined as the continued attempt to bend the beloved to one's own will. Here is the tableau that sticks in my mind. It is evening. We boys are prepubescent, perhaps I am eight, Paul is ten, the girl is six. We have dutifully done our homework and had it inspected by Obersturmbannführer-Mutti. The air is redolent with heavy Teutonic cookery. This is still the time of *alles in ordnung*, before the discovery of That Whore, his mistress, after which our mom more or less gave up on life for a while. We are perhaps watching a small-screen colorless television, perhaps arguing over which channel to watch. Growing tension as six o'clock comes and goes. Will he appear? Will he be in a good mood or not? Six-thirty, and Mutti is banging pots and slamming drawers, and muttering in German. We listen for the clink of bottle on glass. Seven o'clock. A smell of burning, of expensive proteins going dry, of vegetables steaming into inedible slush. We are ravenous, but none dares to enter the kitchen.

Seven-fifteen and the door opens. Our hearts sink when we see his face. No little gifties for the kids tonight, no hearty hi-ho Silvers for the boys, no snatchings up of the little girl and whirlings-around. No, tonight we go straight to the table, and the ruined dinner is flung thumping and clattering on the board, and my father says I'm not gonna eat this shit, and then they get into it, back and forth, in English and then demotic German, in which, even if we can't follow the exact meaning, the violence is perfectly apparent, and then the platters and cutlery start flying, and Miriam ducks under the table and I follow, holding her little weeping head to my chest. Paul stays upright in his chair, and I can see him from my position below, face white, white too the knuckles of the fist that clutches his table knife. The fight grows in volume, ending usually with 'fucking Nazi' from him and 'Jew pig' from her and then he slugs her one and leaves. *Slam!* And we come out again and she makes us sit up straight and finish every scrap of the inedible food while she tells us about how it was to actually starve in poor Germany, after zeh war, and zo we must finish everyting. This isn't why we choke it down, though; it's because what else can we do for her?

But during the trial we didn't do that anymore; now silence reigned. Mutti slapped warmed-up canned goods on the table and retreated into her bedroom, from which the sounds of the German classics emerged, Beethoven, Bruckner, Wagner. She started drinking more, and when she got her load on, the volume went up. Dad might kick the door down then and smash records, or he might just leave and not return for days. Paul also was rarely home. After graduating (barely) from high school he had taken to hanging out with his gang, who had also graduated (as we were shortly to learn) from petty theft to armed robbery.

That left me to cope with the household and with my sister, Miriam, then fourteen. Miri had already developed the remarkable face she would carry into adulthood, a face whose angled planes acted like those on a stealth bomber to allow undetectable penetration deep into the heart of enemy territory, in this case, the male sex. I made no attempt to actually control her, knowing it would be futile, but I could at least ensure that she had meals and clean garments, and between me and Paulie we were successful (I believe) in discouraging the attentions of guys over thirty. One morning, just before Thanksgiving of that year, Dad did not show up in court, nor did he return home. Naturally we feared the worst, that his mob pals had lost faith in his silence (since it was fairly clear by then that he was going to go down for the top counts of the indictment unless he did a deal) and had acted to forestall this. I recall thinking of him stuffed into a weighted oil drum or resting under the asphalt of a highway and trying to feel sad, and failing.

But he hadn't been whacked. After a period of some weeks, the papers reported that he'd been sighted in Tel Aviv. He had skipped bail and followed his mentor, Meyer Lansky, into comfortable exile. Not a card for us, not a call. Later I heard he'd changed his name to something more Hebraic, as encouraged by the Israeli government, although I suppose there are Mishkins enough in that nation. This was all before media frenzy became the rule, and so we only had a couple of reporters come by our house, and Paulie and some of his friends beat the shit out of them, smashing cameras, etc. This was when you could beat the shit out of the press without having it captured on videotape, which made for a more civilized press, in my opinion. Since Dad had put our house and his immovable assets up to make his colossal bail, and he'd skipped with all the cash on hand, we were left essentially destitute. After a decent interval the bailiffs came and took Dad's Caddy and served us with eviction papers.

At this point we had a small miracle. I awoke one Saturday morning to the sound of strenuous packing and *Parsifal* on the stereo. Mutti was back, in charge, shouting orders. We kids were marshaled into action, as well as two guys I'd never seen before, German speakers, probably war criminals in hiding that Mutti had dug up somewhere. It was Regensburg 1945 again, Hitler was gone, the Reds were coming, and life had to be whipped into shape from the ruins. I understand that Ukrainian villages cheered the arrival of the Nazis in 1941, and we kids were in somewhat the same state – anything had to be better than what we'd recently experienced, and maternal fascism was at least a known quantity. The Germans had a truck too, and it moved us from our comfortable brick house in Flatbush to a cramped two-bedroom in a high-rise public project out by the Queens borderline.

So our lives continued without Dad. The salary from the job Mutti obtained as a clerk at King's County Hospital was just enough to keep us in underwear and bratwurst. We kids thereafter devoted ourselves to living the lives we thought would most piss Dad off: Paul became a stupid rather than a clever criminal; I became a star student (i.e., a schmuck); and Miri, not to mince words, became a slut. In short order,

Paul got nailed for a liquor store holdup and went off for his jolt upstate, Miri ran off with a playboy, and I graduated with honors, aced my SATs, and went to Columbia, where I met Mickey Haas. I hope this connects all the dots.

But I started this long digression by describing my children, and I see I have not yet said anything about my son, Nicholas – Niko, as we call him. For a long time we thought, or rather I thought, that there was something wrong with Niko, some form of autism perhaps, or one of the other childhood syndromes lately invented to provide the drug companies with fresh markets. He failed to walk or talk at the usual times, and I insisted on taking him to various specialists, although his mother maintained that there was nothing seriously wrong with him. In time, his mother was proven correct. He began to talk at around four, and from the start in perfect paragraphs, and demonstrated at around the same time that he had taught himself to read. He is some kind of prodigy, but we're not really sure what kind. I admit now that I have never felt entirely comfortable in his presence. To my shame. When he was six, before our home dissolved, he used to come into the little room that I used as a study or den and stand staring at me and would say nothing at all when I asked him what he wanted. Eventually, I used to ignore his presence, or try to. I imagined sometimes that he could see into me, into my deepest thoughts and desires, and that he, alone of my family, knew then how perfectly rotten I was.

He goes to Copley Academy with Imogen and has special tutoring in mathematics and computer science, at both of which he excels. Izzy the Book thus struck, in a fashion, across the generations, skipping me, for I never received more than a B – in the few math courses my education required. Niko is a solid, grave little man, and in his features he has already started to resemble his paternal grandfather, the dark, canny, opaque eyes, the schnoz, the wide mouth, the thick curling dark hair. As far as I know, he has never learned anything from me. The last time I tried it was at the pool, when I attempted to teach him to swim. Not only did I fail, but my efforts sent him into a hysteria so profound and long-lasting that no one has ever tried to teach him again, and he remains a terrified sinker. On land I suppose he is reasonably happy; Copley is the kind of place where, if you are not disruptive, they leave you alone. They don't give out grades, and they charge twenty-eight-five a year. I don't begrudge this in the least, as I make a good living. I bill on average seven-fifty an hour, and my annual billings are usually well in excess of two thousand hours per annum. You may do the math. I have no expensive hobbies (or only one, I should say), I dislike travel, and I have moderate tastes. I bought a loft in Tribeca before the prices went nuts, and Amalie also leads a fairly simple life and has a substantial income of her own, although given free rein she would surrender our entire substance to the poor and suffering and live with the children under an elevated highway instead of in a nice brownstone on East Seventy-Sixth Street.

I love my children as much as I love anything, which I have to say is not all that much. I am able to maintain the simulacrum of a good father simply as an act of imagination, as previously I maintained that of a good son, a good brother, a friend, and so on. It is more easy than you might think to fool people, and until I met Amalie I thought everyone was like that, I thought people picked a script from a cultural box and played it out, I thought that, really, there was no difference between Jake Mishkin playing Mercutio and Jake Mishkin playing Jake Mishkin, except that Mercutio was better written.

That was, by the way, why I didn't go into acting professionally. I told myself that I gave up the theater (and what a gross self-pitying phrase that sounds!) because I required a sure source of income to support my family, but in fact it was because once I got into a part it was nearly impossible for me to get out of it. What was funny-eccentric in high school became funny-peculiar when I got a little older, and then not funny at all. I imagined myself spending my days in a locked ward, stuck in Macbeth or Torvald Helmer. Or Estragon. And there was also, I don't know, something seriously toxic about the people who were involved with theater, or maybe I just projected that because I was scared. So I switched to prelaw and have had little reason to regret it since. I don't go to plays.

I've returned after a break to drink some coffee and have a doughnut. I bought two dozen at a place in Saranac Lake and have been living off them and coffee for some time. The house is well stocked with canned goods and staples, some of them of considerable age, and there is a freezer with fish and game in it. Mickey said I could stay here indefinitely, although he added that in the event of a nuclear attack I would have to share it with him and whichever of his three wives he decides to bring along. There is a town twenty-six miles off, New Weimar, but I have not visited it. I thought it best if no one local knew I was here. The house is quite isolated, standing at the end of a long dirt driveway that comes off a gravel road, that diverges from a secondary state road that comes off Route 30 west of Saranac Lake. The isolation is purely physical, however, for some years ago Mickey installed a satellite dish, and so you can get the usual two hundred channels, and more significantly there is broadband Internet access via the dish. I like to feel that with a few button pushes I can send this out to the whole world. This may be a bargaining chip at some point, with whom I don't yet know.

Reading this over I see I have screwed up the line of the narrative beyond all repair. It might have been better had I simply set out to write out my life story straight up, as if, like Bracegirdle, I were on my deathbed, instead of merely dwelling in the probability of meeting some violent end in the not-too-distant future. Death, I suppose, concentrates the mind, assuming one has a mind left. The problem is that I started out to tell a simple story like you used to find in cheap thrillers, the electronic equivalent of the last-gasp message, the cryptic scrawl on the plaster, the note in blood – '*the emeralds are in the p* [illegible scrawl]'; or '*It wasn't Har* .' And from this arises the plot. But it seems that my life has become mixed up with the story, as was Bracegirdle's, viz.:

> *Though God did not call mee to stande among the greate still I am a man not a clod & my story bears telling if onlie to holpe in the breding of my sonne: who needs muste rise to manhoode lacking what ever poore model I might have supply'd.*

So saith Bracegirdle and so say I.

To take up the tale then, I see by my diary that the next two days passed without significant incident, as did the weekend, blank except for a lone 'Ingrid,' which meant I must have gone up to Tarrytown for dinner drinks a brace of reasonably satisfying acts of sexual intercourse breakfast and bye-bye Ingrid.

No, this slights a very nice woman, a choreographer, whom

I met at a music company gala, and whom I caused to fall for me by being courteous, sympathetic, generous, and large. She is not the first, was not the last, to make this misstep. I don't know what's wrong with men nowadays, but the isle of Manhattan seems to be full of attractive, classy, sexy women between thirty and fifty years of age, both married and single, who find it nearly impossible to get laid. I do my best, but it is a sad business. Let me not enter into all that now.

On the Monday, we had our usual partners' meeting in the morning and afterward, as I usually do, I called my driver and went to the gym. I noted above that I live a fairly simple life, no expensive hobbies, etc., but I suppose that having a driver perpetually on call might be counted an extravagance. With the car, it costs me a little shy of fifty grand a year, but on the other hand much of it is deductible as a business expense. There is no good rapid transit connection between my home and my office, and I do not fit into a regular cab, or so I tell myself. The car is a Lincoln Town Car, in midnight blue to distinguish it from all the black ones. My driver, who has been with me for nearly six years, is called Omar. He is a Palestinian and, like me, a heavy-class weight lifter. He was driving a cab when we met, and we both complained about how the regulation cabs they had in New York were not designed for men like us, either as passengers or drivers, and from that came my decision to get the Lincoln and have Omar drive it. He is a terrific driver, both safe and speedy, doesn't drink, and keeps the car spotless. His only fault (if you can call it one) is that when it is time for prayer, he feels obliged to pull over, get his rug out of the trunk, and kneel down on the sidewalk. This has not happened more than a few times with me aboard, however.

I am not devout myself, although I am not an atheist

either. Nor an agnostic, a position I consider absurd, and excessively timorous. I suppose I am a Catholic still, although I do not practice the faith. Like the demons in hell, I believe and tremble. If people ask, I say this is because certain positions of the hierarchy or the Vatican are repugnant to me, as if the Church were not quite good enough to contain the glory that is Jake Mishkin, but this is not true. I abandoned worship so that I could be a devil among the women. Yes, my single expensive hobby.

Back to Monday . . . I was in the gym, which is at Fifty-first off Eighth Avenue. Part of the gym is a regular carpeted Nautilus operation for the locals, but the weight room is unusually well appointed. This is because the proprietor, Arcady V. Demichevski, formerly lifted heavy for the old Soviet Union. Arcady will give you weight-lifting advice if you ask him, and he has a Russian-style steam room with a masseur on site. This end of the gym smells of wintergreen, sweat, and steam. Arcady says the great lifters lift with their heads more than their bodies, and this I have found to be true. It should be impossible for a human being, however muscled, to heave a quarter ton of deadweight into the air, but it is regularly done. As noted already, I have done it myself. It is all about concentration and, who knows, some strange form of telekinesis. It is marvelously relaxing for me to spend an hour or so in the middle of the day lifting weights. When I am done lifting, and have had a steam, I can barely remember that I am a lawyer.

In any case, I had just finished a set of three-hundred-pound bench presses with Omar spotting me. As I was filling my water bottle at the fountain on the Nautilus side, I spied two men entering the gym. They spoke to Evgenia, Arcady's daughter, at the front desk and I saw her point me out. They came over to me, showed their badges, and introduced themselves as police detectives: Michael Murray and Larry Fernandez. We are so prepped by the cop shows to be interviewed by the police, we have all seen it a zillion times, that when it happens in real life it is oddly anticlimactic. The actual cops looked like the guys who just missed getting the TV part: an ordinary medium-size Jewish-type New York guy and a ditto Hispanic. Murray was somewhat more overweight than they like to show on TV, and Fernandez had misshapen teeth. It was somewhat hard to keep a straight face as they asked me if I knew Andrew Bulstrode, because I imagined what we were doing playing out on the small screen, and I sensed also that they did as well, that they had even learned how to behave from watching *N.Y.P.D. Blue* and *Law & Order*.

I answered that he was a client of mine, and they asked me when I saw him last, and I said the first time was the last time, and then they asked if I knew why anyone would have wanted to harm him. I said no, but also that I didn't know him all that well, and I asked them why they'd come to see me. They said they had found a binder agreement in his room in a residence hotel on upper Broadway that Columbia keeps for visiting faculty, at which point I asked them *had* anyone harmed him? They said that someone had visited him in that room on Sunday night, tied him to a chair, and, apparently, tortured him to death. They asked me what I was doing Sunday night, and I told them about Ingrid.

Tortured to death. They didn't supply any details and I did not pry. I recall being shocked but, and this was strange too, not surprised. I neglected to tell the police about the package he had given me, for I considered that it was none of their business, not, at least, until I had taken the time to examine it myself.

The Bracegirdle Letter (3)

So we began & I found I had a head for this worke – the numbers stuck hard as Latine never did. I learnt me what is twice two, twice three &c until sixteen sixteens & he expounded & I did fix it in my mynde how to figure therebye using but a pensille & paper: & also Division, as if a man wished to packe 2300 jarres twelve to a boxe how many boxes to be builded & what left in the last one alle figured with no board. He gave me besides a booke which was a wonder to me named DISME: or the Art of Tenths by a Dutchman Simon Stevins, & although you will be hard put to understand Nan I will any way tell you that Disme is a kind of Arithmeticke consisting in Characters of Cyphers; whereby a certain number is described & by which also all accounts which happen to humane affayres, are dispatched by whole numbers, without fractions or broken numbers. When I had shewed I was master of that he let me looke into his Euclid lately englished by Billingsley Lord Mayor of London. Which I ate as foode to a stervyng man or lyke one bounde in fetters, of a sodden set free. Beside this he instructed me in the art of the quadrante & other philosophickal devises that were I thinke ne'er seen on Fish Street before & taught me to make plats to scale from measoures wee took with quadrante & chaynes: also the elements of astronomick figuringe such as takynge Latitudes from the sun & divers stars: mee that when I began I sweare I knew not a Latitude from a cheese. So it was a greate thinge for me to accomplish this who had been accounted a slugg at schole.

This all in one sommer my twelft year: but now my father seeyng this taxed us sayyng what shal you not only be idle thyselfe but also tayke my clerke into idlenesse with thee? But Mr Wenke stod his grownde lyke a man quoth he sir this lad you have is as apt at the Mathematicks as any I have seen: in some few moneths he has learned near all I have to teach hym & will shortly exceede me. He, that is my father, saith how will this Mathematicks sell me more iron? Mr Wenke then says what I have taught the boye will grately spede the workynges of accountes, and to me saith, do you shew your father your Arithmeticke.

So I took pensille & a bit of paper from the fire-box & wishing to mayke a vainglorious shew I Multiplied two numbers of seven figures together. My fathere looked & he saith pah that is mere scribbling. Nay sir, Mr Wenke sayde he has it right. My fathere sayde how can you say so? For it would take an houre or more to mayke certayne that figure working with my borde. So we were at a stand; also my fathere had it in his heade besides that there were some thing papistical about such workynges as cominge mayhap from Italie or other landes under sway of the harlot Rome.

Nexte day he ruled I should studie no more with Mr Wenke & be made a foundry-man insteade, saying we shall see if you founder in this as well & laughed heartie at his witte. Soe amid many teares of my deare mother & I too wept most bitter, I wase sent off to my Bracegirdle cozens at Titchfield. The night I left Mr Wenke sought me privily & pressed on me the first ten bookes of his Euclid, saying I have them by heart in the maine & can buy more at Pauls if needbe & make thou good use of them. Soe I departed my home.

My cozzens workes at Titchfield were as unlyke the countynge-house in Fish Streete as one could well imagine for makeing iron is as different from sellyng it as slaughteryng oxen be from the sarving of a mete pye: by that I intend dirty hard callous brute work. My cozzen Matthew the maistre of the place was harde as the stoffe he mayde. Looking down at me for he was a tall grete beare of a man he sayde what a paltrie thinge thou art but we will toughen you or kill you before a yeare be out we shall see which it shalbe & laughed. But though I worked lyke a slave & slept hard on straw with the other prentyces this was not the hardest of my newe lot for I had been blessed by nice breding never a curse in my house & all orderly nor had I ever been much among sinners in the way of the flesh. But now I thought I was amongst verey devils. My maistre though he professed the true faith was a vile hypocrite verey sober in church of Sundays but otherwise a roisterynge knave he kept a punke in the towne & dranke & beat his wyfe & servantes when in cups & fed we prentices short commons in oure kennel. The prentices themselves I swear were become little more than beastes of the field fighting & stealing & drunk when they could filtch ale. They were upon me from the start like crowes at a carcasse on account of my manneres & that I was a relatioun of the maistre & mayde my lyfe a miserie, which I bore as I must, weepeing onlie in secrete & prayynge for release whether by deathe or some othere mercie I cared not. But now one of them Jack Carey by name a lowde booreish fellow spied me at my Euclide & ripped it from my hande & mocked me for a mere clerke & made to throw it in the fyre, then I lept up lyke a fiende, & tooke up a stave & stroke him upon his heade so that he dropped the booke & fell senselesse down & three of them muste holt me then or I would have done grete evil upon hym even murther I think for being overcome with my rage, for which may God forgyve me. But afterwards my waye was more easie amongst them.

4

The crying lasted for approximately five minutes and ended in a series of deep shuddering breaths. Crosetti asked Carolyn what was wrong several times, but received no answer; as soon as the spasms had died down she pulled away from him and vanished behind the bathroom partition. He heard water running, footsteps, the delightful swishing sounds of a girl changing clothes. She's slipping into something more comfortable, thought Crosetti with unaccustomed anticipation.

But when she emerged, he found that she was dressed in a gray mechanic's coverall with her hair tightly bound up in an indigo scarf, below which her face had been scrubbed clean of even the light makeup she normally wore. Upon it no trace of the recent outburst. She looked like a prisoner or a nun.

'Feeling better?' he asked as she walked by him, but she didn't answer. Instead, she began to replace the blotting paper in the wet books.

He walked over and started to pull sodden toweling out of volume three. After a few minutes of silent working he said, 'And . . . ?'

No response.

'Carolyn?'

'What?'

'Are we going to talk about what just went down?'

'What do you mean?'

'I mean you going hysterical just now.'

'I wouldn't call it going hysterical. I get a little weepy when I drink.'

'A little *weepy*?' He stared at her and she stared back at him. Aside from a slight reddening of her eyelids there was no sign she had ever been anything but cool Carolyn Rolly. Who said, coolly, 'I'm sorry if I disturbed you. I really don't want to discuss it, if you don't mind,' and returned to her work.

Crosetti had to be content with that. Clearly, there was to be no leap into intimacy, no sharing of dark secrets, and no further physical contact. They worked in silence. Crosetti cleaned up the scant debris of their supper and the used paper towels. Rolly sat on a stool and did arcane things with her medieval tool-kit and the half-ruined books.

Something at a loss, Crosetti retrieved the manuscript pages, now barely damp, and spread them out on the kitchen counter and the spool table. He grabbed a magnifying glass from Rolly's worktable and examined a page at random. Some of the letters were obvious – the vowels were similar to modern ones, and short familiar words like *the* and *to* could be picked out easily. But actually reading the thing was another matter. Many of the words seemed to be mere sawtooth squiggles, and there were enough completely indecipherable letters to obscure the meaning of well over half the words. Besides that, several of the sheets seemed to be inscribed in some unfamiliar foreign tongue, but he couldn't be sure of that because the orthography was so difficult to make out. Was he really seeing such a word as *hrtxd*? Or *yfdpg*?

He decided to ignore the text and focus on the fabric and character of the sheets. All forty-eight were folio sized, and they appeared to fall into three classes. The first, consisting of eighteen sheets of fine thin paper, were closely written, neatly but with many crossed-out words and lines; they had at one time been deeply creased both vertically and horizontally. The second group consisted of twenty-six sheets of heavier paper, inscribed on both sides, and on these the writing was larger and messier, with a number of blots: despite this, it was written – at least to Crosetti's inexperienced eye – in the same hand used on the first eighteen sheets. On each page of this second group, the paper was evenly punctured along one side, as if it had been torn out of a book. Another peculiarity of this set is that they seemed to be overwritten upon faded brownish columns of figures. The word *palimpsest* popped into Crosetti's mind, and gave him an obscure satisfaction, although he understood that this was not a true example: palimpsests were normally parchment, where an old manuscript had been scraped down to make way for new text. But clearly this set of pages had been written on paper pressed into duty at need. The remaining four were the pages that had correction marks in pencil, and were clearly a different sort of paper and in a different hand. Crosetti held each of the pages up to the overhead lights and confirmed his guess: three different watermarks. The eighteen sheets of fine paper were marked with a curled post horn and the letters A and M; the twenty-six punctured sheets were marked with some sort of coat of arms; and the last four bore a crown.

But how did this collection wind up padding a binding in the mid-eighteenth century? Crosetti imagined a bookbindery of that era. There was a bale of wastepaper by the binder's table, a table probably not very different from the one at which Rolly now worked under the light of an articulated desk lamp, her slim neck shining bright and vulnerable against the dark matte of her scarf. It would have been stout English oak, scarred and stained, instead of laminated pallet-wood. The bookbinder sitting before it would have reached into the stack and pulled out six sheets, trimmed them to size with a razor knife against a steel rule, and laid them neatly against the boards.

It was just sheer luck, thought Crosetti, that so many sheets of what seemed to be from the same hand had ended up in this copy of the Churchill *Voyages*; but on second thought, maybe not. He imagined some old guy dying, and the widow or the heirs deciding to clean out the deceased's papers. They stack it all in bundles on the front step and send a kid to fetch the dealer in old paper, who comes, makes an offer, and carries the stuff away. Now they'll have room for a proper pantry, says the heir's wife, all that dusty old rubbish, pooh! And the old-paper guy tosses the bale into his bin, and after a while, he gets an order from a London bindery, regular customer, say, for a bale of scrap paper . . .

And because the pages with the pencil marks were not written in the same hand, the binder must have by chance mixed some unconnected printer's copy in with the scrap from Crosetti's tidying heiress. Yes, it could have happened that way, and this thought made him happy: he did not desire a miscellany, but a discovery. Although it was giving him a headache now, the peering through the glass, the way the black-brown squiggles refused to surrender their meaning. He put the magnifier down and walked the length of the loft.

'Do you have any aspirin?' he asked Rolly, and he had to ask twice. 'No,' said Rolly, in a near-snarl.

'Everyone has aspirin, Carolyn.'

She threw down the tool she was using, sighed dramatically, dismounted her stool, strode away, and returned with a plastic bottle that she shoved into his hand so hard it rattled like a tiny castanet. Motrin.

'Thank you,' he said formally and took three at the kitchen sink. Ordinarily he would have reclined in a quiet place until the pounding pain ceased, but chez Rolly had no comfortable seating, and he was wary of using her bed. He sat therefore on a kitchen chair and was glum and shuffled the sheaves of old paper. Were Carolyn Rolly an actual sane human person, he thought, we could puzzle this out together, she probably has books on watermarks and Jacobean secretary hand or at least she knows more about this shit than I do . . .

But as soon as he had this thought, he brightened and drew his cell phone from his pocket. He checked his watch. Not eleven yet. At eleven his mother watched the *Tonight Show* and would not answer the phone during that hour to hear of the Apocalypse, but now she'd be in her lounger with a book.

'It's me,' he said when she answered.

'Where are you?'

'I'm in Red Hook, at Carolyn Rolly's place.'

'She lives in Red Hook?'

'It's gentrifying, Ma.'

'It's dockies and gangsters. Why is a classy girl like that living in Red Hook?' Mrs Crosetti had met Carolyn on several occasions, at the shop, and delivered this assessment to her boy afterward, with the implication, like a thrown brick, that if he had any sense, he would put on some moves. She resumed, with a hopeful note, 'And how come you're there? You got something going with her?'

'I don't, Ma. It's the fire. She had to work on some heavy books at her place – she's kind of an amateur bookbinder – and I helped her carry them over here from the city.'

'And you hung around after.'

'We ate. I'm just about to leave.'

'So I shouldn't rent the hall. Or alert Father Lazzaro.'

'I don't think so, Ma. Sorry. Look, why I called . . . do you know anything about seventeenth-century watermarks, or Jacobean secretary hands? I mean how to decipher them?'

'Well, for the secretary hand, that would be Dawson and Kennedy-Skipton, *Elizabethan Handwriting, 1500–1650*. It's a manual, although I understand there's some good stuff on the Web, more like interactive tutorials. For the watermarks, there's Gravell . . . no, wait, Gravell starts at 1700; just a second, let me think . . . oh, right, it'd be Heawood, *Watermarks Mainly of the 17th and 18th Centuries*. What's this about?'

'Oh, we found some old manuscript in the covers of a book she wants to repair. I'd like to find out what it is.' He wrote the references down on a Visa counterfoil from his wallet.

'You should talk to Fanny Doubrowicz at the library. I'll call her for you if you want.'

'No, thanks. It's probably not worth her time until I know if it's not just an old shopping list or something. Part of it, some pages, are in a foreign language.'

'Really? Which one?'

'I can't tell. A funny one, anyway, not French or Italian – more like Armenian or Albanian. But that could just be because I can't really read the script.'

'Interesting. Good. Anything to keep that brain working. I wish you'd go back to school.'

'Ma, that's what I'm doing. I'm saving money to go to school.'

'I mean real school.'

'Film school *is* real school, Ma.'

Mrs Crosetti said nothing, but her son could well imagine the expression on her face. That she herself had not settled down to what became her profession until she was years older than he was now did not signify. She would have helped him pay for serious grad school, but making movies? No, thank you! He sighed and she said, 'I got to go. You'll be home late?'

'Maybe real late. We're interleaving wet books.'

'Really? Why don't you use a vacuum? Or just send them to Andover?'

'It's complicated, Ma. Anyway, Carolyn's in charge. I'm just the help.' He heard music faintly in the background and applause, and she said good-bye and hung up. It never failed to astonish him that a woman whose profession had given her an immense store of knowledge and who typically finished the *Times* Sunday crossword in twenty-two minutes could waste her time watching a celebrity gabfest and listen to a moderately talented comedian tell a skein of leaden topical jokes, but she never missed an evening. She said it made her feel less lonely at night, and he supposed that lonely people were in fact the main audience for such shows. He wondered if Rolly watched the *Tonight Show*. He had not seen a television in the place. Maybe vampires didn't get lonely.

Crosetti rose from the terrible chair and stretched. Now his back ached too. He checked his watch and walked the length of the loft to where Rolly was still bent over her tasks.

'What?' she said as he drew near.

'It's time to change the blotter. What're you doing?'

'I'm putting the cover of volume four back together. I'm

going to have to completely replace the covers on volumes one and two, but I think I can get the stains out of this one.'

'What're you using to replace the manuscript pages as backing?'

'I have some contemporary folio scrap.'

'Just happen to have it around, eh?'

'Yes, as a matter of fact,' she snapped back. 'There's a lot of it available from books broken for their maps and plates. Who were you talking to on the phone?'

'My mom. Look' – he gestured to the walls of bookcases – 'do you happen to have a book about watermarks? I have a reference . . .' He reached for his wallet.

'Well, I have Heawood, of course.'

Unfolding the counterfoil and smiling: 'Of course. How about Dawson and Kennedy-Skipton?'

'That too.'

'I thought you weren't a paleographer.'

'I'm not, but Sidney asked me to take a course on incunabula and early manuscripts and I did. Everyone in that field uses D & K-S.'

'So you can read this stuff?'

'A bit. It was some years ago.' Here again he heard a tone creep into her voice that discouraged probing.

'Can I take a look at those books after we do the interleaving?'

'Sure,' she said, 'but early secretary hand is a bear. It's like learning to read all over again.' They changed the blotters and then she extracted the two books from her shelves. She went back to work at her table and he sat down with the guidebooks at the spool table.

It *was* a bear. As the foreword to D & K-S has it, 'The Gothic cursive hands of the fifteenth to seventeenth centuries in England and elsewhere in Europe are among the hardest to read of all the scripts normally considered by paleographers.' Crosetti learned that the contemporaries of Elizabeth and James I made no distinction between *n* and *u*, or *u* and *v* or *i* and *j*, nor did they dot their *i*'s. *S* appeared in two different forms, and *r* in four, and there were strange ligatures tying *h* and *s* and *t* to other letters, distorting the shapes of each. They punctuated and spelled as they pleased, and to save expensive parchment they had invented dozens of incomprehensible abbreviations, which had remained in common use even when paper came in. Doggedly, however, he applied himself to the exercises provided by the manual, starting with Sir Nicholas Bacon's *An Exhortacion gyuen to the Serieaunts when they were sworne in the Chauncery in Anno domini 1559*. By the time he had reached line three, checking nearly every word against the translation provided, it was well past midnight. Rolly was still at her task, and he thought that if he could just rest his eyes and his aching back for a few moments he would get a second wind. He slipped off his sneakers and lay down on one edge of the pallet.

Then there was a weird clatter sounding in his ear. He sat upright with a curse and grappled in the bedclothes until he had the source of it in hand: an old-fashioned alarm clock, the kind they draw in cartoons, with twin bells and a clapper on top and a wide white face, and Carolyn had taped the bells so that when the thing went off it would not awaken her as well, a typically elegant low-tech solution. He shut it off and saw that there was a note affixed to it with a bit of ribbon:

Your turn; I did the last two myself.

It was written on a slip of heavy antique paper in black ink, the hand an elegant italic. Crosetti's violent annoyance instantly evaporated. He examined the deeply breathing shape in the bed next to him. He could see a shock of hair on the pillow, an ear, a curve of downy cheek. Cautiously, he leaned over and placed his face close to this, mere inches away. He breathed in long and deep and got soap, some kind of shampoo, a note of glue and old leather, and underneath this something more personal, eau de girl. Crosetti was no stranger to the delights of women, specializing in those that liked nice guys rather than the type (more numerous, in his experience) that preferred the other kind, nor was he even sure he particularly liked this woman. No, actually, he was sure he did not, and also sure that never in his life had he obtained an erotic charge as powerful as the one he now received, sniffing absurdly at the skin of Carolyn Rolly.

Incomprehensible, but there it was. He peeked under the duvet and found that she was wearing a dark T-shirt. He could just make out the little knobs of her spine bulging the thin fabric. Below that, dim whiteness. He had to know, and so he reached out and touched her, barely touched her haunch with the back of his hand, and felt tight, sheer fabric; a shock like an electric current flowed up his arm; she stirred and murmured.

He was out of the bed in a flash, and stood there feeling a jerk, with (could it be?) his knees actually trembling and his penis turgid. Holy shit, he said to himself several times, and then Uh-uh, no thank you, this is *not* happening. He marched like a soldier to the sink, where he drenched his face with cold water. He wished he could take a shower, but there was none, nor any bath either. An image of the occupant standing nude on a towel dabbing at her body with a warm sponge suddenly inhabited his mind. He forced it away by an act of will and started on the changing of the blotters.

After which he found himself with a couple of hours to kill before the next change, scheduled for 5 a.m. Briefly he considered poking through Rolly's things, checking out her underwear, her pharmaceuticals, her papers. He let this notion play for a while on his interior TV, and then dismissed the idea. The point was not to penetrate more deeply into whatever weird shit she had going on but to finish this stupid project and escape. Thus the mature Crosetti lectured Crazy Al, a new person who was dying to dive back under that duvet and yank Carolyn Rolly's panties down, or failing that, gather sufficient material to become a successful stalker.

But he did explore the kitchen and found in a cabinet (constructed of the ever-present pallet boards) a package of sugar cookies and one of those tin boxes of flavored instant coffee, hazelnut in this case, that he often saw in racks in the supermarket, when he often wondered who bought that crap. Now he knew. He boiled water in a pan and made the disgusting brew and drank it down for the caffeine's sake, and ate all the cookies, which were stale and like sweet gypsum in the mouth. On the evidence of her larder, Rolly obviously preferred live prey.

Somewhat pumped up now from the coffee and the sugary snack, Crosetti reset the alarm for five o'clock and renewed his investigation into the old papers. Before half an hour passed he was convinced that either he was going crazy or that the eighteen sheets marked by the post horn watermark were all in a language he did not know, or in some code . . . no, not code, cipher. Well, well, that might be interesting. The four crown-marked sheets, in a different and easier hand, appeared to be some sort of religious screed:

> *Worldly tears fall to the earth but godly tears are kept in a bottle. Judge not holy weeping superfluous. Either sin must drown in them or the soule burn*

He wondered briefly which kind Rolly had wept, and then put these pages aside. He was much more interested in the twenty-six sheets marked with a coat of arms, which were in the same hand as the ones written in the odd language. Within minutes he was gratified to discover that these were obviously in English. He could pick out the familiar short words – *of, and, is*, and the like – and after a while he located the beginning of the manuscript, or at least he thought it was the beginning. There was an inscription on the upper right, above the body of the text, the date *25th Octobr. Anno. Dom. 1642*, and the place, *Baubnmy*. No, that couldn't be right, or maybe it was Welsh, or . . . he examined the text again, and suddenly something clicked and he saw it was *Banbury*. Crosetti felt an odd thrill, akin to his delight when his film editing was going well, the emergence of meaning out of the raw stuff. It was a letter, he soon discovered, from a man named Richard Bracegirdle to his wife, called Nan, and not just a letter, but a final letter, and a . . . Crosetti knew there was a word for this sort of statement but could not recall it. Bracegirdle seemed to have been mortally wounded in a battle, although Crosetti had as yet no idea where the battle was fought, which contestants fought there, or in what war. Like many Americans, he had only the sketchiest idea of European history. What was going on in 1642? He'd look it up, and would have done so immediately, except that a computer with broadband access was another thing that Rolly lacked. He finished the first page and picked up the next; it had a signature on it, so was clearly the last page of the letter. He began it anyway, for the pages were unnumbered and there was no way of putting them in order without first reading them.

So he plowed on, line by line, slowly increasing his facility at translating Bracegirdle's hand. And there came at last a moment when Crosetti realized that he was reading the text somewhat more easily, and that the long-dead soldier was as alive to him as any chat room correspondent. The thrill redoubled at this realization, and the romance of paleography struck him like a blow: *no one else knew this!* No human being had read these lines for over three and a half centuries, perhaps no one had *ever* read them except for Bracegirdle and his wife. It was like looking out a rear window in an apartment building and observing some intimate act in the domestic life of strangers.

Some more thinges of import for my time groweth short I can scarce make out the page though it be clare day & I am griped by my mortal agonie you know well my leathern boxe that I keep in my privy closet, in it you shall finde the letteres cypher'd in the fasioun I devized. Doe you keepe them safe and show them to no one. They tell all the tale nearlie of my Lord D. his plot & oure spyeing upon the secret papist Shaxpure. Or so wee thought him although now I am lesse certayne. In that manner & bent of lyfe he wase a Nothinge. But certayne it is hee wrought the playe of Scotch M. I commanded of him in the Kinges name. I find it passing strange that all though I am dead and him also yet the playe lives still, writ in his own hande & lying where onlie I know & there maye it reste for ever.

Crosetti was so intent on deciphering each word into English sense that he missed it the first time through and it was only upon rereading this section that the connection between *Shaxpure* and *playe* actually penetrated his mind. He froze, gasped, cursed; sweat popped out on his back. He stood staring at Bracegirdle's squiggles, expecting them to fade away like fairy gold, but they stayed put: *Shaxpure, playe.*

Crosetti was a cautious fellow, and tight with a buck, but he occasionally picked up a lottery ticket, and once he had sat in front of his TV and watched the girl pull the numbered Ping-Pong balls out of the drum and followed the numbers on his ticket and let out a whoop when the numbers matched. But his mother had come in at the sound and informed him that where the winning number needed 8–3, his ticket read 3–8. Actually, he'd never won anything in his life, had never really expected to, had grown up a fairly happy kid from a working family with no sense of entitlement at all, and now this.

Crosetti was no scholar, but he had at least been an English major, and had done Shakespeare in his junior year. So he understood that what he held in his hands was a colossal find. Shakespeare (for he also knew that the man's name could be spelled in a vast number of ways) had not to his knowledge ever been the subject of an official government investigation. And for papism! What, if any, religion William Shakespeare had espoused continued as one of the big questions in the field, and if some official contemporary had believed it . . . and who was this Lord D.? For that matter, who was Richard Bracegirdle? And the cherry on top was the mention of a manuscript of one of the plays, extant at least until 1642. Crosetti tried to think what play it might be that was 'commanded of him in the Kinges name.' Oh, God! Why hadn't he paid more attention in that class? Wait a second! Something to do with King James, some noble had tried to kill him in a Scottish castle, and witchcraft, something in a BBC documentary he'd watched with his mother on TV. He grabbed his cell phone – no, still too early to call – maybe Rolly – no, he didn't want to think what she'd be like awakened at ten to five with a question about . . .

And just like that it popped into his mind. Shakespeare's company, the King's Players, had wanted a Scottish play to compliment the new king, and refer to his narrow escape, and flatter his ancestral connection, Banquo, and pander to the peculiar monarch's obsession with witchcraft, and the house playwright had come up with *Macbeth*.

Crosetti now recalled the necessity of respiration. He gasped. He knew there was nothing in Shakespeare's hand but a few signatures and some suspect lines in a manuscript of a play that he supposedly worked on. No autograph on any play of his existed, none. The possibility that an autographed *Macbeth* was still buried in an English cellar somewhere . . . it boggled the mind. Crosetti knew a little about manuscript prices and he could extrapolate. It was too immense to consider; Crosetti could not wrap his head around it and so he simply stopped thinking about the possibility. But even the thing in his hands now, the Bracegirdle ms. plus what might be a ciphered account of the investigation of William Shakespeare for recusancy, would be enough to send him to film school. Film school! It'd do that and fund his first movie as well . . .

Assuming always that the eighteen sheets of thin paper with the post horn watermark were in fact the secret letters Bracegirdle mentioned – and these ciphered English rather than a foreign language. Everything depended on the tidy heiress theory again: papers from the same stack of waste at the bindery being used in sequence to stuff the volumes of the *Voyage*. He spread out one of the sheets and examined it through the magnifying glass.

Ptuug u kimn If rmmhofl

Or maybe not. Maybe that first series of characters was *Ptmmg* or *Ptmng*. He found it impossible to derive even the actual ciphertext accurately, because deciphering secretary hand depended so much on context, on knowing what English word was meant. Or at least it was for him. He imagined that the original recipient was familiar enough with Bracegirdle's hand to read the ciphered letters and actually decipher it into plaintext. Crosetti knew little about ciphers except what he had picked up from movies, spy novels, and television. He knew what a ciphertext message was supposed to look like: equal blocks of five or six letters or numbers marching across the page. This didn't look like that at all. It looked like regular writing, with 'words' of differing length. Maybe that was how they wrote cipher in Jacobean times. He knew nothing of that subject, yet by analogy with other technical progress, such a cipher must have been fairly primitive. As he considered this, he recalled the difference between a cipher and a code. A code required a code book, or a memorized list of words that meant something other than what it appeared to be. But then it would have looked more like plain English, something like 'the parson failed to buy the pig' might mean 'the subject suspected of hiding a priest.' And that would limit what an intelligencer could relate. No, he simply knew that this was cipher; indeed, Bracegirdle had called it a cipher in his final letter.

The alarm rattled and Crosetti hurried over to squelch it. In the bed, Rolly turned over murmuring. Her eyes flicked open. Crosetti saw an expression of terror cross her face and her whole body jerked. He was about to say something soothing when she closed her eyes again and turned away, pulling the duvet over her head.

'Carolyn? You all right?'

No answer. Crosetti shrugged and went to change the

diapers. The blotters. They were barely damp now and the pages seemed almost dry to the touch, maybe a little cool: the miracle of capillary action. They were still buckled along the edges, in the way of paper that has been wetted, and the gilt edges of the text block no longer had the perfect smoothness of the pristine book. He wondered how she was going to fix that.

As he worked he heard sounds from the sleeping zone: throat clearing, the swish of fabric, the sound of running water, a toothbrush in action, more cloth sounds, the water again, the clunk of a pot, openings of cabinets. He was just finishing the last of the volumes when she appeared at his side, dressed in yesterday's overalls and black Converse high-tops with bright blue socks; she held two mugs of aromatic bad coffee, one of which she handed to him.

'I'm sorry I don't have any cream. Or milk.'

'That's okay,' he said. 'I'm sorry I startled you when the alarm went off. You looked like you were going to jump out of your skin.'

A blank look here, a small shrug. She opened a volume of the *Voyages* and felt the paper. 'This is good. It's almost dry.'

'What are you going to do about the buckling?'

'Press it out, or use heat. This kind of linen rag paper is a lot like cloth. I'll iron every edge if I have to and then trim and regild.' She turned to face him and smiled. 'Thanks for the help. I'm sorry I was cross with you last night. I'm not very social.'

He said, 'You let me sleep with you on our first date. I'd call that social,' and instantly regretted it when her smile faded, replaced by a wary look and a very proper sniff. Then, in her characteristic way, she pretended nothing untoward had been said and announced her plans for that day. She had to go out and buy leather for the covers and arrange for the patterned endpapers to be re-created; there were specialty shops in New York that did this sort of work.

'You want me to come along?' he asked when she had finished.

'I don't think that'll be necessary. It's going to be quite tedious. A slog, really.'

'I'm a slogger.'

'No, thanks. I think I have to do this by myself. And, ah, I'd like to get started right away.'

'You're booting me out?'

'I wouldn't put it that way. I'm sure you have things to do . . .'

'Nothing more important than traipsing around after you, carrying packages and hoping for the tiniest smile.'

He got it, just. Desiring to build on this, he asked, 'Don't you want to see what I discovered in those manuscripts we found in the cover padding?'

'Like what?'

'Well, for starters, they were written by a man who knew William Shakespeare.'

This got a reaction, although not exactly the one he desired. Her eyes widened, startled, and then rolled in disbelief. 'I find that rather unlikely.'

'Come here and I'll show you,' he said, and led her over to the spool table, where the folio sheets were stacked. He pointed to the key lines and explained about the ciphered pages. She examined the writing with the magnifying glass, and took her time doing it. He sat next to her and inhaled the scent of her hair. He did not kiss the back of her neck, although he had to actually grit his teeth not to.

'I don't see it,' she said, at last. 'Shakespeare was a fairly common name in some parts of England, and that name could also be "Shawford" or "Sharpspur," not Shaxpure.'

'Oh, please!' he exclaimed. 'Sharpspur who wrote plays? For the king? *And* who was suspected of being a papist *and* was significant enough to prompt an intelligence operation against him?'

'Shakespeare wasn't a papist.'

'He might have been. There was a program on PBS I saw that was pretty certain he was one, in secret, or at least that he was raised Catholic.'

'Uh-huh. So on the basis of – what is it? – two hours' experience in interpreting Jacobean secretary hand and a TV program you think you made a major literary discovery?'

'And the cipher letters?'

'They're probably Dutch.'

'Oh, fuck Dutch! They're in cipher.'

'Oh, you're an expert on ciphers too? Jacobean ciphers?'

'Okay, fine! One of my mother's best friends is Fanny Doubrowicz, who happens to be head of the Manuscript and Archives Division at the New York Public Library. I'll show it to her.'

He was watching her face as he said this and so was able to observe the quick intake of breath and the slight whitening around the nostrils that signaled . . . what? Spinning wheels, hatching plots? He'd seen it before when he'd called her on her current scam about the books and now here it was again.

She shrugged. 'Do what you want, but I think it's unlikely you're going to find a world-class expert on Jacobean secretary hand in the New York Public Library. Ninety percent of their holdings are American, mostly the paper of local writers and prominent families.'

'Well, it looks like you know everything, Carolyn. I guess I'm just a big asshole, who will now' – here he made a show of stacking the manuscript sheets – 'get out of your hair, and take my pathetic manuscript to my low-end pathetic expert who will *obviously* tell me that it's a letter from some Jacobean pissant about his case of gout.'

He strode over to her workbench and snatched up the brown paper that had wrapped the *Voyages* yesterday and began to secure the manuscript in it, using the jerky, clumsy motions that indicate irritation.

'Oh, don't,' she said from behind him in an uncharacteristically high voice. 'Oh, I'm sorry, I don't know how to behave. You were so excited about it and I just . . .'

He turned around. Her mouth was turned down into an amusing inverted U like many of the indeterminate bumps that made Jacobean secretary hand so confusing. It looked like the start of another wailing session. But she continued in the same strangled voice: 'I never see anyone. I haven't got a life. The only person I've talked to in years is Sidney, and he just wants to be like my *mentor*, which means mainly he gets to paw me and . . .'

'Sidney paws?'

'Oh, he's harmless. He thinks he's some kind of big-time rake, but all he does is take me to expensive lunches and squeeze my leg under the tablecloth and sometimes in the shop, if we make a big sale he'll grab my ass and hold on for a little too long, and he'll kiss me semi-quasi-paternally on the mouth. He's the last man in New York who chews Sen-Sens. That's the extent of my whoredom. I need the job and the food. You're the only one I ever told this to. Talk about pathetic. I have no friends, no money, no place to live . . .'

'You live here.'

'Illegally, as you guessed. This building is condemned for human habitation. They used to store DDT here and it's totally contaminated. The guy who owns the building thinks I just work here. He'd like to paw me too. You're the first person my own age I've been with in, I don't know . . . *years*.'

Who is also dying to paw you, thought Crosetti, but said only, 'Gosh, that's sad.'

'Yes, pitiable. And you're decent to me and I treat you like shit. So typical! If you were a complete shithead I'd probably be slavering at your feet.'

'I could *try* to be a shithead, Carolyn. I could write away to the Famous Shitheads School and take a course.'

She stared at him and after a moment laughed. It was an odd barking sound not too distant from a sob. 'But you hate me now, right?'

'No, I don't,' said Crosetti with as much sincerity as he could cram into the phrase. He was thinking about why she should have chosen to isolate herself so. She was not a fatty, not disfigured, presentable, 'classy' as his mother had observed, no reason for someone like that to skulk in the shadows of the city. And she was, if not actually a beauty, a . . . what was the word? A fetching woman. When her face was together, as now, when she was not scowling or scarily vacant, she could have fetched him from Zanzibar.

'On the contrary,' he added. 'Really.'

'No? But I've treated you so badly.'

'Yes, and now I'll give you a minute to think how you're going to make it up to me.' He hummed and looked at his watch, and tapped his foot.

'I know what I'll do,' she said after a moment. 'I will introduce you to a *real* expert on Jacobean manuscripts, one of the best in the world. I'll call him and set it up. And you can come with me on my errands and be bored stiff while I talk about split calf and marbled endpapers and then we'll go see Andrew.'

'Andrew?'

'Yes. Andrew Bulstrode. Sidney introduced us. That was who I took that course on English manuscripts and incunabula from.'

'Does he want to feel you up too?'

'No. You, maybe.'

'I can't wait.'

'You'll have to, a little. I need to visit the bathroom and then I'll make the call. Why don't you wait for me downstairs?'

The Bracegirdle Letter (4)

Despyte his unseemlie lyfe Mr Matthews workes did prosper mightilie for he knew his art welle, better they sayde than any iron-maistre in the Weald of Sussex. He had contract with the Royal Ordnance & that wase oure chief labour: makeyng of iron & casting gonnes. I was first put to loading & hauling & such donkey-taskes being as I was ignorant of all arte & if I grieved for my lost ease & tyme to studie that which I loved, still I balked not for as God speaketh: whatsoever thy hande findeth to do, do it with thy might: for there is no worke nor device, nor knowledge, nor wisdome in the grave whither thou goest.

Now you can onlie caste iron from winter through springe: for in summer you have not the flow of water to werke the mills that empouwer the bellowes that maketh the blaste for the furnaces & the hammers for the forging of your bar-iron: & in summer must you bryng ironstone & charcoal & tayke away what you have mayde, before the roades myre. Soe they muste werke us like dogges in those few moneths: & in every werke we did whether hoisting pigges or carrying iron-stone & charcoales to feed the furnace, or clayeyng the mandrel, or layyng the mould, or heavinge the coolled peeces from the pitte, or knockyng off the sprues, or fileing smoothe, the maistre poynted out mee for being the moste laxe or a blockheade or clumsy withal &

maney a harde blow I got from his hande or staffe, & called Sloppy Dick & Malhand Dick & other like naymes or worser. Yet I rebelled not & turned the othere cheeke, as commanded by oure Lord Jesu Christ & I vowed I would learne the worke, all though it went hard gainst my graine, so that he would have no cause for despising mee or but a little. And in the heate & smoakes of that place which wase the nearest I ever came to what we trust shalbe the fate of all sinners (& that is Hell) to my surprize I found some delight. For it wase a joy to see the blazyng iron spoute from the mouth of the furnace into the mould tossyng up sparkes like the stars in the skye & to thinke that it was, if only in littel, lyke the work of God in the makeyng of our worlde: for if I loved not the werke it self still I loved the werkes done. For these gonnes would be a sheeld against the enemies of England & the reformed religion: as all men acknowledge Englishe gonnes have no equal in the world, & oure shotte as well, soe let Spaine lament.

In this wise a year passed & two & cometh then Ladye Day in the Yeare Three as I stoode before Maistre Matthew to get my wage he sayde well Richard think you I have used you harde? And being honeste I sayde yes Mr that you have. He laughed & sayde still you have grown two span & waxed more than a stone o' weight & no more art thou the clerkely puling thynge thou wast but a true foundryman: for you know wee pound on iron not because wee despise it but to mayke it stronge.

After that he used me more kindly & beggan to instruct me in all the mysteries of the founders art, viz. how to tell good iron-stone, that there wase enough shell in it else addyng more shellstone & when to tap heats & controll the bellowes its ayre so that the heat did not sicken the iron & what divers heats were goode for as: the first mere pigge iron, the seconde, bar & firebacks, the third tooles, the fourth smalle gonnes, as sakers & falcons & the last alone for the greate gonnes, viz. culverines, demicannon & cannon royal, &c. Also how to prepare the mandrel with corde & clay & how to packe the mould so it cracke not nor leake & how to rigge cordes & pulleys for the liftyng of heavie weightes. Soe another yeare passed, me growing in craft & art & size too for he sate me at his own tabel & fed me welle. Then at the ende of this yeare he shewed me how to loade & fyre the gonnes.

Hard it may be for you to understand Nan being but a woman, but when first I heard the cannones roare I wase a lost man I had a luste beyond alle tellyng to heare it again & see the flyte of the balle, it wase a drunkenesse of pouwer & might. Soe my cozzen sees this & of his goodnesse says – and this wase nowe sommertyme of the Yeare Fyve me being aged fifteen yeares & a littel – lad, I must stay & over-see the mending of the mill-race & wheel, do you goe along with oure brace of culverines to the Tower & see them assayed by the Ordnance. I was verey eager to do so having not seen my mother & father alle this tyme, so off I went in two cartes the gonnes bedded in strawes, six oxen to each & men hyred to drive &

keep, from Titchfield to Portsmouth, thence by lugger to Gravesende & changed to barge up river to the Tower, me never ben on boat before now & lyked it well, nor was I sea-sick lyke some others that were aboard.

The gonnes delivered to the Tower without mishap for which I thanked God most heartilie for the moveing of two loades of 48 cwt each is no smalle thynge with the roades as they were in those daies & the drovers much given to drinke & the common perills of the sea. I repaired to Fish Street & wase welcomed with all friendlinesse bye my family who were much surprized at my mans appearance & kept me late with telling of what had befallen in the yeares since I last had seen them. But my fathere wished to uze me as he once hadde which I could hardlie stande, beinge now a man not a boy, yet I did beare it for my motheres sake & for the peece of the house & in accord with the commandment honor thy father &c. We had a new servante mayde Margaret Ames a sour canting creature if a goode Christian who for what raison I never descryed lyked me not.

Then the nexte morn earlie I made to the Tower for the assaye. The officer of the Ordnance Peter Hastynges by name wase amazed at my youth as he had expected my cozzen as in times before. So both culverin were double-charged to see if they brake but thank God did not. Aftewarde I sat at mete with Mr Hastynges & some other officers, the talk very merrie but bawdy as many of the companie were cannon-

maistres lately come from the Dutch warres. Such talk lyked me well for I yearned to be familiar with these artes & pressed them to answer my questions viz. how to site a gonne for best advauntage in the field, how to best aim to strake your marke, the divers sortes & qualities of poudre, how to mix & preserve it, & how to know how farre distant be your marke. This laste put them at a stande for they contended amongst them, one sayde by truste of eye another sayde nay by tryal of fire, looking close where the ball fell at everie shotte adding or taking away of poudre & also changing this according to the heate of the gonne as the day spent, for a hot gonne will throw farther of the same charge.

So I asked why they did not use the methode of triangles & sines & at this they were amazed haveing not heard aught of this beforre. Soe I drew a little picture shewing how a gonners quadrant, a square & a yard-sticke could be soe used to take the distance from one point to another far offe. They had to see & trye this methode without delay & I arranged all & tried to a distant tree & wee paced it out after & they were greately pleazed thereby how it accorded with my figures. Then a bigge heartie man Thomas Keane clapped my shoulder saying lad I would make a true gonner of you, be you ever wearie of making gonnes you can come with mee as matrosse to the warre & shoote them at Spaniardes, for a matrosse you know is a gonneres holpe. Soe I thanked hym kindlie but sayde I had no thought of warre then, how little we know Lord of youre devizynges or youre werkes.

5

To my credit, I suppose, I did not immediately race back to the office after the two detectives left. I finished my normal routine at the gym and took a shower and had a steam before returning. In the car, I admit I was not as engaged as I usually am with Omar's conversation. Omar worries a little obsessively about our involvement in Iraq and in general about the relations between his adopted nation and the Islamic world. His experience in this city after 9/11 has not been pleasant. This particular morning, as the radio murmured the latest bad news, and Omar put in his comments, the only atrocity that engaged me was the grim fate of my late client, Bulstrode. Could he actually have found a document that led to an invaluable manuscript? And had someone killed him to find out where said document was? There followed the even less pleasant thought: torture meant a desire for information, and what information did Bulstrode have to give out but the name of the person to whom he had given his manuscript, which was me? I did not really know the man, but I did not consider for one second the possibility that when they put the pain on him he would be able to conceal the location of that fat envelope.

Again, as with the cops, the feeling of unreality, the slipping into the forms established by fiction. Shortly after I graduated from college, that being still the era of the draft, and not being the resistant type, I yielded to the inevitable and volunteered myself (virtually alone among my graduating class I believe) as a draftee. They made me into a medic rather than an infantryman, and I ended up in the Twelfth Evac Hospital in Cu Chi, in South Vietnam. Unlike my S.S. grandfather, I was an entirely undistinguished soldier, being what was then known as a rear-area-motherfucker, or white mouse, but I did see an ammo dump spectacularly explode after being hit by an enemy rocket, and I recall all the witnesses thereto, in order to validate the experience, repeatedly using the phrase 'it was just like the movies.' Thus, although life is by and large unthrilling, when we do find ourselves in the sort of situation upon which thrillers dote we cannot really experience it, because our imaginations are occupied by the familiar tropes of popular fiction. And the result of this is a kind of dull bafflement, and the sense that whatever it is cannot *really* be happening. We actually think that phrase: this *can't* be happening to *me*.

Back at the office, I obtained the safe-deposit box key from the place where Ms Maldonado keeps it, having waited for her to be away from her desk. I retreived the Bulstrode envelope and took it back to my office. Ms Maldonado looked at me inquiringly when I returned her key, but I did not offer to explain, nor did she ask. I said I wanted to be undisturbed until further notice and locked my office door.

I am no expert, but the papers from the envelope looked genuinely old. Of course, they would, if forgeries, but clearly *someone* believed in their validity, assuming Bulstrode had been tortured to reveal their whereabouts. There were two separate series of papers, both clearly in English, although using a style of handwriting I could not easily read, except for the shortest of words. One was marked up in what looked like soft pencil.

I put the papers into a fresh manila envelope and shredded the old one, after which I returned them to the bank. Then back to business for the rest of the afternoon. The next day, my diary tells me, I had lunch with Mickey Haas. We do, or did this, on average once a month or so, with him usually making the call, as he did this time as well. He suggested Sorrentino's near my place, and I said I would send Omar to pick him up. This is our usual practice when he comes downtown. Sorrentino's is one of a large number of nearly interchangeable Italianoid restaurants that dot the side streets of midtown on the East Side of Manhattan, and which live by serving somewhat overpriced lunches to people like me. The more prosperous denizens of this great mass of Manhattan office space each have a favorite Sorrentino's; it is much like being at home, but with no domestic stress. They all smell the same, they all have a maître d' who knows you, and what you like to eat and drink, and at lunch they all seat at least two interesting-looking women upon which the solitary middle-aged diner can rest his eyes and exercise his imagination.

Marco (the maître d' who knows me in particular) seated me in my usual table in the right rear and brought me, unbidden, a bottle of his private *rosso di Montalcino*, a bottle of San P., and a plate of anchovy bruschetta for nibbles while I waited. After about half a glass of the delicious wine, Mickey walked in. He has gained a good deal of mass over the years, as I have, although I am afraid that his consists almost entirely of fat cells. His chin has clearly doubled, where mine retains something of its former line. His hair, however, is still thick and curling, unlike mine, and his mien confident. On this occasion I recall that he appeared uncharacteristically haggard, or maybe haunted would be a better word. The skin under his eyes was bruised looking, and the eyes were bloodshot and pinched. He was not exactly twitching, but there was something wrong. I've known the man for years and he was not right.

We shook, he sat down and immediately poured himself a glass of wine, of which he drank half in one go. I asked him whether anything was wrong and he stared at me. Wrong? I just had a colleague murdered, he said, and asked me hadn't I heard and I told him I had.

Reading this over, I just decided that from now on I'm going to concoct dialogue, like journalists seem to do with impunity nowadays, because it is a pain in the ass to paraphrase what people say. The fellow who invented the quotation mark was no fool; if only he had established the copyright! Thus:

I asked, 'When did you hear about it?'

'My secretary called me in Austin,' he said. 'I'd just given my paper at the morning session, and of course, I had my cell off and as soon as I turned it on there was Karen's message. I flew back right away.' He drank off his glass and poured another. 'Can I have a real drink? I'm turning into an alcoholic behind this.'

I gestured to Paul, our waiter, who was there in an instant. Mickey ordered a gimlet.

'And then when I got back, chaos, needless to say. The university was going ballistic, with the implication from my chairman, that asshole, that somehow it was my fault for obtaining the appointment for someone of dubious moral status.'

'Was he?'

Mickey flushed at this and snapped back, 'The *point* is that he was also one of the great Shakespeare scholars of his generation. Our generation. And his only crime was that he was duped by a swindler, which could have happened to any one of the people who now condemn him, including my fucking chairman. Do you know this story?'

I assured him that I had perused the available material on the Web.

'Right, a fucking catastrophe. But that wasn't what the police were interested in. They had the nerve to imply that he was living, how did they delicately put it? An irregular lifestyle. By which they meant to imply that he was queer, and that his being queer had something to do with his death.' He drank down the remains of his gimlet. Paul floated over and asked if he wanted a refill and also presented him with a menu nearly the size of a subway billboard. He glanced at it without interest, which confirmed my earlier impression that he was seriously distraught: Mickey loves food; he loves to eat it, and talk about it, and cook it, and recall it.

'What are you having?' he asked.

'What am I having, Paul?' I inquired of the waiter. It has been years since I ordered anything off the menu here.

'*Carciofi alla giudia*, gnocchi *alla romana*, osso bucco. The osso bucco is very good today.'

Mickey handed back the menu. 'I'll have that too.'

When Paul left, Mickey continued, 'They had some theory he got involved in rough trade. I mean the police imagination, right? They see Brit and gay and it's some rent boy he hired to tie him up and it went too far.'

'Not possible?'

'Well of course *anything's* possible, but I happen to know that Andy had a discreet long-term relationship with a fellow don at Oxford. His tastes did not run that way.'

'He might have changed. One never can tell.'

'One can, in this case. Jake, I have known the man for over twenty years.' He took a drink from his second gimlet. 'I mean it'd be like finding out *you* were chasing boys.'

'Or you,' I said, and after a moment we both laughed.

He said, 'Oh, God, we shouldn't be laughing. The poor bastard! Only I'm damn glad I was a thousand miles away when it happened. The cops were looking at me with uncomfortable interest, sniffing me for the telltale signs of perverted inversion.'

'The cops were Murray and Fernandez?'

He stared at me, his smile gone. 'Yeah, how did you know?'

'They came to see me, to see if I could shed light.'

'Why would they do that?'

'Because he was my client. He came to me with some story about a manuscript he'd turned up. I assumed that you sent him.'

Mickey gaped at me. Paul appeared and laid down our Jewish artichokes. When we were alone again, Mickey leaned toward me and, with lowered voice, said, 'I didn't send him. No, wait a second – he did ask me once if I knew an intellectual property lawyer and I said my best friend was one, and mentioned your name. I asked him why he was interested and he told me he'd come across some manuscripts that might be publishable and wanted to know their status under law. And he actually came to see you?'

'Yes,' I said. 'He told me he had a manuscript that revealed the whereabouts of an unknown Shakespeare manuscript . . .' I was beginning to relate what I had told Bulstrode when Mickey swallowed a half of an artichoke heart and coughed violently and had to wash it down with San Pellegrino before he could speak.

'No, no, he had a manuscript that *mentioned* Shakespeare. Or so he claimed. I never saw the thing myself. Because of what happened with Pascoe, he was more than a little paranoid. He made a trip to England about that time – it was last summer – and when he came back he was, I don't know, not himself. Nervous. Irritable. He refused to talk about what he had, except that it was a completely unknown mention of William Shakespeare in a genuine contemporary manuscript. He didn't tell me where he'd found it, by the way. I bet that's some story!'

'You mean somebody just *mentioning* Shakespeare in a manuscript, that would make it valuable per se?'

He stopped mopping sauce with his bread: another gape here and an incredulous laugh.

'Valuable? Christ, yes! Cosmically important. Epochally significant. I thought I explained this to you any number of times, but obviously not enough.'

'Then once more, please.'

Mickey cleared his throat and held his fork up like a classroom pointer. 'Okay. Aside from his work, the single greatest literary achievement by an individual human being in all of history, William Shakespeare left practically no physical trace in the world. You can just about write down everything we know for sure about him on a wallet card. He was born, christened, got married, had three kids, wrote a will, signed a few legal documents, composed an epitaph, and died. The only physical evidence of his existence besides those records and his grave is a suspect sample of what looks like his handwriting on a manuscript of a play called *The Book of Sir Thomas More*. Not a single letter, or inscription, not a book with his name in it. Okay, the guy was a luminary of the

London theater for nearly twenty years, so there are a whole bunch of references to him, but they're pretty thin soup. The first one is an attack on someone called 'Shake-scene' by an asshole called Robert Greene, and an apology for printing it by a guy named Chettle. Francis Mere wrote a book called *Palladis Tamia*, *Wit's Treasury*, which would have been justly forgotten except that he mentions Shakespeare as the best English dramatist. He's mentioned by William Camden, the headmaster of Westminster, and by Webster in the preface to *The White Devil*, and there's a mention by Beaumont in *The Knight of the Burning Pestle*. And there's a bunch of legal stuff, contracts, lawsuits, leases, plus various theater references, plus, of course, the central fact of the First Folio. His pals thought enough of him to publish all his plays in one book after he died, and name him as author. That's basically it – what is that, a couple dozen or so substantive contemporary references. And on this has been built an absolutely enormous scholarship, mining the plays and poems for suggestions about the man, completely speculative, of course, because we just don't know. It drives us crazy because the guy was smoke. I mean there's *nothing* there.'

'It was a long time ago.'

'Yes, but we know shitloads more about Leonardo, just to name an obvious example, and *he* lived a century earlier. For the sake of comparison – just one example – we have an actual letter from Edmund Spenser to Walter Raleigh explaining some of the allegories in *The Faerie Queene*. We know a *lot* about Ben Jonson. Michelangelo – there are nearly *five hundred* of his letters surviving, notebooks, fucking *menus*, and from Shakespeare, the greatest *writer* of all time, and an important theatrical entrepreneur besides, not a single letter. And the problem is that the vacuum sucks fake stuff in. There was a vast Shakespeare forgery industry back in the eighteenth, nineteenth centuries, and there's even some today, which is how Bulstrode got caught. Not to mention the cottage industry represented by the so-called authorship question: we haven't got anything from him except the work, ergo someone else did the work – Southampton, Bacon, *extraterrestrials* . . . I mean I can't express to you how intense the desire is to find out stuff about the son of a bitch. If Bulstrode actually did find a contemporary manuscript that mentions Shakespeare, especially if it contained substantive information – why it would absolutely resurrect him in the field.'

When Mickey talks about his work he drops twenty years and resembles more than he usually does now the youth I met in that scabby apartment on 113th Street. I confess that I can't imagine such a transformation in my case, should I wish to expatiate on the intricacies of, say, the Digital Millennium Copyright Act. He loves his profession, and I admire him for it. And am a little envious too, I suppose. But now, as he mentioned Bulstrode, his eyes clouded. And was that moisture? It was hard to tell in the friendly gloom of the restaurant.

'Well,' he resumed, 'not anymore, obviously. I would have given a lot to take a look at those papers though. God knows what happened to them.'

Here I thought he looked at me in a somewhat disingenuous fashion. All decent lawyers are close-mouthed about their clients' affairs, nor does mere death spring open their lips, but they are casual gossips compared to us IP lawyers. So I did not rise to the bait, if bait there was, but asked, 'Is there something wrong?'

He said, 'You mean besides Bulstrode getting killed? Isn't that enough?'

'You look like you're carrying more than that, pal,' I said.

'I've been noticing it the last couple of times too. You're not sick or anything?'

'No, aside from the fact that I'm fat as a hog and get no exercise, I'm a horse. Arteries like shotguns according to my doc. No, what you're observing is the physical stigmata of the current market.'

Here I should mention that Mickey and I have different attitudes toward investment. My pile is with a mutual fund started in 1927 that has never paid much more or much less than 7 percent per annum. Mickey calls this irresponsible conservatism, or did when the market was roaring some years ago. He is a hedge fund guy, and he used to regale me with tales of his fantastic returns; no longer. I said, 'Well, you still have the industrial fasteners,' at which he barked a laugh.

'Yeah, if I didn't have to share them with the two dozen cousins. My family suffers from an excess of heirs.'

I sensed he wished not to pursue this subject so I said, 'Speaking of which, do you know if the late professor had any heirs? I take it there were no children.'

'There's a niece: Madeleine or something like that. Picture on his desk. His late sister's kid, and he doted on her. I expect she'll inherit whatever he had. Or the longtime companion.'

'Has she been notified?'

'Yeah. She's coming down this week.'

'From England?'

'No, from Toronto. The sister emigrated years ago, married a Canadian, had the one kid. Ah, here's our gnocchi. You know, I think I'm getting my appetite back.'

As we dug into the meltingly tender dumplings, I said, 'So the manuscript doesn't actually lead any further – it's not a clue to something even bigger?'

Through gnocchi Mickey responded, 'Bigger than a

contemporary reference to Shakespeare? I can't imagine what that would be. Did he tell you that?'

'He suggested that his manuscript mentioned another manuscript actually by Shakespeare.'

'Oh, right! Pure fantasy would be my guess. As I said, Andrew was utterly desperate to get back in the game. With good reason. When the will is cleared up and what's-her-name has possession, we'll take a look at it and see if it's anything. Although, given the man's desperation to recoup his career, I rather think it'll be nothing much.'

We spoke no more of Bulstrode during this meal (in which Mickey actually did get his appetite back and joked about the garbage they had to eat in Texas) or his mysterious manuscript, or even more mysterious demise.

As far as I recall, that is, since the above is a complete fabrication. I have eaten those dishes and drunk such wine at Sorrentino's, perhaps with Mickey Haas in attendance, and there is a Marco and a Paul, but I am in no position to attest that we ate those things on that day, many months ago. I can hardly recall what I had for lunch last Tuesday, nor can anyone else. I did garner some facts about Shakespeare, but whether on that occasion or later, I could not say. I recall that he was upset, and I recall that it was the first occasion at which I learned of the existence of that young woman. Miranda, not Madeleine, as it happens. Aside from that it is fiction, but even as I wrote it, it became the truth, because in point of fact we have virtually no real memories. We make it all up. Proust made it up, Boswell made it up, Pepys . . . I have actually a great deal of sympathy for the increasingly common sort of person, often one with a high position, who is caught fabricating. You mean I *didn't* go to Harvard Med School? I did not have sex with that woman . . . It's not the collapse of morality (for I think there has never been truth based on memory) but rather the triumph of intellectual property, that blizzard of invented realities – artificial lives, Photoshopped photos, ghosted novels, lip-synched rock bands, fabricated reality shows, American foreign policy – through which we daily slog. Everyone, from the president on down, is a novelist now.

I suppose we can blame Shakespeare himself for starting it, because he made up people who were *more* real, though false, than the people one knew. Dick Bracegirdle understood this, which was why he set out to smash Shakespeare and all his works. I took a history course at Columbia – Haas will recall it too, because I took it on his recommendation – a man named Charlton taught it. It was English medieval history, and although I have expunged the Domesday Book and all the kings and queens from my mind, I recall very well his take on history in general. He said there are three kinds of history. The first is what really happened, and that is forever lost. The second is what most people thought happened, and we can recover that with assiduous effort. The third is what the people in power wanted the future to think happened, and that is 90 percent of the history in books.

(Anyway, reading over this scene in the restaurant I find I am absurdly pleased with it. Yes, it could have happened that way. That *is* Mickey's voice I've put there, and I expect that people who know him, if they read the above, would agree. And I find that reality has swum in to inhabit the fiction I created, and I am absolutely sure that if Mickey read it he would say, Yeah, I recall it just like that. So I write the second kind of history here. As did Bracegirdle, I imagine, although he was an honest man, and I am not.)

I should mention now that shortly after this event I stopped into one of those electronics shops on Sixth Avenue to buy a cell phone battery and for reasons I can't quite recall . . . no, actually I do recall. As noted, I have a mind more disorderly than I would prefer and have been in the habit of scrawling down random notes about this and that when they occur to me, in the pages in the back of that aforesaid diary. Unfortunately, I sometimes find I can't read what I've written: *see urty abt. srtnt* would be a typical notation. But while I was in the shop my eye fell on a digital voice-activated recorder, a Sanyo 32, and I thought to myself that here was a solution to my disorder and I purchased it for seventy-two bucks. It is the size of a cell phone and it records two solid hours in high-quality mode. Since I bought it, the last two hours of my life's sound track has been saved for later listening. It has been invaluable to the present exercise.

After lunch, I ran Mickey back uptown in the Lincoln. He'd drunk most of the wine with the couple of gimlets and he was fairly well oiled. When Mickey gets like this he invariably talks about his three wives. The first Mrs H. was his college sweetheart, Louise, a strapping blonde from a fine old New England family, who doled out sexual favors standing up under the balcony and the hanging ivy of her Barnard residence hall, as we all did in those days, and somewhat more intimate ones in our apartment. She started letting him fuck her in senior year after she had the ring, another jolly tradition of those times. I recall weekend mornings in the apartment, Mickey in his maroon velour bathrobe (or dressing gown as he pretentiously called it) making fussy coffee with a Chemex, and Louise swanning in, faintly embarrassed at the sight of me at the kitchen table, but carrying it off with class. She usually appeared on these occasions in black tights with one of Mickey's Oxford dress shirts on top, an outfit I have ever since considered wildly erotic. (Tights were underwear in those days; I have never quite become used to girls racing around town exhibiting their bodies in them – always a certain vibration in the scrotum.) She also appeared without bra, as she was an early adopter of that style, and she had lovely, pointed, jiggly ones too.

The assumption at these matinees was always that Mickey was the big stud with the mistress, while I was the poor but honest sexually deprived grind, and didn't we all giggle at this play! In fact, at the time I was getting rather more sex than I could handle from a woman named Ruth Polansky, a thirty-six-year-old librarian at the Farragut Branch of the New York Public Library. This I kept secret from my roommate and everyone else, out of embarrassment for myself and a credible fear for Ruth's job. Is this germane to the story? In a way, if only as evidence of how early my training in sexual dissemblage began. I suppose there is nothing quite so explosive as an affair between a teenaged boy and a woman of a certain age, in which the peak capacity of the male is matched by the hunger of the female. The French exhibit a certain awe at such affairs and have a whole literature on this subject, but in America it is (Mrs Robinson!) treated only as farce.

Our particular affair was farcical enough, for our major problem was finding a place to do it in. She lived with her mother and I lived with Mickey Haas, neither of us had a car, I was destitute, as I've mentioned, and a librarian's pay did not run to springing for hotel rooms. Miss Polansky and I had been acquainted for years, and she had been an interested observer of my adolescent growth and the accumulation of heavy musculature that attended it. She was a small, pale woman with silky colorless hair that she wore in a ponytail, making her look younger than her age. Unusually, for that era, she was divorced, which added a certain spice to my fantasies about her, which began at about age twelve. As

I (falsely, I suppose) reconstruct it, she brought me along quite skillfully, using my interest in theater to turn my thoughts toward the sort of erotic life not generally available in high schools at the time. She gave me books, plays: Williams, Ibsen, *Tea and Sympathy*, erotic French poetry, and *Ulysses*, these last on loan from her private collection. It is in any event not hard to seduce a teenage boy in a book-smelling, steam-heated library on a drowsy winter afternoon. She didn't mind the pimples. She complimented my eyes. Sexy, she said, bedroom eyes.

The primary seduction occurred in the staff room at the library. She had a fifteen-minute break, the other librarian was at the front desk. We did it in a chair, close to a radiator that hissingly leaked steam, although it had nothing on Mrs Polansky. I lasted only a few minutes but that was enough to send her into a remarkable paroxysm, during which, because she did not wish to attract the attention of the library patrons, she caused volumes of air to issue from between her clenched teeth, since which time I have always found the whistle of escaping steam to be lubricious. I did not get to hear her full-throated cry of ecstasy until the city began closing libraries on Tuesday and Thursday afternoons and I was able to start using my old room in the family apartment while Mutti was working at the hospital.

We had a window of about three hours between noon and when my sister returned from school, of which a good deal was consumed by the subway ride from uptown Manhattan to eastern Brooklyn, so that we were clawing off our clothes from the instant the front door clicked shut. Mrs Polansky was not the noisiest orgasmer I have ever encountered, but she was a contender, producing at the peak a series of deep, loud organlike groans; and it was only to be expected, given the farcical nature of our affair, that one day, after our typical exertions and having arranged our clothes for the world, we should have encountered Mutti sitting at the kitchen table. She'd taken the afternoon off for some reason, and I never knew how long she'd been sitting there. Her face was unreadable as I introduced Mrs P. as a math tutor helping me with my algebra. Ruth extended her hand and Mutti shook it, quite correctly, and offered coffee.

I haven't thought of that afternoon in quite some time. I really don't like thinking about that apartment at all, especially the kitchen.

Back to Mickey and his wives. Louise, as I said, was the first, and lasted the usual seven years. By then it was the height of the sexual revolution, and Mickey wanted his share, which was not all that hard for a professor to pick up, and so then there was Marilyn Kaplan, the eternal grad student. By this time Mickey had a couple of kids and a dog in his big Scarsdale house, and so it cost him a bundle to slake his lust for Marilyn. Of the three wives, Marilyn is the most classically beautiful: big black eyes, glossy long chestnut hair, and the great American girl body, long legs, thin waist, cannonball breasts. She was a staunch feminist of the high 1970s school, utterly contemptuous of the male gaze, while attracting it without cease, and waxing great upon the advantages it conferred. She produced another child, and after some three years vanished with a fellow from, I think, Berkeley, an epicene bisexual of flawless politics, or so I gathered. As Mickey explained it, the problem was largely intellectual: he simply was not on her level with respect to literary theory. This was something nearly as important to her as sex, at which, according to Mickey, she was the dominant partner and of boundless energy and inventiveness.

I heard her lecture once. Mickey took me, a lecture called something like 'Privileging the Text in the Late Comedies:

Speech Act Theory and Discursive Formation in Shakespeare.' I did not understand one single word of it, and told Mickey so, and he tried to explain to me about Foucault and Althusser and Derrida and the revolution in the study of literature of which Marilyn was an ornament, but I could see that his heart was not in it. Mickey's problem, I gathered, was that while he could talk the current critical talk, and did it surpassing well, his heart was not really in it, for he *loved* Shakespeare, and loving anything was apparently a bourgeois affectation concealing the machinations of the oppressive patriarchy. Marilyn thought she could change him, thought she could blow some fresh air into his paternalistic, bourgeois view of literature, but no. And he had never made her come, not like Gerald-from-Berkeley could, or so she told him. She left him the kid, though.

Number three was, or is, Dierdre, who was his editor at Putnam, a Kevlar and piano-wire item, who pursues perfection in all things. She is now (we are back on our drive) the main subject of complaint, for Dierdre is à la mode to the max. For Dierdre to have the wrong refrigerator, attend the wrong party, appear at the wrong club or resort, or have the wrong sort of house in the Hamptons, would be a kind of social cancer, and she now wishes to produce a perfect child, at which Mickey is rather balking, having three already. He told me a long anecdote about . . .

You know, I forget what it was about. Tiles? A German appliance? Conception strategies? Who gives a shit, but the point was that she was costing him a bundle, as was the first wife and the first set of kids, and the boy from Marilyn (Jason) was acting up, and he was spending a fortune in special schools and psychiatrist bills, and because of the market and the too numerous fastener heirs, he was seriously pinched. (I offered a loan, got laughed at, ha-ha, it's not that bad yet.) Such bitch sessions are a normal part of my friendship with Mickey. I suppose he's listened enough to mine, although I have had only the one wife. The peculiar thing, though, about Mickey's wives is that, by chance, I have fucked each of them, although not ever during the period in which they were married to him. I would never do that.

Louise and I had a single long afternoon about two weeks before she got married. She said she loved him and wanted to have his children, but simply could not bear the thought of never doing it with another man and she said she always had a sneaker for me (her word) and wanted to see what it was like before the gate clanged shut. She was a somewhat nervous lover, and it was clear that Mickey had not proceeded past the introductory course, whereas Mrs Polansky had given me an entire curriculum. That was it, and she never mentioned it, or sought more, and I don't think she ever told Mickey, even when he took up with Marilyn.

Who I'd met at a literary cocktail to which I was invited by one of my clients, about six months before he hooked up with her. She was ranting on about *fascists* in her English lit department, and I made a mild comment about how that word had a technical meaning and it was not particularly wise to use it in so broadly figurative a sense, lest we be unguarded if the real thing came along again, as it very well might, since it had its attractions, obviously. She laughed at me, because to her *fascist* was what you called someone you disliked, and their response was always to deny it. Nobody except some brainless hicks in Indiana or Idaho ever admitted to actually espousing fascism. For obvious reasons, I have read deeply in the history and literature of that philosophy, and, being a little drunk, gave her a massive dose. I don't think she'd ever heard a coherent argument that did not start with *her* assumptions, but with a completely different set – that sexual and racial oppression were natural, for example, and that it was as absurd to be ashamed of them or to suppress them as it was to be ashamed of sex; that absolute power to grind the faces of one's enemies was delightful and also not something to be ashamed of; that democracy was pitiful; that it was ecstasy to bind one's will to that of a leader; that war was the health of the state . . .

When I was finished, she asserted that nobody could possibly believe any of that shit, and I pointed out that, historically, many people did, that it had in fact been wildly popular some decades ago among people just as smart as her, including Martin Heidegger and my grandfather, who, I informed her, had been a member of the Waffen-SS. She thought I was joking, I assured her I was not, and I invited her to my place to see my collection of inherited Nazi memorabilia, something that I am almost certain she had never previously been invited to do. She came along, I showed her my stuff and told her my stories. It had a perverse erotic effect on her, for I suppose it represented the instantiation of the famous line by Plath, although every woman does not love me and I am not an actual fascist. She did actually want the boot in the face, however, in the form of violent sex and some other rough stuff. I don't much care for that sort of thing, but I felt obliged to play the gentleman (in a manner of speaking) on this occasion. She was a sewer-mouth orgasmer, another thing I don't much like, and I did not call her again, nor see her until Mickey invited me out for a drink to meet his new amour sometime later and there she was. We pretended we had never met.

Dierdre publishes a client of mine. We met at my office, something to do with this author using characters that had appeared in previous work jointly copyrighted with another author. We exchanged glances. She was wearing a shimmery blouse and very tight slacks, and when she rose to rummage something out of her briefcase, I admired her ass and the thin thighs that depended from it, and the clear-cut interesting space between them, as wide as a pack of cards. She gave me another look as she returned. This was, I must admit, a *Sex and the City* sort of thing. I called her, and the usual. She turned out to be one of those women who likes to get well impaled on one and then masturbate. She had no padding at all and left a painful bruise on my pubic bone from the grinding. As against that, she was a nightingale, which I rather enjoy, a long series of tuneful notes during her several drawn-out climaxes. We had a few dates – this was about five years ago – and then I called and she was busy and called again and the same, and that was it. I did not regret the termination. I think she found me a little stuffy, and I found her a little shallow. When I met her some months prior to her wedding to Mickey, she also pretended not to have met me, and perhaps she had indeed forgotten our routinized little fling.

Somewhat depressed now by these reminiscences, I vouchsafe them only to lay the groundwork, necessary to the unfolding of this tale, of my increasingly pathetic yearning for the erotic. Dierdre was sexy but not erotic; there is no deep life in her. Ingrid is erotic, if a little detached, there is always a distance when we're together and I suppose that's why I visit her. Artists, I have found, are often like that; it all goes into their work. My estranged wife, Amalie, is far and away the most erotic woman I have ever known, the life force boils out of her, and everything she touches attains beauty. Except me.

Does 'erotic' have an antonym? Thanatotic, perhaps. Is that a word? Clearly the thing is itself real, for don't we all delight in death? Violent death especially, what pleasure! Don't we show it in all its fictive detail to our children tens of thousands of times? Although not the reality: no, NASCAR racing excepted, here's the one remaining area where we acknowledge the difference between IP and Real Life. Real death is the last embarrassing thing. And there's surely an aesthetics of death, the opposite of all those sprightly Impressionist scenes and the luscious nudes of Boucher, an aesthetics that I believe reached its apogee during the regime for which my grandfather made the supreme sacrifice. Contra Mies, this appeal has nothing to do with mere functionality. The American P-47 Thunderbolt was an effective and formidable weapon, arguably the best fighter-bomber of the war, but it *looks* like something out of the Disney studio, plump and bulbous, as if it should have its prop emerging from a smiley face. The Stuka on the other hand looks just like what it is: terror from the skies. Again, the Sherman tank looks like something a toddler would pull on a string; the Panzer VI Tiger is obviously an elaborate machine for killing human beings. Not to mention the terrific uniforms, the regalia. And this thing here in my hand.

The Germans call it a *Pistole*-08, a *null-acht*, but everyone else calls it a Luger. This is in fact the very item brandished when Mom and Dad met: yes, she lied about that, for here it is. It is a special presentation model awarded to old granddad when he won the Knight's Cross with Oak Leaves and Swords. God knows what it's worth, thousands and thousands to the peculiar little men who collect this shit. On the left side of the walnut grip is an inlaid diamond lozenge quartered red and white with black letters inlaid in the center

II

ϟϟ

Pz.

and on the right side we find an inlaid miniature in silver of the decoration; the recipient's name, his rank, and the date are engraved on the receiver. Himmler apparently conferred it with his own pudgy white hands. My mother was unclear as to what the medal citation was, but it involved killing a truly spectacular number of Russians while commanding a panzer regiment on the eastern front during the late summer of 1943. It still makes me sweat a little to look at it and hold it, it is so totally awful a thing, but for some reason I have never been able to sell it or toss it in the river. It's loaded too, with the original Parabellum 9 mm. And I know it works. Perhaps I will do some plinking with it later. I am a pretty good pistol shot as a matter of fact. My brother, Paul, taught me how during a leave after his first tour. I met him down at Fort Bragg and we went out into the piney woods one afternoon and blazed away with a military Colt .45 and a Soviet Makarov 9 mm he had picked up in Vietnam. He taught point-and-shoot combat style, speed above everything because the average pistol target was seven feet away or less.

Anyway, I dropped Mickey off at Columbia, and as he left the car he said, 'Let me know when the niece calls – if she finds that manuscript, tell her I'd love to have a look at it.'

I said I would and we drove off south. On the ride back I thought about my long relationship with Mickey Haas, especially its sexual aspects. I had to acknowledge a certain contempt for the man, which is, I believe, inevitably a part of any really intimate long-term friendship. My brother, Paul, would call this feeling part of our fallen state, that we cannot love unreservedly, that we must consider the beloved less than we believe ourselves to be, in at least one way. I suppose this is, though hurtful, a good thing. We all have a tendency toward self-worship, and one of the prime functions of a good friend is to keep this in check. I know he thinks I am a dull old dog, and not nearly as smart as he is. Perhaps true; certainly I am not nearly as famous. I don't write popular best-selling books, I am not worshipped by legions of students, I am not a premier member of the National Academy of Arts and Letters, nor do I have his Pulitzer Prize. He must also think I am something of a fool for love, or at least sex. He is certainly privy to the tale of my peccadilloes, save the three exceptions I have noted. He was terribly affected when Amalie and I broke up. She's perfect for you, he said at the time, listing her virtues. He was correct. Too perfect for me by far, but it's hard to get that notion across to another.

Several days later, according to my diary, Ms Maldonado put through a call; I had alerted her to its possibility and stressed the importance thereof. The voice was young, pleasant, somewhat throaty. You know what this is about then, eh? The *aboot* and the terminal syllable marked her as a Canadian. Foreign – nearby, as the ads used to say. I found it immediately attractive, and I invited her to drop by the office, but she demurred. She'd rather meet me in a neutral place, for reasons she would explain when we met. Where, then? She was working, she said, in the New York Public Library, in the Brooke Russell Astor Reading Room of the Rare Books Division. I said I had some things to clear up, but that I could meet her there at four. She said she looked forward to meeting me.

I resumed my task of the day, which was suing some poor slob of an artist on behalf of a giant corporation. This is the daily bread of the IP lawyer. Someone had appropriated the logo of a national chain to comment on the madness of consumerism. The original logo is a little risqué (tits), and the artist had made it more so, and it had shown up on popular posters and T-shirts and the corporation was not amused. I can do cease-and-desist orders of this type in my sleep, or on this occasion, with my mind on my coming date with the mysterious heiress of Bulstrode, whose name I now knew was Miranda Kellogg.

Omar dropped me off at the Fifth Avenue entrance to the great Beaux-Arts pile of the library at a quarter to four. The two stone lions, Patience and Fortitude, who according to New York lore are supposed to roar when a virgin ascends the steps, were mum. I took the elevator to the third floor and arranged admission to the locked Astor room, just off the main reading room. Memories here: I spent a significant portion of my middle-school years sitting at those long wooden tables. I would subway up from Brooklyn and stay the whole day, supposedly researching a school paper (this was before the Internet, of course, and before Mrs Polansky struck) but mainly enjoying the anonymity, the company of strangers and scholars, and the utter un-Mishkinity of the place. My first really adult experience.

I spotted her right away, at a long table in one corner. Apart from a gentleman manning the official desk, she was alone in the richly paneled room. Her hair was blond, worked into two miniature braids pinned up over the ears. Amalie wore her hair that way when we were courting, and absurd as it is I have always been a sucker for that style. Her neck was bared and deliciously vulnerable; women's necks are, in my view, the most underrated secondary sexual characteristic in our culture, and one that always gets me in the vitals. I stood there for minutes just watching her turn pages. Then, in the mysterious way that has never been successfully explained to me, she became conscious of my stare and turned abruptly. Our eyes met. I nodded. She smiled dazzlingly and rose and came toward me. She didn't really look like the young Amalie, not feature by feature, but she had that same leonine grace; somewhat shorter than average, she wore a short gray skirt and a beautiful glowing pink silk blouse. Dark stockings, elegant ankles. She held out her hand and I grasped it. She had grape-green eyes, just like Amalie's. She said You must be Mr Mishkin. I'm Miranda Kellogg. I couldn't speak for a moment. Electricity ran up my arm and I am afraid I held the grip a little too long. This is ridiculous, I recall thinking.

The Bracegirdle Letter (5)

As I neared my house that even I hearde the noyse of womans cryes & entering therein I found my father laying harde upon my poore mothere with his sticke, which I had never seen before now nor ever thought to see. The case was this: Margaret the mayde had founde in my motheres presse a papiste crucifixe & beades & brought them straightways to my father, & hym thinkynge all these yeares he had tabeled & bedded a secrete papiste grew mad with it & stroke oute in a furie, my mothere protestynge that such kickshows were alle she hadde of her mother mere keep-sakes, yet it availed naught. And though I knew my father was in his rights I could not beare it & made to stay his arm saying have mercie she is your wyfe: but he cryed she is no wyfe to me anie more & stroke at mee too & at that I coulde not holpe but presse hym away & he felle harde upon the floor. Wee two – I mean my mother & mee then kneelt to aide him if we could: in truth he was not hurt sore but in his pryde & he cried plague take you both, you shalnot stoppe a night more in my house, I have not wyfe nor sonne no more.

So weeping both full bitterlie I left with my mother & a few thynges of our own, me hyring a barrow to carry these fornitures, she near dieing for shame. Now by chaunce I had the gold from the Ordnance that payed for the gonnes £68 12s. so wee were not paupered & could hyre a room for the night in an inn the Iron Man in Hart Lane by the old Crutchedfriars, 3d. the night & keep. The next morn leavyng some smalle monnaie with my mother I took boat to Gravesend & then back to Titchfield as I had come up. My maistre was well-pleazed his gonnes had assaied well but frowned harde when I told hym what had come to pass at my fatheres house & harder stille when I sayde I had uzed his gold to keep us the night & my mother some daies after: & promised I would paye it back everie pennie, & pleadeth the necessitie. But he gave me the lie saying I had gamed or drunk it up & hoped to gull hym with this tayle of papistes: in short, we fought, me not able I feare to keep Christian forebearance as I should nor honor my maistre as I should, for I could not beare his cantings hym being hymselfe a greate liar & keeping a whore besydes. Which I tolde oute to the whole house & his wyfe there too & was greate dissensioun in that house after. Next day I was dismissed with but the clothes on my backe & no ticket of leave neither.

Titchfield being 65 Englishe myles from London it ben some tyme for me to walk back, slaepyng under hedges & stealing fruit & egges may God forgive my sinne. Arrivyng late at the Iron Man I found my mother well enow being kept goode compagnie by a faire young mayde the master's daughter of the house, which wase you my Nan from what connexion we first met & afterward loved, as thou knowest. But mayhap oure sonne grown to a knowinge age, which may the good Lord allow, knows it not so I tell it heere.

Now had I to earn oure bread & keepe, mee a lad not 16 years & I thought mee of the Tower & those I had met there & would they give me werke & so I repaired there straightway & asked for Mr Hastynges: he cometh, I tell him alle oure lamentable plight as I have heere tolde & he scries me close saying, well, lad, we can have no papistes nor yet puritans in the Tower, one it would be my head to doe & the other I cannot beare to have around mee, for I sit but one sermon in the weeke & that o' Sunday & need not prayeres & canting other daies. Where-upon I sayde I too was done with them. Then Mr Keane hearing this sayeth Hastynges we must trye him like a gonne, ho to Southwark. So over-bridge went wee, & drank much sacke (which I never did before) & saw bear-baytes & dogge-baytes, lewde shews, &c.: and they carried me to the stewes & bought me a punk but God be thanked I spewed & was soe sick I mounted her but scarce enow to count a sinne & they laughed much & made bawdry jestes upon me, but Mr Keane sware I wase no puritan withal but a mere two-pounder falconet, could spew little shotte well enow but did not burst my breech & so wast proved.

6

Crosetti, bearing the rolled and wrapped maybe-invaluable manuscript under his arm, waited out on the deserted street for nearly half an hour, which he thought excessive. What was she doing in there? Although he had occasionally waited as long for women to get ready to go out. Although they weren't going to the prom. He looked at his watch and paced and felt the craziness pluck at his mind.

She emerged wearing one of her black outfits, as if going to Glaser's to work, and he wondered why. Maybe Bulstrode insisted on a certain formality, in which case he would be disappointed in Crosetti, who needed a bath and a shave and was wearing a T-shirt from a Springsteen concert, grubby jeans, and Nikes. He did not, however, complain to her about the waiting.

Nor did she apologize. Instead, she nodded at him casually and started off. He did not ask any questions about their destination, resolving to play it cool. He could be an international man of mystery too. They walked to Van Dyke and took the 77 bus to the Smith Street station, where they boarded the F train and rode noisily in silence to Manhattan.

At Houston Street she got up and trotted from the car, and when he caught up with her he could not resist asking her about where they were going. Crosetti was not at heart cool.

'Mermelstein's,' she answered. 'They're the last wholesaler of fine binding leather in the city.'

'They'll sell you retail?'

'Mr Mermelstein likes me.'

'Really. Does he . . . ?' Crosetti made a pawing gesture. They were walking on the station steps, and she stopped abruptly and said, 'He does not. You know, I'm really sorry I told you that about Sidney. Are you going to trot it out every time I mention a business connection with a man?'

'It's erased from my mind as of this very minute,' said Crosetti, genuinely abashed, but also feeling a little manipulated. He also wondered why she was going to a wholesaler. Everyone in the old book trade in New York knew that the center of the bookbinding business was in Brooklyn, in Borough Park. He was about to ask her that but then stopped and figured it out for himself. Book dealers and major collectors had contacts among the regular bookbinders. If one of them were offered a Churchill *Voyages* at a fire-sale price, he'd check around with the bookbinder trade to see if the book had been doctored. It would not occur to any collector to imagine that the seller had done it solo, from raw materials. He was rather pleased with himself for having figured this out, any penetration of Rolly's deviousness being to the good.

They walked east on Houston to an old commercial building near Second Avenue, where, in a pungent loft containing perhaps an acre of various animal skins, Crosetti leaned against a bale of the stuff and watched Rolly negotiate for a considerable time with an elderly man in a skullcap, a rusty black suit, and carpet slippers. They seemed to be having a good time, and Crosetti noticed with interest that Rolly had subtly changed her delivery. She smiled more with Mermelstein, actually laughed a time or two, and in general seemed a louder, more aggressive person than the one he knew, more . . . dare he think it? . . . more Jewish? Her speech had also taken on the pace and accent of the outer boroughs.

He remarked on this as they left with a small roll of fine calf wrapped in brown paper.

'Everybody does it,' she replied lightly. 'You talk to someone, you take on a little of their shtick, their affect. Don't you?'

'I guess,' he said, but thought, Yeah, but I'm something to begin with, and what, my sweet, are you? He rehearsed this line, thought about voicing it, declined. Instead he said, 'So, where to now?'

'Take the F to Fourteenth Street and the Broadway train up to Columbia. We have an appointment with Dr Bulstrode in forty-five minutes.'

'Can we get something to eat first? I haven't had anything to eat since last night.'

'You ate all my cookies.'

'Oh, right, sorry. Your elderly cookies. Carolyn, what is going *on* with you? Why don't you live like a regular person, with furniture and food in the house and pictures on the wall?'

She started walking toward the subway entrance. 'I told you. I'm poor.'

He hurried to catch up with her. 'You're not *that* poor. You have a job. You make more than I do. Where does it go?'

'I don't have a mother I can live with,' she said tightly.

'Thank you. That puts me in my place.'

'That's right. I'm not sure you understand. I am *completely* alone in the world, with no backup at all. No brothers, sisters, cousins, aunts, uncles, godfathers. I have a clerk's salary with no benefits. If I got sick I'd be on the street. I've *been* on the street, and I'm not going to go back.'

'When were you on the street?'

'That's none of your business. Why are you always so snoopy? It gets on my nerves.'

The train came and they boarded it. When they were under way and in the zone of privacy generated by the subway's roar, he said, 'I'm sorry. I get it from my mother. She sits down next to someone on the subway and in two stops they're spilling their life's story. You know, Carolyn, most people *like* to talk about themselves.'

'I know and I think it's a waste of time, people blathering on about their hard luck. Or fishing for compliments. Oh, no, Gloria, you're not really that fat. Oh, your son's at Colgate? How proud you must be!'

'But that's what people *do*. I mean what else do you talk about? Books? Bookbinding?'

'For starters. I told you I wasn't a very interesting person, but you don't seem to want to believe it.'

'You're a fascinating person, in my opinion.'

'Don't be stupid! I have a very dull life. I go to my job, I come home, I work at my craft, I count the days until I can get to a place where I can really learn what I'm interested in.'

'Movies,' said Crosetti. 'We could talk about movies. What's your favorite movie?'

'I don't have one. I can't afford to go to movies. And as you obviously know, I don't own a television.'

'Come on, girl! Everybody has a favorite movie. You must have gone to movies in your hometown.' This got no response. He added, 'Which was where?'

'Okay, what's *your* favorite movie?' she asked without much interest, after a pause.

'*Chinatown*. You're not going to tell me where you come from?'

'No place special. What's it about?'

'What's it about? You never saw *Chinatown*?'

'No.'

'Carolyn, *everybody* saw *Chinatown*. People who weren't born when it came out saw *Chinatown*. There are movie houses in . . . in *Mogadishu* for crying out loud, that ran it for weeks. Best original screenplay ever written, won an Oscar for that, nominated for eleven other awards . . . how can you not have seen it? It's a cultural monument.'

'Not of my culture, obviously. This is our stop.'

The train screamed to a halt at 116th Street and they left the car. She took off with her characteristic impatient stride, and he trotted after her, thinking that his initial impression of Carolyn Rolly as a vampire or some other sort of unearthly creature had been fairly accurate, if she really hadn't seen *Chinatown*.

They arose from the underground and walked through the noble gates into the Columbia campus. Crosetti had occasionally come up here to catch movies at film society showings and always felt, as he now did, a vague sense of regret. At age twelve his mother had brought him up to the campus and shown him around. She'd received her library science degree here, and he knew she had wanted him to attend. But he was not the kind of grind who could get the grades necessary for a white New Yorker to win a scholarship, and paying cash for an undergraduate degree on a cop's pension and a librarian's salary was out of the question. So he'd gone to Queens College, 'a perfectly good school,' as his mother often loyally remarked, and also, 'if you're a success nobody cares where you went to college.' It did not rankle a lot, but it rankled; and on the occasions when he had to come up to the campus, he found himself studying the faces of the undergraduates and listening to snatches of their conversation to see if he could observe a major gap between their supposed Ivy-level smarts and his own. Which he could not.

Carolyn Rolly, he knew, had attended Barnard, just across the street. He knew because he was the filing system at Sidney Glaser Rare Books and had used this position to examine her résumé in detail. He did not at the moment think much of a Barnard education, since it had failed in her case to provide a familiarity with *Chinatown*. This was why she was so stuck-up, a Seven Sisters girl, after all, and probably brilliant too, since she said she was poor and clearly *she* hadn't failed to get a scholarship.

In a mood to needle, he said, 'So . . . back at the old campus, hey, Carolyn? I guess it brings those dear old Ivy League college days back. Look, if there're any special customs like not walking on a particular plaque or bowing to a statue or something, you'll let me know – I wouldn't want to embarrass you or anything.'

'What are you talking about?'

'You and your college days. Class of '99, right? Barnard?'

'You think I went to *Barnard*?'

'Yeah, it was . . .' Here he stuck, but she instantly understood the reason.

'You little spy! You read my résumé!'

'Well, yeah. I told you I was interested. I went through your underwear drawer too while you were sleeping.'

At this he thought he noticed a look of real fear whip across her features, but it was gone in a flash, replaced by one of amused contempt. 'I doubt that,' she said, 'but for your information I didn't go to Barnard.'

'You lied on your application?'

'Of course I lied. I wanted the job, and I knew Glaser was a Columbia alumnus and his wife went to Barnard, so it seemed like a good idea. I came up here, picked up some of the talk, learned the geography, audited a couple of classes, studied the catalogs. They never check résumés. *You* could say you went to Harvard. If you had, I bet Glaser would be paying you a lot more money.'

'Good God, Rolly! You don't have any morals at all, do you?'

'I don't do any harm,' she said, glaring. 'I don't even have a *high school* diploma, and I don't want to work in a sweatshop or do cleaning, which is the only kind of jobs a woman can get without one. Or whore.'

'Wait a minute, *everyone* goes to high school. It's compulsory.'

She stopped walking and turned to face him, dropped her head for several breaths, and then looked him straight in the face. 'Yes,' she said, 'but in my case, when my parents were killed in a car wreck I went to live with my crazy uncle Lloyd, who kept me locked in a root cellar from age eleven to age seventeen, as a result of which I didn't have the opportunity to attend high school. I got raped a lot though. Now, is there anything else you'd like to know about my goddamned past life?'

Crosetti gaped and felt his face flush. He could see liquid trembling on her lower eyelids. 'I'm sorry,' he croaked. She turned and strode rapidly away, almost running, and after a miserable moment he skulked after her into a tan brick building with a columned entryway and up two flights of stairs, stumbling a little because he was kicking himself so hard. Okay, end of story, expunge her from his mind, he'd done it God only knew how many times before, no stranger to rejection, not usually *quite* this stupid, not *quite* so much his own stupid fault, but still he could go out classy, do this business with Bulstrode, a little correct nod and handshake afterward, walk off. God! How could he have been so tooth-hurtingly dumb! Woman tells him she doesn't want to talk about her past, so of course he does nothing else, and . . . but here they were, she knocking tap-a-tap on frosted glass and a plummy voice from within, 'Yeh-ehss.'

The man was wearing a vest, or what he would have called a waistcoat, and as they entered he was slipping on the brown tweed suit jacket that went with it: a short plump man in his fifties, with smooth dull pale brown hair worn medium long and arranged so as to hide a bald patch in the center. Jowly, with round tortoiseshell glasses. Hand when shaken unpleasantly soft and moist. Crosetti hated him already; it made a pleasant change from the current self-contempt.

They sat. She did the talking. Bulstrode was interested in the provenance, the age and origin of the volumes of the Churchill in which the manuscript had been found. She gave these details tersely and, as far as Crosetti could tell, accurately. While this went on he looked around the office, which was small, not much larger than a suburban bathroom, with one dusty window looking out on Amsterdam Avenue. A single glassed-in bookcase, books on only one shelf, otherwise full of stacked papers, untidily arranged. Besides that, two wooden armchairs (in which Rolly and he were sitting), a standard wooden desk somewhat battered, a scatter of papers and journals thereon, and a large framed photograph, whose image Crosetti could not see, although he shifted and peered to the extent propriety allowed.

'Very interesting, Miss Rolly,' the professor was now saying. 'May I examine the documents?'

Both Rolly and Bulstrode now looked at Crosetti, and he

felt his heart sink, as we do when an unfamilar doctor asks us to slip out of our clothes and into a gown. The papers were *his*, and now they were passing out of his hands, to be confirmed as genuine or rejected as spurious, but by someone else, someone he didn't know, whose eyes were all funny behind those thick lenses, avid, crazed really, and Rolly's eyes were blank blue fields with less feeling in them than the sky itself, and he had to resist the urge to grab up his package and flee. But what he did was to pull out only the letter from Richard Bracegirdle to his wife. It was easy to distinguish these pages by feel from the rest of the sheets. Let's see what this geek had to say about the letter before exposing the ciphered letters, was Crosetti's thinking.

He slumped in his chair as Bulstrode took the letter and spread the pages out on his desk. It was fear that made him hand them over, a chicken-guts fear of appearing even *more* stupid in the damned woman's eyes than he was already. He knew he would never remove the shame of that moment with Rolly from his mind, it would be a lifetime image, bubbling up at random time and again to blight his joy and deepen depression. And also the image of the girl locked in the root cellar listening to the approaching steps of her tormentor, and he'd never now be able to help her with that through love, he'd screwed that up too, you asshole, Crosetti, you complete turd . . .

'Can you read it, Professor?'

This was Rolly; the sound of her voice jerked Crosetti from the dear land of self-flagellation, Bulstrode cleared his throat heavily, and said, 'Oh, yes, indeed. The hand is crude but quite clear. A man I imagine who did a good deal of writing. Not an educated man, I think, not a university man, but a writing man all the same. A clerk perhaps? Originally, I mean.' Bulstrode returned to his reading. Time passed, perhaps half an hour, that seemed like time in the dentist's chair to Crosetti. At last the professor sat up and said, 'Hm, yes, in all, a very interesting and valuable document. This,' he continued, pointing, 'seems to be the last letter of a man named Richard Bracegirdle, who apparently was wounded at the battle of Edgehill, the first major battle of the English Civil War, which took place on October 23, 1642. He is writing from Banbury, it seems, a town close to the battlefield.'

'What about Shakespeare?' Crosetti asked.

Bulstrode regarded him quizzically and blinked behind his thick spectacles. 'Excuse me? Did you think there was some reference to Shakespeare in this?'

'Well, yeah! That's the whole point. This guy says he spied on Shakespeare. That he had an autograph copy of one of his plays, in fact, that he was the one who got Shakespeare to write one of his plays for the king. It's right there on the signature page.'

'Really. Dear me, Mr Crosetti, I assure you there's nothing of that sort. Secretary hand can be quite confusing to ah . . . an amateur, and people can see all sorts of meanings that don't exist, rather like finding pictures in clouds.'

'No, look, it's right here,' said Crosetti and came out of his chair and around the desk. Picking up the manuscript and indicating the relevant lines, he said, 'This is the part I mean. It says, "They tell all the tale nearly of our spying upon the secret papist Shaxpur. Or so we thought him although now I am less certain. In that manner and bent of life he was a nothing. But certain it is he wrought that play of Scotch M. I commanded of my Lord D. his plot and of him in the king's name. I find passing strange that all though I am dead and him also yet the play lives still, writ in his own hand and lying where only I know and there may it rest forever." '

Bulstrode adjusted his eyeglasses and issued a dry chuckle. He picked up the magnifier he had been using and placed it over a line of text. 'Very imaginative, I must say, Mr Crosetti, but you're quite mistaken. What this says is, "I shall tell to you of the sale of gems secretly proper Salust." The man must have been some sort of factor in Salisbury for this Lord D. Then it goes on, "Of these thefts I lack shriving. In that manner and bent of life I was a nothing." And further along he writes "the pearls live still willed by his own hand," and he says he alone knows where they are. I'm not entirely sure of what "willed by his own hand" means, but in any case the man was clearly dying and probably in intense distress. He seems to flit from subject to subject. In fact, much of this may be pure fantasy, going through his life in a kind of terminal delirium. But the document is interesting enough as it is without bringing in Shakespeare.'

'What does the rest of it say?'

'Oh, it contains a quite vivid description of the battle itself, and these are always of interest to military historians. And apparently he served in the early stages of the Thirty Years' War, ditto. He was at White Mountain, Lützen, and Breitenfeld, although he gives no detail about these. Pity. A professional artillerist, it seems, and trained as a cannon-founder. He also claims to have made a voyage to the New World and been shipwrecked off Bermuda. A very interesting seventeenth-century life, even a remarkable life, and potentially of great value to certain narrow fields of study, although I suspect there's also a touch of Munchausen in his narrative. But nothing about Shakespeare, I'm afraid.' A pause here. Leaden silence for a good thirty seconds; then, 'I would be happy to purchase it from you, if you like.'

Crosetti looked at Carolyn, who returned a neutral stare. He swallowed and asked, 'For how much?'

'Oh, for a Jacobean manuscript of this quality I should think perhaps, ah, thirty-five would be the going rate.'

'Dollars?'

An indulgent smile. 'Hundred, of course. Thirty-five hundred. I could write you a check now if you like.'

Crosetti felt his belly twist, and the sweat started to bead up on his forehead. This was wrong. He didn't know how he knew, but he did. His father had always talked about instinct, although he always called it his gut, how you always went with your gut when you were out on the street in harm's way. Crosetti's gut made him say, 'Uh, thanks, but I think I'd like a second opinion. I mean on the translation. Um, no offense, Dr Bulstrode, but I'd like to eliminate the possibility that . . .' He gestured haphazardly, not willing to put it into words. He had remained standing after handling the manuscript, so it was an easy matter to snatch the papers from Bulstrode's desk and slip them into the brown paper wrapper. Bulstrode shrugged and said, 'Well, suit yourself, although I doubt you'll get a better price.' Turning then to Carolyn, he asked, 'And how is dear Sidney these days? Quite recovered from the shock of the fire I hope.'

'Yes, he's fine,' said Carolyn Rolly in a voice so unlike her own that Crosetti stopped wrapping and looked at her. Her face was pained in a way he could not interpret. She said, 'Crosetti, would you step outside for a minute with me? Excuse us, Professor.'

Bulstrode smiled a plump formal smile and gestured to his door.

Outside, a scant summer population of students and professors passed to and fro; it was clearly the interval between classes. Rolly grabbed Crosetti's arm and pulled him into an alcove, the first time since the crying jag of the previous evening that she had touched him. She clung to his arm and spoke vehemently in a hoarse tense voice. 'Listen! You have to let him have those goddamn papers.'

'Why do I? He's obviously trying to pull the wool over our eyes.'

'Not our eyes, Crosetti. He's right. There's no mention of Shakespeare. It's some petty clerk running a scam and dying and confessing his sins.'

'I don't believe it.'

'Why not? What's your evidence? Wishful thinking and three hours' experience with secretary hand?'

'Maybe, but I'm going to show it to someone else, someone I trust.'

As he said this, he saw her eyes grow fat with tears and her face begin to crumple. 'Oh, God,' she cried, 'oh, God, don't let me come apart now! Crosetti, don't you get it? He *knows* Sidney. Why do you think he mentioned him just now?'

'Okay, he knows Sidney – so what?'

'So what! Jesus, man, don't you see? He knows the manuscript came out of the *Voyages*, so he knows I'm taking the book apart. And that means . . .'

'You're not just breaking it, like Sidney told you to. You're trying to doctor it, which means you're going to try to sell it. And he's, what? Threatening to tell Sidney unless we give him the manuscript?'

'Of course! He'll tell him, and then Sidney . . . I don't know, he'll fire me for sure and he might call the cops. I've seen him do it with shoplifters. He's nuts that way, people stealing books and I can't . . . I can't take the chance . . . oh, God, this is horrible!'

She was frankly crying now, not hysterical yet as she was the night before, but building up to it, and that was something Crosetti had no wish to see again. He said, 'Hey, calm down! You can't take what chance?'

'The cops. I can't be involved with the *police*.'

Lightbulb.

'You're a fugitive.' It wasn't a question. Obvious, really; he should have picked it up right off the bat.

She nodded.

'What's the charge?'

'Oh, please! Don't *interrogate* me!'

'You didn't whack Uncle Lloyd?'

'What? No, of course not. It was some stupid dope thing. I was desperate for money and I moved packages for some people I knew. This was in Kansas, so of course the sky fell in and . . . oh, God, what am I going to do!'

'Okay, get yourself together,' he said, resisting the urge to wrap his arms around her. 'Go back in there, and tell him it's a deal.'

He started to move away and her face stiffened in what seemed like panic; he was happy to note that she clutched at his arm, as at a plank in a shipwreck.

'Where're you going?'

'I just need to do something first,' he said. 'Don't worry, Carolyn, it's going to be fine. I'll be back in ten minutes.'

'What should I tell him?' she demanded.

'Tell him I got the runs from the excitement of his generous offer and I'm in the bathroom. Ten minutes!'

He turned and raced down the stairs, three at a time, holding the rolled manuscripts under his arm like a football. Out of Hamilton at a run, he threaded through a quad full of strolling young people who had higher SATs than he did and ran into the vast columned bulk of Butler Library. One advantage of having a well-known research librarian for a mother is that she knows nearly all the other research librarians in the city and is pals with a number of them. Crosetti had known Margaret Park, the head research librarian at

Butler, since childhood, and it was an easy matter to call her up and get permission. All big libraries have large-format Xerox machines that can reproduce folio pages; Crosetti used the one in the Butler basement to copy all of Bracegirdle's papers. He explained to the bemused but amenable Mrs Park that this was all to do with a movie he had a chance to make (somewhat true) and could he also cadge a mailing tube and buy some stamps?

He rolled the copies into their tube and added the originals of the ciphered letters and the sermons. As he did this, he wondered why he hadn't shown them to Bulstrode along with the Bracegirdle letter. Because the guy was an asshole and he was screwing him in some way on this deal, although Crosetti couldn't prove it, and besides there was Carolyn to consider. But keeping the ciphers to himself gave him an obscure pleasure. Shakespeare or not, the sheets had kept their secrets for four centuries and he was reluctant to let them out of his own hands, he who had brought them into the light. He sealed the tube, wrote out an address label, added postage, dropped the tube into the outgoing mail cart, and trotted back to Hamilton Hall.

Fifteen minutes later he was walking with Rolly down the center of campus again, but in the opposite direction. Crosetti had a check for thirty-five hundred folded in his wallet and was feeling not exactly good, because he felt he'd been ripped off in a number of ways, but that he'd done the right thing. Doing the right thing had been a major expression around the house while he was being raised. His father had been a detective second grade with the NYPD in an era when to be a detective was to be on the pad, but Charlie Crosetti had not been on the pad, and had suffered for it, until the revelations of Serpico, when the chiefs had cast around for the straight and clean, and found him and promoted him to lieutenant in command of a Queens homicide squad. This was taken as a sign in the Crosetti household that virtue was rewarded. The present Crosetti still tended to believe this, despite all the evidence to the contrary that had accumulated in the years since. The woman walking beside him, however, seemed to set the moral universe on its ear. Yes, she'd been hideously abused (or so she said) but had responded with a kind of desperate amorality, a stance he found hard to condone. Every skell has a hard-luck story, his dad used to say. But he could not consider Carolyn Rolly a mere skell. Why not? His gonads? Because he lusted for her? No, not that either, or not only that. He wanted to ease her pain, make her grin, release the girl he glimpsed hiding under the dour, ascetic bookbinder.

He studied her trudging along, silent, her head down, gripping her roll of book leather. No, he was not going to end it with a handshake at the subway and let her roll off into her own astringent universe again. He stopped and placed his hand on her arm. She looked up, her face blank.

'Wait,' he said, 'what are we doing now?'

'I have to go to the paper guy in Brooklyn for the endpapers,' she replied glumly. 'You don't have to come.'

'That can wait. What we're actually going to do now is go to the Citibank branch over there, on which this check in my wallet is drawn, and cash it. Then we're going to cab to Bloomie's, where I will buy a jacket and pants and a shirt and maybe a pair of Italian loafers, and you will buy a dress, with colors in it, something for the summer, and maybe a hat, and we'll change into our new clothes and we'll take a cab to a fancy restaurant and have a long, long lunch with wine, and then we'll – I don't know – do city stuff, go to museums or art galleries or window-shop until we get hungry again and then go out to dinner and then I will take you in a *cab* back to your spare and illegal loft and your two chairs and your lonely bed.'

What was that on her face, he wondered: fear, surprise, delight? She said, 'That's ridiculous.'

'No it's not. It's exactly what felons are supposed to do with their ill-gotten gains. You can be my moll for a day.'

'You're not a felon.'

'I am. I converted my employer's property to my own use, probably grand larceny if you want to get technical. But I don't care. Come on, Carolyn! Don't you ever get tired of grunging around, squeezing every penny while your youth withers a little every day?'

'I can't believe I'm hearing this,' she said. 'It sounds like a bad movie.'

'But you don't go to movies, so how would you know? Putting that aside, you happen to be absolutely right. This is exactly the kind of thing they put in movies, because they want people to feel joy, they want people to identify with beautiful people having fun. And now we're going to do it, we're going to imitate art, we're going to be in our own movie and see what it's like in real life.'

He could see that she was thinking about it, testing it, as we do with a limb lately out of a cast, gingerly, afraid to let it take the weight. 'No,' she said, 'and if the money's burning a hole in your pocket why don't you just give it all to me? I could live for three months on –'

'No, that's not the *point*, Carolyn. The point is experience, for once, not prudence, red meat not ramen fucking noodles!' With that he grabbed her arm and hustled her across 116th Street.

'Let go of my arm!'

'No, if you won't come along of your own free will, I'm kidnapping you. This is now a major felony.'

'What if I scream?' she said.

'Scream away. The cops will arrest me, and they'll get the whole old book and manuscript story out of me, and then where will you be? Up shit's creek is where, instead of dressed in a gorgeous new dress drinking champagne in a fine restaurant. You better choose right now, baby, because here's the bank.'

He found a cocoa silk-and-linen Varvatos jacket on sale for three-fifty and some linen slacks and a nubbly black silk shirt and woven Italian loafers to go with it and she was yelled and chivied into a Prada ruffle-front flowered dress, a matching silk scarf and shoes, a couple of sets of devastating La Perla underwear, and a big Panama hat with an upturned brim like an English schoolgirl, all of which did not leave much change from a thousand bucks, and then they had lunch at the Metropolitan Museum and took in the Velázquez show and then went to an afternoon concert at the Frick that he happened to know about because his mom had tickets from her library mafia and had pressed them upon him (go, take a date!), another example of magic, because he'd been carrying the damn things around in his wallet for two weeks with no intention of going and now here it was that very afternoon. So they went, and it was the Concerto Vocale doing a program of Monteverdi sacred music. They sat in folding chairs and were lifted, to the extent their spiritual development then permitted, up to the divine regions.

Crosetti was no stranger to this world, his mother having made sure that American barbarism was not an option for him, but his covert glances at Carolyn revealed a person stunned. Or bored senseless, he really couldn't tell; and after the concert he was hesitant to ask her which it was. But she said, after one of her long intervals of silence, 'Wouldn't it be nice if the world was really like that, the way that music says it is, just flowing along in beauty?' Crosetti thought it would be exceedingly fine, and used the Hemingway line about it would be pretty to think so, without attribution.

They walked down Madison and he got her into pretending to be not just temporarily rich and to select choice items from the windows of the great boutiques, and when they grew tired of that he steered her down a side street and into the first restaurant they encountered, because he was sure that anyplace they went to would be perfect and this one was, a tiny *boîte* specializing in provincial French cuisine, where the patron took a liking to the nice young couple and kept sending out exquisite little tastes from the kitchen and recommended the wine, and watched them eat the entrées, beaming; and except that he did not actually break out singing in an accent it was exactly like, as Crosetti noted, *The Lady and the Tramp*. Which she had actually seen, it turned out, and they talked about that and about other Disney movies, and about the films he loved and the ones he was going to make, stuff he hadn't ever told anyone, and she talked about beautiful books, their aesthetics, their structure and the cryptic subtle beauties of paper, type, and binding, and how, as she put it, she wanted to make things that people would be handling and loving a thousand years from now.

He had to wave a hundred-dollar bill in the rearview mirror before the cabby would consent to take them to Red Hook, something he had never done before, nor ever dreamed of doing, and they arrived in the dark industrial street, and when the cabby had roared away with his C-note, Crosetti grabbed Carolyn Rolly, spun her around, and planted a good one on her wine-and-coffee-tasting mouth, and she kissed him back. Just like the movies.

Unlike, they did not tear off their clothes as they staggered up the stairs, into the loft, and into bed. Crosetti had always thought this a cliché and unrealistic; such a thing had never happened to him nor to anyone he knew who was not either drunk or cranked to the gills. So it was not going to happen in his movie. Instead, he sighed deeply and she sighed. He held her hand lightly, as if it were a dried blossom, as they slowly ascended. They entered the loft, they kissed again. She pulled away and rummaged in a drawer. She's going to light a candle, he thought, and she did, a simple plumber's candle, which she stuck carefully in a saucer and set by the bed. Crosetti did not move. Then she looked straight at him, her face set in its lovely grave lines and silently and slowly took off her new clothes in the candlelight, folding them tenderly, which was exactly the way he would have shot it, maybe a little more blue coming in from the window, and as he thought this he laughed.

She asked him why he laughed and he told her, and she told him to undress, that this was the part they didn't show in the regular movies, this was the fade-out. But after they were in bed together he thought of the horrible uncle and was abashed and too tentative until she used her nails and a harsh urgent command to unleash the animal. They did not practice safe sex, which he considered a little odd, a thought he entertained just before all thinking ceased.

After that, the director was out of the building for a long time. When he returned, Crosetti was on his back, feeling the sweat and other fluids drying on his skin, staring up at the tin ceiling. The candle was only an inch high. He had nothing to say, and his mind was quite blank: dead air, white screen. They'd had the setup, the development, the first plot point (discovering the manuscript), the second plot point (this incredible evening), and now what? He had no idea what the third act was going to be, but he was starting to feel fear. He'd never had anything like this happen to him, except in dreamland. He reached over to caress her again but she held on to his hand and kissed it. She said, 'You can't stay.'

'Why not? Are you going to turn into a bat?'

'No, but you can't stay. I'm not ready for . . . mornings. And all that. Do you understand?'

'A little. I guess. Well, Red Hook at . . . where's my watch? Three-ten a.m. with a roll of cash and smelling like a bordello. That sounds like fun.'

'No,' she said, 'I'll wash you.'

She took him by the hand and led him to the sink behind the screen, lit two candles set in wall sconces made of tin cans, and filled the sink with steaming water. She stood him on a thick straw bath mat and washed every inch of him, slowly, with a washcloth and Ivory soap. Then she drained the suds and washed him with clear water, kneeling lightly on one knee like a courtier before the prince. She had small flattish breasts with broad pink nipples. Despite the night's epic exertions he hardened painfully under this treatment. It had an unnatural appearance, like one of her bookbinding implements, something suitable for burnishing leather to a high gloss. She looked up at him and said, 'You can't go out in Red Hook at three a.m. in that condition.'

'No, it would be unwise,' he said in a hoarse croak.

'Well, then,' she said.

He noticed that she held it at the base with two fingers, the other three extended, like a duchess sipping tea. Her dark little head moved slowly back and forth. How did they learn how to do that, he thought, and also: Who are you? What are you doing to me? What's going to happen?

The Bracegirdle Letter (6)

Thus I began my lyfe as an ordnancer of the Tower 10s. the moneth wage, prentice wages that but beggars cannot be chusers. We took lodgings two mean roomes in Fenchurch St. by Aldgate, verey poore were wee but had liverie from the Tower so saved on my cloathes. One yeare spent thus: in the winter of the second yeare came a chill & my mother sickened & wee had not coales enow to warme her. Methinkes she wase besydes wearied from her sorrowes. Alas to come to this end through no fault of hers: all ways a good, sober, virtuous woman & no papiste neither, as I asked her then, she sayinge no sonne but I did pray for the sowles of my dead babes & for the sowles of my parentes as wee learnt in the olde religion a great sinne I know & wille burn in Hell for it though I praye God not. Soe she died 2nd February AD 1606 & is buried in St Katherine Colemanchurch. Now you know, my Nan, that after that sadde tyme you gave me comfort soe that I wish to marry you but your father sayeth what, nay nay, no man can marry on prentice wages how will you keepe my daughter & I hadde no answer & left sad & wast sad many daies.

Comes now Thomas Keane saying ho Dick what say you to Flanders? For I am off to-morrow to deliver four cannon royal to the Dutch at Sluys & shoot em too against Spain. Come & be my mate & matrosse: wee will eate cheese & drinke genever & blaste papiste dogges to Hell. I answer him yes by G-d & my hand on't & the thynge is settled. We must needs goe from the Tower at night for the Kinges majestie had late made peace with Spain so 'twould be thought ille to arme Spaines foes. But some at court (that Prince Henry I think mee who after untimely died) thought it a shame on England to shrink cowardly from warre gainst wicked King Phillipe who pressed so cruel on the reformed faith. Besides the Dutch had payed for the gonnes before this so wase it justice too, for the King would not yield a pennie backe & thus we went for the honour of England besydes.

Wee brought out the cannon & theyre carriages braken all in peeces & all necessaries as: 500 shottes, rammers, worms, port-fyres, &c. by barges & then to the Pool where mariners swayed them into the holte of the ship Groene Draeck a saloop of 6 gonnes belonging to Captain Willem van Brille. Soe with a fair wind wee sayled down river. A three-daye voyage wee had & a goode enough sea for winter not too colde & wee ate fresh: bread & cheeses, pickel-herrynge, ale. At Sluys a flat dreare place to my eye all brick dun or red & verey goode businesse since the Spanish have tooke Ostende these many moneths tis the onlie port in western Flanders. Soe we off-lade the gonnes & placed them on theyre carriages.

Nay I am too longe about my foolishe youth & I fear I have but little tyme. My wound now gripes me more than before & the surgeon saith it is fowle & gives me two daies no more.

7

Yes, ridiculous. Did I give the impression that I am a famous lecher about town? Not true. I seem to keep falling in love, which is not the same thing. Yes, Dr Freud, I am compensating for withdrawal of maternal affection, and yes, Dr Jung, I am unable to make peace with my negative anima, and yes, Father, I have sinned through my own fault, in what I have done and what I have failed to do. Yet it is not, I must insist, merely sex. I have never had a better sexual relationship than the one I had with Amalie, but clearly, it was not enough. From very early in our marriage I was in the habit of having one on the side, and as I believe I've already noted, there is no shortage of such opportunities in New York City.

Ingrid, my current girlfriend, is a good example, and the clever and impatient reader may be thinking, Oh, he's avoiding getting to Miranda, he's stalling. This is true, and tough shit. I may die, but I am not actively dying like poor Bracegirdle; perhaps I have all the time in the world.

Ingrid was happily married for nearly twelve years to Guy, a successful television executive, and by all accounts a prince among men, and especially princely compared to many others in that business, but one day in his fifty-second year he got out of bed, walked into the bathroom and began to shave, whereupon something popped in his brain and he died right there. No symptoms, perfectly healthy, good blood pressure, low cholesterol, but dead. Ingrid spent the next three years in the most intense mourning, after which her naturally sunny disposition burst through again, and she decided to get on with life. She had not gone out at all during those three years but now accepted an invitation to one of those anonymous award or fund-raising galas that enable the rich to mingle with the creative and thereby draw some of the divine afflatus into their desiccated lives. She went to a spa and got done, had her hair cut at the salon of the moment, bought a new outfit and made her appearance.

She has such a nice appearance: just forty, quite tall, perhaps too fleshy to dance at the highest levels, which is why she switched early to choreography. Her hair is boy-short and light brown, very fluffy, and she has those long wolf eyes in gray. Terrific wide mouth too with a little overbite, which I find quite attractive. And the dancer's body. I was at the party too, being myself a rich person needing a whiff of the real stuff, and as soon as I saw her, I grabbed the arm of my law partner Shelly Grossbart, who knows everyone in the music business, and asked him who she was. He had to think for a moment before he said, 'Christ, that looks like Ingrid Kennedy. I thought she was dead.' He made the introductions. We chatted about dance and intellectual property and actually had a fascinating conversation about the extent to which dance was protected by the laws of copyright. I found her intelligent and amusing; I suppose she found me likewise.

Later in the evening, the two of us having consumed what

I suppose was the better part of two bottles of Krug, she caught me up with those long gray peepers and inquired whether she could ask a personal question. I said she could and she said, 'Do you like to fuck women?'

I said that, given an appropriate other, I rather did.

'Well,' she said, 'I actually haven't had any sex since my husband died three years ago and you seem like a nice man and lately I've been having these incredibly horny feelings and just masturbating doesn't seem to work.'

I replied that it didn't for me either.

And she said, 'So if you don't have any STDs . . . ?' I assured her in the negative, and she continued, 'I live in Tarrytown and I always take a room when I come to these things so I don't have to drive home drunk, but tonight I was hoping to meet a halfway decent man whom I could take upstairs to it.'

Yes she was drunk, but not off-puttingly so. We slipped out of the ballroom without further discussion and took the elevator. She was, and is, a laugher, in my experience the rarest orgasmic sound. Not yucks, as at the Three Stooges, but a rippling glissando somewhere between what you produce when you smack your funny bone and the joyous hysteria of tickled little girls. It takes some getting used to but is truly delightful, like you're with a real friend and not engaged in yet another grim skirmish of the war between the sexes.

So it began. Ingrid and I have little in common. We mostly talk about our former spouses, these sessions occasionally ending in tears. I used to have several Ingrids at one time, but no longer. I believe this is not through any sudden impulse of fidelity but simple exhaustion. Some men I know (and I believe Mickey Haas is one of them) delight in the maintenance of a network of deceptions, playing one woman off against another, provoking operatic scenes, and so on, but not me. I am not even a decent rake. It's simply that I have no power of resistance, and while it is conventional to suppose that it is the man who does the pursuing and wooing, I have not found this to be so. The little story above about me and Ingrid is not at all unique, not even that unusual. They look at you, they make remarks, they hold their bodies in a certain way, and perhaps there are secret pheromones too; the availability is in any case announced and one says, Oh, why not? Or I do, at any rate.

The only real campaign of seduction I have ever carried out was directed against my wife, Amalie, née Pfannenstieler, and I will have to tell about this too before continuing with the story of Miranda.

(Pretend that time is suspended for now, Miranda and I are still in the paneled room at the library, our hands touching, the electricity flowing like Boulder Dam, pheromones beading up on all slick surfaces . . .)

So – my first job out of law school laboring as an associate at Sobel Tennis Carrey, on Beaver Street in the financial district. The firm had a modest practice in trademark and copyright, but anyone could see then – some twenty years ago that was – that intellectual property was going to be big, and I was working like mad in the usual manner of young associates. This was during the high tide of the sexual revolution, the first time in recent history when any reasonably well-set-up young fellow could have sex ad lib with females other than whores or courtesans, and in pursuit of this delicious horror I repaired nearly every night to one of several saloons (meat markets, they were amusingly called) in the East Village and uptown to continue and extend my revenge on the girls.

One Saturday morning, hung over and having detached

myself from my meat market conquest of the previous evening, I went down to my office to complete some work I had scanted so as to get a good start on my Friday-night hijinks. I was in the firm's library, quite alone in the office, when I heard a distant tapping, which I soon determined was coming from the office's locked outer door. Investigating this, I found a young woman standing in the deserted hallway. I recognized her as someone who worked at Barron & Schmidt, a financial outfit with whom we shared the fourteenth floor. We had often risen on the elevator together, me dull with the night's excess, she quiet and neatly turned out but carrying that look on her features that parries the male glance nearly as well as a Pathan burka.

She introduced herself and told me she had locked herself out of her office. I could see she was wretchedly embarrassed by it, especially as it was a trip to the john that had occasioned the flub. Charming little blossoms of red had appeared on her cheeks as a result of conveying this tale. She had fine, white-blond hair gathered in little twisty braids wound around her ears, rather a Pippi Longstocking effect, and she was wearing white jeans and a black Kraftwerke T-shirt, the black-letter text nicely distorted by her pretty pointy breasts, a Saturday outfit quite unlike the proper and cryptomammary suits she always wore to work. Her eyes were preternaturally large, just short of goggly, her mouth a little pink bud. She looked about seventeen but was (as I found later) nearly twenty-six. She was about five inches shorter than I was, tall for a woman, and had an athletic body (winter sports as I also learned – she was Swiss), slim of waist, with legs to the chin.

I invited her in and she made her call to building maintenance and they said they'd send a man around, but it'd be a while. She was truly stranded, since her bag with all her money and ID was locked up in Mr Schmidt's office. She was his private secretary and was learning the international finance business. Did she like international finance? No, she thought it was silly. She could not get excited about money. One needed enough, it was horrid to be poor, but beyond that there was something not healthy about wanting ever more and more and more. It was sometimes almost wicked, she said, and cutely wrinkled her nose. She asked me what I did at the firm and I told her and added that I thought I would never make a good IP lawyer because I felt most of the cases were sort of dumb and weren't really about the true purpose of IP law, which was to make sure that the creative act was rewarded, with the better part of the money going to the actual creator. Unfortunately this was, I informed her, hardly the rule; rather the opposite was in fact the case. Well, said she, you must fix that.

And she said it with such confidence – first, assuming such a fix was possible, and second, assuming I was the man for the task – that I was amazed. Perhaps I gaped. She smiled: light filled the dreary room and the dreary place in my head. I felt an unfamiliar shock. To recover, I asked her if she was ever really wicked herself. She said she tried to be, because everyone said it was such fun, but it was not fun at all, more sick-making than anything else, and she hated to be poked by men she didn't know.

Poked? I questioned the word. A little idiomatic slip; she meant pawed. In any case, this is what had drawn her from stuffy old Zurich to naughty New York. Her family was devoutly Catholic and so was she, she supposed, but she craved a little more zing in her life. Is that right? Zing?

It was, I assured her. And I informed her that today was her lucky day, because I was certainly among the wickedest men in New York and I would be pleased to take her among the depraved in their fleshpots, to provide zing but no poking. Unless she desired it, which was, of course, my wicked plan, but I did not voice this then. Her eyes lit up and again that smile. Waves of goodness broke upon my bitter brow.

Thus began my first date with Amalie. The building manager took his time getting up to the office, for which I blessed him in my heart, and we spent the interval talking about the one thing we found that (remarkable!) we had in common, which was that we were both Olympians. She had competed for Switzerland (alpine skiing) at Sapporo. And about our families, or rather about her family, which was like something out of Heidi. (Later, when she got her bag back she showed me pictures of colorfully parkaed upper-middle-class Switzers on the slopes, in front of the chalet, eating fondue. No, a lie, none eating fondue, but they *did* eat fondue, and I ate a lot of it too during our marriage.) I had not realized that there *were* Catholic Swiss, since I associated the tiny mountain republic with grim old Calvin, but of course there are the pope's Swiss Guards, who are really Swiss, and Amalie's mother's brother was one of them. Very *hoch* were the Pfannenstielers. And what of your family, Jake?

Oh, what indeed? Mother dead by then, Dad 'traveling,' brother studying in Europe (I boasted a bit here), sister . . . I thought of lying, but I never can keep my lies straight (I mean in personal life; as a lawyer I am, of course, a perfectly competent fabricator), so I said my sister was Miri de Lavieu. At that time in New York you would have had to be more or less blind to not know who she was, that, or perfectly out of tune with popular culture. 'The model,' I added to her blank look. I asked her if she had ever heard of Cheryl Tiegs, Lauren Hutton, or Janice Dickinson. She asked me if these were also my sisters? I have never met anyone, before or since, as uninterested in celebrity. Not of this world entirely, was Amalie. I should have taken warning from this, but I did not.

Now came the guy from the building and opened her office, and after she had done some final bits of work we left. I had at that time a BMW R70 motorcycle, upon which I commuted to work in nearly all weathers. She mounted the pillion, I spun up the machine. She placed her hands lightly around my waist.

Is there anything better than riding on a powerful motorcycle with a girl clutching on behind, her thighs pressing against your hips, her breasts making two warm ovals against your back, which pressure you can subtly augment whenever you like by tapping a little harder on the brakes than traffic conditions require? If so I have never found it. I took her up to Union Square, where in that season there was an immense billboard covering the entire side of a building showing an ad for a liquor that featured a blond woman in a slinky black evening gown. I stopped and pointed. That's my sister, I said. Amalie laughed and pointed to another billboard, this one showing a bare-chested young fellow in jeans. My brother, she said, and laughed again. I drove on, a little deflated, but in a nice way. I had scored plenty by being my sister's brother, so lustful are many in the city for even indirect contact with celebrities, and I was a little thrilled by the strangeness of being with someone to whom it meant nothing at all.

I bought her a meal in a Caribbean restaurant frequented by big-time *guapos* and their molls, noisy with salsa music, and vibrational with contained violence, and then we toured various dives and music clubs, the kind with drug markets in the john and blow jobs available in the alley behind. I was not famous enough to get into some of them, but Miri's name and the fact that I knew a number of the bouncers from my weight-lifting avocation served to breach the velvet ropes, that and the remarkable-looking woman on my arm. She turned out to be a terrific dancer; I was not bad at the time, but she danced me into the floor. People stared at her with peculiar looks on their faces that I couldn't quite interpret – contempt, longing? The damned contemplating the saved, perhaps; I'm sure the same look was on my face half the time.

Long story short: I took her back to her place, a condo sublet on First off Seventy-eighth, and to my immense surprise and dismay, I got a crisp Swiss handshake and a chaste cheek kiss. Same on the second date, same on the third. After that a little light canoodling, but she would not, as we used to say, put out. She said there'd been a boy at school and she'd slept with him and he'd broken her heart and she'd realized then that she was not made like the other girls she knew, not like they showed in the films, she couldn't bear sex without commitment, she didn't agree with everything the Church said, but she thought it was right on that score, and had been perfectly celibate since. Waiting for Mr Right? I asked her, and she, ignoring my irony, said yes. This colloquy took place, by the way, in the middle of an infamous club that was practically a petri dish for sexually transmitted diseases.

At this time in my life, I should add, I was entertaining at least four women, all lovely, all sexually available, and I can barely recall their names and faces now, so completely did Amalie take over my erotic life. And I had always been perfectly casual about allowing my girls to know I had others, it was after all the sexual revolution, and I did the same with Amalie, and amazingly she said I had to stop if I wanted to keep company with her, and even more amazingly, I did. I called up my current ladies one after another and kissed them off, so to speak.

Because – and this is the whole point of this long excursion – being with Amalie was better than sex. It was mystical. It was as if you could lean into a sunbeam and it could support you. Colors were brighter, music was more enticing, everything moved slowly, elegantly, like a grand entrance of ancient royalty, caressed by perfumed zephyrs. I had heard of stuff like this, but I thought it was all figures of speech. The moon did not hit my eye like a big pizza pie, but short of that, all the songs came true.

Eventually, I did seduce her, in the time-honored and honorable old way: that winter we were married, in the Liebfrauenkirche in Zurich, with her large and very proper Swiss family in attendance, banker dad and professor of linguistics mom and the six siblings, all blond and rosy-cheeked, and none of them thinking that she had carried off the prize, but everyone was as polite and correct as could be. My sister and brother came too. Miri happened to be on a fashion shoot in Paris and arrived with her coke-fiend Eurotrash husband, Armand Etienne Picot de Lavieu, and Paul came from his studies in Italy, so it was convenient. Maybe they would have still come had it not been, but that's something I was not sure of at the time. Dad was uninvited and absent. It was all something of a blur, actually, as I imagine weddings always are to the principals. The only thing I recall is Paul gripping me hard above the elbow and saying, This is a keeper, kid, don't fuck it up. And that Miri cried and, as far as I could tell, remained drug-free during the event.

We went on our honeymoon to Zermatt and stayed in the family chalet and skied. Or she skied. I mainly fell down and watched her zoom gorgeously down the pistes, and afterward participated in what was then and yet remains the most terrific sexual experience of my life. An orgasmic calliope. She made a sound like doves, the delighted *uohh uohh uohh* they produce, from almost the moment we started, and she was able to generate a nearly epileptic crescendo in which Time quite stopped, as it is supposed to do in heaven, existence without duration. Naturally, within six months, as I said, I had started sleeping around again, although I was able to keep this secret for many years, taking clever advantage of Amalie's near inability to think badly of anyone. No excuse, sir: it was evil plain and simple, evil black as night. I did fuck it up, as Paul feared, which is why he grasped my arm so tightly on my wedding day, leaving a bruise.

And having ruined paradise, I have for years desired to return there (without, naturally, having to make any major changes in my spiritual state) and have nurtured a longing for a new and fresh Amalie, but this time one not quite so good, someone more along the lines of me, but not *too* much like me, if you take my meaning, but with the same electricity and without the unbearable burden of guilt that I bring to relations with my wife. Which is why I have made this long excursion, to make it clear what was happening in the Brooke Russell Astor Reading Room. A fresh start, and there she was with her tiny blond braids and her Amalie-esque look, shaking my hand with the tingles goosefleshing up my arm.

I asked her what she was doing, and she pointed to a thick volume open on the desk. Something my uncle wanted me to research – family history. I gestured to chairs and we sat down. It was a library, so we had to speak softly, and since we had to, it was necessary for me to have my head closer to hers than ordinary interlocution would require. She wore a light perfume, floral.

'You're an academic too, I gather?'

'No, I work for the ministry of education in Toronto. This is more of a sideline, and to help him out.'

'But he's deceased.'

'Yes. I thought I could finish up the work and arrange for a posthumous publication. I think he would have liked that.'

'You were close, then?'

'Yes.'

'Although separated by oceans?'

'Yes.' Then, somewhat impatiently, with a little wrinkle forming across her fine high forehead, 'My uncle Andrew was a very important part of my life, Mr Mishkin. My father left my mom when I was four, leaving us in a very precarious financial position. He was something of a wild boy and not at all interested in fatherhood. He's dead now, as is my mother. Uncle Andrew, meanwhile, paid for my education, had me over to England during practically every summer vacation starting at age eight and . . . oh, God, why am I telling you all this? I guess I haven't quite recovered from the shock of what happened to him. I'm sorry. I hadn't intended to spill my guts like that.'

'It's quite all right,' I said. 'Losing a close relative through violence can be a devastating thing.'

'You sound like you speak from experience.'

'Yes,' I said, but in a tone that did not encourage further queries. Changing the subject, I asked, 'How long have you been in the city?'

'Toronto?'

'No, here. I'm sorry – when New Yorkers say "the city" they always mean the island of Manhattan.'

She smiled at this, our first shared smile. 'Since Monday. Two days.'

'In a hotel, are you?'

'Yes, the Marquis on Eighth Avenue. I was expecting to stay in Uncle Andrew's place, but there are legal complications. It's still a crime scene and they won't release any of his things, although Professor Haas very kindly let me look through his office and take some personal items.'

'You're comfortable there?' Making conversation here, God knows what I was thinking, I suppose I just wanted to keep her talking, prolong the moment. Ridiculous, as I say, but in the interests of an honest tale . . .

She replied, 'Well, to be frank, it's fairly grotty. It's supposed to be cheap, but cheap in New York is more than I can afford, especially with Canadian dollars.'

'You've seen the police?'

'Yes. Yesterday. I thought I would have to identify the body like they do on TV, but that had already been done. They asked me some questions, really, pretty awful questions.'

'This is their theory that he was killed as part of some gay sexual ritual?'

'Yes, but my God! – and I told them this – Uncle Andrew wasn't like that at all. He made no secret of his, um, romantic orientation, but he was devoted to Ollie. He's a don at Oxford. They were like an old married couple when they were together.' Her tone abruptly changed and she asked, 'Do you think we can conclude our business today?'

'Our business being . . . ?'

'Uncle Andrew's manuscript.'

Oh, that! I asked her what she knew about it.

'Oh, he didn't tell me much, only that it was a Jacobean manuscript. He paid several thousand dollars for it, but he thought it might be a lot more valuable if some things checked out.'

'Like what?'

'I don't know. He didn't say.' Again she produced that adorable wrinkle. 'And frankly I can't see that it's any business of yours. It's my property.'

'Actually, Ms Kellogg,' I said, somewhat prissily, 'it's the property of the estate. In order for you to claim it, you have to demonstrate both that you are who you say you are, and that you are the sole legal heiress of Andrew Bulstrode. In order for that to happen, you must produce a will and have it probated in surrogate's court for the County of New York. Only then will the executor of the will have the authority to instruct me to hand over the estate's property to you.'

'Oh, gosh! Will that take long?'

'It could. If the will is faulty or contested, it could take weeks, months, even years to settle. As in Dickens.'

At this she gave a despairing cry, bit her lip, and brought her hands to her face. The clerk at the desk looked over at us disapprovingly.

'I can't wait that long,' she wailed. 'I could only get these few days off. I have to be back in Toronto on Monday and I can't afford to stay in a hotel. And . . .' Here she stopped and dropped her eyes, as we do when we are about to reveal something it's best not to reveal. Interesting, that; I thought it might be part of why she was reluctant to come to my office. I decided to push on that door.

'And . . . ?'

'Nothing.' A poor liar, I thought, observing the delicate flushing below the jawline.

'Well, *not* nothing, I think. You ask me to meet you in a secluded place, you keep looking up at the door, as if you expect someone to barge in, and now you seem to be concealing something. Add to that the fact that your uncle died in mysterious, even frightening circumstances, and you strike me as a woman with something of a problem. A woman who, if I may be so bold, needs . . .'

'A lawyer? Are you volunteering yourself?' Suspiciously.

'Not at all. You need an estate lawyer who can help you get through probate. I am not that kind of lawyer, but my firm has some good ones. I was thinking of volunteering myself as your friend.'

'You think I need a friend?'

'You tell me. I'm guessing that you were approached about this manuscript and that this approach was of a disturbing nature.'

She nodded vigorously, causing her braids to wiggle. Delightful!

'Yes. I got a call just after the police called me and told me Uncle Andrew had died. It was a man with a deep voice and an accent.'

'An English accent?'

'No, like Slavic or Middle Eastern. I sort of yelled at him because I was so upset, I'd just found out that Uncle Andrew had died and here was this vulture circling. I hung up and he called right back and his tone was . . . I mean it sounds stupid to say "threatening" but that's what it felt like. He offered me fifty thousand Canadian for the documents, and I told him I'd think about it. He wasn't happy with that answer, and he said something like, I forget his exact words, something like it would be better for you in every possible way to agree to these terms. It was like that line from *The Godfather*, an offer you can't refuse, and it was so unreal, I almost giggled. Then, after I got to the Marquis, I got called again, same voice. How did they know I was there? No one at home knew where I was staying.'

'No significant other?' Concealing the hopefulness.

'No. And my office has my mobile. Anyway, when I left

the hotel this morning there was a car, one of those big SUVs, black, with smoked windows, parked down the block from the hotel and there was a man, a big man, with a bullet head and sunglasses, leaning against it. And I looked back after I passed him and he was looking at me with this really horrible smile and then he got into the car, and I took the bus here, and when I got to the library the car was there again.'

'That's worrisome,' I said.

'Yes, it is,' she said after a long pause. Her voice was a trifle shaky.

'Look,' I said, 'let's say that the police are wrong about your uncle's death, as you suggest, and that he was murdered. Murdered for this, um, document. Melodramatic, yes, but such things must happen occasionally. So assume for a moment that this item is extraordinarily valuable for some reason, way more valuable than fifty grand Canadian, and that criminals have somehow learned about it and are trying to obtain it by fair means or foul. Does that make sense?'

She nodded slowly. I thought I saw her shiver, and I wanted to fling my arms around her, but forbore.

'Yes, in a horrible way,' she replied, 'but I can't imagine what it could be. I mean the value part. Uncle Andrew said he paid a few thousand for it and that's probably near what it's worth, or else why would the seller have sold it? And if for some reason it turned out to be *more* valuable, why would criminals be involved?'

'That's the question, of course, but my sense is that it's not the document itself that's valuable, but what it leads to. Did your uncle tell you anything about that?'

'No. As far as I knew it was a Jacobean letter of some sort, of purely academic interest. He was really excited about it, and made a special trip to England last summer to check up on some things related to it, but he didn't imply that it had any, well, *pecuniary* value. Did he tell *you* what it was? I mean what it might lead to.'

'Yes, he claimed it was an actual Shakespeare autograph manuscript, but I'm afraid he might have been unduly optimistic. Later, I spoke with Mickey Haas, and he suggested that this was unlikely, and that your uncle seemed to be somewhat desperate to, as it were, recoup his fortunes.'

'Yes, he was, he tended to be like that since the scandal. You know about that?'

'I'm familiar with the facts, yes. But he must have been aware of this criminal interest, since he deposited the damned thing with me. He must have suspected he might be attacked and wanted to preserve it from being taken. So . . . to continue, the first order of business would seem to be securing you personally. You clearly can't return to your grotty hotel. We could change hotels . . .'

'I can't afford to change hotels. It was all paid in advance anyway. Oh, God, this is turning into a nightmare . . .'

'. . . or, if I may, I have a large loft downtown. There are two bedrooms in it where my kids stay when they're on school holidays. You could have one of them. It's probably nearly as grotty as the Marquis, but free of charge. I also have a driver to take you around town. He used to be sort of a bodyguard.'

'A bodyguard?' she exclaimed and then asked, 'Whom did he guard?'

'Yasser Arafat, actually. But we like to keep that part quiet. I can't think of anyplace you'd be more safe.' Except from me, but let that pass for the moment. Honestly, I was not thinking of that at all when I made the offer. I recalled the terror on her uncle's face quite well and did not want that look ever to appear on hers. 'Once you're stashed, we can see if we can learn something about the people involved from their vehicle. I'll alert the police to this development and leave that part to them.'

She agreed to this plan after the usual polite demurrers. We left the reading room and then the library. At the top of the steps I steered her into the shadow of the porch columns and peered out at Fifth Avenue. There was no black SUV with smoked windows in sight. I called Omar on my cell and told him to meet us on the Forty-second Street side and then we hurried through Bryant Park and were waiting for the Lincoln as it pulled up.

My loft is on Franklin Street off Greenwich. It's four thousand square feet in area, and the building used to be a pants factory, later a warehouse, but now it is chockablock full of rich people. I got into it before downtown real estate became psychotic, but it still set me back a bundle, and that doesn't count the improvements. We used to live here as a family, Amalie, the kids, and me, until she moved out. Usually the guy moves out, but Amalie knew I really liked this place and also she wanted to be closer to the kids' school, which is on Sixty-eighth off Lexington. They're all now on East Seventy-sixth in a brownstone duplex. We split expenses right down the middle, because she has a good income and sees no reason why I should be beggared simply because I am a sexual asshole.

At the time under discussion, however, I was not thinking about that. I was showing Amalie 2 (aka Miranda Kellogg) around my dwelling. She was suitably impressed, which I found an improvement over Amalie 1, who was never impressed by things money could buy. I ordered Chinese takeout and we ate by candles at a low table I have from which you get a nice, if narrow, view of the river. I was a gentleman, and reasonably honest as we ate and exchanged histories. It turned out she was a child psychologist by training, working as a midlevel bureaucrat. We talked about Niko, my boy, and his problems. She was sympathetic in a rather distant way. As I became more familiar with her face, I decided that she did not resemble Amalie quite as much as I had originally thought, not feature by feature, but still there was that feeling of bubbling excitement when I looked at her. How little we know, how much to discover, from lover to lover, as the song has it.

She began to yawn, and perfectly proper, I made up the bed in Imogen's room. I gave her a new white T-shirt to sleep in, and of course I had fresh toothbrushes because of my kids. I got sleepy thanks and a nice kiss on the cheek. What was that perfume? Elusive, but familiar.

The next day, we rose early, breakfasted on coffee and croissants, in a mood that was more companionable, I must admit, than it would have been had this been a Morning After. She had a certain distancing air about her that did not encourage aggressive intimacy seeking, which was fine with me: another reminder of Amalie back when. She dressed in the same little department-store wool suit she had worn the previous day, and Omar took us up to my office. Once there, I introduced her to Jasmine Ping, our brilliant estate lawyer, and left them to plumb the mysteries of probate and also help arrange for the transfer of Bulstrode's body back to England.

My diary tells me I spent the morning dissuading a writer from suing another writer for stealing her ideas and from them producing a far more successful book than the writer's own, and later on the phone with a fellow at the U.S. Trade Representative setting up a meeting about (what else?) Chinese IP pirates. A typical morning. At twelve-thirty or so Miranda appeared up at my office and I suggested lunch. She refused, I insisted, at which she shamefacedly admitted that she was still too frightened to wander freely in public and wished to eat in the office or be driven back to the loft.

We therefore ordered from a deli, and while we were waiting, Miranda broached the subject of the manuscript. She said that under her uncle's tutelage she'd become an efficient reader of Jacobean secretary hand: could she not look at it now? I hesitated but saw no real objection. Heirs often make independent judgments on the value of prospective inheritables. I sent Ms M. down to the vault.

While we were waiting our lunch arrived and we ate, sitting at my glass coffee table. She was a precise eater, tiny bites. We talked about IP and her uncle's visit here, but she had no more idea about why he wanted or needed an IP lawyer than I did. Ms Maldonado came back with the folder.

Miranda pulled on cotton gloves before she handled the stiff brown pages. She held several up to the window to examine watermarks. But the day had gone dark, with the beginnings of a spattering rain. She had to use the desk lamp instead.

'Interesting,' she said, and again as she passed the pages before the light. 'This heavier paper is what they call a crown folio sheet, marked with the coat of arms of Amsterdam, which comes from a well-known paper house and quite common in the seventeenth century. The pages look like they were ripped out of a ledger. These other sheets seem to be printer's copy and unrelated.' She mentioned the name of a paper maker, but I have forgotten what it was, and then she discoursed briefly about the provenance of paper. In one ear and out the other. She drew a folding magnifying glass from her handbag. 'Do you mind?' she asked.

I did not. I was content to watch her. She studied the pages; I studied the swan of her neck bobbing above them and the tendrils of hair that moved delicately in the faint breeze from the heating system. Time passed. I doodled at some paperwork, without enthusiasm. The noises of the office outside my door seemed to come from another world. She read four pages. From time to time she would mutter. Then she positively gasped.

'What?'

'The writer of this thing, Richard Bracegirdle – he claims to have sailed with Somers. He was on the wreck of the *Sea Adventure*. Oh, God! My hands are shaking.'

I asked what was handshakingly important about it.

'Because it was a famous event. The governor of the Virginia colony was aboard. They were wrecked on Bermuda and they lived off the land and built a ship and got back to Virginia. Some of them wrote accounts of it, and we believe that Shakespeare used them to create the atmosphere of Prospero's island in *The Tempest*. But if this guy knew Shakespeare in 1610 as he claims . . . I mean he might have been with him, feeding him tropical color while he was writing. This alone makes it . . . look, Mr Mishkin . . .'

'Please, you're a guest in my house. I wish you'd call me Jake.'

'All right – Jake. I *have* to study this manuscript. Would it be possible for us to take it back to your place?'

My first instinct as a lawyer was, of course, to refuse. Lawyers famously have free access to money and valuables belonging to others, and the first step on the slippery slope is handling these with anything but the most rigid propriety. Carry a manuscript out of the office for the perusal of a putative heiress and pretty soon you're hanging the client's Renoir in the small bedroom and taking the family to Saint Bart's on the decedent's yacht.

Yes, that, but she was looking at me with hope, her cheeks still aflush with the thrill of discovery, and here I thought of

Amalie, who never asked me for anything, who expected me to know what she wanted through mystic bonds of affection. At which I inevitably failed. It's nice to be asked. So I said that I supposed that would be all right, since legally they would not be out of my personal possession. I obtained a stiff folder and placed the Bracegirdle material into it. I called Omar, grabbed an umbrella and my briefcase, and after speaking with Ms Maldonado about various things, I left the office with Miranda beside me. As it happened, I had promised to pick my children up at school and take them home. This was somewhat awkward, but Miranda was after all a client and not radioactively intimate with Daddy, or not yet, anyway. I made the pickup, introduced the kids, and it was a perfectly pleasant ride. Imogen was unusually charming and wanted to know if Miranda spoke French, being Canadian, and was told she (embarrassingly) had no talent for languages at all, and Niko entertained us all by making knots in a piece of rope, many many knots, all carefully explained as to provenance and use and topological features. I was delighted that Miranda was kind to the boy – many people are not, including me – and thought it presaged well for our future.

After dropping them off, we continued south (slowly, because of the gloom and the increasing rain), and during this ride, after the obligatory compliments about the kids, Miranda was uncharacteristically chatty about the wonders of Bracegirdle's screed. I should recall this conversation but I do not and don't feel up to fabricating it, as I have the others above. It's nearly three and I will need to get some sleep shortly. In any case, we arrived. Omar departed.

But no sooner had his taillights vanished around the corner than we heard the high whine of spinning tires against wet paving and a large black SUV, a Denali, came barreling around the Greenwich Street corner, skidded to a halt in front of us, and disgorged three men. These men were all wearing hooded sweatshirts and leather gloves, and they all three came rapidly toward us in a menacing manner. One of them made a grab for Miranda and I stabbed him in the face (quite ineffectively I'm afraid) with the ferrule of my umbrella. This was wrenched from my hand by the larger of the other two men while his companion slipped behind and grabbed my arms. The big fellow moved in to deliver a disabling blow to my midsection; probably he was planning a few others to make up for the umbrella-stabbing.

I am not much of a fighter, but I have spent a good deal of my free time in saloons, and there is a certain species of feisty little guy who, when loaded, cannot resist picking a fight with a big guy, especially when they look somewhat out of shape and un-Schwarzeneggerish, as I do. So I was not as unused as most men in my profession are to physical violence. There are not that many heavyweight lifters around, and these people simply had no idea what I was.

First I flexed my arms and broke the grip of the man behind me and in the next instant I had squatted down and spun on my heel, so that I faced the thighs of my erstwhile captor. I grabbed both his legs around the knees. My hands are immense and very, very strong. I felt the big man on whom I had just turned my back starting to clutch at my neck, but now I stood up again, raising both arms above my head. The man I had grabbed only weighed about 180, so he went up quite easily. I took a step away, pivoted again, and hit the big man on the head with his friend. A human body makes a very inefficient club, but as a demonstration of strength and as a way to demoralize one's opponents, especially the club person, it is hard to top. The big fellow staggered back, slipped on the wet pavement, and went down on his butt. I whipped my club around my head a couple of times and flung him out into the street.

Regrettably, in order to perform these feats I had to drop my briefcase, and the man who had grabbed Miranda threw her roughly against the side of my building, snatched up the briefcase, shouted something to the others in a foreign tongue, and made for the Denali. The others picked themselves up from the ground and also fled, screaming imprecations. The vehicle screeched away too quickly for me to get the plate numbers. I went to see if Miranda was all right, which she was, although her wrist was strained and bruised where the thug had held her and her hand and knee were scraped.

She impatiently dismissed my concern over her injuries and asked, 'Did they get your briefcase?'

'I'm afraid they did and I hated to lose it. I've had it since I passed the bar.'

'But the *manuscript* . . . ,' she wailed.

'The manuscript is perfectly safe,' I assured her. 'It was in the lining pocket of my raincoat.' I was about to tell her that I always carry items of particular value on my person, since the day when, still in law school, I had left my old briefcase on the Boston subway and in it the only copy of a Con law paper representing several hundred hours of tedious work, but instead she seized my face and kissed me on the mouth.

THE BRACEGIRDLE LETTER (7)

Now on a daye some weekes after oure coming Mr Keane was killed by a great balle: one moment I spake him & the next there stoode he without a head & fell. And where was I then? The gonnes were let to another maistre who hadde his owne people & so stoode I in Sluys with scarce a dodkin in purse & no Dutch in my mouth neither: but one day wandering idel by the harbour there I spied the Groene Draek & went on it & spake to Captain & sayde I can serve gonnes as well as anie man & he said well I know lad but say thee, knowest thou my trade? For he spake good Englishe & I saying no sir he sayde I am a pirate & a smuckler, a word I knew not & he opened the meaninge as: one who defraudeth His Majesty of duties, tonnage poundage &c. Soe will you serve my gonnes in that trade he asketh, it be bloudie & cruel, but we earne gold. And I sayde yes sir being verie hungrie & I said to myself privilie well it is but papistes we kill. And I wished verey earnest to have gold.

Wee sayled out from Sluys & othere portes of Hollande a scourge to the Spanish shipping from the German Sea to Biscays Bay & took many a vessel & slew many Spanish & some French & also ran in to England by night & landed cargoes of silks, spices, wines & spirites under the noses of the coste guardes. Meantimes whilst wee layde in port I made perfect my fancie of a distance-quadrant, having a man in Rotterdam fashioun one out of brasse, the lines cut in with aqua fortis upon the quadrantes with thereto a little mirroir so one could see through bouth sightes at one glance. With this set upon a raile wee then laded all oure gonnes with such quantitie of poudre as would carry shotte a certayne distance, I will saye eight hundred yards. Thus ready I peer into my device set with the angle before-figured to that distance on the moveable arm & peering down the sight I wait until the target appears in both mirroir & plain sight & there you have your range exact & give the order to fyre & all balles striking home all at once without warning or casteing shottes they are surprized & overcome & we board & take them easie.

Soe two yeares on the seas & I have 80 sovereigns in gold that I left with a Jewe of Sluys to keep. For the crew spent all in drink & whores but not I. In the Yeare Nine as all knoweth a truce wase signed between the King of Spain & the Dutch & the Stadthouder orders no more robbyng of Spainish shippes. But Van Brille says wee are not ordered to stoppe smuckling as that is no affayre of the Stadthouder d-mn his eyes. So we continued in this wise but I was uneasey & one daye I went to my Jewe & he writes me a bill of paper saying that what Jewe soever I should shew it to from Portugale to Muscovy will give me suche a sum in gold. Wee went over to England one night & whilst wee were ashore a-trading oure stores with certayne men of Plymouth I walked off into the darke & was done with smuckling or so I thought.

In Plymouth some daies passed at the Anchor Inn thinking upon what I should do when comes a man seekyng mariners & others for the voyage of the Admiral Sir Geo. Somers to Virginia in the New World & I thought me this be a sign what I should do & I says to hym I am a gonner afloat or dry & can take the starres in sight by crosse-staff or back-staffe to tell latitudes & can make survey if required. & he says canst walk upon water too or need you a boat, & all there assembled laughed: but he bade me come with him to see Mr Tolliver the master of the flag-ship Sea Adventure. He greetes me kindly & askes I show him my mettel: soe I doe & he being well-satisfied I can doe all I profess with passynge skille I sign as maistre gonner is 4d diem.

We sayled on second June the Yeare Nine. After the Groene Draeck I find the ship like almost the palace of some lord so spacious was it & well-appointed & the food far better, no Dutch cheese & fish & hock wine but goode beer & English beefe: soe I wase well contente. I fell in friendlie with Mr Tolliver & learned from him more of the art of the compass & use of the back-staffe & how to figure longitude from the starres, a thyng most difficult to doe well. He was a most strange man his lyke I had never met before this, for he did not credit Gods grace & thought there wase not a farthing to chuse between the papist superstitioun & the reformed faith: for he believed God had made the worlde & then left it to be what it might, like a wyfe setting cakes out to cool & cared not for us creatures a whit. Wee would argue such matteres on the night watch til dawn brake: but it booted little for wee never did agree as he would not accept the authoritie of Scripture at all. Wast thou there he sayde when it was took down? Nay? Then how know you it is Gods word & not wrote by some foole such as yoursen? He had no feare of Hell-fyre neither, sayde he had never seen a devil nor an angel nor had hee ever met one fellow (saveing a few mad) who ever had. He thought church could doe no harme for the moste of mankynde & went glad enough o' Sunday but cared not what was the service or the sermon: if the Kinges grace should saye worshipe a mere stone or else the Pope he wold be content to doe it. It was all one to hym: & I was amazed at this for how could all the world think these thynges the most grave of all thynges & hym not: & hym yet a goode, kynde man with all his wittes?

8

Crosetti's mother, Mary Margaret Crosetti (Mary Peg as she was universally known), possessed a number of personal characteristics useful for both a high-end research librarian and a mother, including a prodigious memory, a love of truth, a painstaking attention to detail, and an industrial-strength bullshit detector. Thus, while she tried to give her son the privacy suitable to the adult he was, the ordinary business of life in a smallish Queens bungalow produced enough mother–son interactions to give her a good idea of his interior state of being at any particular moment. Ten days ago this state had been extraordinarily fine. Al tended to the dour, but she recalled that for a day or so he sang in the shower and glowed from within. He's in love, she thought, with the mingling of joy and trepidation that this perception raises in most parents, and then, shortly thereafter, came the crash. He's been dumped, she concluded, and also that it was an unusually quick end to what had appeared to be an unusually intense joy.

'I'm worried about him,' she said on the telephone to her eldest daughter. 'This is not like Albert.'

'He's always getting dumped on, Ma,' said Janet Keene, who besides being her mother's chief coconspirator was a psychiatrist. 'He's a nice guy with no smarts about women. It'll pass.'

'You're not here, Janet. He's moving like a zombie. He comes home from work like he spent the day in the salt mines. He doesn't eat, he goes to bed at eight-thirty – it's not natural.'

'Well, I could see him . . . ,' Janet began.

'What, as a *patient*?'

'No, Ma, that's not allowed, but if you want a second opinion.'

'Look, darling, I know when my children are crazy and when not, and he's not crazy – I mean not *crazy* crazy. What I'm going to do is this Saturday I'll make a nice breakfast, I'll sit him down, and I'll get it out of him. What do you think?'

Janet, who in her wildest professional fantasies could hardly imagine having her mother's ability to make people spill their guts, produced some noncommittal affirmative remarks. Affirmative remarks were what were required when Mary Peg called to ask for advice, and Janet did her duty. She thought the main thing her baby brother needed was a girl, a decent job, and to vacate his mother's roof, in ascending order of importance, but she declined to pursue that line of argument. She and her two sisters had bailed out at the earliest opportunity: not that they didn't dearly love their mother, but she cast a good deal of very dense shade. Poor Allie!

Mary Peg always felt better after soliciting professional advice from Janet and was pleased that this accorded so well with her own instincts. She was one of seven children of a subway motorman and, unusually for one of her class and culture, had succumbed to the lure of the '60s and gone the whole countercultural route – rock band groupie, communard in California, a little drugging, some casual sex – and then the semishamefaced resumption of real life in the form of a B.A. from City College and an M.S. in library science. Her own parents had known nothing of the wilder part of this history, for she was not one of the many of that time who were naughty to get back at the folks; naughtiness for its own sake had been quite sufficient. But she had always felt a bracing Catholic guilt at deceiving them and had resolved, when she came to have children of her own, that intergenerational deception was not going to be part of the deal. She occasionally thought that this was why she had married a cop.

As planned, she presented the nice breakfast, her son shuffled up to the table, sipped some fresh orange juice, took a few forkfuls of French toast, and announced that thanks but he wasn't really very hungry, at which point Mary Peg banged a teaspoon against a glass in a good imitation of a fire alarm. He jerked and stared.

'Okay, spill it, Buster!' she said, fixing him with her eyes, these being the color of gas flame and, just now, about as hot.

'What?'

'What, he says. You've been doing a scene from *The Night of the Living Dead* for nearly two weeks. You didn't think I noticed? You're a wreck.'

'It's nothing, Ma . . .'

'It's something. It's that girl, what's-her-name, Carol.'

'Carolyn.' Followed by a great sigh.

'Her. Now, you know I never pry into the personal lives of my children . . .'

'Ha.'

'Don't be fresh, Albert!' And in a milder tone, 'Seriously, I'm starting to worry about you. You've broken up with girls before but you never acted all weird like this.'

'It's not a breakup, Ma. It's not . . . I don't know what it is. That's the problem. I mean basically we had one date, very nice, but then she . . . I guess she sort of vanished.'

Mary Peg sipped coffee and waited, and in a few minutes the whole confused story came out, the convoluted tale of Rolly, and the manuscript, and Bulstrode. Her husband had described any number of interrogations to her, for he was not among the majority of police detectives who thought their spouses too tender to listen to cop stories; nor was she. This was how it was done, she knew, a sympathetic ear, an encouraging word. She was disturbed to learn that her son had abetted what an unsympathetic person might regard as a felony, nor did she like anything of what she heard about Ms Rolly. But she declined comment; and now her son arrived at the period subsequent to their first date: he had not of course filled in the moister details, but she had the experience and imagination to provide these herself.

'Well, like I said, we had a nice time and I was feeling pretty good. I went to work the next day expecting to find her in the shop, but she wasn't there. I asked Glaser and he said she'd called and said she had to go out of town for a couple of days. I thought that was a little peculiar, I mean I thought we had something going, that she would've called *me*, but like I said, she was a strange bird. So I was, you know, cool about it. Anyway, the day comes when she's supposed to come back and no Carolyn. Mr Glaser calls her – the phone's disconnected, so now we're a little freaked and I told him I'd go by after work and see what was up. And when I got to her street there was a big dump truck parked outside and a wrecking crew was all over her building. They were just finishing up for the day, but I could see they had set up one of those chutes that wreckers use to slide debris and stuff down to the Dumpster and it was stuck in her window on the top floor. I talked to the crew chief and he didn't know anything. He'd gotten a call from the building management that they needed a rush job, the building had to be gutted down to the brick shell and made ready for renovation. I got the name of the management company from him but he wouldn't let me go into the building. Like I told you, Carolyn had built all this furniture out of pallet boards, beautiful work, and there it was, all smashed up, her worktable and everything. It was like seeing her corpse.'

Crosetti seemed to shiver. He pushed French toast around with his fork.

'In any case, I couldn't do anything there, and I was, like, totally stunned. I started to walk away and I noticed that the street and the sidewalk were strewn with scraps of paper. It was a windy day and I guess some of the lighter stuff had blown off the truck, or the wind had picked it up between the chute and the pile of trash in the truck. So like an idiot I went down the street bent over picking up stuff, thinking to myself, Oh, she'll want this, this photograph, this postcard, whatever; stupid really, because she would've taken whatever she wanted.'

He took out his wallet and showed her a folded postcard, a folded photograph.

'Pathetic, right? Carrying this stuff around? It's like magical thinking, if I hold on to something of hers, there's still a connection, she hasn't totally vanished . . .' He placed the items back in his wallet and looked so forlorn that Mary Peg had to control an atavistic urge to take him on her lap and kiss his brow. Instead she said, 'What about these famous volumes? You think she took those?'

'I hope so. I didn't see them. For all I know they were at the bottom of the truck. That'd be ironic, like the gold dust in *The Treasure of the Sierra Madre*.'

That last made Mary Peg feel a little better; if he was making movie references, he couldn't be that far gone. She said, 'You called the building manager, of course.'

'Of course. I even went up to their offices. Able Real Estate Management, up near Borough Hall in Brooklyn. A receptionist who knew zip and a boss who was never in. When I finally got him on the phone, he said he didn't know any Carolyn Rolly, and that the top floor had never been rented out as a residence, that it wasn't certified for human occupancy in any case, which was why they were gutting the building. I asked him who owned the building and he said that was confidential. A consortium, he said. Then I called Professor Bulstrode, and the departmental secretary said he'd left for England the previous day and they weren't sure when he'd be back. Visiting professors were more or less free to go where they pleased when they had no classes to meet and he didn't. It was the summer. She wouldn't give me his number in Oxford.'

He gave her a look so bleak that it zapped a little shock of pain through her heart. 'I don't know what to do, Ma. I think something happened to her. And somehow I think it's my fault.'

'Well, that's just nonsense. The only thing you did wrong was to go along with this scheme of hers. Look, I know you were fond of this girl, but why isn't it likely that she simply absconded with her ill-gotten gains?'

'Ill-gotten gains? Ma, it's not like she knocked over a liquor store. She was a bookbinder. She was fixing a beautiful set of books that their owner had given up for scrap. Glaser wouldn't suffer a penny of loss – he only wanted the money he would've gotten from the sale of the prints . . .'

'Which he didn't get, don't forget.'

'Hey, I'm not making excuses, but if she was a crook, she was a certain kind of crook. There was stuff she wouldn't do, and bugging out like this and not giving Glaser what he had coming were in that zone. I mean, she was in the middle of a project that she really wanted to do, and . . . you didn't see her place, but she'd created this whole little world in this crummy loft in Red Hook, I mean she'd built it with her own hands, it was her work space, and work was all she had. She never would've just ditched it.'

'I don't know, darling: she seems like a very unpredictable young woman and almost . . . can I say "unstable"? I mean according to her she's been horribly abused. And you said she was some kind of fugitive – maybe that caught up with her? You're shaking your head.'

'No, and I'm not sure about the fugitive part either. I did a massive search on the Internet. You'd think an incident like a guy named Lloyd keeping a girl named Carolyn Rolly locked up for ten years as a sex toy would have generated some hits, but I came up blank. I called the *Kansas City Star* and the *Topeka Capital-Journal* and the *Wichita Eagle,* a couple of other Kansas papers, and got zilch: nobody had ever heard of the case. Okay, she could've changed her name but still . . . so I called Patty.'

Mary Peg noted that her son's face showed a tinge of embarrassment at this admission, as well it should have, she thought. Patrica Crosetti Dolan, the second eldest girl, had followed her dad into the New York City Police Department and risen to detective third grade. Members of the NYPD are not supposed to do little investigative tasks for their families, but many do anyway; Mary Peg had occasionally availed herself of her daughter's connections in this way while doing research, had taken substantial flak off her son on the subject as a result, and now ha-ha!

She refrained from gloating, however, satisfying herself with a simple but freighted 'Oh?'

'Yeah, I asked her to do a records check, whether she was a fugitive or not.'

'And . . .'

'She didn't show up, not as Carolyn Rolly anyway.'

'You mean she lied? About the uncle and about being a fugitive?'

'I guess. What else could it be? And that's what sort of knocked the stuffing out of me. Because . . . I mean I really liked this woman. It was chemical; you know, you and Dad always talked about the first time you saw each other when you were working behind the desk at the Rego Park Library and he used to come in for books. You just *knew*? It was like that.'

'Yeah, but, honey, that was mutual. I didn't pack my bags and split after the first date.'

'I thought it was mutual too. I thought this was going to be it. And if it wasn't, I mean if it was all something I cooked up in my head, then, well, where am I? I must be crazy.'

'Please, you are not any kind of maniac, take my word for it. I would be the first one to tell you if you were going off the rails. As I would expect you to do for me when senile dementia rears its ugly head.' She clapped her hands briskly, as if to demonstrate how very far off lay that event, and said, 'Meanwhile, what are we going to do about this?'

'We?'

'Of course. Now, clearly, everything revolves around this Professor Bulstrode. What do we know about him?'

'Ma, what're you talking about? What does Bulstrode have to do with Carolyn disappearing? He bought the papers, he split. End of story. Although I did run a search on him and he's sort of a black sheep.' Here Crosetti explained about the famous quarto fraud, which, as it happens, she recalled.

'Oh, *that* guy,' she exclaimed. 'Well, the plot thickens, doesn't it? Now, the very first thing we have to do is get Fanny in on this, just like you should've done originally.' He stared at her blankly and she went on. 'Albert, you don't imagine that Bulstrode gave you the real translation of that thing! Of course he lied. You said your gut was telling you that you were getting rooked, and you wouldn't have sold it to him if that woman hadn't turned on the waterworks and told you those whoppers. They were in it together.'

'That's impossible, Ma . . .'

'It's the only explanation. She played you like a fish. I'm sorry, honey, but the fact is, we sometimes fall in love with unsuitable people, which is why Cupid carries a bow and arrows and not a clipboard with a stack of personality tests. I certainly did when I was a kid, and not just once.'

'For example,' said Crosetti with interest. His mother's supposedly wild past was a subject of fascination to all her children, but one she only mentioned in the form of admonitory hints like this one. Her answer when questioned was invariably, as now, 'That's for me to know and you to find out.' She added, 'In any case, my boy, I'll call Fanny right now and set it up. You can see her after work on Monday.'

Against which Crosetti had no compelling argument. Thus at six that day he presented himself with the papers in their mailing tube at the manuscript department of the New York Public Library. He found Fanny Doubrowicz at her desk. She was a tiny woman, less than five feet tall, with a pleasantly ugly pug face and bright mahogany eyes, deep sunk behind thick round spectacles; her coarse gray hair was drawn back in a librarian's bun, stuck with the canonical yellow pencil. She had come over as an orphan from Poland after the war and had been a librarian for over fifty years, most of them at the NYPL, specializing in manuscripts for the last twenty or so. Crosetti had known Aunt Fanny for his whole life and considered her the wisest person within his circle of aquaintance, although when complimented upon her encyclopedic brain, she always laughed and said, 'Darling [or *dolling*], I know nothing [*nozhing*] but I know where to *find* everything.' When he was a child he and his sisters had tried to think of facts that would be impossible for Aunt Fanny to discover (how many bottles of Coke got sold in Ashtabula in 1928?), but she always defeated them and provided remarkable stories of how the information had been obtained.

So: greetings, questions about his sisters, his mother, himself (although Crosetti was sure she had been elaborately briefed on this by Mary Peg), and swiftly to business. He drew the pages out of the tube and handed over the roll. She carried them to a broad worktable and spread the sheets out in three long parallel rows, the copies of what he had sold Bulstrode and the retained originals.

When she had them spread out she uttered some startled words in what he supposed was Polish. 'Albert, these eighteen sheets . . . they are *originals*?'

'Yeah, they're what looks like enciphered letters. I didn't sell them to Bulstrode.'

'And you are rolling them up like calendars? Shame on you!' She walked off and came back with clear plastic document envelopes, into which she carefully placed the enciphered sheets.

'Now,' she said. 'Let us see what we have here.'

Doubrowicz looked at the copies for a long time, examining each sheet with a large rectangular magnifying glass. At last she said, 'Interesting. You know there are three separate documents in all. These copies are of two different ones and these originals.'

'Yeah, I figured that part out. Those four sheets are obviously the printer's copy of some sermons and I'm not interested in them. All the rest is the letter from this guy Bracegirdle.'

'Umm, and you sold this letter to Bulstrode, your mother said.'

'Yeah. And I'm sorry, Fanny, I should have come straight to you.'

'Yes, you should have. Your dear mother thinks you were cheated.'

'I know.'

She patted his arm. 'Well, we shall see. Show me the part where you thought he mentioned Shakespeare.'

Crosetti did so, and the little librarian adjusted a goosenecked lamp to cast an intense beam at the bright paper and peered at it through her lens. 'Yes, this seems a clear enough secretary hand,' she remarked. 'I have certainly had to deal with worse.' She read the passage aloud slowly, like a dim third-grader, and when she reached the end exclaimed, 'Dear God!'

'Shit!' cried Crosetti and pounded his fist into his thigh hard enough to sting.

'Indeed,' said Doubrowicz, 'you have been well cogged and coney-catched, as our friend here would have said. How much did he pay you?'

'Thirty-five hundred.'

'Oh, dear me. What a shame!'

'I could have got a lot more, right?'

'Oh, yes. If you had come to me and we had established the authenticity of the document beyond any reasonable doubt – and for a document of this nature and importance, that in itself would have been a considerable task – then there's no telling what it would have fetched at auction. We would probably not be in it, since it's a little out of our line, but the Folger and the Huntington would have been in full cry. More than that, to someone like Bulstrode, having possession, *exclusive* possession, of something like this – why, it's a career in itself. No wonder he cheated you! He must have seen immediately that this thing would place him back in the center of Shakespeare studies. No one would ever mention that unfortunate fake again. It would be like an explosion opening up an entirely fresh field of scholarship. People have been arguing for years about Shakespeare's religion and his political stance and here we find an official of the English government suspecting him not only of papistry but papistry of a potentially treasonous nature. Then you have a whole set of research lines to explore: this Bracegirdle fellow, his history, who he knew, where he traveled, and the history of the man he worked for, this Lord D. Perhaps there are files in some old muniment room that no one has ever explored. And since we know that Shakespeare was never actually prosecuted, we would want to know why not, was he protected by someone even more powerful than Lord D.? And on and on. Then we have a collection of enciphered letters apparently describing a spy's observation of William Shakespeare, an actual detailed contemporary record of the man's activities – an unimaginable treasure in itself, assuming they can be deciphered, and believe me, cryptographers will be fighting with sticks to get hold of them. But at least we have *these* in original.'

Doubrowicz leaned back in her chair and stared up at the coffered ceiling, fanned herself dramatically with her hand, and laughed her sharp little bark. It was a gesture familiar to Crosetti from his childhood, when the children had brought what they imagined was an utterly insolvable puzzle. 'But, my dear Albert, all that, enticing as it is, is mere trivia compared to the real prize.'

Crosetti felt his throat dry up. 'You mean that an autograph manuscript might still exist.'

'Yes, and not just that. Let me see, does he give a date anywhere?' She lifted her magnifier and cast over the sheets, like a bird seeking a scurrying bug. 'Hm, yes, here is one, 1608, and here, ah yes, he seems to have begun his spying career around 1610. Do you understand the significance of that date, Albert?'

'*Macbeth*?'

'No, no, *Macbeth* was 1606. And we know how it came to be written and there were no secret Bracegirdles involved. The year 1610 was the year of *The Tempest*, and after that, except for some small things, collaborations and the like, Shakespeare wrote no more plays, and that means . . .'

'Oh, God, it's a new play!'

'An unknown, unrecorded, unsuspected play by William Shakespeare. In autograph.' She placed her hand on her chest. 'My heart. Darling, I think I am a little too old for this kind of excitement. In any case, if genuine, I say again, *if* genuine, well . . . you know we say "priceless" very easily nowadays, by which we mean very expensive, but this would be truly in a class by itself.'

'Millions?'

'Pah! Hundreds . . . hundreds of millions. The manuscript alone, if proved authentic, would be certainly the most valuable single manuscript, perhaps the most valuable portable object, in the world, on a par with the greatest paintings. And then, whoever owned the manuscript would have the copyright too. I am not an expert here but that would be my guess. Theatrical productions – every director and producer on earth would be selling their children for the right to mount the premiere, and don't even mention films! On the other hand, lest we build too high a castle in the air, the whole thing could be an elaborate fraud.'

'A fraud? I don't get it – who's defrauding who?'

'Well, you know Bulstrode was caught once by a clever forger. Perhaps they thought he was ripe for another try.'

'Really? I'd think he'd be the last person to go to. Who'd believe him? The whole point is that his credibility is shot, that's why he's so desperate to recoup.'

She laughed. 'You should go up to Foxwood sometimes, to the casino. If those who lost heavily did not desperately try to recoup, as you put it, they would have to close their doors. Of course, were I a villain, I would not attempt such a scheme.'

'Why not?'

'Because, darling, how would you create the prize? The play itself? It is one thing to forge a bad quarto of *Hamlet*. We have *Hamlet* and we have bad quartos and we have some idea of Shakespeare's sources for the play. And the text does not have to possess any particular quality. In parts it need not even make sense; bad quartos often do not. You know what a bad quarto is, yes? Good, so you must realize that here it is entirely different. Here you must invent an entire play by the greatest dramatic poet who ever lived, and who was then at the height of his powers. It can't be done. Someone tried it already once, you know.'

'Who tried it?'

'A silly little fellow named William Henry Ireland, back in the eighteenth century. His father was a scholar, and Willie wanted to impress him, so he started finding documents related to Shakespeare in old trunks. Completely ludicrous, but with the state of analysis and scholarship that then was, many people were taken in. Well, nothing would do but that he had to find a new play by Shakespeare, and he did, an abortion he called *Vortigern*, and Kemble produced it at the Drury Lane Theatre. It was howled off the stage, naturally. Meanwhile the great scholar Malone had exposed all the other manuscripts as fraudulent and the whole thing collapsed. Now, Ireland was a dullard and easily exposed. Pascoe, the man who tricked Bulstrode, was a good deal smarter, but what we're talking about is of another order. It could not be a mere pastiche, you see: it would have to be *Shakespeare*, and he is dead.'

'So you think it's the real deal.'

'This I cannot say without examining the original. In the meantime, I will type out for you a Word document from this Bracegirdle's letter so you will not have to learn Jacobean secretary hand and you can read what he has to say. Also, I will prepare another Word document based on these supposed enciphered letters so at least you can see what the ciphertext looks like. If you don't mind, I would like to keep the letters here and run some elementary tests on them. If they are not genuine seventeenth century, of course, we can all have a good laugh and forget the whole thing. In fact, I will do that first, and if they prove genuine I will send to you the two documents by e-mail, and also I will give you the name of a man I know who is interested in ciphers and such things. If we can generate a solution, it gives us a bit of bargaining against Bulstrode. For he has not got these, and they may hold information about the location of the autograph play, do you see?'

Crosetti did. He said, 'Thanks, Fanny. I feel like such a jerk.'

'Yes, but as I say all is perhaps not lost. I will be happy to meet this Bulstrode and tell him what I think of his sly tricks. Let me begin with the transcription of the cipher first. It should not take too long. Will you stay?'

'No, I have to get back to work. I don't know a lot about crypto but maybe it's a simple substitution. They couldn't have been all that sophisticated back then.'

'Oh, I think you would be surprised. There are ciphers in French of the *ancien régime* that have never been broken. Still, we could be lucky.'

'Who's this cipher expert you mentioned?'

'Oh, Klim? He is a Polish person too, but a more recent immigrant. He was a cryptanalyst with the WSW in Warsaw, that is, military counterintelligence. Now he drives a hearse. If you leave me alone now, I will have this done in a little bit. And don't feel too bad about yourself, Albert. There was a woman involved, after all, and you are still young.'

Feeling as old as Fanny, however, Crosetti slumped out of the library and took the Madison bus uptown to the bookstore. There was a new woman working there, Pamela, this one genuinely ex-Barnard: short, earnestly intellectual, attractive, well turned out, engaged to someone on Wall Street. It was as if Carolyn Rolly had never been, except that occasionally Glaser would mention that she had vanished without telling him what she had done with the prints from the Churchill *Voyages*. When Crosetti entered the shop today, however, Glaser hailed him and ushered him into the little office he kept in the rear of the shop.

'You'll be interested to know that Rolly has surfaced,' Glaser announced. 'Take a look at this.'

He handed Crosetti a brown envelope with the slick crinkly feel that announced it as foreign. It had a British stamp and a London postmark. Inside Crosetti found a letter written in Rolly's beautiful italic hand, black ink on heavy cream paper. He felt his face grow hot and a pang darted down his center, and he had to restrain himself from raising the paper to his nostrils and sniffing it. He read:

Dear Sidney,

Please forgive me for leaving you in the lurch like this, and for not contacting you to let you know what I was doing. Since I didn't know when the shop would reopen, I thought it would not be too much of a burden on you and would give you sufficient time to find a replacement. But I was rude not to call you earlier and I *am* sorry. What happened was that I was called away to London on urgent family business, which then turned into a career opportunity, so it looks like I will be staying here in the UK indefinitely.

The good news, from your perspective, is that I was able to sell the maps and plates from the broken Churchill for what I believe was a far higher price than we would have received on the American market – 3,200 British pounds! They seem to have an insatiable appetite here for good-quality prints from their glory days. I enclose an international money order for $5,712.85. I paid the various fees out of my pocket, to make up for any inconvenience you might have suffered.

Do say good-bye to Mrs Glaser for me and to Albert. You've all been far kinder to me than I deserved.

Best,

Carolyn Rolly

Crosetti handed the letter back with lead in his belly. He had to clear his throat heavily before saying, 'Well. Good for her. I didn't know she had family in England.'

'Oh, yes,' Glaser replied. 'She once mentioned that the name was originally Raleigh, as in Sir Walter, and she implied that there was some connection to the famous one. Maybe she inherited the family castle. That's quite a sale, anyway. I always figured our Carolyn was heading for higher things than bookstore clerking. Did you print out those auction notices I wanted?'

'This morning. They should be in your in-box.'

Glaser nodded, grunted an acknowledgment, and walked off, and Crosetti clumped down the stairs to his cave. It was a more pleasant work environment than it had been before the fire, for the insurance had paid for a complete renovation, including neat steel shelves and a new Dell computer with all the latest stuff attached. The cellar now smelled of paint and tile adhesive instead of dust and cooking grease, but the improvement did not noticeably help Crosetti's mood. Each time 'How could she?' appeared in his mental theater, the answer came swiftly: 'Schmuck! You had one date. What did you expect, love forever? She got a better deal and split.' On the other hand, there was Crosetti's devout belief that the body never lied, and he could not accept that Rolly had lied to him in that way, that one night. She was a liar, sure, but he could not accept that sort of falsehood. Why should she? To repay him for a nice evening? It made no sense.

And speaking of lies, went the inner voice, that letter was complete horseshit. We know she didn't break those volumes, therefore didn't sell the prints. He was as sure of that as he was about the honesty of the flesh. So where did she get the nearly six grand she paid out to Glaser? Answer: someone supplied it, plus the costs of travel to England, and for this the only suspect was Professor Bulstrode, for there was no one else on the scene who both had that sort of money and was in England. She had gone to England with Bulstrode. But why? Kidnapped? No, that was absurd: professors of English did not kidnap people except in the sort of preposterous movies that Crosetti despised. Then why did she go?

Two possibilities presented themselves, one unpleasant, one frightening. The unpleasant possibility was that Carolyn saw the opportunity for a big score, the possibility of actually finding the supposed Shakespeare treasure. She'd read Bracegirdle's letter and called Bulstrode behind Crosetti's back (that long wait outside her loft!), set up the sale of the Bracegirdle manuscript, pressured Crosetti to sell, and then – he wanted to think – fallen a little in love but not quite enough to make her willing to miss the opportunity to get out of a life of crushing poverty.

The frightening possibility was that she was acting under duress, that Bulstrode had something on her, a threat far worse than just losing her clerk's job and having to deal with the cops. No, that was another lie – the cops were not after any Carolyn Rolly, not according to his sister anyway. But maybe it was a little of both, a carrot and a stick. He had to have new information. Information was what allowed you to separate the lies from the truth.

As soon as this thought appeared, Crosetti swiveled in his chair and faced his new computer. He actually did have some new information, and because of the moping he'd been doing lately he hadn't thought to use it. From the back pocket of his jeans he extracted the two items he had scooped from the street outside Carolyn's former home. The photograph was a one-hour-photo print of two women and two children, a boy of four or so and a baby girl. One of the women was a younger Carolyn Rolly, with her hair jammed up under a feed cap, and the other woman was a pretty blonde. They were sitting on a bench in some kind of park or playground, in summer sunshine, the trees around them, heavy with leaf, throwing dark shadows on the ground. They were looking at the photographer and smiling, with the sun in their faces making them squint slightly. It was not a good photograph; Crosetti knew that the cheap instant camera it was taken with could not deal with the contrast between bright sun and shade, and so the faces were washed out, especially those of the kids. But Carolyn had kept it and then walked away from it, as if abandoning her life once again. He studied the silvery faces, looking for signs of family connections, but again there was too little information.

He scanned the photograph into the computer, called up PhotoShop, and played with the contrast for a while, and then downloaded a program he'd used before that enhanced just such photos, using statistical methods. The result was a better look at the family, because now it was clear that it *was* a family. This had to be Carolyn's sister, or at least a first cousin, and the two kids were clearly related to either or both of the women. Crosetti could not have said exactly why he knew this, but he was from a large family, and from a social and ethnic stratum where large families were common, and the fact was instinctively clear to him.

The picture on the postcard bore the legend CAMP WYANDOTTE done in what was supposed to look like birch sticks, and depicted a fir-lined mountain lake, a dock, and some boys canoeing. The message side had a three-year-old postmark and said, in childish block printing: Dear Mommy Im haveing a good time at camp. We catched a snake. I love you Emmett. It was addressed, in an adult hand, to Mrs H. Olerud, 161 Tower Rd., Braddock PA 16571.

Turning to the computer, Crosetti generated a map of the address, which turned out to be in western Pennsylvania, near Erie. He used Google-Earth on the address and brought up the roof of a modest frame house with outbuildings, surrounded by scrubby woodlands. Zooming out from that image showed a semirural neighborhood like those that surround the smaller, tired towns of the American Rust Belt: five-acre plots, broken cars and appliances in the yards, woodpiles: scruffy zones inhabited by people who used to have good manufacturing or mining employment and now barely got by on sporadic work or McJobs. Did this milieu spawn the exotic creature that was Rolly? He looked again at the photograph of the two women and the kids at the playground and wished that he were thirty years in the future when Google (he was sure) would let you google the interiors of all the houses and study the faces of all the inhabitants of the planet. At present, however, a journey would be required.

BRACEGIRDLE LETTER (8)

We crost the seas with fayre windes until 23rd July when the skye came all over black as night & commense a greate wind. The fleete wase scattered entirelie & oure ship drave upon a rock & wracked but through the mercie of God none perished save three men & Mr Tolliver one of them, may God have mercie on his sowle & now is all his quizzing done for he seeth face to face. When the storm abates wee had greate feare for wee find we are upon the Bermoothes, which all mariners dight Isle of Devils, for dwelleth salvages there that eate mens fleashe or soe twas thought. But we landed having no other choyce & found not salvages but a place near to Paradise, waters, meadowes, fruite trees &c. with pleasaunt flowered aires most swete. Was good cedern timber abounding too & wee set to building two boates fit to carry all o' wee & passed there near one yeare before sayling & I gayne greate credit for steeryng by starres and Sun & did arrive with the Lords holpe at Jamestown 23rd Maye the Yeare Ten. All this tale has been tolde before in bookes wrote by Mr Wm Strachey of oure partie which you have read, soe I will saye no more of this.

Now returning to England on the first ship landeing Plymouth 6th July & wisht to goe to London for I desyred to turn my bill to gold coyne at some Jewes counting-house & shew youre father that I wase a fit man to have my deare Nan. Soe I did takeing boat next daye & found my Jewe and walked in my pryde with a heavie purse; but comeing thereafter to the Iron Man Inn & askeing wase told that some moneths before this thou wast wed to Thomas Finch fishmonger of Puddyng Lane.

Then was my heart sore for I had lade all my hopes on that marriage, haveing mee now no familie nor friendes nor home: & besydes Mr Tollivers fancies had worne to nubbin my olde faith in the pure religione & knew not what to think but considered I wase likely damned to Hell & did not cayre, or not much. Thus are sowles lost. Yet I had gold: & friendes of a sorte can always be got if you have it, so roistered many weekes Nan, I would I had not nor will I saye what foul thynges I did doe in that passage but awoke one morn in Plymouth in a trulls bedde & 2s. 3d. was all I had in purse. Now among my fellowe sottes there wase one Cranshaw who called hymself a gentleman of the coste, which interpreted is a smuckler & he says you are a stout fellow Dick & know the shiftes, come we wille grow rich together with bringeing in canary, sacke & other goodes from sea. Soe we did for some time. But that Cranshaw was as fond of drinking sacke as selling it & worked so ill & clumsy, boasting in tavernes & the lyke that one night the coste guardes took us & clapped us bothe in fetteres & soe caste in the Tower.

There Mr Hastynges kindlie came & visited me & he says lad you are for the rope sure nothynge can save thee, caught with uncustommed goodes: what foole thou – why camest thee not to mee, shall I denie thee worke? And I was sore ashamed to be brought so low. Yet I commenced to praye agaen which I had not for soe long & it did me confort, methoughte Gods mercie mayhap wold save e'en one such as mee, for Christ came to save sinners not the righteous.

Now Nan you knew all this or almost all, and twas for younge Richard I have wrote it out so I may speake fatherly to hym from the Grave: but now I shall tell what no man knowes except they were there & I alone yet live. Of a morn, mee lying in filthie straws in chaynes & thinking of how many better than I wast once so enchayned for Gods sake and wishing I was one of theyre number instod of what I wase a kynde of robbinge knave, there comes a warder saying, here rise & he unshackels mee & bringeth water to washe and attend my bearde and new cloathes. Soe he beckones & I must followe. Thus to a small roome in the White Tower, new rushes on the floore and a good fyre, tabel and chayres and meate upon the tabel & canary in cuppes & a man there, a stranger saying sit, eate.

9

'Gosh, I'm sorry,' she gasped, pulling away from me in confusion. 'You must think I'm awful. I don't even know why I did that.'

'An instinctive reaction to danger escaped?' I suggested. 'A kind of inherited reflex. The male rescues the female from danger, and saves the woolly mammoth cutlets, and the female repays him with a sexual display.' I added, after a pause, 'I'm sure it was nothing personal,' hoping the opposite. She just stared at me. I opened the door to the building. 'Are you all right? You're not hurt?'

'A little bruised. And my knees are scraped. Ow!' At this, she staggered against me, trembling.

'We're three flights up,' I said and put my arm around her shoulders. 'Can you walk?'

'I don't know. I just went all weak in the knees.'

'It's the adrenaline. Here, let me help you.' With that I picked her up in the approved carrying-over-threshold manner and ascended the stairs. She slumped against me and did not object. Myself, I was still dizzy from the kiss.

I settled her on a sofa, supplied us both with a cognac,

and went to fetch my first-aid kit and a plastic bag of ice. She had removed her ruined panty hose and had her skirt hitched up to expose her naked thighs. I gave her the ice bag to use on whichever of her bruises seemed most to need it while I bathed and dressed her knees as I had learned to do long ago in the army. I had to lean fairly close in order to pick out the tiny pieces of street debris. The erotic charge I received from this labor was nearly too much to bear, my face there close to, inches from, her delicious thighs, these lolling slightly open to enable my ministrations. I imagined she felt this too, but she said nothing, and I was able, just, to keep from diving headfirst into the shadow of that hitched-up skirt. I suppose I wished to hang a little longer under that delicious tension, something I got to enjoy when I was courting Amalie, and which we have most of us lost in this era of copulation lite.

She didn't speak while I worked on her. When the dressing was complete, she thanked me and asked, 'What did you do to that guy? Some kind of judo?'

I answered that I was a stranger to any martial art, but simply very strong, and I explained why. She took this in without comment and asked if I knew any of the muggers.

'No, of course not. Did you?'

'No, but I thought one of them was the same one who was watching me the other day, the big one who you hit over the head with his friend. It looked like the same SUV too. They were speaking Russian, weren't they?'

'I believe so. I don't speak it myself, but I go to a gym run by a Russian and I hear the language a lot. And you had that man on the phone with an accent . . .'

At this Miranda twisted her body so that she faced the back of the sofa and clutched a throw pillow over her head. Muffled sounds emerged.

Is this level of detail important? What does it matter at the present remove what one person said to another? For the record: she cried, I comforted her. And yes, I am enough of a cad to seduce a woman in an extreme state of dependent panic. She sighed and fell against me, her mouth against my neck. I scooped her up and carried her into my daughter's bedroom. I put her on the bed and carefully removed her clothes – blouse, skirt, bra, underpants – she not helping much but not objecting either. I have to say that it was not, despite my ardor, anywhere near the Top 40, not remotely in the same class as Amalie, although their bodies were remarkably similar, the musculature and structure of the limbs, the pointed pink nipples.

Miranda lay not exactly comatose but as one in a dream, eyes closed. Something was going on, because she was making those little puffings with her lips that some women do when they are experiencing sexual pleasure, and she did that head-coming-up-off-the-pillow thing a few times, with her wide brow furrowed, as if in quiz-show concentration. In the end she made a sharp single cry, like a small dog hit by traffic. Then she rolled over without a word and seemed to go to sleep, in the manner of a guy married for years.

On the other hand, the first one *is* occasionally a dud. I kissed her on the cheek (no response) and covered her with a duvet. In the morning, I heard the shower go on early, and when I arrived in the kitchen she was there, fully dressed, looking fresh, asking if we could stop for a new pair of panty hose. No comment on the sexual events of the previous night and none of that familiarity of the body one more or less expects after a fuck of whatever quality. Nor did I raise the subject at that time.

*

I must have drifted off because it is light and my watch says it is after six in the morning. There is a thick fog on the lake and dew gleams on every leaf and needle of the trees. The risen sun is only a bright pink glow in the clouds over the eastern shore of the lake. Very strange and unearthly, like being inside a pearl. My pistol is broken open on the desk, the magazine removed and the seven bright 9 mm Parabellum rounds are lined up next to it like toy soldiers. I have no memory of doing this. Could I have done it in my sleep? Perhaps I'm going slightly nuts, from the tension and the lack of sleep and from my perfectly fucked-up life. Seven rounds. There were originally eight.

You know, you read in the paper about people who have a firearm in the house and the kid gets hold of it and does something awful, the lesson being that kids will always find the gun, no matter how carefully the parent has hidden it, but as far as I know none of us ever found our mother's *Pistole*-08, none of us even knew she had it. I suppose she was a genius at concealment, a trait her children have inherited to an extent. My siblings don't know I have it, or perhaps they are themselves concealing this knowledge. It took some doing, since technically it is an unlicensed weapon, but those with connections can usually get what they want in the city of New York, and at the time of my mother's death I was working for one of these, a fine legal gentleman named Benjamin Sobel. When I explained the situation to him he arranged for the police to return the thing to me, although I did not expatiate upon its provenance. A valuable souvenir of the war, I explained, that could be sold to pay for the funeral expenses. But I didn't sell it, and the expenses were slight. Paul was in jail, and Miri was off on someone's yacht, and so it was a small band of strangers at the cheap funeral home, some people from her church and her work at the hospital, and me; her priest did not show, I assume because of the circumstances of the death, one of the sins for which I have not been able to forgive my church.

I kept her ashes in a tin can in my apartment until I got my first job and then I bought her a slot in a community mausoleum at Green-Wood Cemetery in Brooklyn, not too far from Albert Anastasia, Joey Gallo, and L. Frank Baum, the author of *The Wonderful Wizard of Oz*, so she's in good company. I believe I have forgiven her, although how does one really tell? I have never figured that part out. I know she was making a point because she knew I was on my way back to Brooklyn that Saturday afternoon. As the Official Good Son, I often submitted to mass at St Jerome's, preceded and followed by heavy Teutonic dinners and evenings of TV or cards. This particular Saturday, she had actually put the dinner on, sweet and sour tongue with dumplings, one of my favorites actually, and its odor filled the apartment as I walked into the kitchen and found her. She had arranged the chair she sat in just so and spread newspapers all around so as not to make a mess when she put the muzzle in her mouth.

I relate this to demonstrate my near-perfect insensitivity to the interior states of my dear ones, which I suppose is a key to some aspects of this story. I really had no idea at all, although I saw poor Mutti nearly every week. Yes, Ermentrude played her cards pretty close, but still, shouldn't I have suspected something? Some terminal depression? I did not, nor was there a note. Forty-four years old.

Earlier, before I entered my terrible puberty, we were unusually close. During my ninth year, by some happy coincidence, I had an early school day and my mother had moved to the late shift at her hospital, so we met and had biweekly Oedipal Theater. She would bake treats for me on those days, marvelous Bavarian delights rich with nuts, cinnamon, raisins, stuffed into leaf pastry thin as hope, and the smell would hit my nose in the hallway as I left the urine-stinking elevator, like a presagement of paradise. And we would talk, or she would talk, mainly reminiscences of her girlhood, her marvelous girlhood in the New Germany – the music, the parades, how beautiful the men looked in their uniforms, how wonderful her father, how kind everyone was to her. She actually served as one of those little blondies you see in old newsreels presenting a bouquet to the Führer on an official visit. It was set up through her dad's contacts in the Party, and she recalled every detail, how proud she was, how the Führer had cupped her little face in his hand and patted her cheek. Yes, the cheek I kissed every day. Lucky Jake!

About the bad stuff that came later, not so much talking. I don't like sinking about zose days, she said, only of zhe happy times I like to sink. But I pressed and learned about the rats and the flies, the absence of pets, the smell, what it was like to be bombed from the air, more about the smells, the exploded bodies of her friends and their parents, the peculiar juxtapositions created by blast, the bathtub blown through a school-house wall and resting on the teacher's desk. How the children laughed!

When I cleaned out her stuff I found a trove of family memorabilia that she'd never shown us, but which she must have been carrying around in her suitcase when she met Dad: letters home from the various fronts, photographs of the family, school certificates, vacation postcards. It included a good deal of Nazi stuff, of course, awards from the SS, my grandfather's various medals, and the rosewood presentation case for the pistol. One photograph in particular I rescued and later had framed, and it is still in my bedroom. It is of her family, just before the war started, at some beach resort. She's about ten or eleven, lovely as a nymph, and the two older brothers are there in their old-fashioned knit bathing suits, grinning blondly into the sun, and my grandmother is looking quite svelte in a one-piece suit, reclining in a deck chair and laughing; and leaning over her, sharing the joke, is the then Hauptsturmführer-SS Stieff. He has obviously just come to the beach from work, for he is in tie and shirt-sleeves and carrying his tunic, accoutrements and hat, and unless you look very carefully, you can't see what kind of uniform it is.

I like this picture because of how happy they all look, although they lived under the worst regime in human history and the father of the family worked for an organization bent on genocide. In contrast, there are no such pictures of my family, for although we had our laughs, my father was not into photography, and, unlike his late father-in-law, had a positive horror of being captured on film. The only family pictures we have are stilted department-store poses taken on our birthdays or else records of events – First Communions, graduations, and so on, plus many snapshots taken by neighbors or strangers, for, as I have suggested, with the exception of myself, my family is unusually photogenic.

No, let's tear ourselves away from the distant past (if only!) and back to the main story. Miranda and I agreed that she could not be left alone. I made arrangements for Omar to come by and exercise his protective skills, and further arranged that he should stay over and add a little fire-power in case they tried anything else once they found that the briefcase lacked what they wanted. This left the question of why Russian-speaking toughs had become interested in Richard Bracegirdle's personal history. Could Bulstrode have had some original connection with them? I asked Miranda and she looked at me like I was crazy. Uncle Andrew hardly knew anyone in New York aside from scholars, and he had never so much as mentioned any Russians, criminal or otherwise. Freelance thugs then? More likely. Despite the fictions of TV, organized crime has become somewhat more Russian in the past few decades: the Mafiya, so called, but not by the Russians. Someone looking for frighteners, strong-arm guys, torturers, had found a contractor. Who this person was remained obscure, but finding him (as I now explained to Miranda) was not our job. What we had to do was keep her safe, which I thought Omar could handle, and turn the recent developments over to the police.

Around eight, a fellow called Rashid came by from a hire agency to drive me to work. I left Omar in the loft with Miranda, with instructions not to let her out of his sight, and I cut short his eager description of how well armed he was. I didn't want to know. At the office, I called Detective Murray and related what had happened the previous night. He asked if I had the license plate of the car and I said I hadn't and he said he didn't see that there was much that he could do about the loss of a briefcase, and he'd transfer me to an officer who'd give me a case number for my insurance. I got a little steamed at that and pointed out that this incident must be related to the murder of Andrew Bulstrode, which he was supposed to be investigating, and there was a pause on the line after which the detective asked with heavy patience how I figured that. And then I told him about Ms Kellogg and how someone with an accent was trying to get an old manuscript from her, one that Bulstrode had owned, and how the men who had attacked us had spoken in what seemed like Russian, and it had to be all connected. He asked me what this manuscript was worth and I told him Bulstrode had bought it for a couple of thousand dollars, but . . .

And here I checked, because all beyond that was speculation, all the Shakespeare business, and I knew how it would sound to a New York cop, and so I concluded the conversation rather lamely and suffered being put on hold and, when at last unheld, reported the petty mugging to a bored man and received my case number. Then I called J. Ping and got the scoop on the status of Bulstrode's will, with which she saw no obvious trouble, perfectly straightforward, a month should see it through surrogate's court, and asked me if there was any big rush on, and I said, no, quite the contrary, no rush at all. The decedent's body, I learned, was due to be flown out that day, in care of one Oliver March, presumably the longtime companion I had heard about.

I skipped lunch that day, my diary says, and went to the gym, although it was not my regular gym day. I wished to talk to someone about Russians, and the gym was as good a place to do that as I had at my disposal. When I arrived, however, it was Arkady who wanted to talk to me. He took me into his tiny office, a cluttered industrial-carpeted place with hardly room for a desk and a few chairs, which desk was nearly invisible under a mass of lifting magazines and defective lumps of gear and samples of diet supplements, some of them even legal for use in Olympic events. There was a glass case in the office holding Arkady's remarkable array of medals and cups – the old U.S.S.R. certainly did not stint its darlings – and the walls were plastered with many more triumphant photos than I owned myself. Arkady Demichevski is squat and hairy, with deep-set small brown eyes and a twenty-inch neck. He looks like an early hominid but is a civilized, cultured, and kind man, with a good sense of humor. Today he was uncharacteristically solemn.

'Jake,' he said, 'we need talk.'

I indicated that he had the floor, and noted that he could

not seem to meet my eye. 'Jake, you know I don't care what peoples who come to my gym do on outside. Is their life, yes? They behave in gym, they could stay, if not . . .' Here he tossed an imaginary object over his shoulder and made a zipping sound. 'So, Jake, I know you for long time and I am embarrassed to ask what you are mixed up in, some . . . some . . . *bizniss*, with bad peoples.'

'This would be bad Russian peoples?'

'Yes! Gangsters. What happens, day before yesterday, in evening, I am going to club, in Brighton Beach, for Odessa peoples, you know? Have Russian bath, play cards, drink a little. So two of them sit by me in steam, they have these tattoos, dragons, tigers, this is showing they are *zeks*, from prison in Siberia, they are proud of this, you understand. These not cultured peoples in the least. So they ask me do I know Jake Mishkin. I say yes, I say Jake Mishkin fine upstanding American citizen, heavy-weight lifter. They say we don't care about this, we want to know what he does, is he connected, what his business. I say, hey, I see him in gym I am not colleague of his. Then they want to know other things, all kinds I can't understand what they are saying, some woman, name I never heard of, Raisin Brans or something, so I tell them –'

'Raisin Brans?'

'Yes, some name like that, on the box, I can't remember . . .'

'Kellogg.'

'Yes! Is Kellogg. I say I don't know no Kellogg, I don't know any private business from Jake Mishkin and I don't want to know, and they say I should keep my ears open and find out whatever with this Kellogg and Jake Mishkin. So what I do? I come talk you like a man: Jake, what is with you, all of sudden gangsters?'

'I don't know, Arkady,' I said. 'I wish I did know.' Whereupon I told him about the attack on me and Ms K. and the theft of the briefcase, although I did not expand on what was supposed to be in it. But Arkady was after all a Russian and he stroked his chin and nodded. 'So what is in briefcase, Jake. Is not drugs?'

'Is not drugs. Is papers.'

'You can give them so they leave you alone?'

'I can't. It's a long story, but I would like to know who your *zeks* are working for, if you have an idea.'

'You didn't hear it from me,' said Arkady. He was nibbling at his lip, and his eyes were all over the place. Seeing him like that, this big, confident man nervous as a sparrow, was nearly as shocking as the attack by the thugs. After a pause and in a hoarse voice he said, 'They work for Osip Shvanov. The Organizatsia.'

'The who?'

'In Brighton Beach. Jewish gangsters. You know about this? Twenty years ago the Americans say to Soviets, you are keeping Jews against will, this is like Nazis, you are persecuting, let them go. So the Soviets say, okay, you want Jews, we give you Jews. Then they go to Gulag and they find every criminal what had Jew marked on passport, they say you go to America, you go to Israel, have nice trip. So some come here. Of course most Jews got out from Soviet Union was regular peoples, my accountant is one of these, very nice man, but also very many criminals, and they go back to old doings, whores they have, porno, drugs, what-you-call, extortions. These very bad peoples, like these Sopranos you have on cable, but Sopranos are stupid and these are very smart, are *Jews*! And Osip is worst of all of them.'

'Well,' I said, 'thanks for that information, Arkady.' And I got up to leave, but he gestured to stop me and added,

'They come here too. These men, yesterday morning, and ask me if you going come here today, and they just sit. I could not eat my lunch, they are watching me like animals. So, Jake, I'm sorry, but I think you should not come here to train anymore. I will refund membership, no hard feelings.'

'You're booting me out? I've been coming here nearly twenty years, Arkady.'

'I know, I know, but you can go other places, you can go to Bodyshop –'

'What! Bodyshop is pretty boys and girls in designer outfits and fat guys on treadmills reading the *Wall Street Journal*. Bodyshop sucks.'

'So someplace else. You keep coming here they make me to spy on you and if I say no . . . I don't want my place burned up and I have family. I mean it, Jake. You don't know these peoples. If you got something they want, is my advice give it to them.'

I saw Arkady had a point, so we shook hands and I left, with my gear in a Nike bag. I felt like I'd been expelled from school because someone else cheated. But the mention of family was what had really struck home. I recalled that I had one too.

My diary says simply 'A.' in the slot for six-thirty on the day in question, which was the first Wednesday in November, so it was my evening to dine *en famille* at my ex-wife's brownstone on East Seventy-sixth Street, our arrangement on the first Wednesday of every month. Not exactly 'ex,' because officially, in the eyes of the state, the Church, and my wife, we are still married. Amalie will not agree to a divorce, partly on religious grounds, but mainly because she believes we will get back together after I cure my mental illness. She thinks it would be shameful to desert me while I am sick in this way, and the fact that my mental illness is philandering does not signify. I don't know anyone else who has this sort of relationship, although I don't for a moment believe we are unique. My three law partners have, I think, eight or so wives among them, and in every case I have been treated to the whole litany: the insanity, the vicious revenges, the manipulations of children, the financial extortions, and I find I cannot produce a fair exchange of marriage-hell narratives. I do suffer excruciatingly, but through my own fault rather than via the malice of my wife, for she is generous, kind, and forgiving, and so I have to carry the whole fucking load myself. Jesus had a point, you know: if you really want the evildoers to suffer, just be nice.

These dinners are an example. What could be more civilized? A little family sits down to a meal and demonstrates that despite whatever differences Mommy and Daddy are having there is still love, the daddy who has left the family still loves them very much, or to put it another way (as I recently heard my daughter explain it to her brother), 'Daddy likes to boink ladies more than he wants to stay with us.' In the wrong, in the wrong! Even the babes can see it, even Niko, who has only the faintest interest in other humans, can draw this fact into his vast mental library, and feel (assuming he feels anything) contempt.

I know there is no point to my boinking of ladies, as does my wife, for as I believe I have already mentioned, Amalie is in that department the acme of delight. How does she know she is tops, having so little experience besides me? Answer: she is great friends, *intimate* friends with my sister, who is an encyclopedia of the fuck, and she has I believe conveyed to Miri every lubricious detail of our sex lives with her Swiss clinical frankness, and Miri has assured her that she lacks nothing in that department, and further, that I am the Asshole of the Western World for cheating on such a prize. I can't bear it; but I go anyway to these ghastly meals, as penance maybe. It doesn't work.

Before I went over, I had the driver take me, as on many of these occasions (penitentially perhaps), to an obscure little shop off First Avenue in the Forties that sells very expensive orchids, and I bought one for Amalie. She collects them, and although she could buy out the Amazon herself with her own money, I think it is still a nice gesture. This one was pale green with magenta speckles on the usual pudendalike blossom, a *Paphiopedilum hanoiensis*, endangered in its native Vietnam and illegal as hell. I believe Amalie knows these orchids are smuggled, but she always accepts them, and it gives me a perverse pleasure to see my saint debauched by her lust for flowers.

Rashid dropped me off and the door was opened to my ring by Lourdes Munoz, my wife's servant, a refugee from the Salvadorean wars. Amalie essentially saved her life through one of her do-good charities, and in contrast to the dictum that no good deed goes unpunished, which always works for me, the result of this selfless charity was the creation of the perfect house-servant and nanny. Lourdes does not trust me and has been proven correct. I got the usual stone-faced greeting, had my raincoat taken, and entered my wife's home with my orchid.

I heard the sound of laughter coming from the living room and followed it in, with a little dread building up because I knew the source of the fun, recognizing as I did the loudest contributory voice. The family tableau, minus Dad: Amalie in her working costume of pale silk shirt and dark tailored slacks, her hair piled on her head in its golden coils, sitting in her leather sling chair with her feet pulled up under her;

on a leather sofa soft as thighs sits Miri, my sister, and on either side of her my children, Miri and Imogen as beautiful as the dawn, pink and blond, and then there is poor Niko, our dark little Nibelung. Both children love their aunt Miri. Imogen loves her because she is a font of stories about celebrities. Miri knows everyone (that is, everyone rich and famous) in New York, and a good many in London, Rome, Paris, and Hollywood, and sometimes it seems she has been married to or had affairs with around 10 percent of this population. She has a Rolodex the size of the nosewheel on a 747.

Niko likes her because Miri was married briefly to one of the most famous stage magicians in the world, and learned during this time to do sleight of hand, a skill that fascinates him. She claimed that the man was as stupid as one of his hat rabbits, and if he could make things disappear so could she. She's pretty good at it, for it is generally hard to attract Niko's attention, and this she can do nearly as well as Amalie or Lourdes. Also she burns with love for them; she can't have children of her own apparently and so aunting is one of her chief joys.

The laughter died away as I entered the room. They all looked at me, each in their different ways, except for Niko, who hardly ever looks at me. He was still staring at my sister's hands, which semiconsciously twirled and vanished several small colored sponge balls. My daughter's look challenged me to be something I was not, a perfect father to complement her own perfection, and my sister's was, as usual, ironic and tolerant. She is no longer the most beautiful woman in the city, but she is still pretty rare and has the means to preserve and enhance her looks to the fullest extent medicine and fashion allow. She was wearing black Dior head to toe and glittered with chunky jewels. As for Amalie, she can never help herself, she always smiles at me with love in her eyes, before she recalls the situation and retreats behind her formal Swiss persona. Still a lovely woman, Amalie, if no longer exactly the one I fell in love with. Two kids and the strain of marriage to me have added soft flesh on the body and lines on the face. I could not help thinking of Miranda at that moment, and the long-sought second chance.

I kissed them all on both cheeks in the European fashion that has long been our family custom (Niko flinching slightly as usual) and presented my orchid. Polite thanks from Amalie, eye-roll from Imogen and Miri (and it is exactly the *same* expression of amused contempt on both lovely faces; is it genetic or was it taught?) and from Niko a brief recitation in his curiously robotic voice of the taxonomic position of this particular species, and the details of blossom morphology that make this obvious. Niko is interested in orchids, as he is in nearly any complex subject requiring memory and a minimum of human relationship.

I asked Miri what they had all been laughing about when I came in and she retold the story of the world-famous actress and the woman famous for breasts-and-appearing-on-talk-shows and how they were getting face packs at the same high-end salon when their tiny dogs got into a dogfight, and it was a fairly amusing story about dripping mud and flying fur and screaming homosexuals, and she continued it as we went down to the dining room and sat around the oval teak and glass table. Amalie had cooked our dinner herself, a kind of cassoulet made with chicken sausage, lamb, and white beans, one of my favorite meals as it happens, with an artichoke salad and a bottle of Hermitage. Given what her time was worth nowadays, it was probably among the most expensive meals on earth. Niko had his bowl of Cheerios, which foodstuff comprises 90 percent of his diet.

During dinner, Amalie and I struggle to keep the conversation flowing, and some of what we talk about is business. My wife, despite her disdain for making money (or perhaps because of it), is a financial whiz. She publishes an on-line report called *Mishkin's Arbitrage Letter*, in which she tells her fifteen hundred or so subscribers where the currency markets are going during the next week. Naturally, the smart players take her info into account, which changes the market, and the even smarter players are taking *that* into account and planning their yendinar-renminbi swaps accordingly, in an infinite regress that makes some of them billionaires. I consider myself a useless parasite compared with people who do real work, like writing songs, but I am a civil engineer compared with these guys. Amalie, however, has no problem charging twenty-five grand a year for a subscription, since she pumps maybe a third of her profits into good works. I occasionally run into people who have business in this rarefied world and they often ask me if I know *that* Mishkin. I always say no, but feel an odd pride all the same.

The meal ended and Aunt Miri went off to play with the kids, as is the custom. Having none of her own she has her fill of adult conversation. Lourdes served coffee; Amalie and I could now talk companionably about our children. We are civilized. She asked about Ingrid. She knows about Ingrid, we are very open about this aspect of my life. I said Ingrid was fine, and she said, 'Poor Ingrid.' I asked her why and she said, 'Because you have a new woman.' I felt the blood rise to my face, but I pasted on a smile and asked her why she thought that, and she sighed and said, 'Jake, I am neither stupid nor unobservant. In the years when I trusted you, of course, I never looked for these signs, or misinterpreted them, but now that I know to look it is all very transparent. Who is she?'

'No one,' I lied. 'Honestly.'

She stared at me for a long moment, then dropped her eyes to the table and sipped her cooling coffee. 'Whatever you say,' she said. She put the cup down and rose and walked out of the room without another word or look. Lourdes came in and started clearing the plates, also ignoring me.

Then the Invisible Man went upstairs to the children's playroom. Niko was at his computer with headphones on, and Miri and Imogen were watching MTV, sitting closely together on a ratty velvet love seat, made rapt by glitz.

Feeling more of a jerk than usual, I upped the fool ante by asking Imogen if she had done her homework and without taking her eyes off the screen she answered in a tone laden with tedium, 'I did it at school.' I thought of asking for it. I also thought of taking the aluminum ball bat in the corner and smashing the television, and the computer, and holding the children hostage until they gave in to my demands. Which is for everything to be different, for me to have the love and admiration of my children and the devotion of my wife, but also the thrill of romance, and to never grow up and forever fly in and out on a wire, dressed in green tights . . .

Instead I sat down next to Miri and studied for a while the tiny scars of her face-lifts and the peculiar shiny dead areas left by the Botox and I was nearly overcome with compassion and I reached out and grabbed her hand. Miri is, I suppose, the person I feel closest to in the family now. We were a refuge for each other all during childhood, and she turned out even worse than me, so we have a basis of understanding. I was thinking about how she always came and grabbed my hand when Dad was on one of his rampages; I have no idea what she was thinking now, if anything, but she squeezed my hand back, and we stayed that way for a while watching the soft-core porn that our civilization uses to entertain the young. Then a little tune played and Imogen pulled out her cell phone, checked its tiny screen and disappeared for an episode of chat with some acolyte.

Miri muted the set, turned, and gave me an appraising look. 'So who's the new lady?' she asked.

'You too?'

'It's obvious. You have that fevered look, and you're less morose than usual. You need to grow up, Jake. You don't want to end up like one of those old farts chasing little girls.'

'Oh, that's rich, getting recommendations on continence from you.'

'Don't be nasty, Jake. We're a pair of sluts, you and I, but I at least don't have a family I drag into it. And especially doing it to someone like Amalie.'

This was not a conversation I wished to have at the moment, so I said, 'How's Dad?'

Miri is the only one of we three who retains any contact with the old gangster. She is parsimonious with information about this relationship, however, perhaps at his insistence. That would be like him.

'Dad is fine. I saw him about three weeks ago. He looks good. He had to get a stent put into a coronary artery.'

'I hope they used an especially corrosion-resistant material. Brick would be my suggestion. Where was this meeting, by the way?'

'Europe.'

'Could you be more specific? Cannes? Paris? Odessa?'

She ignored this. 'He asked after you and Paul.'

'Oh, that was kind of him. I hope you conveyed to him that he's always in our thoughts. What's he up to nowadays?'

'This and that. You know Dad, he always has some kind of hustle going. You should go over and see him. Take Amalie and the kids.'

This made me laugh. 'That's a good idea, Miri. I really can't think of anything that would be more sheer *fun* than such an expedition.'

'You know,' said my sister after an offended pause, 'have you ever noticed that your wife is never sarcastic? You might take a tip from that. You might try a little forgiveness too. I mean you sure *get* a lot of it.'

'And religious advice tonight as well. Are you sure you're not Paul in drag?'

'If you're going to be shitty, then I'm leaving. I need another drink anyway.'

She tried to pull her hand away from mine, but I held on and she fell back on the love seat.

'What?'

'I just thought of something I needed to ask you. In your dealings with the demimonde have you ever come across a Russian gangster named Osip Shvanov?' I was watching her face closely as I asked this and I saw a little tremor run across its sculpted surfaces. She licked her lips with a pink tongue-tip.

'Why do you ask?'

'Because his goons are after me. He thinks I have something he wants. I think.' I provided a brief explanation of the Bulstrode/Shakespeare affair as background, omitting to identify Miranda by name. 'Do you know him?'

'We've met.'

'A client?'

'In a way. He entertains a lot. Some of my girls have been at some of his parties.'

'Could you get us together? I mean socially.'

'I don't think you want to do that, Jake.'

'Because he's such a bad guy.'

'He's pretty evil. I mean *evil* guys think he's evil.'

'Bad as Dad?'

'The same type of person, the two main differences being Dad never played rough and Shvanov is not our dad. Why do you want to meet him?'

'A frank exchange of views. Anyway, will you?'

'I'll suggest it to him. Will he want to see you?'

'I believe so. We share an interest in old manuscripts. I'm sure we'll have lots to talk about. You should come too. It'll be a fun evening. We can plan our trip to Israel to see old Dad.'

She stood up. 'I'll call you,' she said and walked out, leaving me alone except for the strange being tapping away at the keyboard. I stood behind Niko and looked at his screen. It was colored a flat, pale gray, across which field incomprehensible blue letters appeared and vanished like windshield rain. Niko was programming. I should say that for a working lawyer I am computer literate. Most lawyers believe their skin will rot away if they touch a keyboard, but not me. I suppose I am about where Niko was when he was four. I lifted one of his earphones and asked, 'What are you doing?'

I had to repeat myself several times. 'Search engines,' he said.

'Oh, search engines,' I said knowingly. 'What are you searching for?'

'Anything. Let me go.' He shook his head and tried to tug his earphones down, but I lifted them off and spun his swivel chair around so that he faced me.

'I have to talk to you about something important,' I said. His body was starting to stiffen up and his gaze was directed at an upper corner of the room.

'Focus on this, Niko! Gangsters are after me and I think they may want to hurt you and Imogen and Mommy. I need you to help me out.'

This seemed to get through. He asked, bored, 'This is pretend, right?'

'No, not pretend. For real.'

'Why are they after you?'

'Because I have some papers they want. A client of mine gave them to me and they killed him. They tortured him, and before he died he gave them my name.'

Yes, pretty strong stuff for a kid, but Niko is hard to reach. It's not like he was sensitive. I imagine that if someone were torturing me he would watch with fascinated interest.

'Why do they want the papers?'

'I'm not sure. I think they think they could lead to a treasure.' He considered this for a moment, and I imagined the peculiar wheels in his head whirring like a fine clock.

'For real?'

'They think so,' I said.

'We should find the treasure,' he said. 'Then they would probably leave us alone.'

I believe this is one of the few times Niko has used the pronoun *we* to include myself with him. I said, 'That's a very good idea. Now, there are two things I want you to do. The first is I want you to keep careful watch on the street and call me immediately if you see anything suspicious. These guys are Russians and they go around in black SUVs, so call me if you spot them, okay? The next thing is I want you to search for a man named Richard Bracegirdle. He died in 1642 in England.' I wrote this down on a sheet of paper from his printer.

'Who is he?'

'The man who buried the treasure. Find out about him and his descendants, and if there are any of them still alive. Can you do that?'

'Yes, I can,' said Niko. I'm not sure why I engaged him

in this way, although Niko is about as expert a data searcher as any I know, he's won prizes for it, and university professors correspond with him without knowing he is eleven years old. Clearly I could have hired a commercial firm to do the search, or we have people at my office who are good at it. Perhaps I was feeling lonely and here was something Dad and son could do together, like a hike in the piney woods. Thinking on my feet, like philanderers learn to do. Of course, that was the easy part. Now I had to go down and tell his mother all about it.

THE BRACEGIRDLE LETTER (9)

This fellowe says he is named James Piggott and is servant to my lord Dunbarton a man high in counsel to the Kinges majestie & askes me if I am of the pure religion & this man had the whey-faced, cold-eyed look I recollect from daies of my youth as markes youre canting Puritan & so I sayd oh yes sir, truely I am and fall to my meate a capon pastie & ale. Whilst I ate he quizzed mee upon all matters bearing upon religion as: depravity of Man, predestination, inefficacy of workes, revelation soley through Scripture, salvation through faith alone &c. & seemed well-pleazed with my answeres & then sayde Mr Hastynges gives a good reporte of thee & I answer hym Mr Hastynges a goode man and of the true religion I have found & after speaking somewhat of Mr H. he of a sudden says, I heare that your mother was a papiste and brat of a papistical traitor. What say you to that? At this I was much surprized and wroth but I stanche my ire and say that she wase upon a tyme mayhap but repented her error and was a faithfull adherent of the Reformed church her whole lyfe after. He asked of mee was she an Arden of Warwickshire & mee replying she was he saieth that hath saved thee from the gallowes my lad for my lord Dunbarton hath need of someone such as thee, of pure religion but papiste connectiones and those of your motheres family most particular. Now he asketh, hast evere heard a playe?

I sayde I had not for were they not verey wicked thynges? Aye, quoth he, and more than you know. For struttynge actors stand in full light o' day & hatch treason. How you say? By three means. First, playes doe corrupt the mindes and soules of men who heare them by shewing lewd actiouns as: murther, thefte, rapine, bawdrey, fornicatiouns, soe that those heareres may imitate them thereafter and soe disorder the state and lose theyre owne sowles to Hell. Next, these playes o'erthrow Gods lawe for they shew boys dressed as women which is itselfe sinne but far worse they doe unbridyle the filthie lustes of Sodom, which I do not doubt me these playeres doe sinke themselves in soe they are a stenche to heaven. Thirdlie and worste: theye are all but a maske for papistick treasones & he saith again: a maske, but a maske.

And he goeth on: for well you know the Harlot of Rome uzed to delight in rich shewes and silken costumes and men dressed as women to bedazzle the people and turne them away from the true worship of Christ. What is theyre gibbering mass but a playe? Now we have stoppte theyre masses will they not trye another waye to turn folke from true faith? What, quoth I, think you these players are secret papistes? Nay, says he, they are more subtle, more than serpentes. Now what sayest thou if I tell thee there is a man now abroad the chief of these playeres who, item: doth devise secret libels on the true religion: item, doth hold up papiste priestes in such playes to admiratioun: item, whose father wast a papiste fined many tymes for shunning the protestant church and whose mother wase spawn of a family longe reviled for adamant recusancie, doutlesse a papiste herself: item, who conspyred traitorously to ralleye the attainted earle of Essex his forces when he rebelled gainst our late sovereign Quene by meanes of shewing to his followers on the morn of the rebellion the playe of Richard Second as an inspiring exemple of treason & regicide & should have been taken up at that time but was not, for some of worship did protect him, dmn their eyies. What saye you of such a one? Quoth I (which I knew well was the onlie mete answer nowe), to the Tower with him hee should not walk abroade one houre.

Hee then smyled a colde smyle saying marry, you spake the truth boy, yet in the kingdomes now disordered state this wee cannot do, or not yet. For look you, the King surroundes himselfe not with the Godly but with lascivious & corrupt favourites, viz. my Lord of Rochester and otheres lyke, of these manie as near to papistes as your shirt your bodie & these delighteth in such vaine shewes as playes upon the stage: even the King hath a bande of playeres of whom he doth bespeake playes to suit his fancies & the one of whom I tolde thee the chiefest amongst these knaves.

Now, he sayeth further, wee have us a prince Henry as good a protestant as ever ate bread, sober, wyse beyond his yeares: yet his father the King can thinke of nothing but to wed him to a popish princesse & this we cannot suffer to befall this lande for it will be the ruine of Gods church in England, the same as the King hath already begun with his depraved and ungodlie rule of bischopes. Soe my Lord D. and other worthie nobles of the true faith, thinking upon this lamentable past, hath brought forth a plan and have looked long for some one to bring it to particular action. And wee have found hym.

Who, quoth I? You, quoth hee. At hearinge this I wase much afrayde & sayde, for why? Thus he expressed it: you know the Kinges mother wase a vain wicked papiste traitor Mary Queen of Scotlande justlie executed by oure late Quene & this hath long rankled the King that all good Englishmen should despise his mother and mayhap thinke them: lyke mother lyke childe. Soe happlie he would looke with favour upon a playe presentinge Queen Mary as a goode woman wronged, & mayhap he should command this knave of whom I lately spake to write it oute. What then boy?

Then I thought mee be clever as you can Dick for thou art fulle in the power of this one and I sayd 'twould be a scandal to all goode protestants in the kingdom they would not stand it. He says Aye and tis why it is far from the Kinges mind. But suppose one feigning to be in service of some great Lord, a privy councillour even, should go to this maker of playes saying I bear direction from the Kinges majestie: write such a playe and thou wilt be rewarded & gaine favour in the Kinges sight. And suppose such a playe came to be and suppose it were plaied before the King and his courte, what think thee would befall? For know you that no playe can be shewn without a licence from the maistre of the revels: yet in truth no such license would ever issue for such a playe, 'twould be worth the heade of any such officer. Yet suppose further that we have the seal thereof and provide our knave with a false license and then he all unknowing goeth on & giveth the playe. What think you befalls?

Says I he would be ruined I think. You think rightlie boy & gives hym a laugh but with little joy in't, he would be ruined & all this cursed plaieing with hym and not just that: the scandal as thou sayest would race through the kingdom, that the King hath put forth his mother as a goodlie dame unjustlie put down by Elizabeth the Quene, who shall further appear in this playe as a vile scheming bastard. Soe alarums hither & yon: the King denieth all as he must, this knave I spake of is ta'en up and racked, oh yes I shall see to that myself: and racked he giveth forth the names of all who hath complotted this outrage, viz. first Rochester and all otheres who seek a papiste match for oure prince. They are disgraced, deny it how they may & soe do wee put down for ever this papiste match. What think you of this?

Quoth I, sir, a mightie plan methinkes but agen I ask why chuse Dick Bracegirdle? He says, because thou art an Arden by thy dam as is hym we aim at, you are cozens or may seem to be and you can feign at need the same demi-papistrie he professeth if truth be knowne. Soe if my Lord Rochester wisht to sende a privy messenger to this one who shall he chuse better than one such as you. Recall this is all to be done close, or so you shall give out, for my Lord desireth to surprize the King at his birthday with a new playe. But say now, are you oure man?

To this there was but one answer an I ever wished to see free aire again soe I said yes and he sware me a greate oathe on a Bible and warned it should at my grave perill should I ever betray't. After-ward I asked pray what is the name of this fellowe and he says William Shaxspure: this the first tyme I ever heard the name.

Soe I wase freed next night and in darkness passed wee by boat from Tower stayres up-river to a greate house in the Strand belonging to my Lord Dunbarton and was presented to my Lord, a verey grave fat man much burdened by affayres, but uzed me kindley enow & sayde I would doe greate worke for England if wee could but brynge oure devizes to fruite. But wee did not in the end, God willed other wise in His greate wisdom & in later yeares I oft thought mee had wee won all wee had forecaste & hoped mayhap the present broiles that bid fayre to ravage oure sad countrie had therebye been checked. Yet I wase but a smalle peece upon the board & verilie is it sayde His thoughts are greater than oure thoughts Amen.

I stopped some weekes at Dunbarton House, well-tabeled, dressed in cloathes finer than aught I had before but verey sober. Of daies Mr Piggott taught me how to write & reade cypher'd messauges & he wase amazed how well I did in this & I tolde hym my minde had been trayned up in the Mathematick artes long since & your cyphers be somethyng lyke. Soe he was pleazed there-bye. I reade deepe in the Tracktee de Chiffres a French booke late Englished & Sigr. Porta's De Furtivas verie subtle werkes & too the grilles of Mstr. Cardano & this arte lyked mee so welle that I did labour longe at it in the night-tyme, for there was no lack of candels at Dunbarton House and shewed Mr Piggott my werkynges: and after some wekes wase hee not full amaz'd for I had mayde a new cypher the lyke hee had not seen before & hee sayde e'en the Pope could not mayke it oute.

Afterward he had mee increase my skill at recollection of wordes hym saying many score of them and set mee to recall them in the self-same order & set down in writing. Besides, he shewed me lykenesses of men & women & viewes of townes & countrie-sydes all verey prettilie made with paintes & mee made to describe them after onlie a little scant looke. The same: hee & another feigned a discourse of poperie and treasoun, mee conceeled behind a screen & later I am made to tell him all the plot. Here again he admitteth I doe well. Soe now I aske hym be this all the intelligencers art and he answereth nay, this be but the smaller parte, which answer puzzel'd me much.

Yet later I understood hym, for next cometh a man Henry Wales a leering coxcombe he seemed, in modern pretty cloathes fit for one of higher state, but Mr Piggott spake civillie to him & gave him a purse and spake me Dick, here be your true friend Henry Wales that you have knowne since youth in Warwickshire, now met in London amid greate joie. He is an actor of the Kinges Companie & knoweth Mr Wm. Shaxespur right well. Then Mr Piggott caste on me such a looke as I knew his meaning afresh: that I too wase to be actor but in lyfe not upon stage & this is what it is to be an intelligencer not mere cyphers, listening & recollection & I thought mee then of my first yeare in the foundry when I acted the boorish prentice rough in word and harsh in dede whilst keepyng my true selfe within & thought yea this can I doe & lett the papistes & traitoures feare.

All that befell thereafter you will finde writ in the letteres that I passed to Lord D. viz: my approache to this Shaxspure, what passed between us, the playe he wrought of that wicked queene of Scots, and what became of it, and at laste how wee fayled and so I shalnot repeate here for I feare me I have not more than a few houres & it straineth me to write more. You know well Nan my lyfe thereafter & I am saddened that I can not relate it to hym as I have those yeares before. Say to hym your sire was a gonner in the German warres in the goode Protestant cause: was at White Mountain and vanquished by the papistes & at Breitenfeilde and Luttzen holped vanquishe them: but trying of warre & sore hurt in the foote by a bullet then returned, my father having since died & your fishmonger dying also (the which I had prayed for & pray you and God forgyve mee for it!) and were married 3rd Aprill 1632 St. Margaret Pattens & yeare after had a son, praise God & maye hee live long and thee.

Some more thinges of import for my time groweth short I can scarce make out the page though it be clare day & I am griped by my mortal agonie you know well my leathern boxe that I keep in my privy closet, in it you shall finde the letteres cypher'd in the fasioun I devized. Doe you keepe them safe and show them to no one. They tell all the tale nearlie of my Lord D. his plot & oure spyeing upon the secret papist Shaxpure. Or so wee thought him although now I am lesse certayne. In that manner & bent of lyfe he wase a Nothinge. But certayne it is hee wrought the playe of Scotch M. I commanded of him in the Kinges name. I find it passing strange that all though I am dead and him also yet the playe lives still, writ in his own hande & lying where onlie I know & there maye it reste for ever.

As to the letteres: if the King should prevail in this present affarye, which God forbid, and his ministers come at you with ill intent, these leaves may holpe to secure your fortune, yours and that of oure son. You know how to worke the cypher and I recollect you the Keye be the Willowe where my mother lieth and if thou'rt able I wish that my bones may lye besyde hers hereafter.

Fare thee well my girl & with Gods grace I hope I shall see you agen in the incorrupt bodie promised us by oure Lord & Saviour Christ Jesus in whose name I sign this yr. husbande
RICHARD BRACEGIRDLE

10

Crosetti sat in his father's car, a black 1968 Plymouth Fury, and watched 161 Tower Road, feeling stupid. The house was a two-story frame model in need of a coat of paint, set in a weedy lawn behind a low chain-link fence. A row of brownish junipers bordering the house seemed the limits of H. Olerud's horticulture. This name was displayed on a battered black maibox nailed to a crooked post. In the driveway sat a rust-flecked green Chevy sedan with the hood up and a scatter of tools on a tarp next to it. In the open shedlike garage that adjoined the house, he could see a red tractor and a tangle of shapes that could have been agricultural implements. The place had a tired look, as if it and the people who lived there had been knocked down and were waiting for breath to return. It was a Saturday. Crosetti had left the city at dawn and driven across the state of Pennsylvania, nearly three hundred miles on I-80 and 79, and reached Braddock a little past three. Braddock was built around a single intersection with two gas stations, a McDonald's, a pizza joint, a VFW hall, two bars, a 7-Eleven, a coin laundry, and a collection of older brick-built commercial buildings, most of the shops in them

Wal-Marted into oblivion and now occupied by junk dealers or storefront services for the distressed. Behind this strip were dozens of large homes that must have been built for the commercial and industrial aristos when the steel mills and mines had been working. Crosetti couldn't imagine who lived in them now.

Tower Road and the sad house on it had not been hard to find with his Google map, and after arriving there he had knocked on the front door with no result. Crosetti had pushed the unlocked door open and called out, 'Hello! Anyone home?' and felt the hollow sense of an empty house. Inhabited, though: messy but not filthy, toys on the floor, little cars and a plastic gun, a TV tray with an empty plate set up in front of the large-screen TV. They had satellite too – behind the house a white dish scanned the heavens. In front of the TV a La-Z-Boy lounger in brown vinyl attended a sagging chenille-covered couch. A narrow mantelpiece held photographs in frames, but Crosetti could not see them from the door and did not wish to venture within. No dogs barked, which he thought was strange. Didn't all rural households have dogs? Another clue to he knew not what. He walked around the house. In the backyard there was a plastic playground set much faded by the sun and sized for very young children. In the center of the yard stood a clothes-drying contraption of the kind that resembles an inverted parasol. It was empty, and several of the lines had broken away and dangled, waving feebly in the light breeze. On the back porch stood an elderly cylindrical washing machine. He checked it; dry and spidery.

After his brief exploration he sat in the car and thought about all this and also how really dumb it had been to drive all this way because of a postcard he'd found in the street. He had no idea whether Carol Rolly had any connection whatever to this house. She could have picked the card up off the sidewalk or found it marking an old book. No, he thought, don't think about that. Let's go with the gut. This has something to do with her and that photograph of the two women and the kid. Well, there *was* a kid here, a boy. He took the photo and looked at it once again. He judged that it had been snapped around five or so years ago, given the apparent age of Carolyn's face in it, and so the boy would be around eight or nine by now. Crosetti studied a bicycle tossed casually down on the driveway. That would fit a kid of that age, and the various toys scattered around the house and yard suggested the same. There were no girl toys in sight, nor was there another bike, and Crosetti wondered what had become of the baby girl in the photograph . . . no wait, there in a sandbox attached to the playground set, a single, weathered, naked Barbie. So that checked out too, unless Barbie had been dropped by a visitor. Or stolen.

He considered the backyard. A sunny day, a Saturday, no clothes on the dryer and it in disrepair, nor had he spotted an electric dryer exhaust, nor did the washer look much used. Which meant that probably there wasn't a woman in residence. The guy lived here with his kid (or kids), and on Saturday he went to town and did his laundry in the Laundromat, because it was ignoble for a man to do laundry at home, and by going to town on a Saturday he got to meet women and advertise his availability, and maybe he'd go across to the VFW and have a couple of beers while the dryer spun. The kid(s) could play video games at the 7-Eleven and get a Slurpee.

Crosetti caught himself spinning this tale and wondered where it came from even while he understood that it was as true as if he had made a documentary of the life of H. Olerud. That he was the child of a legendary police detective and a well-known research librarian did not at the moment present itself as an explanation, for he had always made up stories about people, even as a kid. It was one reason why he wanted to make movies, and why he thought he'd be good at it. He took his powers of observation and inference for granted, much as natural musicians think little of causing an inert appliance to sound the secret music they hear in their heads.

He hadn't eaten since a gas stop at ten and now it was close to four and he was feeling hungry. He thought he would drive back to town and get a bite, and was about to start his car, when he saw a plume of dust coming from the direction of town, which soon resolved itself into a green pickup truck that slowed, passed him, and turned into the driveway of 161 Tower Road. He saw with some satisfaction that the cab contained a man and a boy of about nine, whose small head just showed above the dashboard. The truck was going a little too fast as it made the turn, and its off-front wheel crashed into the boy's bike that lay in the driveway.

A bellow of rage from the driver as he slammed on his brakes and a shrill cry from a child. The driver's door of the truck flew open and out jumped a stocky man a few years older than Crosetti, dressed in jeans and a clean white T-shirt. He had a sizable gut, and a reddish buzz cut topping a tight flat red face of the kind that always seems a little angry. He ran to the front of the truck, cursed again, kicked the bike out of the way, and jerked the passenger door open. From the cab came shrill screams, and Crosetti realized that there was another, younger passenger, and also that the man had not secured either of the children with seat belts. The man reached in and yanked the boy out by his arm. Still holding the arm he batted the boy several times across the head, heavy blows that made awful meaty noises Crosetti could hear from where he sat, all the while demanding of the boy how often he had told him not to leave the fucking bike in the fucking driveway and also whether he thought he was ever going to get a new bike or anything new ever again you little piece of shit.

Crosetti was wondering in a helpless sort of way whether he should take some action, when the man stopped beating the boy and reached again into the cab of the truck and pulled out a girl of about four. The child's face was bright red and screwed up in a paroxysm of pain and fright. Some of the red was blood from a wound on her mouth. She squirmed like a lizard in the man's grasp, her back arched. The man told the child to shut up, that she wasn't hurt, that if she didn't shut up this minute he'd really give her something to yell about. The screaming subsided into horrible wheezing gasps, and the man strode into the house with the little girl.

Shortly thereafter Crosetti heard the sound of a television going at considerable volume. He left his car and walked over to the boy, who lay crouched on the ground where the man had flung him. He was crying in a peculiar way, sucking in great gasps and letting them out in strangled almost noiseless sobs. Crosetti ignored the child and squatted down to examine the bicycle. Then he walked up the drive to where the sedan was under repair, selected a few wrenches and a heavy pliers from the tools scattered about, and addressed the injured bike. He removed the front wheel, straightened the handlebars, set his foot on the front fork to straighten that as well and used the pliers to bring the front wheel spokes into some semblance of their original alignment. He felt the boy's eyes on him as he worked and heard the child's sobbing die away to sniffles. He twisted the rim back into approximate circularity by eye, set the wheel back on its fork, and with the bike upside down, he gave it a spin. It wobbled but spun freely around its axle. Crosetti said, 'Some say a wheel is just like a heart, when you bend it, you can't mend it. You're going to need a new wheel there, partner, but it'll ride if you don't go over too rough of a road. What's your name?'

'Emmett,' said the boy after a pause, and wiped his face with the back of his hand, making an ugly smear of tears and dust. Bingo, thought Crosetti, the name on the postcard, and examined the child with interest. He was a good-looking kid, if a little too thin, with wide-spaced intelligent-looking blue eyes, and a thin-lipped mouth whose genetic provenance Crosetti thought he knew. His hair was cropped so short that it was hard to tell what color it was.

Crosetti said, 'My name's Al. Look, Emmett, would you like to help me out with something?'

The boy hesitated, then nodded. Crosetti took an enhanced printout of Carolyn Rolly's photograph from his back pocket, and unfolded it for the boy.

'Do you know who these women are?'

The boy studied the photograph, his eyes wide. 'That's my mom and my aunt Emily. She used to live with us but she died.'

'*This* is your mother?' Crosetti asked with his finger on the younger Rolly.

'Uh-huh. She run off. He locked her in the cellar but she got out. She got out at night and in the morning she wasn't there. Where did she go, mister?'

'I wish I knew, Emmett, I really do,' said Crosetti absently. His mind had been set whirling by the boy's appearance and this confirmation of his guess, and his belly churned with tension. To his shame, what he was thinking of was the single night he had spent with Rolly and what she had done and what he imagined she had felt, and whether she had done the same for her husband, that brutal man, in the bedroom of this crummy little house. A powerful urge seized him, to get away from this place and also (although this would be more difficult) to vacate the place in his heart occupied by the person he knew as Carolyn Rolly. He was sorry for the children, stuck with this father, but there was nothing he could do about that. Another blot on Carolyn's record.

He started to walk away and the boy called out to him, 'Did you know her? My mom?'

'No,' said Crosetti, 'not really.'

He got into his car and drove off. The boy ran forward a few steps, with the photograph flapping in his hands, and then stopped and was lost in the dust of the road.

Crosetti found a McDonald's and had a Big Mac, fries, and a Coke. He finished the junk and was about to order more but checked at the counter. He ate when he was upset, he knew, and if he didn't watch it he was going to look like Orson Welles, without that person's early achievement to balance out the flab. He tried to calm himself, an effort hampered by the fact that he'd somehow lost his MapQuest driving directions and made a couple of wrong turns on the way back.

When he was on the right interstate at last, he composed in his head the script of the film *Carolyn Rolly*; not a bad title, and he could probably use it without a release because Mrs Olerud had probably fabricated her name too. Okay: brutal childhood, use that, the girl-in-the-cellar angle, although maybe the uncle's serial rape business was a little too X-rated. Let's make Uncle Lloyd a religious fanatic who wanted to keep his niece from the corruption of the world. He dies or she escapes and there she is at seventeen, say, knowing nothing, having had zero contact with mass culture, a little homage to Herzog's *Kaspar Hauser* there.

There's some local celebrity around the weird case, and let's say the cop who found her falls in love with Carolyn, he falls for her purity, her innocence, and marries her, which she goes along with because she's all alone, she knows nothing about how the world works, and they set up house. He's a control freak, a cop after all, Crosetti knew guys like that on the cops, but she submits, and that's the first act.

Then we show her life, she has the kids and then she starts taking them to the local library, where she meets the wise librarian and the librarian turns her on to art and culture and it lights her up, and then there's a traveling exhibit of fine books that the librarian gets her to go to without her husband's knowledge, maybe they go to Chicago (they would shoot it in Toronto, of course), and she realizes she wants to make books, she wants books all around her, but what can she do, she's got two kids, she's trapped, but she decides to apply for a bookbinding course by mail and her husband finds out and beats her up, and after that it gets worse and worse, and he locks her in the cellar just like her uncle did, and she escapes and that's the second act. Then in the third act she goes to New York and . . . no, you couldn't do that, the male lead has to come in earlier, you'd have to show the backstory in flashback, the humble clerk who maybe has a past of his own, he's an ex-cop maybe, and they get together and fall in love and she disappears and . . .

Why does she disappear? Crosetti didn't know, and he found he could not generate a fictional reason that would hold water either. Was she kidnapped? No, too melodramatic. Did she see an opportunity to get enough money so that she could get the kids away from the bad dad? That made more sense. She'd run off with Bulstrode in pursuit of the Shakespeare manuscript. There was a clue in the Bracegirdle letter, Bulstrode had found it, and they were off to England to where X marked the spot. Hundreds of millions, Fanny had said. That had to be it, and the next thing was for the hero to work out the clue himself and find where they'd gone and confront them there in England, you could fake that in Canada too, right, and there'd have to be a subplot, someone else looking for it, and the cruel dad cop also in there somewhere and they'd all come together in the old castle, in the dark, grabbing the briefcase with the manuscript in it away from one another, with plenty of business about false briefcases, a little reference to the *Maltese Falcon*, of course, and the only last-act problem would be the hero and Rolly, would he save her, would she save him, would they get out with the treasure, or would it be lost? Or maybe the cruel dad would get killed and she'd give up the treasure to be with the hero and the kids . . .

He didn't know how he'd end it, but the more he thought about it, about the intersection between fiction and the real, the more he thought that he had to get some advantage over Bulstrode, the Shakespeare expert, and the best way to do that was to crack the cipher, because with all his expertise, that was one thing Bulstrode did not have. So besides having to learn a lot more about Shakespeare, he had to decipher and read Bracegirdle's spy letters. Such were Crosetti's thoughts during the long drive back to the city, peppered by the usual fantasies: he confronts the angry husband, they fight, Crosetti wins; he finds Carolyn again, he acts wry, cool, sophisticated, he has understood all her plottings and forgives; he earns a fortune via the manuscript and explodes upon the cinematic world with a film that owes nothing to commercial demands yet touches the hearts of audiences everywhere, obviating the necessity for a long apprenticeship, cheap student films, playing gofer to some Hollywood asshole . . .

He arrived back in Queens at around eight on Saturday evening, fell immediately into bed, slept for twelve hours straight, and awoke vibrating with more energy than he'd felt in a long time and frustrated because it was Sunday and he would have to wait before getting started. He went to mass with his mother therefore, which pleased her a good deal, and afterward she made him a colossal breakfast, which he consumed with gratitude, thinking of the scrawny kids in that house and being frankly grateful for his family, although he knew it was totally uncool to have such thoughts. While he ate he told his mother something of what he had learned.

'So it was all lies,' she observed.

'Not necessarily,' said Crosetti, who was still a little entranced with the fictional version he had concocted. 'She *was* obviously on the lam from a bad situation. Parts of it could have been true. She changed the location and some of the details, but this guy actually locked her in a cellar, according to the kid. She could have been abused as a child and fallen into an abusive situation.'

'But she's married, which she didn't bother to mention, and she ran out on her kids. I'm sorry, Allie, but that doesn't speak well for her. She could have gone to the authorities.'

Crosetti abruptly rose from the table and brought his plate and cup to the sink, and washed them with the clattering movement of the angry. He said, 'Yeah, but we weren't there. Not everybody has a happy family like we do, and the authorities sometimes screw up. We have no idea of what she went through.'

'Okay, Albert,' said Mary Peg, 'you don't have to break the dishes to make a point. You're right, we don't know what she went through. I'm just a little worried about your emotional involvement with a married woman you hardly knew. It seems like an obsession.'

Crosetti turned off the faucet and faced his mother. 'It *is* an obsession, Mom. I want to find her and I want to help her if I can. And to do that I have to decipher those letters.' He paused. 'And I'd like your help.'

'Not a problem, dear,' said his mother, smiling now. 'It beats playing Scrabble in the long, long evenings.'

The next day Mary Peg began rounding up cryptography resources from the Web and through her wide range of contacts in libraries around the world, via telephone and e-mail. Crosetti called Fanny Doubrowicz at the library and was heartened to learn that she had puzzled out Bracegirdle's Jacobean handwriting and entered the text of his last letter into her computer. She had also made a transcript of the ciphertext of the spy letters and sent a sample of the paper and ink from those originals to the laboratory for analysis. It was, as far as the lab could determine, a seventeenth-century document.

'This Bracegirdle tells quite a story, by the way,' she said. 'It will make a revolution in scholarship, unless it is a pack of lies. If only you had not been so foolish as to sell the original!'

'I know, but I can't do anything about that now,' said Crosetti, expending some effort at keeping his voice pleasant. 'If I can find Carolyn I might be able to get it back. Meanwhile, has anything surfaced on the library grapevine? Blockbuster manuscript found?'

'Not even a peep, and I have called around in manuscript circles. If Professor Bulstrode is authenticating it, he is being very quiet about his doings.'

'Isn't that strange? I figured he'd be calling press conferences.'

'Yes, but this is a man who has been badly burned. He would not want to go public with this until he had made absolutely sure. However, there are only a few people in the world whose word on such a manuscript would be probative, and I have spoken to all of them. They laugh when they hear Bulstrode's name and none have heard from him recently.'

'Yeah, well, maybe he's holed up in his secret castle, just gloating. Look, can you zap those documents over by e-mail? I want to get to work on that cipher.'

'Yes, I will zap now. And I will also send the number of my friend, Klim. I think you will need help. I have looked a little and it does not seem to be a simple thing, this cipher.'

When he had the e-mail, Crosetti made himself print out Fannie's transcription of the Bracegirdle letter instead of reading it immediately on the screen. Then he read it several times, especially the last part, about the spying mission, and tried not to be too hard on himself for letting the original go. He almost sympathized with Bulstrode, the bastard – the discovery was so huge that he could well appreciate what was going through the guy's mind when he saw it. He did not allow himself to think about the other, larger prize, as Bulstrode had obviously and immediately done, nor did he keep Carolyn and how she was connected to all this uppermost in his thoughts. Crosetti was an indifferent student most days, but he was capable of intense focus when he was interested in something, like the history of movies, a subject on which he was encyclopedic. Now he turned this focus onto the Bracegirdle cipher and on the tall stack of cryptography books his mother had brought home from various libraries that evening.

For the next six days he did nothing else but go to work, study cryptography, and work on the cipher. On Sunday he again went to church and found himself praying with unaccustomed fervor for a solution. Returning home he made for his room, ready to begin once more, when his mother stopped him.

'Take a break, Allie, it's Sunday.'

'No, I thought of something else I want to try.'

'Honey, you're exhausted. Your mind is mush and you're not going to do yourself any good spinning around like a hamster. Sit down, I'll make a bunch of sandwiches, you'll have a beer, you'll tell me what you've been doing. This will help, believe me.'

So he forced himself to sit and ate grilled-cheese sandwiches with bacon and drank a Bud, and found that his mother had been right, he did feel a little more human. When the meal was over, Mary Peg asked, 'So what have you got so far? Anything?'

'In a negative sense. Do you know much about ciphers?'

'At the Sunday paper game-page level.'

'Yeah, well that's a start. Okay, the most common kind of secret writing in the early seventeenth century was what they called a nomenclator, which is a kind of enciphered code. You have a short vocabulary of coded words, *box* for *army, pins* for *ships*, whatever, and these words and the connecting words of the message would be enciphered, using a simple substitution, with maybe a few fancy complications. What we got here isn't a nomenclator. In fact, I think it's the cipher Bracegirdle talks about in his letter, the one he invented for Lord Dunbarton. It's not a simple substitution either. I think it's a true polyalphabetic cipher.'

'Which means what?'

'It's a little complicated. Let me show you some stuff.' He

left and came back with a messy handful of papers. 'Okay, the simplest cipher substitutes one letter for another, usually by shifting the alphabet a certain number of spaces, so that A becomes D and C becomes G and so on. It's called a Caesar shift because Julius Caesar supposedly invented it, but obviously you can crack it in a few minutes if you know the normal frequencies of the letters in the language it's written in.'

'ETAOIN SHRDLU.'

'You got it. Well, obviously, spies knew this, so they developed ciphering methods to disguise the frequency of letters by using a different alphabet to pick every substitution in the ciphertext.'

'You mean a literally different alphabet, like Greek?'

'No, no, I mean like this.' He pulled a paper out of the sheaf and smoothed it on the table. 'In the sixteenth century the architect Alberti invented a substitution cipher that used multiple alphabets arranged on brass disks, and a little later in France a mathematician named Blaise Vigenère supposedly invented what they call a polyalphabetic substitution cipher using twenty-six Caesar-shifted alphabets, and I figured it or something like it would be known to Bracegirdle if he was studying the cipher arts at that time. This here is what they call a tabula recta or a Vigenère tableau. It's twenty-six alphabets, one on top of the other, starting with a regular A through Z alphabet and then each successive one starts one letter to the right, from B through Z plus A, then C through Z plus A and B and so on, and there are regular alphabets along the left side and the top to serve as indexes.'

'So how do you use it to disguise frequencies?'

'You use a key. You pick a particular word and run it across the top of the tableau, lining each letter of the key up with each column and repeating it until you reach the end of the alphabet. For example, let's pick *Mary Peg* as a key. It's seven letters with no repeats, so it's a good pick.' He wrote it out several times in pencil and said, 'Now we need a plain-text to encipher.'

'Flee, all is discovered,' suggested Mary Peg.

'Always timely. So we write the plaintext over the key, like so . . .

F L E E A L L I S D I S C O V E R E D
M A R Y P E G M A R Y P E G M A R Y P

'And then to encipher, we take the first letter of the plaintext, which is *F*, and the first letter of the key, which is *M*, and then we go to the tableau, down from the *F* column to the *M* row and we write the letter we find at the intersection, which just happens to be *R*. The next combination is *L* from *flee* and *A* from *Mary*, so *L* stays *L*, and the next is *E* and *R*, which gives *V*. And now see how this works: the next *E* is over the letter *Y* in our 'Mary Peg' key which gives *C*. The two *E*s in *flee* have *different* ciphertext equivalents, which is why frequency analysis fails. Let me knock this out real quick so you can see . . .'

Crosetti rapidly filled in the ciphertext and produced

F L E E A L L I S D I S C O V E R E D
R L V C P P R U S U G H G U H E I C S

	A	B	C	D	E	F	G	H	I	J	K	L	M	N	O	P	Q	R	S	T	U	V	W	X	Y	Z
A	A	B	C	D	E	F	G	H	I	J	K	L	M	N	O	P	Q	R	S	T	U	V	W	X	Y	Z
B	B	C	D	E	F	G	H	I	J	K	L	M	N	O	P	Q	R	S	T	U	V	W	X	Y	Z	A
C	C	D	E	F	G	H	I	J	K	L	M	N	O	P	Q	R	S	T	U	V	W	X	Y	Z	A	B
D	D	E	F	G	H	I	J	K	L	M	N	O	P	Q	R	S	T	U	V	W	X	Y	Z	A	B	C
E	E	F	G	H	I	J	K	L	M	N	O	P	Q	R	S	T	U	V	W	X	Y	Z	A	B	C	D
F	F	G	H	I	J	K	L	M	N	O	P	Q	R	S	T	U	V	W	X	Y	Z	A	B	C	D	E
G	G	H	I	J	K	L	M	N	O	P	Q	R	S	T	U	V	W	X	Y	Z	A	B	C	D	E	F
H	H	I	J	K	L	M	N	O	P	Q	R	S	T	U	V	W	X	Y	Z	A	B	C	D	E	F	G
I	I	J	K	L	M	N	O	P	Q	R	S	T	U	V	W	X	Y	Z	A	B	C	D	E	F	G	H
J	J	K	L	M	N	O	P	Q	R	S	T	U	V	W	X	Y	Z	A	B	C	D	E	F	G	H	I
K	K	L	M	N	O	P	Q	R	S	T	U	V	W	X	Y	Z	A	B	C	D	E	F	G	H	I	J
L	L	M	N	O	P	Q	R	S	T	U	V	W	X	Y	Z	A	B	C	D	E	F	G	H	I	J	K
M	M	N	O	P	Q	R	S	T	U	V	W	X	Y	Z	A	B	C	D	E	F	G	H	I	J	K	L
N	N	O	P	Q	R	S	T	U	V	W	X	Y	Z	A	B	C	D	E	F	G	H	I	J	K	L	M
O	O	P	Q	R	S	T	U	V	W	X	Y	Z	A	B	C	D	E	F	G	H	I	J	K	L	M	N
P	P	Q	R	S	T	U	V	W	X	Y	Z	A	B	C	D	E	F	G	H	I	J	K	L	M	N	O
Q	Q	R	S	T	U	V	W	X	Y	Z	A	B	C	D	E	F	G	H	I	J	K	L	M	N	O	P
R	R	S	T	U	V	W	X	Y	Z	A	B	C	D	E	F	G	H	I	J	K	L	M	N	O	P	Q
S	S	T	U	V	W	X	Y	Z	A	B	C	D	E	F	G	H	I	J	K	L	M	N	O	P	Q	R
T	T	U	V	W	X	Y	Z	A	B	C	D	E	F	G	H	I	J	K	L	M	N	O	P	Q	R	S
U	U	V	W	X	Y	Z	A	B	C	D	E	F	G	H	I	J	K	L	M	N	O	P	Q	R	S	T
V	V	W	X	Y	Z	A	B	C	D	E	F	G	H	I	J	K	L	M	N	O	P	Q	R	S	T	U
W	W	X	Y	Z	A	B	C	D	E	F	G	H	I	J	K	L	M	N	O	P	Q	R	S	T	U	V
X	X	Y	Z	A	B	C	D	E	F	G	H	I	J	K	L	M	N	O	P	Q	R	S	T	U	V	W
Y	Y	Z	A	B	C	D	E	F	G	H	I	J	K	L	M	N	O	P	Q	R	S	T	U	V	W	X
Z	Z	A	B	C	D	E	F	G	H	I	J	K	L	M	N	O	P	Q	R	S	T	U	V	W	X	Y

'And notice how the double *L* in *all* is disguised too,' he said. 'Now you have something that can't be broken by simple frequency analysis, and for three hundred years no one could break a cipher like that without learning the key word. That's mainly what they tortured spies for.'

'How *do* you break it?'

'By finding the length of the key word, and you do that by analyzing repeating patterns in the ciphertext. It's called the Kasiski-Kerckhoff Method. In a long enough message or set of messages, *FL* is going to line up with *MA* again, and give you *RL* again, and there'll be other two-and three-letter patterns, and then you count the distance between repeats and figure out any common numerical factors. In our example, with a seven-letter key you might get repeats at seven, fourteen, and twenty-one significantly more than would be the case by chance. Obviously, nowadays you use statistical tools and computers. Then when you know our key has seven letters, it's a piece of cake, because what you have then is seven simple substitution alphabets derived from the Vigenère tableau, and you can break those by ordinary frequency analysis to decrypt the ciphertext or reconstruct the key word. There are downloadable decrypting programs that can do it in seconds on a PC.'

'So why haven't you cracked it?'

He ran his hand through his hair and groaned. 'If I knew that, I'd *know* how to crack it. This thing's not a simple Vigenère.'

'Maybe it is, but it has a really long key. From what you said, the longer the key, the harder it would be to factor out the repeating groups.'

'Good point. The problem with long keys is that they're easy to forget and hard to transmit if you want to change them. For instance, if these guys wanted to change the key every month to make absolutely sure that no spy had discovered it, they'd want something an agent could receive with a whisper in the dark or in a totally innocent message. What they do nowadays is that the agent gets what they call a onetime pad, which is a set of preprinted segments of an infinitely long, totally random key. The agent enciphers one message and then burns the sheet. It's totally unbreakable even by advanced computers. But that kind of method wasn't invented in 1610.'

'So what else?'

'It could be a grille, in which case we're screwed.' Seeing

her puzzled look, he added, 'A Cartan Grille, a literal piece of stiff paper with holes punched in it that reveals the message when you place it over the page. That would mean it's not a cipher at all. For example, assume the ciphertext I wrote is just random noise, but if you slide a grille over it you can get *RUG* or *USE* or *RUSE* . . .'

'But surely, if they were using a grille, the ciphered message would look like a normal letter. "Dear Mom, having a great time in London, bought a new doublet, baited some bears, wish you were here, love, Dick." And the grille would reveal the plaintext: "flee, all is discovered." I mean the *point* would be to allow the concealed message to pass as innocent, no?'

Crosetti tapped his head in the what-a-jerk gesture. 'Of course. Obviously, I'm losing it. Anyway, I'm stumped – I have no idea where to go from here.'

'I rest my case. Like I said, you need a break.'

'You're right.' He rubbed his face with both hands and then asked, 'What day is this?'

'October 14. Why?'

'There's a Caribbean film festival at BAM, and I wanted to catch *Of Men and Gods*. Maybe if I lose myself in gay Haitian voodoo, I'll come back to it fresh.'

'That's a good plan, dear,' said Mary Peg.

Something about her tone and the expression on her face made him pause. He regarded her narrowly: 'What?'

'Nothing, hon. I thought that if you didn't mind I'd take a look at it myself.'

'Hey, knock yourself out!' said Crosetti, with just a trace of smugness. 'It's not a crossword puzzle.'

He was gone for over four hours because after the movie played he ran into some film freak pals of his and went for coffee and they took the film apart technically and artistically, and he enjoyed the usual amusing and astringent conversation common to such groups, and made a couple of good points and got to talking with a small intense woman who made documentaries, and they exchanged numbers. Crosetti felt like a real person for the first time in what seemed to him a long while. It had been nearly two months since that thing with Rolly started and ended, leaving a peculiar emotional ash. Not love, he now thought. Chemistry, sure, but as his mother had pointed out, in order for chemistry to transmute into connection there had to be reciprocity and a modicum of commitment, which he had certainly not got from Rolly . . . just a nothingness and that stupid letter, oh, and P.S., bid a heartfelt bye-bye to Albert. It still griped him, not so much as a blow to his self-regard but as an insult to his aesthetics. It was wrong; he would never have written a plot point like that into a screenplay, and since he was a realist sort of *auteur*, he believed that such an event could not exist in the real world. Thus the subway thoughts of Crosetti.

When he got home, he found Mary Peg in her living room, drinking vodka with a strange man. Crosetti stood in the doorway and stared at his mother, who coolly (rather excessive, *suspicious*, coolness, Crosetti thought) introduced the man as Radeslaw Klim. This person rose to a considerable height, perhaps six inches more than Crosetti's, and shook hands with a stiff little bow. The man had an intelligent aquiline face, a foreign face, although Crosetti could not have pinned down why it was not an American one. Washed blue eyes looked out through round wire-rimmed glasses, under a great shock of stiff silver hair, which stuck up above his broad forehead like the crest on a centurion's helmet. He was about the same age as Mary Peg, or a little older, and he was wearing a baggy rust-colored suit with a dark shirt under it, no tie, the suit a cheap one that hung badly on his long slender frame. Despite this, the man had a nearly military bearing, as if he had temporarily misplaced his beautifully tailored uniform.

Crosetti sat in an armchair and his mother supplied him with a glass of iced vodka, a substance for which he found an unfamiliar but urgent need. After he'd drunk a slug he looked challengingly at Mary Peg, who said blandly, 'Mr Klim is Fanny's friend. I asked him to come by and take a look at your cipher. Since you were stuck.'

'Uh-huh,' said the son.

'Yes,' said Klim. 'I have looked, examined it somewhat. As you have guessed, it is a polyalphabetic substitution cipher and it also is true that it is not a simple Vigenère. That is of course elementary.' He had a slight accent that reminded Crosetti of Fanny's; his mien was gentle and scholarly enough to at least partially assuage Crosetti's nascent resentment.

'So what is it?' Crosetti asked sharply.

'I believe it is a running key,' said Klim. 'From a book of some kind. You understand how these work? The key is of very long extent compared to the plaintext, so the Kasiski-Kerckhoff Method is of no use.'

'Like a book code?'

'No, this is not the same thing. A book code is a code. The codetext is, let us say, 14, 7, 6, and that means you go to *World Almanac* or some such and look at page 14, line 7, word 6. Or you can use letters if you like, the fourth letter, the tenth letter. A running key uses a book, the same, but uses the book text as a continuous key. These are not so secure as people think, however.'

'Why not? It's similar to a onetime pad.'

Klim shook his head. 'Not so. Onetime pad has very high entropy, because the letters are randomly generated. That is, given one letter of your key you have no idea which of the other twenty-six will follow. Whereas, in a running key based on any English text, let us say, if you see *Q*, what is next letter for sure?'

'*U*.'

'Exactly. Low entropy, as I say. How we break these is we run probable plaintext alongside ciphertext until we see something intelligible.'

'What do you mean by "probable plaintext"?'

'Oh, words always appearing in English text. *The, and, this*, and so on and so forth. We run against ciphertext and suppose we find once that *the* gives us *ing* or *shi* when we work back through the tableau? We use such clues to discover more English words in key. Eventually we recognize actual source of running key, I mean, the book it comes from, in which case we have completely broken cipher. It is not very complex, but we would need a computer, or else large squads of intelligent ladies.' Here he smiled, showing small stained teeth, and his glasses glinted. Crosetti got the impression that Klim had at one time supervised such squads.

'Would mine do?' asked Crosetti. 'My PC, not my squads of ladies.'

'Yes, if networked to others, which can be done. There are numbers of people in the world who like cracking ciphers for amusement and they will let one borrow computer cycles they are not using, late at night for example, and is always late at night somewheres. I can set this up if you like. Also, we are fortunate this is cipher from the year 1610.'

'Why so?'

'Because there are many less, many *fewer*, printed texts that could be used as running key source. In fact, taking what your mother has informed me of the character of these people, I would venture that the text is almost certainly the English Bible. So, shall we begin?'

'Now?'

'Yes. Is there objection?'

'Well, it's kind of late,' said Crosetti.

'Does not matter. I sleep very little.'

Mary Peg said, 'I've offered Radeslaw Patty's old room.'

Crosetti finished his vodka and suppressed the usual shudder. He stood up and said, 'Well, you seem to have arranged everything, Mom. I guess I'll just go to bed.'

In the morning, Crosetti woke not to the buzz of his alarm but to the brisk knock and then the vigorous shoulder shaking of his mother. He blinked at her. 'What?'

'You have to read this.' She rustled the *New York Times* at him, opened at the pages devoted to local crime, corruption, and celebrity.

English Professor Found Murdered in Columbia Faculty Housing

This headline brought him up to full wakefulness. He rubbed the blur from his eyes and read the article, then read it again. It was a short one, the police being their usual closemouthed selves, but the reporter had used the word *torture*, and that was enough to start Crosetti's belly fluttering.

'Call Patty,' he said.

'I already did,' said Mary Peg, 'but I got voice mail. She'll call back. What do you think?'

'It doesn't look great. He disappears right after I sell him the manuscript, he's probably in England for a couple of months, maybe with Carolyn, maybe not, and then he comes back here and someone tortures him to death. Maybe the play manuscript really exists and he found out where it was and someone found out he knew and tortured him to get him to give it up.'

'Albert, that's a *movie*. Things like that don't happen to English professors in real life.'

'Then why was he tortured and killed? Not for his ATM password.'

'Maybe the mother of another silly boy he cheated took her revenge. From what we know about his character, he may have been mixed up in any number of sleazy deals.'

'Mom, believe me, movie or not, that's what went down. I need to get up.'

This was the signal for his mother to leave, and she did. Crosetti in the shower found his thoughts floating back to Rolly and the plot of his movie and the possibility that she could actually be the villainess of the piece, Brigid O'Shaughnessy as played by Mary Astor in *The Maltese Falcon*. His mother was wrong. Not only was life like a movie, movies were *why* life was like it was. Movies taught people how to behave, how to be a man, how to be a woman, what was funny and what was horrid. The people who made them had no idea of this, they were just trying to make money, but it was so.

And here they were in the *Falcon*, his next favorite after *Chinatown*, which was essentially a reimagining of the same movie, updated for the '70s, and why did he like movies about bad girls? *Bonnie and Clyde*, naturally, and *La Femme Nikita* and dozens more. He wondered what part he was playing, the dead Miles Archer, or the dead sea captain in the backstory, or Sam Spade. *You killed Miles and you're going over for it*. And, *I hope they don't hang you, precious, by that sweet neck. Yes, angel, I'm gonna send you over*. He had nearly the whole script by heart and now he said those lines to the showerhead with the Bogart hissing lisp and wondered whether, if it ever came to it, he could send Carolyn Rolly over, if she'd really helped kill Bulstrode. Or maybe he would be her sap. The mere imagination of it made his heart race. He turned the temperature of the water down a notch and let it run onto his heated face.

The First Ciphered Letter

My Lord It has now passed two weekes and some daies since I left your howse and have had passing success as I heere shal tell. Upon a Friday I left my lodging at the Vine in Bishopsgate in company with Mr Wales, who hath lain with mee all this tyme & a sore tryall hath it been, he beyng a verey coxcombe cracking sot & oft hazarded the safetie of oure enterpryse with hys hintes & vauntes in tap-room. Oft have I had to carrie hym to oure chamber with a buffett & threat; but when sober is craven & doth then as hee is bid under menace. Whilst not in cuppes, he hath instructed me divers popish tricks and sayinges as they doe in theyre masses & superstitious shewes, so that at need I may pass for one of theyre number.

Of the lodgeres heere the greater parte be drovers & some plaiers; of these last, half of them demi-papists & the rest plain damned atheists, scarce a Christian man among them. Soe we stride down Bishopsgate, hym pale & asweat from drinke & wants to stop heere & about for more sacke, but I doe prevent hym saying mind on oure business Mr Wales & I see feare well-marked in his face. Soe we arrive at the Swan in Leadenhalle Street where he saies W.S. frequently lieth. Mr Wales saies his fancie is to take roomes here and about, when he is not being tabled at some greate house. Formerly he dwelt near Silver Street but no longer & formerly he went every day to the Globe or Black-Friers play-howse but now he withdraweth som from those stewes as he hath grown rich off it, the bawd. A low company at the Swan, players punks decoygamesters & other rogues & Waley inquiring of the tapster is told Mr W.S. is up-stayres in a leased chamber, his habit seemingly to lay there the morning at his papers. So Waley do send a wench up to say there is a kinsman of his to see hym: which wase mee. Soon comes he in the room a man scannt-bearded a middling height bald-pated a little fat in a good doublet dead-spaniard coloured & hath the looke of a mercer. Mr Waley doth make us acquainted, Will Shakespur here is your cosen of Warwick, Dick Bracegirdle.

Saith he then it must be through your mother we are cosens for never was there such a name in Warwickshire & I say yes my mother was Arden born. At that he smyles & clapps me upon my backe & carries me to the table & calls for my pleasoure & the pot-boy bringeth us ale, but Mr Waley calls for canary though he wast not asked & calls some varlets he knows & a trull over & proffers them from his jack of wine. Now W.S. speakes me direct but I can not make out a word in three that he sayes, so strange are his accentes; seeing this he makes a halt saying thou wast not Warwick-bred & I say nay but born in London and passed my youth in Titchfield & he says he hast been oft at Titchfield a-visiting my lord of Southhampton & this he says in as plain a Hampshire voice as could have ben mine uncle Matthew, which amaz'd me much. But after I bethought me, he hath ben a playere, 'tis his arte to ape the speache of anie man.

Next we spake of our families and found that his dam was bred ancientlie from Sir Walter Arden of Park Hall as soe wase mine but his hath descent through Thomas that gentlemans eldest son not Richard as mine was & this contenteth hym much & I tell howe my grand-sire wase hanged for papistrie but they sayde traisoun & hee looketh grave sayinge aye mine nuncle was served soe in the olde quenes tyme. Soe wee further converse, hym demanding of me my storie & I tell hym it pretty much in truth, of my lyfe as a boy and prentice in the foundrie, & of the grete gonnes & the Dutch warres; nor have I ne'er met a man so content to heare another man out in fulle; for men chiefly love to tell of them selves & paint them selves out in finer colours than wast in lyfe; but hym not. Herein I spake but the trewth for Mr Piggott saith if wouldst tell a grete lye, guard it close with a thousand trew tales, so that it shalbe passed amongst theyre number. Bye now Mr Wales hath drunk a pint & more of beste canary & wase drunk withal & commenced to rail at W.S. sayinge he hath not employment these manie weekes with players less skilled than he uzed in his roome & W.S. saith nay, hath not Mr Burbadge manie tymes warned thee? If thou attend the playhouse as full o'canary as yon butt so you stumble and misremember your lines thou shalt lose thy place; and thou hast soe done; and thou hast indeed lost place, as wase promised; & I can do naught for thee, but here's an angelet for thee thou wast a goode Portia once. Yet Mr Wales spurns the coin; saith he, thou vain scut He see thee hangd & broke & e'en nowe are the snares set for thee that will & then I kick him in his ankle-bone & he cry out & draw or tries to &

I serve hym a blow on's heade with a stone-jack & down goes he in blodd. Now those friends he lately wined make to start affray with me & I stand to draw but W.S. calls sacke & safron cakes for the table & speakes so sweetlie & jestinglie to these low fellowes that they are assuaged & he has a wench & pot-boy to carry off Mr Wales to a settle & payeth alle & then he carries me out of that place saying let us goe to a more quiet howse for I wishe to speake further with thee.

Soe down Bishopsgate we walke, then on Cornhill & West Cheap toward Paul's & again he quaeres mee upon my lyfe & I doe as best I am able, recalling manie thinges I have forgot & when I tell how I wase late a smuckler he halts & hath me saye agen that worde which he sware he never before heard & writes it that moment with a wad penselle in a littel booke he carries & seems as well-pleazed as if he found a shillinge in the myre of the waye. Arrive at the sign of the Mer-mayde on Friday Street hard bye Paul's & were manie there that knew W.S. & greeted hym with affectioun & after greeting alle moste courteouslie he brought me to a corner bye the fyre that was I thinke his accustomed place: for the pot-boy brought hym smalle beere without the asking & a jack for mee as well & he presses mee agen to speake of my lyfe especially that at sea: & when he heard I wase on the Sea Adventurer & was wracked upon Bermoothes Isle he was much excited & plaisure shon on his face & takes up his little booke again & wrote much in it as I spake. He desired to know of the Carribans, theyre character & customes & did they eat the fleshe of men, & I sware hym I never met a Carriban in my lyfe, there are none in the Bermoothes: but I spake much of how we builded boates and scaped oure prison of that Isle & sayled to Virginia safe & of the Indians which the Englishe there living saye doe eat mens fleshe & are verie fierce salvages. He sayde he had reade accountes of this before now; but it were best to heere it from lips of one who was there & again questioned me upon the ship-wracke, viz: how the mariners comported & how the passengares of quality, did they waile & crie oute in feare of the present perils & I tell hym how oure boat-swaine cursed Governour Thom. Gates when he ventured upon the deck in the midst of the storm & chased hym down a hatch-waye with a rope's ende; for which the Admiral cried he should be whipped but was not for the ship strook upon the rock soon after.

Now as I tolde this tayle, W.S. calls to some who came in or were there alreadie: come & heere this tayle, this is my cosen who hath been to the New World & hath ben ship-wracked &c. Soon had we a goode company about us, sitting & standing. Some did not beleeve me thinking my tale a mere fardel of lyes such as mariners tell; yet W.S. spake up to these sayeing nay the man speakes fayre for there are no dragons nor monsters, nor yet water-spoutes, nor anie fantastique thinge, but onlie such perrils as shippes meet in theyre voyages; further saith he, I have read an accounte of the verie wrack of which he speakes & agrees in all particulares.

Thus was I justified before that assemblie. After mye tale was done, they sit about & talk, & this talk such as I nevere before heard & it is hard to recall for it is the jesting sorte that sticks not to the minde.

Or not my minde. It was verie bawdy, all prickes & cuntes, but disguized in othere & innocente speeche, & they said not a worde but another would twist that word into one lyke it & yet again & again, so that I never knew what they meant. This they account Witt: & one of these Mr Johnson can shew Witt in Latin & Greek & did so but few there comprehended his meaninges: yet laughed all the same & rated hym for a dull pedant. He is an other maker of wicked plaies thought greate by these wretches & seconde onlie to W.S.: except in his owne reckoninges first. A prowd conceited man & I thinke an arrant papiste & rayles much gainst the reformed faith & preacheres. W.S. now boastes of me that I wase in Flanderes fighting Don Spainiard & Mr Johnson saies he too was & quaeres me close what battels & seiges was I in & under what commander & when. Soe I answer hym; but when he findeth I was with the gonnes, he says pish that is not soldiers woork but mere cartage & dunnage & tells how he trayled his pyke before Flushinge & Zutfen & it was clare it ben a tale they all had hearde before & they mocketh hym & make witt of his pyke & sayde he had pricked more Flanders maydes than Spainiards with it; by which I thinke they meant his privy member. W.S. listeneth mainlie but when he speaketh all give hym attencioun. Thus, Mr Johnson vaunting his witte largelie with many Latin tagges & drinking largelie too & hadde a meate pye & bye & bye he lifts haunch & letts a great blaste of winde & W.S. upon the instant saies, so speakes a Batchelor of Artes, list well & learne;

and all laugh, even Mr Johnson. But I did not understand the jest.

Houres so passed I think til it grew neare darke without & W.S. saith to me Dick I have business at Black-Fryares playe-howse wilt come with me for I wish to speake privilie to you more. So I go with him & he asks of me what I will now for my trade, shall I goe back to sea? Quoth I nay I am done with it having been wracked soe & done with my travells nor have I taste anie more for warre, but to have some place whereat I could be sure of my meate & my bed a-nights & a goode fyre & make my fortune; for I had it in mynde to wed one daie. He saies what canst doe to earne thy bread Dick, besydes warre & smuckling & making of cannones? I sayde I wase clever with numbers & mought fynde worke as surveyoure of landes an I could fynde me a maistre. But here we come to the playe-howse after the play has done & the audience still comes forth, many rich-dressed in furs and brocades but also the common sorte & we must press through a croude of litters carriers horses servants groomes &c. who await. So through the greate room all ablaze with candels but one is snuffing them all ready & we pass to a smale room behinde the stage where are some men, one all in black velvet verie fine with paint still on's face; and two otheres apparent marchants & one little scriveninge sorte; & two stout fellowes armed with hangers & of these one hath no eares & t'other but one eie. By name, as I learned, the first, Dick Burbage, playere; John Hemmynge, a sharer in the Playeres company; Henry Watkins, a sharer in the House-keeping company; Nicholas Pusey, who kept the purse of the

King's Men Company & the accompte booke. Spade & Wyatt are the two men-at-armes, Spade hath the one eye. Save the laste pair, all these stood quarrelling calling each-other rogues cheateres &c.

W.S., comeing amongst them all, saith what betides gentlemen, why this affray? And soe the tale: of the monies payd each night. Players sharers must have such portion, Housekeeper sharers yet another & further fees out of the nightes purse variously figured. Mr Pusey hath a booke in which all monies are wrote down, yet I o'erlookinge it see it is done poorlie in the olde fashioun as it were some pettie fishmonger & not a greate enterpryse such as this theatre: for wickednesse yieldeth up much proffit. W.S. saith good Mr Pusey fetch thee thy board and jetones & we will see the figuring done before oure eies, are we not alle honest fellowes who can cut a figure with the beste; and made them smyle with this witte & off Mr Pusey goes. Now I inquire of W.S. what are the shares of each & how figured & I studie the accomptes booke laid open & look close at the scratchinges men maketh when they use compters & board to keep theyre talleyes & I see the faulte of castynge-off he hath made. Mr Pusey not retourning, Mr Burbage shouts for Spade to fetch him & whilst he is off I take my wad penselle and doe the needefull sums & divisiouns into partes. Soe returneth Spade with Mr Pusey in tow carrying his board with the compters dropping out of his sleaves; he hath been at drinke & now too fuddled to make sence of his papiers: which no man could any way make sence of even if sober. I spake up then upon the matter & shew them my reckoninges & discourse upon my methodes. Which were a wonder to them & I see W.S. smyling upon me: for he doates upon clevernesse in anie thinge. Further I saye gentlemen it is vain to quarrell upon who warrantes what sum, for with this accomptinge there be no waye under heaven you can saie what gaine you hath. Further, though I saye naught gainst this gentleman, who anie waye I knowe not, yet as thinges stand anie man could rob you all at will nor would you ever knowe of it. It is as if you walked blind-folde down Shoreditch at mid-night with full purses held in youre fingeres & expect not to have 'em snatched. Soe some further talke & twas agreed that I should be hyred to re-caste the accompte bookes in the Italian style with double-entreys & have charge of the divisioun of the shares: here W.S. saith he will stand bond for me as I am hys cosen.

After this W.S. carreys me to supper at the Mer-mayde & verie merrey with hys friendes as I have sayde before & later to bed in chamberes neare hys owne in a howse he leases neare to Black-Fryres & whilst theyre I laughed oute lowde & he quares why & I saye you intended Batchelour of Fartes, for hee hath broke winde then. He smileth, sayeing wee will make a witt of you Dick, one daye wilt thou catch the jest at the instant & not further in the weeke. To bed thereafter & methinkes I have done well enow for I am in the verie bosome of these wicked villeynes, which I think doth advance greatlie oure venture. With alle honour & my humble duty to yr. Lordship & may God protect you & blesse oure enterprizes, from London this Friday the 10th Januarye 1610 Richard Bracegirdle

11

Someone once said, Paul Goodman I think, that stupidity was a character defense and had little to do with intelligence, one reason the so-called best and brightest got us into Vietnam and why people who are smart enough to accumulate huge piles of wealth persist in doing things that get them major jail time. *Mit der Dummheit kämpfen Götter selbst vergebens*, as, reportedly, my maternal grandmother used to say, quoting Schiller: against stupidity the gods themselves struggle in vain. In any case, it was stupid to tell my son about the gangsters and then my wife – no, wait, the *font* of the stupidity was not *immediately* surrendering the Bracegirdle manuscript, after which no gangster would have had any interest in me or mine.

As I've said, Amalie is ordinarily of saintly mien, but like Our Lord when confronted with hypocrisy or injustice she has the ability to generate anger sufficient to wither fig trees. After she had wormed the whole tale out of me, in horrible little snips mixed with futile lies, I got the full blast of it, such that the resources of even her perfectly fluent English for insulting my intelligence were exhausted and she had to switch over to German: *saudumm, schwachsinnig, verblödet, verkorkst, vertrottelt, voll abgedreht*, and *dumm wie die Nacht finster sein*, to recall just a few. German is rich in such expletives, and they often filled the air of my childhood home. 'Stupid as the night is dark' was in fact one of Mutti's favorites. Finally: *du kotzt mich an*, which is quite vulgar and means roughly, 'you make me puke.' With that, I was out on the street. I had received the reaming in near silence, conscious of a perverse pleasure in having at last violated the holy patience of my spouse. I called Rashid, he arrived in minutes, he stepped out to open the door for me (something that Omar has been told not to bother with), and I noticed he was looking upward and I did too as *Paphiopedilum hanoiensis* came flying from the top floor of Amalie's house, just missing my car and smashing its new pot on the street. I had made her both angry and violent – a good night's work and another down payment on my condo in Hell.

That, as it turned out, was the *best* part of the evening. After Rashid dropped me off and I stuck my key in the street door I noticed that it swung open before I'd had a chance to turn the lock. Someone had jammed the latch with a bit of duct tape. Heart in mouth I raced up the flights. The door to my loft hung open. Inside, in the narrow hallway that leads to the bedrooms, I found Omar. He was on his hands and knees groaning and seemingly examining a bright red oval on the polished oak floor, for blood was dripping down either side of his face from a wound in the back of his shaved skull. I lifted him up and into an armchair and obtained a clean dishcloth, a basin of water, and a bag of ice from the kitchen. When I had the wound washed and the bleeding under control, I asked him what had happened. I recall feeling an unnatural calm as I sat there listening to his groggy mumbles – in Arabic to begin with – a calm that recalled my army days as a medic, when the wounded were unloaded in large numbers from the dust-off helicopters after a firefight: the first moment you wanted to run away screaming and then came the unnatural calm that enabled you to work on mangled boys. I wanted to run screaming now through my loft to see what had happened to Miranda, but I made myself sit and ask and listen. There was not much to tell. He had heard a woman's shout and a heavy thump and come running in from the living room where he had been watching cable news. That's all he remembered. He didn't see anyone. Miranda, of course, was gone, as was the original of the Bracegirdle manuscript.

I found Detective Murray's card in my wallet and called him and left an urgent message and then dialed 911. After this we had the sort of confused interaction of many strangers, of the sort that's always cut away in television dramas about crime and emergency, but which in real life absorbs many frustrating hours. Paramedics removed Omar, although he insisted upon walking down the stairs under his own power, and I entertained the police, first a pair of uniformed officers and then a pair of detectives, Simoni and Harris. They examined the front door of my loft and declared that the lock showed signs of picking, which made the affair more serious, not so much a domestic thing, which is what I imagined they thought when they arrived – a bleeding man, a missing woman, rich people, unholy liaisons . . . still, they couldn't keep the snarkiness out of their voices. I imagined they were searching for some witty remark, of the sort that the scriptwriters used to put in the mouth of Jerry Orbach on the old *Law & Order*. They wanted to know who Omar was and where he came from and what was his relationship with the missing woman; and there was Omar's pistol to explain, and my idea of the threat against Ms Kellogg and what had happened out on the street with the maybe Russian thugs. Ms Kellogg was staying here with you? Why wasn't she at a hotel? Was she your girlfriend, Mr Mishkin?

No, she was not; no, I did not know why anyone would have taken her; they only wanted the manuscript. Why did they want the manuscript, Mr Mishkin? Was it very valuable? Not as such, but some people thought it could lead to something very valuable. Oh, like a treasure map? Here the eye rolling started, the smirking. And here I said something like, 'You can smirk all you want to, but a man was tortured to death to reveal the whereabouts of that thing, and now a woman has been kidnapped, and you're still treating the whole thing as a joke.' And then we had a discussion about Professor Bulstrode.

In fairness, this was the sort of thing that urban police detectives rarely encounter. They *wanted it* to be a domestic with elements of rich-guy looniness. The police covered surfaces with black fingerprint powder, took many photos, took Omar's gun and samples of the blood he had shed in my service, and left, saying they would be in touch. As soon as they were gone I went out myself, to the garage on Hudson where Rashid had parked the Lincoln, and drove to St Vincent's Hospital to check on Omar. I was unsurprised to see the two detectives there, and I couldn't get in to see him until they had finished extracting the nothing he knew. The hospital wanted to keep him overnight for observation because of the concussion, and so I left him with the assurance that I would contact his family and that he must not worry about the expenses.

I made that unpleasant call from my cell phone and I was just putting it away when it buzzed again and it was Miranda.

'Where are you? Are you all right?' was naturally (and

stupidly) the first thing out of my mouth, although I knew she could not answer the first question and that the answer to the second was dreadfully patent.

'I'm fine.' In a voice that was not fine at all.

'Where are you?' *Stupid!*

'I don't know. They put a bag over my head. Look, Jake, you can't call the police. They said I should call you and tell you that.'

'All right, I won't,' I lied.

'Is Omar all right? They hit him . . .'

'Omar is fine. What do they want? They have the goddamned letter – why did they have to take you?'

'They want the other letters, the ones written in cipher.'

'I don't understand – I gave you everything that your uncle gave me. I don't know anything about any cipher.'

'No, they were there in the original find. There's a woman here, Carolyn – I think they're holding her too . . .'

'A Russian?'

'No, an American. She says that there were coded letters in the package but someone didn't deliver them like they were supposed to.'

'Who didn't?'

'It's not important. These people say they own the documents, they say they paid my uncle cash for them, a lot of cash, and that he tried to cheat them. Jake, they're going to . . .'

Actually it's too painful to try and reconstruct this dialogue. We were both yelling into the phone (although I am ordinarily careful never to raise my voice into a cell phone as so many of my fellow citizens do, so that the streets often appear to be taken over by the mad; and I often wonder what the truly mad think of this) and someone cut her off in midsentence. The burden of the conversation was clear; unless I came up with some ciphered letters mentioned by Bracegirdle they would handle her as they had her uncle, and also that, if they thought that the police were involved, they would dispose of her instantly.

Gunshots in the fog, three flat, concussive noises from the lake, and there is definitely the sound of a motor craft, an insectile buzz that sounds as if it comes from a long way off. Hunters? Is this duck season? I have no idea. In case not, I have just reloaded and cocked my pistol, a comforting activity I find. I should have said before this that Mickey's cabin is at the extreme southern end of Lake Henry. There is a detailed hydrographic chart of the lake framed on the living room wall, and on it you can see that it was originally two lakes. Around 1900, the summering plutocrats who owned the land dammed an outlet and the water rose and left a string of islands extending out from the eastern shore, an excellent place to play pirates, Mickey has informed me, but you can't drive a boat of any size between them because of hidden rocks. You get to this house either via New Weimar and a long slow drive down a third-rate road and a further drive on a gravel one (which is what I did) or you can get off the thruway at Underwood and take a short drive on a good road to the town of Lake Henry at the lake's extreme northern tip and get into your mahogany speedboat and, after a twelve-mile jaunt, arrive in more style, which is the route Mickey and his family almost always traveled. The land route is actually shorter by a little over an hour, but a lot less comfortable. If I were a stylish sort of thug, I would rent or buy a motor craft, come south from the town, whack my guy, and then on the way back dump the corpse, suitably weighted, into the lake, which is nearly sixty feet deep at its greatest depth, not quite farther than did ever plummet sound, but deep enough.

Examining my diary for the following day I find that the morning meetings are scratched out and I remember that I called in after a nearly sleepless night and spoke with Ms Maldonado. I asked her to cancel these appointments and reschedule them and asked her one important question, to which the answer was yes. Ms Maldonado makes two copies of absolutely everything, she is the Princess of Xerox, and it turned out that she had indeed made copies of the Bracegirdle manuscript. Then Omar called me begging to be rescued from the hospital, so I went and got him. He took the wheel gladly, looking in his white medical turban more like his desert ancestors than he usually did. As he proudly informed me, he had another gun; I did not wish to inquire further.

At my direction, we picked up the Bracegirdle copies at my office and proceeded north on the East River Drive to Harlem. Although I questioned him again about the previous night's events, he could add nothing, except an apology for having been cold-cocked and losing his charge. He could not imagine how someone had got into the loft and into position to surprise him in that way, and neither could I – another mystery added to those already accumulated in this affair.

Our destination that morning was a group of tenement buildings on 151st Street off Frederick Douglass Boulevard that my brother, Paul, owns, or rather operates, since he doesn't officially own anything. He picked them up as burned husks at a tax sale some years ago when buildings of this type were burning almost daily and has renovated them into what he refers to as an urban monastery. Paul is a Jesuit priest, a perhaps surprising revelation, since the last time I mentioned him he was a jailed thug. He is still something of a thug, which is why I went to visit him after Miranda disappeared. He has a profound understanding of violent evil.

I suppose that one of the great shocks of my life was the discovery that Paul was smart, probably smarter than me in many ways. Many families assign roles to their members, and in our family Miriam was the dumb beauty, I was the smart one, and Paul was the tough one, the black sheep. He never did a day's work in school, dropped out at seventeen, and as I mentioned, did a twenty-six-month jolt in Auburn for armed robbery. You can imagine the fate of a handsome, blond, white boy in Auburn. The usual choice is to be raped by everyone or raped exclusively by one of the big yard bulls. Paul chose the latter course as being healthier and safer and submitted to this fellow's attentions until he had fashioned a shank, whereupon he fell upon the yard bull one night while he slept and stabbed him a remarkable number of times (although fortunately not quite to death). Paul spent the rest of his prison time in solitary, along with the child molesters and Mafia informants. He became a reader there, which I know about because every month I used to make up a package of books for him in response to his requests. In two years I observed in amazement his progression from pulp fiction, to good fiction, to philosophy and history, and finally theology. By the time he made parole he was reading Küng and Rahner.

Upon his release, he immediately joined the army, having no other prospects and desiring an education. This was at the height of the Vietnam War and they were not being too particular. I suppose the grand-paternal Stieff genes must have kicked in because he proved to be an exemplary soldier: airborne, Ranger, Special Forces, Silver Star. He spent his two tours largely back in the Shans, as we used to say, in the contested region where Laos, Vietnam, and Cambodia come together, running with a band of montagnards just like Marlon Brando in *Apocalypse Now*. This is virtually Paul's only comment on that experience: *it was just like the movie*.

Strangely enough, the horror, did not make him into a monster but into something like a saint. He went to St John's on the G. I. Bill and then signed up for the Jesuits. When he told me this I thought he was joking, I mean the notion of Paul as a priest, much less a Jesuit, but it goes to show that you can never tell about one's near and dear. I was, as I say, totally flabbergasted.

In any event, he returned to New York with the idea of building a kind of settlement house in a blighted neighborhood, and so he did, but being Paul and considering the social experiment tradition of the Society of Jesus, the thing had a certain twist; he was easily distinguishable from Jane Addams. I say he was a saint, but he also remained a thug. There are a number of these types in the calendar of the saints, including, for one, the founder of Paul's own order. Paul's theory is that our civilization is collapsing into a dark age and that the advancing edges of this are visible in urban ghettos. He says dark ages are all about forgetting civilization and its arts and also the increasing reluctance of the ruling classes to pay for civic life. This sealed the fate of Rome, he claims. He doesn't think that the ghetto needs uplift, however, but rather that when the crash comes, the poor will survive better than their masters. They need less, he says, and they are more charitable, and they don't have to unlearn as much. This was why Jesus preferred them. Yes, quite crazy; but when I observe the perfect helplessness of my fellow citizens of the middle class and higher, our utter dependence on electricity, cheap gas, and the physical service of unseen millions, our reluctance to pay our fair share, our absurd gated enclaves, our 'good buildings,' and our incompetence at any task other than the manipulation of symbols, I often think he has a point.

So Paul has constructed, under the guise of a mission church and a school, a kind of early medieval abbey. It consists of three buildings, or rather two buildings and the empty space between them once occupied by a tenement totally gutted by the fire and later demolished. This space is fronted on the street by a wall and a gate and through this gate walked Omar and I that day. It is always open. (We left the limo on the street. Such is the authority of the place that I was sure no one would molest it.) The footprint of the former building is now a sort of cloister, with a vegetable garden, a little terrace with a fountain, and a playground. One of the buildings is a K-12 school, partially residential, and the other consists of offices, dormitories, and workshops. There is a L'Arche community on site, which is a group that lives with and cares for severely disabled people, and there is also a part-time medical clinic and a Catholic Worker soup kitchen. The place was its usual chaos: the halt, mad, and crippled doing their thing, clumps of robed rehabilitated gangsters working at various tasks, and neatly uniformed schoolchildren racing about, quite the medieval scene. Omar always feels entirely at home here.

I came to Paul on this occasion because his intelligence has a devious edge to it, rather like that of our dad. I am an infant in comparison, and although it often galls me to depend on my brother in this way, I occasionally do. He says it is good for my soul.

We found him in the basement of the school building discussing a boiler with some contractors. He was wearing a blue coverall and was quite filthy, although Paul makes even dirt look good. He is somewhat shorter than I am but far more elegantly built. To my eye he has not changed much from what he looked like when I picked him up at the airport on his return from the army nearly twenty-five years ago, except his hair is longer on top. He still resembles Rutger Hauer in *Blade Runner* or an SS recruiting poster. He gave us a big smile, white teeth gleaming in the dim basement, and embraced both of us. Leaving the contractors to their work with a few more words, he ran us up to his office, a tiny cramped room with a view of the terrace/cloister and the playground, and of course he wanted to know about Omar's head. I think he likes Omar somewhat more than he likes me. No, that's a lie, but let it sit there on the page. Paul loves me, and it drives me nuts. I am not at all nice to him. I can't help it. I think it is Izzy's introjection boiling up from inside me, full of contemptuous disdain.

After Paul got the whole story out of Omar, and after he'd heard a good deal of tedious data about Omar's family and the suffering of his relations on the West Bank, Omar excused himself for his noon prayers. Just after he left, an exquisite brown boy trotted in with a message, looking remarkably fine in his school uniform, which is a navy blazer, gray slacks, white shirt, and a white-and-black striped tie. When he had gone I said, rolling my eyes, 'Getting any of that now? Peachy buttocks glowing in the dim sacristy lamplight . . .'

'Elderly nuns satisfy my residual lusts, thank you,' he said, still smiling. 'And speaking of sexual excess, you seem to have got yourself in a jam again over a woman. Who is this Miranda?'

'No one special, just a client. I only had her stay at my place because some people seemed to be following her.'

'Uh-huh. You know, Amalie called me this morning. She seemed pretty upset.'

'Well, gosh, Paul, I'm sorry Amalie's upset. I know! Why don't *you* marry her. Then you can be all perfect together and I can sink further into depravity. Me and Miri –'

'Miri's worried about you too. What's all this about Russian gangsters?'

Another thing that drives me crazy is my family talking about me behind my back. One reason I try to live a blameless life (the sex part aside) is to reduce the zone of gossip, but clearly I have failed in this. I suppressed whatever I might have felt at the time because the entire purpose of my visit was to seek Paul's counsel in this affair. No one I know has a wider network of contacts at all levels of society in New York, from street bums to the mayor. So I gave him the whole tale – Bulstrode, the Bracegirdle manuscript, the murder, the mugging, the conversation with Miri (although he knew about that already from her), meeting Miranda, her abduction, and the phone call.

He listened more or less in silence and when I'd finished, he made a rotating motion with his hand and said, 'And . . . ?'

'And what?'

'Did you? With Miss Kellogg? No, don't bother to lie, I can see it on your face.'

'And this is the most important thing to you? That I fucked this woman? The murder, the kidnapping, that's all irrelevant compared with where I stick my schlong?'

'No, but where you stick your schlong seems to determine the course of your life, and messes up the lives of a number of people I love. Hence my interest.'

'Oh, I thought that fucking was the *only* thing the Church was interested in. Or were you not speaking *ex cathedra*?'

'Yeah, you persist in thinking lust is your problem. Lust is not your problem, speaking *ex cathedra*, and in a dozen or so years it'll have taken care of itself. It's a miserable little sin after all. No, your problem is acedia and it always has been. The refusal to do necessary spiritual work. You always took on the responsibility for every bad thing that happened to our family, probably including World War II, all by yourself . . .'

'You were in jail.'

'Yes, but irrelevant. God wasn't in jail but you didn't ask for any help in that direction. No, you took it all on and failed, and you never forgave yourself, and so you think you're beyond all forgiveness, and that gives you the license to hurt all the people who love you because after all, poor Jake Mishkin is so far outside the pale, so bereft of all hope of heaven, that anyone who loves him must be delusional and thus not worth considering. And why are you grinning at me, you turd? Because you've made me say the same thing I always say when you come up here and now you can forget it again, even though you know it's true. Sloth. The sin against hope. And you know it's going to kill you someday.'

'Just like Mutti? Do you really think so?' A high-pitched grinding sound came from the machine shop below, where they repaired bicycles. He waited until it stopped and said, 'Yes, I do. As you know. Like the man said, God who made us without our help will not save us without our consent. Either you'll cry mercy and forgive and be forgiven, or die the death.'

'Yes, Father,' I said, looking piously upward.

He sighed, tired of the pathetic old game I make him play. I was tired of it too but could not keep my clawed fingers away from the unendurable, unsalvable itch. He said, 'Yes, you've manipulated me into preaching and you have therefore won yet again. Congratulations. Meanwhile, what are we going to do about this problem of yours?'

'I don't know. That's why I came to see you.'

'You think this Russian, Shvanov, is involved?'

'As muscle, yes. But I can't figure out who's behind it.'

'Why bother? The manuscript is gone, and this woman disappearing seems like a matter for the cops.'

'I was told not to involve the cops. She said they'd kill her.'

'And you feel it's your responsibility to rescue her.'

'I said I'd protect her and I didn't; so, yes I do.'

'You want to continue the affair. You're in love.'

'What the hell does that matter? She's a human being in mortal danger.'

He steepled his hands against his chin and gave me an uncomfortably penetrating stare, which is what he does now instead of kicking my ass. Then he said, 'Well, of course I'll help in any way I can. I have a couple of contacts down at Police Plaza. I'll make some calls, get some background on this guy Shvanov, and also get the word out that this is serious –'

'No, don't do that! Don't involve the cops at all. You have other kinds of contacts.'

'I do. All right, I'll see what the street has to say.'

'Thank you. The main thing I'm worried about is Amalie and the kids. If they want to put more pressure on me . . .'

'I'll take care of that too,' he replied, after a brief considerate pause. This, of course, is what I had come for. Paul knows a lot of tough kids, what they call original gangsters, in that neighborhood, and he has an odd relationship with them. He thinks they're exactly like the Germanic or Slavic barbarians that the missionaries who were sent out in the dark centuries met and converted – proud, violent, hungry for they know not what. In the early days of the mission Paul had to literally fight people on the street to demonstrate that he was tougher than they were, which he was. That he had a rep, that he was known to have stabbed people in prison, didn't hurt. That he had personally killed more people than all of them put together, and looked it, was another plus.

Also, Paul claimed that compared with the montagnards, New York gangbangers weren't very tough. None of them had ever missed a meal and if imprisoned had been housed in what would have seemed luxurious spas to the average Hmong. He said his guys over there could have eaten all the Crips, Bloods, and Gangster Disciples for breakfast. And their pathetic bravado inspired compassion in him rather than the terror common among the better classes. (Paul is not afraid of anything mortal, nor was he at ten.) But he took them seriously as tribes, and like the Jesuits of old he targeted their leaders, the most violent of the violent, and over time had come to a concordat of sorts with them, which was that there was to be no dope sold and no whores run within a certain pale around Paul's buildings, and that people fleeing the vengeance of the street could find sanctuary within. Some few of the street lords have actually been converted. A larger number sent their children or their younger brothers and sisters to be educated at his school. It was a very Dark Ages arrangement and perfectly natural to a man like my brother.

Now I could see that Paul, having made his decision to help, couldn't wait to get me out of there. Not a comfortable man, my brother, sort of like Jesus in Matthew, always at the run, impatient with the apostles, conscious of the shortness of the time, the need to get the successors up and ready for when the founder must leave the scene. He just turned away and started talking to some boys, and so I collected Omar and made my grateful exit.

In the car we headed west and south until the Columbia campus hove into view. I generally have a pretty good idea of Mickey Haas's schedule and so I knew that Thursdays he held office hours all morning. I called him and he was in and yes he'd be glad to have lunch with me, at the faculty club for a change. I have always found the dining room on the fourth floor of Faculty House at Columbia one of the more pleasant places to lunch in New York: a beautifully proportioned airy chamber, with one of the best views of the city from its high windows, and a perfectly adequate prix fixe buffet, but Mickey prefers our usual Sorrentino's. I think it's because he likes to get somewhat drunk at our lunches and prefers to do this out of sight of his peers. Perhaps he also enjoys having my limo sent for him.

Just before we reached the club, my cell rang and it was my sister.

'You were right,' she said. 'Osip would really like to meet you.'

'That was fast,' I said. 'He must owe you a favor.'

'Osip doesn't owe favors, Jake, he collects them. As a matter of fact, *he* called me and asked me to set it up. That's not a good sign.'

'I'm sure it'll be fine,' said I, not at all sure. 'Where and when?'

'Do you know Rasputin's? On Lafayette?'

'You have to be kidding. That's like meeting John Gotti in a Godfather's Pizza place.'

'What can I say? Osip has a sense of humor. Anyway, he says he'll be there after ten tomorrow night. I would say "be careful," if it weren't too banal for words. But you *will be* careful, won't you? If not, I assume you'll want to rest beside Mutti in Green-Wood. I'll send the most vulgar wreath imaginable.'

*

I recall that Mickey and I had the roast beef and shared a bottle of Melville cabernet, so appropriate, he joked, for a professor of English. Mickey was actually in a pretty good mood, and I asked him if his financial position had improved at all and he said it had: here followed a blizzard of information about hedge funds and REITs and commodities trading that went in one ear and out the other. Sensing my disinterest, he politely changed the subject and asked me what was new with me. In answer, I drew out the copy of Bracegirdle's letter I had picked up from Ms M. that morning and slid it across the table. 'Only this,' I said.

'This is it? The Bulstrode thing? Good God!' Naturally he could read the Jacobean scrawl as easily as you read Times New Roman, and he began to do so at once, rapt, and ignored the waiter when he came to ask about dessert, a unique occurrence in my experience. Twenty or so minutes passed as he turned the pages, occasionally making a quiet exclamation – 'Holy shit!' – and similar while I drank coffee and gazed at the diners and played eye games with an attractive brunette at another table. My inner theater was showing what it usually did after a meeting with my brother: a thoroughgoing denigration of him and his works, who did he think he was playing the great blue-eyed white god descending upon the ghetto unasked to bring salvation to the darkies! It was absurd, nearly obscene, nearly Nazi in its colossal arrogance. The sad pleasure of this shadow play ceased only when Mickey beside me said 'Wow!' loud enough to draw the attention of the brunette and several others.

He pounded the papers with a stubby digit. 'Do you realize what this is?'

'Sort of. Miranda read it and explained its value, although I'm sure I don't have a scholar's sense of it.'

'Miranda Kellogg? She's seen this?' He seemed a little upset.

'Well, yes. She's the legal owner of the original.'

'But you have custody of it at present?'

So I related the events of the past twenty-four hours. He was stunned. 'That's terrible,' he said. 'Absolutely catastrophic!'

'Yes, I'm extremely concerned about her.'

'No, I meant the manuscript, the *original*,' he said, with a callousness worthy of a lawyer. 'Without that, this is valueless,' he added, tapping the pile of copy paper again. 'My God, we have to get it back! Do you have any idea what's at stake?'

'People are always asking me that, and my answer is "not really." Ammunition in some literary squabble?' My tone was cold but he ignored it, for this was a new Mickey, no more the laid-back gentleman-scholar, amusingly contemptuous of how his confreres struggled to climb the greasy poles of academe. He had the fire in his eye. The new Mickey expatiated upon the colossal academic value of Mr B.'s screed; I listened, as to someone describing the details of a complex and tedious surgical procedure.

At length I put in, 'So it's a big deal if Shakespeare was a Catholic?'

'It's a big deal if Shakespeare was *anything*. I already went through this with you. We know almost *nothing* about the interior life of the greatest writer in the history of the human race. Look . . . just one example of thousands, and bears on the matter at hand. A woman has recently written a book, she's an amateur scholar, but she's certainly done her research, and in this book she claims that nearly the whole corpus of Shakespeare's work, in particular the plays, is an elaborate coded apology for Catholicism and a plea to the monarch of the day for relief of the disabilities that Catholics then suffered. I mean she gives literally *hundreds* of heterodox readings arguing this theory in reference to all the plays, *and* she also proposes the protective hand of powerful contemporary Catholic peers to explain why Shakespeare wasn't called to account for writing this easily readable code for the public stage. I mean it's a complete and original picture explaining nearly all of Shakespeare's work. How about that?'

I shrugged and asked, 'So – is she right?'

'I don't know! Nobody knows!' This a semishout, provoking more looks from the peers. I could now see why Mickey might hesitate to dine here. 'That's the fucking *point*, Jake! She *could* be right. Or someone could write a book demonstrating through just as thorough an analysis of the same plays that Shakespeare was gay, a good Protestant faggot. Or a monarchist. Or a lefty. Or a woman. Or the Earl of Oxford. That's the basic, intractable problem with *all* Shakespeare studies that bear on intent or biography, and now this!' Tap tap tap. 'If genuine . . . I say *if* genuine, it will be the greatest single event in Shakespeare studies since . . . I don't know, since *forever*. Since the field was born as a rational entity in the eighteenth century.'

'This letter does that?'

'Not as such. It's just the first taste, the first tiny opening taste of paradise. But Jake' – he lowered his voice and moved his mouth closer to my ear in a near parody of a man seeking confidentiality – 'Jake, if this guy *spied* on William Shakespeare, if he wrote down reports, if he described Shakespeare's life the way he described his own miserable life . . . oh, Jesus, that would be something *real*. Not just speculation based on the use of images in the second act of *King* fucking *Lear*, but actual data. Who he saw, what he said, his ordinary speech, what he believed, what he ate and drank, was he a big tipper, how long was his dick . . . Jake, you have no fucking idea.'

'Well, I have some idea what that manuscript play would be worth.' He rolled his eyes and made a show of fanning his face. 'Oh, *that*. We are not going to even think about *that*. No, I will be creaming in my panties if we can even get hold of those ciphered letters he mentions. No wonder old Bulstrode was playing it so close, the poor bastard. Not to speak ill of the dead, but you might've thought that after all I did for him he would've given me a little peek when this fell into his hands.'

'It must've driven him crazy. He didn't say anything to his niece either.'

'Yes. Poor woman. You don't have any idea where these spy letters could be?'

'I don't, but what I want to know now, and maybe you can help me here, is why a Russian gangster is interested in them enough to commit a federal crime. He's probably not in the Modern Language Association.'

'An organization brimful of gangsters and worse,' said Mickey, smiling. 'But I take your point.' He paused, and a peculiar dreamy expression came over his face for just an instant, as if he had just inhaled a mouthful of opium, eyes partly closed, as if contemplating a paradise just out of reach. He came back, however, with an almost audible snap and said, 'Unless . . .'

I knew just what he meant. 'Yeah, unless Bulstrode discovered something on his trip to England that established the existence of the . . . Item. The Item, let's say, really exists, and these guys, or someone hiring these guys, knows about it and wants it. But it turns out that the ciphered letters are part of the trail that leads to it. Do we even know if they were with this letter?'

'You're asking me?'

'Well, yeah. You know more about all this stuff than anyone else but Bulstrode himself and possibly Miranda, both of whom are currently out of reach. Obviously, someone offered Bulstrode a manuscript. What if there were others in the bundle, and he declined to buy them?'

'Impossible! He would've sold both his grandmothers for a package like that.'

'Yes, but absent a bull market in grandmothers, how much would he have had to offer, say for just the Bracegirdle original?'

'I don't know . . . fifty grand, maybe, if the seller wanted instant cash. At auction, God knows what it would have fetched. Maybe twice that, three times . . .'

'And did Bulstrode have that kind of cash?'

'Hell, no. He was skinned by the lawyers over that phony *Hamlet* business. I had to advance him money on his salary when he came over here. Wait a minute . . . !'

'Yeah, right. If he didn't have serious money, how did he get hold of the manuscript? Two possibilities. Either he paid a far lower price to an owner who didn't know what it was, in which case, when the seller was conned into thinking that the Bracegirdle wasn't worth that much, and if he had the ciphers, he didn't offer them to Bulstrode at all. Or, Bulstrode sees the whole package and the seller knows the real value and he wants major bucks for it. So why doesn't Bulstrode go to the Folger? Or to his good pal Dr Haas for that matter?'

A bitter laugh here. 'Because he knew I was broke too?'

'Did he? But let's say it was because the provenance is shaky. The seller is something of a crook himself, but he knows the value of these letters as a key to something even more gigantic. So Bulstrode goes to Mr Big and sells him on a deal – help me buy the package and we'll find the most valuable item on earth and –'

'That's ridiculous! I mean, sure, Andrew could have lowballed a naive seller, but he couldn't possibly have known any Mr Bigs. He hardly knew anyone in New York.'

I thought about this and agreed that Mickey was probably right. Miranda had said much the same thing. I thought for a while and said, 'Then there has to be a tertium quid.'

'You mean someone who knew the value of what Bulstrode had and also knew gangsters? And wanted the big payoff. Are there people like that?'

'Yes,' I said. 'I'm a person like that. I know a distinguished professor of English literature, you, and I also know some hard boys. It's probably not as uncommon as we'd like to believe. Stockbroker types never seem to have trouble finding a thug to knock off their wives. Or vice versa. In any case, Bulstrode may have gone to this person and confided that he had the Item within reach. This person, for whatever reason, lets the hard boys know about it. Bulstrode goes to England and comes back. He knows he's being followed, so he stashes the package with me. Then the gangsters grab him and torture him enough to get my name out of him, which is why I'm in their sights and why Miranda was taken, and why they want to get their hands on the ciphers.'

'Which neither she nor you have, since Bulstrode didn't. Do we know they even exist?'

'Mr Tertium obviously does. Tell me, did Bulstrode ever mention to you the name of the person who sold him the manuscript?'

'Never. Christ! Why *didn't* he come to me? It would've been the easiest thing in the world to arrange a purchase at any reasonable price.'

Here I told him what Miranda had related to me about

Bulstrode's shame over the fake *Hamlet* affair and the extent of his paranoia. Mickey shook his head. 'That poor ass! God, he'd be alive now if he had. But, you know, it shouldn't be all that hard to learn the name of the seller. Andrew had an appointment diary. Or he could've given the seller a check. The trouble is that his diary and checkbook are still being held by the cops.'

'Yes. But there may be ways around that. It occurs to me that I'm the lawyer for the Bulstrode estate and the lawyer for its heiress. I'll see whether the cops will let me examine that material.'

And so on and so on. I'm fairly sure that's where the idea of checking on who sold the papers came up. After I left Mickey, I received a call on my cell phone from Detective Murray returning mine of the previous night. He had, of course, heard about the break-in, theft, and abduction and wanted to talk to me. I concocted a story for him. There had been no abduction, I said. Ms Kellogg had called me and said she was fine, that she had left the apartment before the assault, that she had the papers in her possession. They were her property, technically, and there was really no reason for us to get alarmed because a grown woman had decided to take a hike. He said that was a good attitude because there was clearly no connection at all between the brouhaha around my old papers and the death of Andrew Bulstrode, the investigation of which was closed as of today. He'd been killed by a nineteen-year-old homosexual prostitute named Chico Garza, who was in police custody and had made a full confession, and it was just as they'd thought, a sexual game gone sour. The boy had been caught trying to use Bulstrode's Visa card. So he had been right, I agreed, using a relieved tone. A street mugging, an attempted burglary and assault, a missing woman: all coincidences. I apologized for doubting him, and he graciously replied that citizens, taught by the plots of thrillers, usually tried to complexify things, while *real* crimes were typically stupid and simple, as here. Happens all the time.

I agreed that it probably did and presumed that, since the investigation was completed, there would be no objection to me, as the lawyer in the case, looking into some of his papers on estate business? No objection at all, he said.

The Second Ciphered Letter

My Lord, be assured I am well rebuked by your cypher of 16th Jany & will endeavour to pleaze you better hereafter by writing briefer: for as I am but recently come to this intelligenceing I know not what to put and what is dross & unworthy of yr. worshipes regard. Oure strategem proceedeth thus: upon the Princesse Elizabeth her name-daye as you foretold, there was projected celebratioun & feastinge at White-Hall & we are commanded to playe Much Ado abt. Nothinge & some masques of Mr Johnson. Since the tyme that last I wrote I have become of the company, not a clerke of the bookes onlie but also as indeed all the otheres are too a factotum: I lift & carry, paint & build & beyond these mechanickal labours I also serve to swell a scene, as soldier, attendant-lord, &c. with trumperie robes, basinnets, tinne swords, &c. at perill of my sowle I think, but God will comprehend it and forgive, for I doe not give speche upon the stage. In these weekes I am much with W.S., for he favours me & keepes me at his howse by Black-Friers. On the daye aforementioned I am to be of the Watch & also Lord Attendant to Don Pedro; but verie neare the houre of performance oure Mr Ussher falls from the stage by mischance & can not stand & soe I must play the Boy as well, that is a speaking parte, but two lines, & I sware I would rather face the tercio of Seville in full battel than speke before an audience & this a royal one too; but I did wel enow though I quaked.

The King falleth asleep in Act III which they tell me he doeth always but the Quene & Princesse clap full lustilie & after-ward wee are fed cakes & malmsey wine in a side chamber. Now comes in a noble lord Sir Robert Veney, dressed verie fine & he is of my lord the Earl of Rochester's partie. He hath speche with W.S. & Mr Burbadge & then W.S. beckons me with a confuzed looke upon his face & I go as bid & this Veney carryes me a little way across the chamber & askes me if I know what is afoot. Yea, sir, saies I: for you have told me of it in youre cypher, my Lord, & he giveth me privilie (but onlie seeminge privilie) a sealed letter & he saith boy I would see feare upon thy face now, as one seeing a ghost. And he departs & I thrust the letter into my bosom & it takes no schill at playinge for me to tremmble & shew a timorous face.

Then they all wished to learn what the Lord Veney hath sayde to me, but I would not, sayinge tis a private matter & they all of them mock me, what private matter doth a lord have with lykes of thee save venerie & they make much witt on this, grasping theyre cods & cavorting & callinge me Lord Veneries punk. But I see W.S. doth not join, or but a littel, & regards me some thinge solemn.

Next daye in Black-Friers he cometh in to the closet where I sit alone at my countynge bookes & sitts him down: quoth he Dick you are a brave-looking fellowe but not I thinke so prettie as to make rampant the lustes of Sir Robert Veney & besides you are made to tupp maydes. Come, then, have I not ben your goode cosen? Tell me what hath passed between you & this gentleman; or if you cannot upon your honour tell it in fulle then do you drawe the matter lightly, so I maye know its shape & that it concernes not me & this company. Why think you, sir, saies I, that it might concern you & he then toucheth the sign royal upon his liverie coate & saies lad you are no lack-wit. We are the Kinges Men & this Veney is in the bosom of my Lord Rochester & my Lord rules the King as all men know. Now if My Lord need anie conversation with oure company he will send to me, or Mr Burbadge, or Mr Hemmynge, or anie sharer: so must I aske why he calleth oute a boye; a boye lately come to us, with a storie he is my cosen; a boye who when he sits to meate maketh privilie the sign of the cross upon his harte. Soe my cosen, cozzen me not. And he lookes at me verie close & severe as I have not before seen hym looke at anie man: and I bethinke me he sees alle, I am undone; but I draw up my courage thinkeing too: ah he snaps at the bayte.

Whereupon I fall upon my knees crieing oh my cosen spare your wrath though I am a traitoure; I am set to spye on thee for My Lord Rochester. He groweth pale: how cometh this, saies he, I have done nothinge against that noble lord & it seemeth he still doth smyle upon me. Quoth I: oh sir it has all to doe with weightie matteres of faith & politicks & the devizes of the great & I am just a poore boye a ship-wracked mariner & how come I to meddel with these thinges: & I commence to weepe: & these reale teares, I trowe. He asketh, art my cosen in dede or wase that false invention? I say no twas all trewth & sware on my motheres grave that the

Earle hath chose mee for that reasoun soe thou might truste mee the mor.

Then he raiseth me up to chayre, saying, now doe you be a true man, my lad & tell me all. Soe saie I to hym all we have agreed between us my lord what was all writ in your last cypher, viz: the King desireth a Catholic match for Prince Henry in the cause of peace, the which the Puritans in Parliament right hartilie contemn; my lord the Earle favours this and hath the charge of it, for which the Puritans hate him all; these knaves crie out the late Quene did not treate us so (though I thinke she did, but theyre memorie fadeth with tyme), & mutter this King is but a brat of a papist whore; the King groweth wearie with the comparisoun & with the despisinge of the Quene his mother & wishes to shew himself a greater monarch than Elizabeth. Now my lord Earle hath conceived a plan. What if a playe should be made upon Queen Mary of Scotland, such as would shew her in a better light & shew olde Bess as a tyrannous harridan enslaved to canting Puritans, which when it be broadlie heard shall temper the feelinges of the people toward the Quene of Scotland. For such thinges hath been done before: wase not Harry Bolingbroke the usurper made noble and Crookback Dick shown vile cruel caitiff? And would such a playe not discomforte the Puritan factioun & turn the people gainst them? And who in Englande writes best such playes?

At this he catches my meaning & cries what, he desires me to write this playe? I saie yes cosen, His lordship the Earle thus commands thee. But W.S. cries him such a playe was ne'er heard of before. You know the King hath dismissd the Black-Friars boyes & ruined theyre company for a slight gainst Scotland in theyre Edward Second, what should he doe to a playe that slighteth greate Elizabeth & the Protestant church entire? Zblood! I believe thee not, boye; this mustbe some practice upon me by mine enemies.

At this wase I some-wyse discomfited, my Lord, for I see he is close to uncovering our strategems, but I saie, nay, sir, it is by the Earles own command, for lookest thou: this is why my lord Veney approached me and not you or another sharer. Wee are all overlooked by spyes & this can not be seen to come of the Earle. It must be wrote out in secret, onlie I knowinge & thee & shewn to the Earle & he will soften the King to let it playe. For his majestie is timorous; he would crush the Puritans but dare not, or not now. For this projected playe is but parte of a grander complot that needeth more tyme to hatch: the Spanish marriage, newmade bischops, new lawes gainst Puritain conventicles & relief for papists. As I sayde this I study him close but could find nothinge revealled in his face. Quoth he, why should the King favour papists now, who near slew him in the Yeare Five? And I answer, why should he give his sonne to them that paid Guy Fawkes his fee? It is policie cosen, and the lykes of us can not compass it, but muste do as we are bid by the greate. But one thynge is sure: the King must have his bischops to rule the church & here is he closer to the papists than to the Puritans. And he saies still I can not credit it & heere I take out from my bosom the letter forged with my lord of Rochesters seale: credit then this, saith I &

give it over. Soe he doth reade it; & after saith, my lord desires it by Christmas. Quaere: Canst thou do it by then? Aye, saies he, I have a smale thinge to be done with, a playe of the New Worlde & shipwracke & magickal islandes & thy boat-swaine in it too, another fort-nighte sees it done. Then maye I starte upon this & maye God keepe us alle, upon sayinge so he doth crosse himselfe as doe I, the while thinkynge now sir we have thee.

Then his face that was cast in lines of care doth clear of a sudden & he smileth sayinge you promised to shew me how to worke arithmetick in the new stile & he grasps at the proper word & I say algorism thou meanest & he writes it in hys booke & asks in what tongue is that word & I saye my maistre sayed it wase Arabian & he saith it some few tymes. Soe we commence to studie arithmetick & methinkes my lord that we must go earlie to the field & have oure witts about us if we are to catch this onne. For never saw I man soe close-barred & deep-moated gainst the examination of other men. Mr Burbadge playeth his parte upon the stage to be suire, yet when dismounted is plain Dick: but this Shaxespure playeth ever & all ways & I thinke no man can see the man who lieth beneathe the player. With alle honour & my humble duty to yr. Lordship & may God confound thy enemies & the foes of alle trew religion from London this Friday the 26th Januarye 1610 Richard Bracegirdle

12

Crosetti had been questioned by the police hundreds of times, but never before by one who was not a close relative. He found it a good deal easier to lie to strangers, especially as they were handling him with care. They were all in the living room of the family home, Detective Murray perched on the couch, Detective Fernandez in the facing armchair with his pad out, Crosetti in the other armchair of the worn blue brocade suite, coffee things on the coffee table, coffee having been poured by Mary Peg before her discreet exit. Behind Crosetti's head was the large oil painting, manufactured from a photo, of Lieutenant Crosetti, heroic cop, in his heavily bemedaled blues, with his young family around him.

The eyes of the two cops occasionally flicked toward this icon as they put their questions; there was no danger that they were going to get rough. In any case, aside from complicity in the conversion of Sidney Glaser's property (the Bracegirdle manuscripts) to unauthorized use, Crosetti had not done anything wrong, and the policemen did not press him on this point. They wanted to know about Bulstrode in a routine way, because they had found Crosetti's name in his appointment book and they were going through the usual motions. They were mildly interested in Rolly; that she had disappeared interested them, but when Crosetti told them about the London letter, their interest vanished. Leaving the country wasn't a crime. Crosetti knew better than to try to engage them in speculation about the murder; cops weren't there to supply information but to obtain it. They stayed twenty minutes, some of which were given over to reminiscences of the late Lieutenant Crosetti, and left as cheerful as homicide detectives ever get.

A cop who was your *sister* was a different item, and when Patty Dolan came by forty minutes later, Crosetti was perfectly willing to get into her face. After having established that he was but a minor figure in the life of the victim, he asked, 'So what do you guys think?' Meaning her fellow cops; as he said this, he glanced at his mother as well.

'Well, the guy was a Brit and gay,' said Patty. 'They're figuring it for a sex thing that went sour.'

'I doubt that,' said Crosetti.

'Why, did you have sex with him?' asked the big sister. 'You explored all his little twists?'

'No, did you? The first time I saw him I thought. Gee, Patty would really go for this guy. He's fat and sweaty and bald . . .'

This was a reference to Jerry Dolan, her husband. The Crosettis were the kind of family where physical imperfections were fair game among the sibs. Patty Dolan herself had come in for enough of it while growing up. She was a blocky woman with a strong-featured face not unlike the one her dad wore in the oil painting. She had his black hair too, but with the mom's blue eyes.

'Look who's talking,' said the detective, and her hand

darted out in a practiced move to wring the loose flab above Crosetti's belt. He batted the hand away and said, 'No, seriously. I assume you know the guy was involved in a big-money con a few years back. And he ripped me off on a valuable manuscript. That speaks to bad character.'

'Which could've extended into his sex life. What's your point?'

'I don't know if I have one,' said Crosetti. 'But look at the pattern. He cheats me and disappears to England. Carolyn Rolly ditches her whole life and disappears to England too, or so she says, in a letter that I know for a fact contains nine-tenths bullshit. Then Bulstrode comes back here and gets tortured to death. Did you find that manuscript on him?'

'I don't know. It's not my case.'

'Well, if it's missing, there's your motive.'

'What was it worth?'

'Hard to say. Fanny says maybe fifty grand at auction.'

At this, Detective Dolan raised an eyebrow, protruded her lower lip. 'That's a lot of money.'

'It's chump change compared to its real value.'

'What do you mean?'

Crosetti looked at his mother. 'Should we tell her?'

'Unless you want her to beat it out of you,' said Mary Peg.

Crosetti told her what they knew and what the Bracegirdle letter suggested, after which Patty turned to her mother. 'You believe all this?'

'I don't know,' said Mary Peg. 'Fanny tells us that the original sheets we have here are genuine seventeenth century, so maybe the Bracegirdle letter is legit too. There really might be an unknown manuscript play by William Shakespeare buried someplace. Maybe Bulstrode got a line on it, and maybe not. Maybe he told someone about it while he was over in England looking and maybe the word got out to the kind of people who kill people for money.'

'That's a lot of maybes, Ma. What I don't like is that Allie is mixed up in a chain of events that lead to a really nasty killing. And that he was involved with this woman who disappeared.'

'What's that supposed to mean?' said Crosetti.

'Just that looking at it from the cop point of view, if we assume for a minute that this murder isn't just a sex thing like the guys on the case think, it's much more likely that it was a scam, just like the one that got Bulstrode into trouble in the first place. Someone slips a phony clue into an old book so that it gets discovered by someone – this Rolly woman – who's bound to send it to Bulstrode . . . you're shaking your head.'

Crosetti had been, and now he said, with some acerbity, 'No, the find was genuine. I was there, Patty. It was pure accident that those volumes were burned and sent to be broken up.'

'True, but she could've had those sheets prepared and just pretended to find them in those books.'

'And somehow slipped them into all the volumes hoping for a fire? That's nuts. I saw them come out of those covers with my own eyes.'

'Oh, there's good evidence! Any con man can do that kind of switch. I'm sorry, but when I hear about the secret treasure and the mysterious manuscript, I grab hold of my wallet.'

'This is ridiculous,' said Crosetti, his voice rising. 'This is a real manuscript, by a real guy, and the cipher is a real cipher. Ask Fanny if you don't believe me. Or Klim.'

'Klim?'

'Yeah, our new houseguest. He's in your old room.'

Patty gave her mother a look. Who said, 'Don't give me

that cop stare, Patricia. He's a perfectly respectable Polish gentleman who's helping us with deciphering these letters. And I have to say that you're being unduly suspicious and even unfair to your brother.'

'Fine,' said Dolan, suppressing a sigh. Getting between Mary Peg and her baby was ever a losing proposition. 'But if a smooth-talking character shows up with a package he says is the Shakespeare manuscript and wants ten grand good faith money . . .'

'Oh, don't be ridiculous!' said mother and son almost simultaneously, which was funny enough to discharge the tensions. The family detective said she'd keep track of the Bulstrode case to the extent her duties and department protocol allowed and keep them abreast of any relevant findings.

As soon as she left, Mary Peg said, 'I'm going to see if Radi wants any coffee. I think he's been up all night.'

'Radi?'

'Oh, mind your own business!' said Mary Peg and walked out of the kitchen, leaving Crosetti to ponder the hitherto unrelated categories of Mom and Romance. He went to work, where he had to dissemble about his special knowledge of Bulstrode and his recent doings while Sidney Glaser went on about how shocking it was when someone one knew was actually murdered, and how this was yet another indication of the collapse of the city and of Western civ. On his return home that evening he entered a house full of the rich smell of cooking stew. He found his mother and Radeslaw Klim in the kitchen, drinking sherry and laughing. She was not sitting on his lap, but Crosetti would not have been surprised to see it, given the atmosphere in the room: not all the steam was coming from the pot on the stove.

'Hello, darling,' said Mary Peg gaily, 'have some sherry.'

Crosetti had not before this been so greeted upon entering his home. He looked at his mother and observed that she seemed ten years younger. Two bright bars of pink stood on her cheeks, but there was a touch of nervousness in her eyes, as if she were a girl again, entertaining a boy on a porch swing with her dad nosing around. Klim stood and extended his hand, and they shook formally. Crosetti felt that he was in a movie, not one he ever would have directed or even wanted to see, one of those family farces where the single mom falls for the unsuitable man and the kids conspire to break it up, only to find . . .

But before he could organize his discomfort into an attitude, Mary Peg said, in her hostess voice, an uncharacteristic chirp, 'I was just telling Radi about your interest in Polish movies. He knows a lot about them.'

'Really,' said Crosetti politely. He went to the jug of red wine that stood (as one like it had always stood) in a corner of the kitchen counter and poured a juice glass full.

'Not at all,' said Klim. 'I am a fan only. Of course I do not need the little words under the screen to enjoy.'

'Uh-huh. What Polish films in particular?'

'Oh, recently I have liked *Życie jako śmiertelna choroba* of Zanussi. Very beautiful, although the Catholic . . . what do you say? Preaching?'

'Proselytizing.'

'Yes, just so. This is too crude, too – what you say – *obvious*, to me. Of course, Kieślowski did the same more subtler. He often would say, we don't hit on the head with the church, is as bad as hitting on the head with the communism. It is enough we have a moral cinema without seeming to. As for example in *Trois couleurs* and of course in *Dekalog*.'

'Wait a minute, you *knew* Kieślowski?'

'Oh, yes. It is a very small country and we were from the

same neighborhood in Warsaw and I am only a few years older. Kicking balls on the street and so on. Later I was able to be of some service to him.'

'You mean on the films?'

'Indirectly. I was assigned to spy on him, since I had an acquaintance with him already. I see you are shocked. Well, it is true. Everyone was spied on and everyone spied. Lech Walesa himself was an agent for a time. The best you could hope for was a spy who would be sympathetic and report only what one wished to have the authorities know, and so I was for Krzysztof.'

After this, for some twenty minutes the two men talked about Polish movies, one of Crosetti's abiding loves, and he learned at last how to actually pronounce the names of directors and films he had worshipped for years. The conversation circled back to the great Kieślowski, and Klim happened to remark, 'I was in one of his films, you know.'

'No kidding!'

'Not at all kidding. *Robotnicy* in 1971. I was one of young police in background, crushers of workers' movement. A quite insane time, which I think is very much similar to the time of your man Bracegirdle. I should say also I have made progress of a sort on your cipher.'

'You cracked it already?'

'Alas, no. But I have identified its type. Extremely interesting for a classical cipher, I believe, even unique. Shall I show? Or wait for after this excellent supper of your mother?'

Mary Peg said, 'Oh, please show us. I have to make a salad and we can eat the stew anytime.'

With his usual diffident little bow, Klim left the room. Crosetti immediately caught his mother's eye and rolled his own.

'What?' she challenged.

'Nothing. It's just this is all pretty fast. We're living here all by ourselves for years and all of a sudden we're in a Polish movie.'

Mary Peg made a dismissive gesture. 'Oh, come on! He's a dear man, and he's really suffered – his wife died, he was in jail – Fanny's been after me to meet him for years. You like him, right?'

'Well, yeah. Obviously, not *quite* as much as you do. So . . . are you two . . . ?' He rubbed his palms together, as if smoothing cream between them. She snatched up a wooden spoon and cracked him smartly on the crown of his skull. 'You be careful, buster. I can still wash your mouth out with soap.' And they both laughed out loud.

Klim came in on their laughter holding a thick sheaf of printer paper densely packed with lines of text and a legal pad covered with neat European pencilings. Klim sat down next to Crosetti and smiled politely. 'We are having fun? Good. This also may be fun. So. You can see from my red eyes, I have been up most of this night with colleagues across the world and many have commented on this most fascinating cryptogram. So first of course we work Friedman's superimposition. This is elementary, yes? We must distinguish the many different alphabets used in polyalphabetic cipher so we may do Kerckhoff's solution by frequency analysis; and we do this by superimposition of one string of ciphertext upon another to find coincidences; and if we have done this correctly, number of coincident letters will approach value kappa sub p or seven percent approximately. This is clear, yes?'

'No. Maybe you could just skip to the bottom line.'

Klim looked puzzled and began to riffle through the pages. 'The bottom line? But the bottom line is enciphered like these others . . .'

'No, it's a figure of speech. I mean, please summarize your findings without all the technical jargon.'

'Ah, yes. The bottom line. This bottom line is that we cannot do superimposition upon this cipher because the key does not repeat at all within the number of ciphertext characters we have available, which is 42,466. Also, we find that the key has high entropy, much higher than expected for a running key from a book, so we cannot do simple analysis using common English words. So, either your man is not using an ordinary tabula recta, which I think highly unlikely, or he has discovered onetime system three hundred years earlier than Mauborgne did, in approximately 1918. Which also I cannot believe. There is no record of such a discovery. In fact, even the Vigenère cipher was not widely used. Most European intelligence services were satisfied with simple nomenclators until telegraphy came, and even afterward. There is no need for such very high security. It is a great flounder.'

'You mean a fluke,' said Crosetti. 'So if it isn't a onetime system, what is it?'

'Ah. I have a theory. I think your man started with a simple running key, from a book, as originally we thought. But I also think he was a very clever person and saw quickly how a running key from a book might be compromised through substitution. Now he might have changed his tabula into some mixed alphabet, in order to disguise common English digraphs like *tt, gg, in, th*, and so forth, but we do not think he did that. No, I think he merely combined two methods well known in those times. I think he combined a running key from a book with a grille. It is a way of easily generating a pseudorandom key of arbitrary length.'

'Which means what? I mean as far as deciphering goes.'

'Well, unfortunately it means we are stopped. As you know,

one-time systems are unbreakable. Now, it is true that this is not a real one-time system. If we had ten thousand messages, I suppose we could make some progress, or even a thousand. But these few cryptograms are perfectly secure.'

'Even with computers, brute force . . . ?'

'Yes, even with. I could show you mathematically –'

'No, I got a C in algebra.'

'Really? But you are intelligent person and it is so easy! Still, you will understand if I say it is like an equation with two unknowns, the unknowns being the key text and the ciphertext. Example: what is solution to $x + y = 10$?'

'Um . . . x is one, y is nine?'

'Yes. But also two and eight or three and seven, or one hundred and minus ninety, and so forth, an *infinite* number of possible solutions for such equations, and it is the same with onetime systems. To solve a cryptogram you must have a unique solution for each particular letter, no matter how it is disguised by multiple alphabets and keys. Otherwise, how to distinguish between "flee at once" and "come to Paris"? Both can be derived from exact same ciphertext of a onetime system. Even if you capture some piece of plaintext you are still no better off because it is impossible to work backward from plaintext through ciphertext to determine what is key, because this key changes continually and is never used again. No, this is indecipherable, unless, of course, you have both the book he used and the grille.'

'I thought we had the book. You said it was the Bible.'

'I said *probably* the Bible. I have talked to Fanny of this and she says most probably they would have used the Geneva Bible edition of 1560 or later. This is the most popular Bible of that era, the Breeches Bible, so called, very common and also portable, nine inches by seven. The grille would be pasteboard or thin metal, perhaps punched out in a simple pattern to disguise secret use. Your Bracegirdle places the grille on pages he agreed on previously with control and copies out the letters that appear under these holes. This is his key. He copies out enough letters to encipher message and on the other end his control does the same, but in reverse. For the next message he uses another page. As I say, if we had millions of characters of ciphertext so that he must repeat *same* position of grille on pages, then we can solve by usual methods, but not as it is now. I am sorry.'

He really looked sorry too, the sorriest Crosetti had ever seen anyone look, almost comical, like a sad clown. But at that moment, Mary Peg declared that supper was ready and plopped a huge tureen of steaming lamb stew down before them, and the expression on Klim's face changed in an instant to utmost delight. Crosetti felt a little brighter himself. It always made him secure to be in a movie plot, and now, as he had mentioned to his mother, they were in a Polish movie: people bent almost to breaking under the weight of history and insolvable problems coming alive at the prospect of a warm meal.

Toward the close of which, Klim returned to the subject they had avoided during the pleasant meal. 'You know, I am baffled about one more thing,' he mused. 'Why a cipher at all?'

'What do you mean?' asked Crosetti.

'Well, this man, your Bracegirdle, says he was spying on Shakespeare for the English government. Well, I too was a spy for the government and wrote reports, as did thousands of my countrymen. There are tons upon tons of these in archives in Warsaw and not one of them is in cipher. It is only foreign spies who use cipher. A Spanish spying on English people would use a cipher. Or if your man was abroad and sending messages back, then he would do the same. But government spies do not use ciphers. Why should they? It is governments who open mail, yes?'

'They were paranoid?' offered Crosetti. 'Maybe they thought that the people they were after could open mail too.'

Klim shook his head, making his white crest wobble amusingly. 'I do not think that is possible. Spies *create* secret messages, they do not decipher them. Ciphers and codes are used by governments only when they think other governments will read them. This cipher we have here – it is difficult to use, yes? Every letter must be enciphered by hand, and by a key that is quite laborious to generate. Why not simply write it in clear and give to royal messenger?'

'I know why,' said Mary Peg, after a wondering silence from the party. The men looked at her, the older with delight, the younger with dubiety, who said, 'Why?'

'Because they *weren't* working for the government. They were plotting *against* the king and his policies. Didn't you read all that business in Bracegirdle's memoir about the Catholic match for the prince and how they were going to get King James to turn against the Catholics even more than he was already? I mean that was the *point* of all of it. They were going to destroy the theater and discredit the pro-Catholic policies in one blow. They couldn't let anyone in the king's party or administration find out what they were doing, and so they had to use this powerful cipher.'

After some discussion, they agreed that this interpretation made good sense. Klim was particularly generous in his admiration. Mary Peg modestly attributed it to her Irish upbringing, in which she learned to look for the utmost in deviousness and perfidy among the English. Crosetti was impressed too, but not surprised, having been raised by the woman; but he was pleased to see that it had won the admiration of a secret policeman trained by the KGB. By that stage, the large jug of Californian red that had begun the evening nearly full was nearly empty. The talk now turned rather drunkenly to films. Klim told some Kieślowski anecdotes, giving Crosetti fodder for any number of saloon conversations, after which Crosetti asked what Klim thought of Polanski. Klim sniffed, pulled thoughtfully at the tip of his nose, and said, 'I cannot like him. I am not a friend of nihilism however beautifully done.'

'That's a little harsh, don't you think? You said before that you thought Zanussi was *too* religious. Religion or lack of it isn't the point. He's a great director. He can tell a story on the screen with vivid characters and terrific pacing and mood. It's like saying that if you like *Rosemary's Baby*, you're on the side of the devil.'

'Are you not?'

Crosetti was about to launch into an exposition of the pure aesthetics of film, but this answer to what he had imagined was a purely rhetorical statement checked him. He looked at Klim to insure that the man was serious, at his pale blue eyes, which certainly were, serious as fate. Klim continued, 'If film or any art for that matter has not some moral basis then you might as well look at flickering patterns, or random scenes. Now I do not say what is this moral basis, only that there should be one. Pagan hedonism is a perfectly acceptable moral basis for a work of art, for example, as in Hollywood. Domestic bliss. Romance. It does not have to be . . . what is the word? Where the villain always dies and the hero gets the girl . . .'

'Melodrama.'

'Just so. But not *nothing*. Not the devil laughing at us, or not only that.'

'Why not? If that's the way you see the world.'

'Because then art suffocates. The devil gives us nothing,

only he takes, takes. Listen, in Europe, in last century, we decide we will not worship God anymore, instead we will worship nation, race, history, the working classes, what you like, and as a result of this everything is totally ruined. And so they said, I mean the artists said, let us not believe anything but art. Let us not believe, it is too painful, it betrays us, but art we trust and understand, so let us believe at least in that. But this betrays too. And also, it is ungrateful for life.'

'What do you mean?'

Klim turned to Mary Peg with a smile that quite transformed his face, showing her a faded image of the man he was when he knew Kieślowski. 'I did not expect to talk of such things. We should be in smoky café in Warsaw.'

'I'll go burn some toast,' said Mary Peg. 'But what *did* you mean?'

'So . . . this Polanski. He has had a horrid life. He is born at just wrong time. He is a Jew, his parents taken to death camps, he grows up wild. He makes success through hard work and talents and marries beautiful wife, and she is killed by some madman. Why should he believe anything but that devil rules this world? But I was born somewhat earlier in same time, not a Jew but still, life was not so happy for Poles either, the Nazis thought we were almost so bad as the Jews, and so I say I was, if not same as Polanski, at least, you agree, in the same class. Father murdered by Nazis, mother killed in uprising, 1944, I am on streets, a baby cared for by my sister, she is twelve years old, my first memory is burning corpses, a pile of bodies in flames and the smell. How we survived I don't know, a whole generation of us. Later, I should add, like Polanski I lost my wife, not to a madman but also tortured to death, months of it. I was by that time not very well in with the authorities and it was difficult to obtain morphia for her. Well, not to talk about these personal troubles. I meant to say, after the war, somehow, despite the Germans and the Russians, we look around and discover there is still life in us. We learn, we make love, we have children. Poland survives, our language lives, people write poetry. Warsaw is rebuilt, every brick, same like before the war. Miloscz wins Nobel, Szymborska wins Nobel, and one of us is pope. Who could imagine this? And so when we make art, this art most often says something more than, oh, poor little me, how I have suffered, the devil is in charge, life is trash, we can do nothing. This is what I mean.'

Crosetti considered this statement as much as he could, which was not very much, because he was an American and he wanted to make movies and sell them and he thought he had to at least be a tourist in the dark country. Suffering, nihilism, the devil laughing, all that Polanski stuff was a necessary spice, like oregano, not something you were expected to make a meal from. What he admired in the Poles was the competent surface, the camera movements, the way a face was lit, the way the camera dwelled upon a face.

After a pause, he said, 'So, anyway, do you want to watch some films?'

'Not *Chinatown* please!' said Mary Peg.

'No. We'll watch moral art,' said her son. 'We'll have a John Wayne festival.'

So they did. Crosetti owned nearly five hundred DVDs and several hundred videotapes and they started with *Stagecoach* and proceeded to hit the highlights of the Duke's career. Mary Peg crashed halfway through *She Wore a Yellow Ribbon*, her head drooping against Klim's shoulder. When the film was over, they settled Mary Peg on the couch with a blanket over her, turned off the set, and went back to the kitchen. Crosetti reflected that this was the first time in his memory that his mother had missed seeing the *Tonight Show*, and this produced in him a good feeling, as if she had won some kind of prize.

'I too will go to bed, I think,' said Klim. 'Thank you for a most interesting evening. I confess I have always liked the cowboy films. They are very soothing to me, like a lullaby when one is a child. Tell me, what do you intend to do about this cipher?'

Crosetti was startled by the change of subject and then recalled that his father had said it was an old cop trick to get the suspect off balance.

'I don't see what I *can* do. You said the thing was uncrackable.'

'Yes, but . . . your mother has told me this entire story, as much as she has of it, and so I know that a man has already died. Now you must think: the men who killed this professor do not know that the cipher is unreadable. Let us presume they have the Bracegirdle letter or a copy of it. This letter mentions other letters, ciphered letters. These they do not have and they must begin to want them and I am sure they must have obtained your name from the dead man. This young lady who was with you when you found them, she at least knows the ciphers exist. She has already disappeared, and sends a letter you suspect, which you are correct to do: anyone can write a letter, or force a letter to be written, and mail it from anywhere. She might be on the next street. Or dead as well.'

Crosetti had considered that possibility any number of times and always dismissed it. Carolyn may have run away – from what he didn't know yet – but he refused to admit that she might be dead. At some level he knew he was being infantile: people died, but not Carolyn Rolly. She was a survivor and good at hiding, and the script required that she reappear and conclude her business with Albert Crosetti. A little Polish-movie business was okay, but not that.

'She's not dead,' he said, as much to hear the magic of the phrase as to communicate the thought to Klim. 'Anyway, what's your point?'

'My point is that we are dealing here with violent people and there is no reason why they should not come after you next. You or your mother.'

'My mother?'

'Well, yes. I presume that if they have your mother you will give them anything they want.'

An unwanted laugh sprang from Crosetti's mouth. 'Jesus, Klim! I think it was a mistake to let you watch John Wayne. They can have the damn things right now. I'll put an ad out – "Thugs who whacked Bulstrode, pick up the cipher letters anytime."'

'Yes, but of course they would see that as a ploy. The problem with evil people is that they can see only evil in others. It is one of the worst curses of being evil, that you can no longer experience good. Believe me in this; for perhaps I have seen more evil people than you. Tell me, your father was a policeman – have you any guns in the house?'

At this, Crosetti's mouth fell open and he felt hysteria well up again but suppressed the feeling. 'Yeah, we have his guns. Why?'

'Because when you are gone it will be necessary for me to stay here armed.'

'What do you mean, gone? When I'm at work?'

'No. I mean when you are in England. You should immediately leave for England.'

Crosetti stared at the man. He seemed perfectly calm, but you could never tell with a certain type of crazy person. Or maybe this was how he became when drunk. Crosetti was fairly drunk himself and decided to treat the current run of conversation like drunk-talk, or the type he and his friends got into when they were thinking about how to raise enough money to make a movie. He pasted a humoring smile on his face. 'Why should I go to England, Klim?'

'Two reasons. One is to disappear from here. Second is to find out what Bulstrode learned while he was there, if you can. Third is to find the grille.'

'Uh-huh. Well, that shouldn't take any time at all. They probably have just the grille we want at Grilles R Us. Or Grille World. But first, I think I'll go to bed. Good night, Klim.'

'Yes, but first the guns. Perhaps they come tonight.'

'God, you're *serious* about this, aren't you?'

'Extremely serious. Guns is not a joking matter.'

Crosetti was just in that stage of drunkenness in which one is physically capable of acts that the sober self would never have considered for an instant (Hey, let's drive the pickup out on the lake ice and do skids!), and so he went into his mother's bedroom and took down the carton that contained all his father's policeman stuff – the gold shield, the handcuffs, the notebooks, and the two pistols in their leather zip cases. One was a big Smith & Wesson Model 10, the classic .38 that all New York patrolmen used to carry before the semiautomatics came in, and the other was the .38 Chief's Special with the two-inch barrel that his father had carried as a detective. There was a half-empty box of Federal jacketed hollow-point .38 Specials in there too and he took it out and loaded both weapons on his mother's blond oak bureau. He put the Chief's Special, still in its clipon holster, into his pocket and left the room, holding the Model 10.

'I assume you know how to use this,' he said, handing

it butt-first to Klim. 'You won't shoot your foot. Or my mom.'

'Yes,' said Klim, hefting it in the palm of his hand like a pound of sausage. Crosetti was happy to see that he didn't sight it and put his finger on the trigger. 'It is a John Wayne pistol. All the world knows how to shoot this type.'

'There's a little more to it than that.'

'I was making a joke. In fact, the weapons training I received was quite thorough.'

'Great. Well, knock yourself out.'

'Excuse, please?'

'Another figure of speech. I'm going to bed.'

He did and awakened at 4:10 in the morning, thinking that he had dreamed it all, dreamed that he had given a loaded weapon to a man he hardly knew. He jumped out of bed and went over to his trousers hanging from the closet doorknob and felt the weight of the other pistol there. With a whispered curse he removed it and started toward his mother's bedroom and then thought better of it. Mary Peg invariably woke during the night after falling asleep in front of the TV, and he could barely imagine what she would think if she awakened again and saw her son in her bedroom brandishing a revolver. He placed it in the canvas briefcase he carried on his way to and from work and returned to his bed. Thereafter he slept fitfully, bemoaning during the waking intervals this last evidence of his terminal stupidity.

The next morning he came down to breakfast late, hoping to keep his contact with the house's other two inhabitants to the socially acceptable minimum. When he arrived in the kitchen, his mother was there, fully dressed and made up, and Klim was sitting at the table attired in his bad suit. The pistol was not evident. Mary Peg was making bacon and eggs and chatting brightly with her houseguest. They were going to go out for a drive, maybe out to the Island, have lunch someplace, it looked like a sunny day, not too cold, etc. This amiable chatter only increased Crosetti's depression and guilt. Klim was the reason for the cooked breakfast, obviously, for on weekdays the Crosettis made do with cold cereal and coffee. Crosetti had to eat some out of simple loyalty, and after a decent interval he grabbed his coat and his briefcase and left.

He had thought of asking when Klim would be leaving, now that the deciphering had reached a dead end, but had decided not to, had decided that it would be ill-mannered. It was his mother's house, she could shack up with anyone she wanted. Why was he living with his mother anyway? It was ridiculous and unsuitable and the hell with saving for film school. Carolyn Rolly had figured a way out of an impossible situation, and she had far fewer resources than he did (as she had pointed out to him), and now he resolved to make a change. There were people he knew in Williamsburg and Long Island City who lived in group dwellings, film and music freaks his own age. The rent would be a pinch, but maybe he could forget about film school for a bit, maybe he could get a small script shot and use that to get an internship or a scholarship, or maybe he should start sending scripts to the contests. He was filling his mind with thoughts that were not about pistols and the menace of violence from unknown parties and this worked well enough until he lifted his briefcase to pass through the subway turnstile and he heard a clank when it brushed against the metal of the turnstile housing and he realized that he still had the pistol with him.

THE THIRD CIPHERED LETTER

My lord there is naught of moment afoot, the same as in my laste, for the company are all engaged at the Globe theatre & I praye me it maye not vex you if I write less often, as it is tedious to encypher as it must be for you to interpret. Yet oure plan proceedeth well I thinke. Having done with his playe of the Tempest & the somer arrivynge W.S. travells to Stratford-upon-Avon which is his habbot to goe these manie yeares & hee bids me goe with hym & stop at hys howse. Soe wee leave London 5th June oure partie being besydes W.S. & mee some marchants in woole & the fellowe Spade as guard. Wee arrive upon the 8th inst. & are reseaved with signes of delight by Mr S. his familie: wyfe & two daughters the eldest Susannah & the youngere Judith; also otheres of the town, W.S. being now a considerable man of propertie in those partes, hys howse at New Place most comodiouse. But the wages of sin are death.

W.S. agen shewes hym a false villein for hee plaies a verie other man in Stratford than in London as hee is plaien-spoke in the ffashion of this countrey lyke a playn burgesse of the towne, saies Zir, saies Chil, not I will, saies mortal not verie &c.: speakes not of the theatre nor hys lyfe in towne, no bawdry though hym bawdie enow in London tap-roomes. Wife some thyng of a shrewe, rates hym for keepyng trulls & not sending money sufficient for her keepe & he answereth her not but forebeares. Verilie he doth keep a trull, a singer of Italy methinkes or a Jewess, verie black to look at I have seen hym abed with her thrice or four tymes; but he doth not boast upon her to otheres: hee is a private man in such thynges, nor doth he goe for debauch in the stewes. His talke heerabouts is all of land & buying of landes & rentes & loanes, mortgages &c. Yet with hys daughter Susannah is he seeminge more merrie; to whose company he doth much repaire. She hath more witt than women comonlie have or so 'tis said in the playce. She is marryed to Jn. Hall physician a Puritan man of goode repute. They speake not of religion; so I suspect them: as who doth not who be an honest man & of the trew faithe? They attend church & are not fyned although the talke hereabouts is the father was oft fyned & a damned recusant papist unto death; the mother too. Searched privilie about the howse for priests holes but could fynde none.

W.S. is verie easie with mee & with mee alone speakes of the theatre & plaies & the plaie of Mary he is comanded (soe he thinks) to write; yet for manie daies he doth no writing whilst here, or but a little in hys smale booke. We are abroad muche & I with my new-devized angle-rod holped hym survey som land neare Rowington which hys neighbour disputeth the boundes & pleazed hym muche therbye. His wyfe though passing olde is yet lively and manages alle; her accomptes all a-hoo (I have stolen a looke) yet she knowes her every ell of lande theyre rentes & where lieth the last pepper-corne. The youngere daughter somewhat ill-favoured; not married nor none in prospect; lykes me not & I doe not know why for I traite her with best courtesie.

But I listen behinde door to servantes prattel & heare she is jealous of this elder sister that her father loveeth beste or soe she thinkes; soe too there wase a sonne her twin who hath died some yeares past & W.S. wisheth it ben her who died & not her brother; seeminglie am I of an age with this dead boye or a little younger & am somwhat lyke in hys eies, therefore hee doth favour mee & this daughter hateth mee for it. Thus they speake & whether it be trewe or no shal we see hereafter; but if trewe it doth advaunce oure enterpryse I thinke.

I have scaped a dangeur that I shal relate you. He hath upon an evening come into my chamber in hys howse & I was cyphering with mye grille & he askes what it is I doe & I wase much discountenanced yet spake brave saying I reade holie scripture. He asketh what is that sheete of metall & answered tis a copie I hath made of a lanthorne that adorneth the crypt where lieth my mother, a remembrance of her. Then asketh: art a poet too Dick I see you have quick hid what you write upon when I cam in as som poets doe & I with 'em. Nay cosen saith I tis som mathematick idlinge I doe. He saith: ho, holie writ & nomberes all at onece thou art a wonder, no wonder thy skull lacks room for witte. Soe he left me safe.

Now heere is a secret I have uncouvered of hym: a-Sundaies 'tis hys habbot after divine servise he taketh horse & quits the towne with the fellowe Spade soe hee saies to ryde in the forest of Arden nearebye. Upon such a day I take horse and follow them on a road through the forest north-west up the vale, five miles or more it must have ben & come to a rise in ground and can see at some littel distanse the castle of Warwick, its tours. I come to theyre horses and I dismount too and walk upon a track through the woode. After a tyme I come to a ruine of som olde priorie or such romish howse shut sence King Henries daie where are manie folke about kneylyng & telling bedes & a man there no dowt a popish priest with hys cuppe & mumbles; & W.S. there too among them all. I watch & listen & then the folk leave the place & W.S. speaketh with the priest for a tyme & I venture closer to heere them theyre develish plots mayhap when I am seized from behynde & a grete hande clappit our mye mouth & then pressed to earth with a heavie weight & feele a point gainst my cheke & a voise saith quiet or you are dead man. Soe for a while; then am lifted up & I see there is W.S. & it is Spade who hath me & his daggere still drawen.

Quoth W.S. Dick why skulk in shadoues why not com to mass you are a goode Catholicke are you not? I answer sir I was afeared an it might be a snare set by pursuivantes to take names of thos sekeing holy masse as if oft done these tymes. Nay he saies they are but good folk of the countrey who cleve stil to the olde religioun. And you amongst them, say I. In parte, he saies, for I am a goode Kinges man & temper me to the requisites of pouwer & shew my face a Sundaies where pouwer demandes it. Quoth I: And believeth not? That, saies he, is for God alone & not such as you, nor yet the Kinges majestie to know; but though Jack Calvin & all the bischops saie I can not praye for the sowles of my parentes & of my littel sonne, yet I will: if it damn mee to hell I will do it. And hym sayeing this looketh most fierce. Then smiles, saying come look

I will shew thee a thinge to marvell at, goode Spade putt up thy blade here is a friende.

Soe goe we throew the oulde stones of the priorie all o'ergrowne with brakken & smale trees; it was the priorie of St Bosa as he telleth whilst we goe, onece the abode of holie sisters. Hee pointes variously: here the chapel there the cloister & at last come we to a ring of stones & in the centre a black cercle. This is St Bosa's holy-welle he saies & list thee well to it & droppeth in a pibble & it passeth a long tyme before wee heare but verie fainte the plash. Tis deep saies I. Marry, passinge deep, saies hee they saie no man hath plombed it ever. In past tymes the maydes would gather heere on St Agnes daie & draw up a payle & peer in the water to scrye the face of theyre husband that shalbe. But no more, no more: for God as we nowe are taught loveth not confort, nor plaifulnesse, nor musick, nor glorious shewes, nor anie lovelie thynge, nor yet workes of charitie, but desireth us to tremble in plain dull chamberes, wee cloathed all in mourninge, whilste som whey-face canting parson drones wee are damned, damned, damned to hell. Then laughes clops me on showleder & saies hang such sectish talk for now wee are for home & shall feaste us & drinke & play nine mens morris lyke simple folk.

Soe we did & after meate wee oute to the sward all the familie & Spade with his knife cutteth out some turves to make a board & they commense plaie. I saie I know not this game & W.S. saies what, canst not play morris? Nay you plaie deeper games mye tricksey cosen deep as Bosa's Holiewell; soe I aske his meaninge &

he saies why I meant onlie London games with cartes as pinero & gleake. But I thinke he meant else.

This night he hath a candle late & I heere hym pace his chamber & I listen close & heer the scrach of a pen & shift of paper & I think hee must write oure plaie of Mary now. My lord you ask can I overlook his papers to see what he doth write & I shall try it; but hee is verie close with hys papers & no onne is let see them til he be finished. I praye you my lord doeth well & all your howse prosper, from Stratford-upon-Avon the 19th June 1611 bye your lordshipes most humble serv[t] *Richard Bracegirdle*

13

I am reading a little Shakespeare now, in the intervals between sleeping, eating, and writing this thing. Mickey's got a *Riverside* here, of course, not to mention any number of supplementary texts, lexicons, critical works, and so forth. Shall I add my own little bit of bird shit to Everest? I think not, although I have to say that Bracegirdle has given me a somewhat different take on the guy. As I've already said, I have had some commerce with creative types and I have indeed seen in them the same peculiar blankness that our Dick picked up in W.S. Like they're talking to you and doing business and all but you get the feeling you're talking not to a regular person but to a fictional character they made up? I just mean writers here; musicians are quite different, like large hairy children.

It so happened, my little diary tells me, that I spent the next morning with a musician whose name you would undoubtedly know if you were rockin' in the '80s at all and this fellow had written at least fifteen Top Twenty songs, music and lyrics and (not having taken the precaution of consulting a good IP lawyer) had signed the copyright to these songs over to his label, in return for which the scumbag who owned the label gave him an advance of something like twenty-five grand. And gosh, the scumbag kept feeding him driblets of money, and of course the musician became famous and went on tours and made even more money, and flash forward twenty or so years, with his original group long dispersed and the crowds of fans with them, but the songs are now classics getting tons of airplay on every oldie station in the country and the label scumbag sells his copyrighted list to a media megacorp for close to a billion dollars and what is my guy's share? Zip is what, the same as what he earns for all those zillions of oldie station plays, because, as practically no one understands, when you hear a song on the radio or TV the artist who's singing the song gets nothing: only the copyright holder collects the ASCAP royalty.

So I sat down with the megacorp people and they said that while they agreed my client had been screwed to the floorboards, they had just dropped a bundle on what was basically an industrial commodity and the fact that it had arisen from my client's guts and heart was neither here nor there. The musician took it, I have to say, pretty well. He just grinned and expressed amazement that he'd thought up stuff out of his head that had transformed itself into this huge piece of property, upon which a vast commercial empire now rested, and that he'd have to content himself with all the pleasure he'd given to so many people. As I said, big hairy kids.

In contrast to Shakespeare, who always had a good eye for the bottom line. Sure he sold *Hamlet* for ten pounds, maybe forty large in today's money, but he sold it to himself, since he was a stockholder in the theatrical company that owned it, and he probably made a good deal more after old Dick Bracegirdle became his bookkeeper.

I'm digressing again because this next part is really painful.

After I had the bad-news meeting with the hairy former kid I went across town with Ed Geller and Shelly Grossbart to a monster cluster-fuck involving squadrons of lawyers, something that happens a lot nowadays when one media company proposes to buy another and I was there because I know a lot about foreign copyright law and it's all too tedious to get into. The point is, however, that I was not at my best, because I was thinking about my lost Miranda and also about the poor schmuck of a musician. No one at the long polished table at which we sat was hairy, nor had any of them ever created anything that any normal person would wish to see or hear. Someone raised the issue of ring tones, and how the EU was going to handle them, and Ed looked at me, because I had done the most extensive work on this and I fumphered and gave what turned out to be the wrong answer and Shelly had to cover for me with an artful equivocation.

In any event, I was out of the office when the fateful call came through and Ms Maldonado had not left a regular pink printed message slip in my in-basket but rather a yellow Post-it note on my desk lamp, which is what she does when someone calls and we don't wish to log it in. In most cases this means a mistress (although I am infrequently called by mistresses at the office) but not today. I went out to her desk, flapping the little yellow slip inquiringly, and she said that Miranda Kellogg had called from Toronto. I immediately called the number she gave me and got a voice mailbox at an education ministry office that said Miranda Kellogg was not at her desk and would I like to leave a message? They used the familiar system that generates a machine voice for the body of this polite request, while the name itself is recorded by, presumably, the mailbox's proprietor. It was a pleasant enough Canadian voice, but one I did not recognize. My belly now commenced churning; I declined to leave a message.

After that, I called the cops and arranged with Detective Murray to have Bulstrode's files picked up. I sent Omar to do it and waited, during which time I called the Toronto number three times and the third time lucky, the phone picked up and there was the unfamiliar voice, heavier and slower than the voice of the person I had already started to call 'my' Miranda. I told her who I was and asked her if she were the niece of the late Andrew B. and she said she was and she had just heard about his demise, having only lately come back to Toronto. She'd been in the Himalayas and quite out of touch. The Himalayas? Yes, she'd won a prize; someone had called her up one night and said she'd won a trip trekking through Nepal. It was either Nepal, Tahiti, or Kenya, your choice, and she'd always wanted to see India and Nepal, so she chose that. At first she'd thought it a scam, but no: a package had come in the mail the next day, Airborne Express, containing all the tickets and arrangements, but she had to leave that week or no deal. I asked her when that was, and she told me six weeks ago more or less; that is, early October, just before Bulstrode had returned to the United States. In any case, she'd read about her uncle's death upon her return and thought she should call, even though she imagined the body would be going back to Oxford and Oliver. She said she didn't think that there was any money involved, since she knew her silly old uncle was broke, but would I give her a buzz when I'd read the will? She thought that most of what he had would go to Oliver, but there was a lavaliere that had belonged to her grandmother that she'd been promised. I said I would and hung up, the phone slipping into its cradle on a film of my sweat.

I immediately called our estate law section and left an urgent message for Jasmine Ping. I sweated some more and tried to get interested in IP law but could not, even though I had to get a response ready for that Godzilla-eating-Rodan media merger business from the morning, no, the words would not cling to the appropriate brain tissue, and then in comes Omar with large brown cartons under each arm and I thrash through them and find a copy of the *real* last will and testament of Andrew Bulstrode rather than the phony one that my Miranda had presented. This, as the real Miranda had indicated, left all worldly goods to Oliver March, the longtime companion, aside from some small bequests to individuals, and I was happy to learn that the real Miranda would get her lavaliere. The box also held a small leather-framed desk photograph of Professor Bulstrode with a younger woman who possessed the squat, pleasantly froggy look that was perhaps a mark of the Bulstrodes and who I presumed was the *echt* Miranda Kellogg.

Ms Ping came in while I was on the floor amid the scattered papers. Mutely I handed her the will and told her my suspicions. She sat down and read it, and it was interesting to observe her perfect porcelain face transform itself into the kind of demon mask you see at Chinese folk-dance festivals. It's not a good thing for a trust lawyer to present a fake will to surrogate's court. Jasmine had some harsh words about my private affairs, somewhat unjust I thought, but I did not defend myself. She wanted to know how I had let this happen and implied strongly that (although she was too polite to use such language) I had been led around by my cock. She said that my partners would have to be told; I agreed that this was only right. She wanted my assurance that I had not allowed the impostor to lay hands on any part of the estate prior to probate, and here I had to confess that an item of value had indeed gone missing, along with the impostor. I explained what the item was and she informed me of what I already knew, which was that if the genuine legatee wished to make trouble, and should the issue be brought to the attention of the court, then I had committed a disbarrable offense. In any event, I could have no further involvement in any legal matters pertaining to the Bulstrode estate. She glanced at the strewn papers with a look on her face that was not at all pleasant, a disgusted look, as if I had been trolling through the chattels of the deceased in hopes of looting some overlooked piggy bank. With no further discussion she made a call to our office manager to shift some papers ASAP. While she was thus engaged I managed to toss Bulstrode's appointment diary under my office sofa.

A pair of husky porters arrived, boxed all the Bulstrode papers, and took them away. As soon as my office was empty again I snatched out the diary and riffled through the pages for the weeks prior to his death. In July I found what I was looking for, the twenty-fourth at eleven-thirty: it read 'Sh. Ms? Carolyn R. Crosetti.' That had to be it: the fake Miranda had mentioned a Carolyn who was somehow involved and there was the 'Sh. Ms' as well. Carolyn R. Crosetti had to be either the seller or the agent for same. I rushed outside to Ms Maldonado's desk, made a photocopy of the relevant page, gave her the diary, told her that it was part of the Bulstrode material that had unaccountably been overlooked, and required her to take it immediately to Ms Ping's. I believe that this was the first actual lie I had ever offered Ms M. and it was an even more significant indication of my depravity than the error over the will or Ms Ping's resultant disdain. It is bad, very bad, when a lawyer starts lying to his secretary.

Crosetti is not, fortunately, a particularly common name.

After thumbing through the white pages for all five boroughs and the surrounding counties, I found only twenty-eight of them, but no Carolyn R. Crosetti. I went back to my office with a list I copied and began to punch buttons on my cell phone. Of course, only the elderly or sick were at home at this hour and I did not wish to leave a lot of messages. For reasons I cannot now recall I had started with the suburban names and closed in on the city from outside. Somewhere in Queens, Ms M. popped her head in and informed me that Mr Geller would like to see me right away. I nodded and went on with my number punching. After a spate of answering machines, or empty-house ringing, I got a woman's voice, a throaty New York accent with a layer of cultivation painted over it. I asked if she knew a Carolyn Crosetti and she said she thought that she knew all the Crosettis in the New York Standard Metropolitan Statistical Area and that there was no such person. Then a pause and a short laugh and she added, 'Unless my son married her and didn't tell me.'

'Who?' I asked.

A pause, and in a more formal voice, 'To whom am I speaking?'

At this point I was staring at the page from Bulstrode's diary and I saw that I had made a slight error. Bulstrode wrote in a loose, nearly medical, scrawl and his appointment for the morning of July 24 had leached over into the line for the previous day. What he had written was not 'Carolyn R. Crosetti' but

Carolyn R.
A. Crosetti

I decided to answer the woman semifrankly and said, 'My name is Jacob Mishkin of Geller Linz Grossbart and Mishkin.

I'm the lawyer for the estate of Andrew Bulstrode and I'm trying to trace a transaction Professor Bulstrode entered into this past July. I've located a notation in his diary of an appointment with an A. Crosetti and a Carolyn R. Would you know anything about that?'

'I would,' said the woman. 'Albert Crosetti is my son. I assume this is about the manuscript.'

A rush of relief on hearing these words. 'Yes! Yes it is,' I exclaimed, and then found myself at a loss for words, thinking now about the various possibilities I had laid out for Mickey Haas. Was I talking to a thief, a victim, or a villain?

'And . . . ?' said the woman.

'And what?'

'And is the estate going to make good the despicable ruse through which your late client cheated my son into surrendering a valuable seventeenth-century manuscript for a paltry sum?'

So this was the victim. 'That's certainly one of the issues open to discussion, Mrs Crosetti,' I said.

'I should hope so.'

'We should arrange to meet.'

'I'll have my lawyer contact you. Good-bye, Mr Mishkin.'

I would have immediately called her again, but my office doorway was now occupied by the stout pugnacious figure of Ed Geller. Now, on paper all the partners of Geller Linz Grossbart & Mishkin are equals, but as often happens in such firms, command flows toward where it is most coveted, and it was the case at our firm that Ed was that coveter and so usually got his way. Besides this, he and Marty Linz were the founding partners and somewhat more equal as a result. Ed was twitching-angry, mainly I suppose because I had not come when called, and so he had to deal with me standing, rather than from behind his desk, which is subtly raised above the normal floor level and surrounded by stuffed legless chairs into which one deeply sinks. I knew better than to stand to my full height now.

I said, 'I guess you've talked to Jasmine.'

'Yes, I have,' he said. 'And could you please now tell me what the *fuck* is going on?'

'A misunderstanding is all, Ed. I'm sure it'll be cleared up shortly.'

'Uh-huh. So you didn't convert a valuable part of our client's estate to your own use and convey said property to your girlfriend?'

'No. I was the victim of a fraud. A woman presented herself as the legatee of the Bulstrode estate with a will that appeared genuine –'

'This was a will we prepared?'

'No. I assumed it was found with his effects at death. I . . . we were only retained by the deceased in a particular capacity, which was to hold a document in safekeeping and to advise him on its IP status and the IP status of such other documents that might be derived from it.'

'Derived how?'

I took a deep breath. 'It was a seventeenth-century document purportedly written by a man who knew William Shakespeare. Aside from its scholarly value, which was substantial, it suggested the existence of an unknown Shakespeare play in autograph manuscript and provided what might be clues to the present location of same.'

Ed is a great litigator, as I believe I've mentioned, and part of the litigator's art is to never seem surprised. But now he gaped. 'Holy fucking shit! And this was legit?'

'Unknown, but Bulstrode believed it was, and he was one of the world's great experts on the subject.'

'And this property, this seventeenth-century manuscript, is now in the possession of your fraudulent bimbo?'

'I wouldn't call her my fraudulent bimbo. But, yes it is.'

He ran a hand through his implants. 'I don't understand. How could you have been so stupid? Wait, don't answer that! You were *shtupping* this honey, right?'

'Do you want to hear the whole story, Ed?'

'I do indeed. But let's go to my office.'

Or something to that effect, with rather more obscene locutions. Ed is the sort of lawyer who equates toughness with the liberal use of foul language. On the short walk over, collecting a number of pitying looks from the staff, I briefly considered whether I could withhold any significant facts from one of the best cross-examiners in the New York Bar. No, the painful truth would have to emerge, but not the speculation, and not my plans. When we were ensconced in our assigned places I gave him the basic facts, and after he had drained me to his satisfaction he said that we were going to have to get the police involved and that we had to contact the genuine legatee, Oliver March, and let him know what had happened. I was not to be the one to do these tasks, however. In fact, now that we were on the subject, he had noted a significant slippage in my focus of late and I had to agree that this was the case. We discussed my sorry performance at this morning's meeting and he pointed out that the proposed merger involved the interests of some important clients and that it was unlikely that I was going to do them much good in my present state. He suggested I think about taking a leave for a while, and then he got avuncular, which he hardly ever does with me, a little like King Kong doing social work instead of wrecking Manhattan, and after a while he got to how sorry he had been when Amalie and I broke up and how he thought that I really hadn't been the same man since. As soon as he said that, as soon as those words drifted into the air, I felt a sort of balloon pop inside my head and . . . it's hard to describe, not really a woo-woo type of out-of-body experience, more of a profound detachment, as if Ed were gabbing away at someone who wasn't really me.

It was quite interesting, really, in a hideous way, and I thought unaccountably of my mother in her last days and wondered whether this was how she felt: alone in that crummy apartment, kids gone (yes, there was me, but didn't I make it obvious that it was grim duty alone that brought me to her), a stupid job – why keep going, what was the point? Ed was now talking about turning my work over to various associates – just until you can get back on your feet – and part of that work was, of course, the cell phone ring tones. And this phrase now completely occupied my brain (*cell phone ring tones! CELL PHONE RING TONES!!!*), and the force of the absurdity struck me like a pie in the face: here we were, grown men, actual human beings, the crown of creation, concerned with making sure that money would be paid out in the proper way whenever some idiot's cell phone went *bee-dee-boop-a-doop-doop* instead of *ding-ding-a-ling* and this connected in a strange way with the detached feeling and thinking about my mother and I started to laugh and cry at the same time and could not stop for an excruciatingly long time.

Ms Maldonado was summoned, and she wisely thought to call Omar, who came up and swept me out the side entrance of our suite, so as not to embarrass anyone or frighten the secretaries. On the ride back to my place I asked Omar if he had ever considered suicide. He said he had after his youngest boy had been shot in the head while throwing rocks at soldiers during the first intifada, he said he wanted to blow up himself and as many of them as possible, and there were people in Fatah encouraging that sort of thing then. But he thought it was a sin, both the suicide and killing ordinary people. Dying *after* you assassinated someone in power was a different story, but no one had ever given him the opportunity to do that. So he had come to America instead.

That afternoon was when I retrieved this pistol I have here from its lair in the back of my utility closet and for the first time seriously asked Camus's big question, since, unfortunately, I was already *in* America. I even stuck the barrel in my mouth just to taste the tang of death, and I did a little active imagining, trying to think of anyone who would be at all inconvenienced by my death right then. Amalie would be relieved and free to marry someone worthier of her. The kids hardly knew I was alive to begin with. Paul would be pissed off but get over it; Miriam would up her medication for a month or so. Ingrid would obtain another lover, indistinguishable from me in any important respect. In my will Omar gets the Lincoln and a nice bequest, so he'd be better off as well.

Obviously, I did not at that time pull the trigger, since I am still here and typing. In fact, I recovered from my hysteria fairly rapidly, one of the advantages of being as shallow as a dish. Nor did I go to bed for a week, forgo eating, stop shaving. No, I thought at the time, the Jake persona would click once more into place and I would continue with what passed for my life, only without the ring tones. In the end I think it was curiosity that kept me alive. I wanted to find out how Bracegirdle's spying went, and to see if that play still existed, and I wanted to meet Osip Shvanov. Yes, curiosity and a mild desire for revenge. I wanted to find out whose little schemes had fucked up my life, and I wanted to get my hands on the woman who had played Miranda Kellogg and played me for a fool.

My appointment with Shvanov was at ten in SoHo, but I had a previous appointment uptown, for I had promised to take Imogen to her rehearsal at the kids' school. Mrs Rylands, the drama teacher at the Copley Academy, does *A Midsummer Night's Dream* every third year, alternating with *R. & J.* and *The Tempest*. Last year, Imo played a spirit in the latter play, but this year she has the part of Titania and is insufferably proud. I did not see her perform that spirit because, as I think I've mentioned, I do not go to the theater, and not because I don't like what they're showing nowadays. I literally cannot bear to sit in a darkened auditorium and watch live actors on a stage. My tubes close up three minutes after the curtain rises, I can't breathe, a painful vise clamps around my head, and my digestive system wants to rid itself of its contents from both ends. My sister is obviously correct when she says I need my head examined, a need I decline, however, to satisfy.

I don't mind rehearsals, though, with the lights up and people moving around and the director calling out directions and actors missing marks and lines. It's sort of fun and not at all like being pinned, silenced, in the dark, while living people in ghastly makeup pretend they are not who they are; just as I do.

When I arrived at my wife's house my daughter was waiting on the front steps of the brownstone, chatting with a couple of young men. These had obviously arrived in the white Explorer with gold-plated fittings that stood double-parked on the street with its rear hatch open, the better to share with the neighborhood the thump of its dull chanting music, which was at a volume calculated to shiver stone. She seemed to be having a good time and I was reluctant to break up the party. The young men greeted me politely, for they were from Paul and were keeping an eye on my house, as he had promised. Imogen seemed a little annoyed when I told her this, after we were seated in the back of the Lincoln, since she had thought she was doing something transgressive, entertaining a couple of obvious gangbangers. After this had been straightened out, we rode to the school in silence, at least on my part; Imogen was immediately on her cell phone, speaking to girls with whom she had just spent the entire day and whom she would be seeing in a few minutes. Anything better than a nice chat with Dad.

Well, you know, there is really nothing like Shakespeare, even performed by children. Mrs Rylands likes *MSND* because it lets her use children from a range of ages, from the lower as well as the upper schools; her conceit is to use the little kids as fairies and slightly older ones for the major fairy parts, freshmen and sophomores for the royals and the lovers, and the biggest kids for the rude mechanicals. When the boys get to horsing around and cracking up she tells them that the greatest women's parts in all of drama were created on the stage by twelve-year-old boys, and no one thought it at all ludicrous, and here you are, you big louts, playing men at least! And remarkably, when the golden lines begin to flow from their lips they are able for a moment to leave the shut hell of teenaged narcissism and inhabit a broader, richer universe. Or so it seemed to me. I watched my daughter make her entrance in the first scene of act II and give her great angry speech: *These are the forgeries of jealousy*. I don't know where she gets it, how she knew how to speak:

Met we on hill, in dale, forest, or mead,
By pavèd fountain or by rushy brook,
Or in the beachèd margent of the sea,
To dance our ringlets to the whistling wind

and arrange her face and move her body so as to generate a vision of the fairies dancing. Mrs Rylands was entranced too, and Imogen is a cinch to do Juliet next year at fourteen and shatter hearts.

As I say, I rather enjoy rehearsals and I feel that attending as many of them as I can makes up a little for missing the performances. And the place was full of lovely young flesh and their adorable moms, which was nice too, and I exchanged some melting looks with the moms, and this made me think about Ingrid. I stepped outside after Imogen had finished her scene and called Tarrytown to see if I could come up after my meeting with the Russian, but she was cool and said she had some work to do. I've always had a certain skill at detecting lies over the wires and I did now. This wasn't at all like Ingrid, a fairly straight arrow. Could she have another lover? Probably. Did I care? Yes, a little. I always care, but not all that much; and they can tell, hence the historically rapid turnover in my romantic life.

After the rehearsal I asked Imogen if she wanted to go out for something. In times past, when she was Daddy's darling, she delighted in being taken to a particular local saloon and having made for her a Shirley Temple festooned with fruity garbage, but no longer. Imogen thinks divorce is boring, practically every one of her peers is what we used to call a child of a broken home, and she rather enjoyed the cachet of being unbroken. Or maybe not. I have no entrée into her lovely little head. We therefore rode home in near silence, although she did tell me that Nerd-Boy had spent the last week or so printing out page after page of genealogical data, so much so that nobody else (that is, Imogen) could use the printer and would I make him stop, Mom gives him everything he wants. I said I would talk to him about it and when we got to Amalie's I did.

I suppose I had nearly forgotten the task I had set Niko, what with all the excitement, but as I have learned to my sorrow, my son makes regular obsessive-compulsives look like fairies dancing in the beachèd margent of the sea. I found him up in the computer room arranging sheets of paper on the long trestle table we have there, lining up each sheet precisely square, with all the rows and columns having the same spacing between them. I watched him doing this for a while before I said, 'Niko? Imogen says you found something for me. On Bracegirdle?'

'Yes, I did,' said Niko. One of the advantages of hiring a search firm for something like this is that they come in, give you the best answer they found, take their check, and split. But when you ask Niko for an answer, you get the whole story, in *exhaustive* detail, from the very first effort, with descriptions of the logic involved, plus all the various strategies adopted, sources consulted, false leads exposed, and every last discovered fact displayed. Being a normal human, I will here summarize: Our Bracegirdle had a son, also named Richard, who survived and married and had seven children, of whom five survived into adulthood, and all married and had children. The males tended toward the sea or the army and rose in status to officer rank in the late seventeenth century and through the eighteenth. A Bracegirdle commanded a battery in Wolfe's army on the Plains of Abraham outside Montreal and another was a captain of fusiliers at Plessy. There were whalers and slavers too, and the bottom line was that the last male descendant of our Richard passed away without issue in 1923, from wounds suffered in the Great War.

Okay, a good idea that didn't pan out: I was perhaps thinking of a family trove, a box of old papers in the attic that might just happen to be a Shakespeare play that no one knew about. I looked at my son and his useless work and felt a pang of sorrow, and felt also like hugging him, but knew better.

I said, 'Well, too bad, Niko. It was worth a try. Have you seen any Russian gangsters hanging around?'

'No. There are two pairs of black guys hanging around. One drives a white Ford Explorer New York license HYT-620 and the other drives a green Pacer, New York license IOL-871. I haven't finished with the descendants. I just said the males.'

'There are females?'

'Yes. On average, half of all offspring are females. Three of Richard Bracegirdle's son Richard's children were female. The eldest, Lucinda Anne, married Martin Lewes in 1681 . . .'

And off we went. I did not pay much attention, I have to say. Being with Niko is often like sitting near a rushing brook, oddly soothing. I was thinking about my coming meeting with the Russian, and also about my crack-up in the afternoon and also about where my next sexual encounter was going to come from, and under all of it was the great pulsing wound of Miranda Kellogg. Niko's narrative reached its end. He picked up the various neat stacks of paper and carefully stapled them together. He said I had to take them away because his mother said he had too much stuff in his files and he was no longer interested in Bracegirdle genealogy. He turned to his screen, slipped on his headset, and left the building. I found a big envelope, stuffed the papers in it, and left too. I did not see or seek out Amalie, although I was aware of her presence in the house, like a rumor of war.

Rasputin's is a small chain of semi-fast-food joints started by a couple of Russian immigrants, one of innumerable efforts to find the next pizza. They serve a variety of piroshki, borscht, Russian pastries, and strong tea in tall glasses. The decor is Ye Olde Soviet Union: socialist realist posters, tile floors, servers in peasant blouses and long skirts, steaming samovars, and chunks of Red militaria artfully arranged. The menus are in faux Cyrillic, with the Rs printed backward, and so on. Omar dropped me off at the only one in Manhattan, on Lafayette Street, at five of ten and lurked in the Lincoln on the curb outside, in case our gangster tried any rough stuff.

It was fairly pleasant inside, actually, steamy and redolent of cinnamon and cabbage. I sat under the ornately framed portrait of the eponymous mad monk, a place with my back to the wall and facing the doorway, and ordered a tea and a couple of piroshki. The place was half-full, mainly of local denizens seeking a break from Chinese or Italian or over-priced trendy. At ten past, a man walked through the door and stood in front of my table. I rose and shook his extended hand and he sat down, looking smilingly around the place. He was about my age and half my size, with a thick head of salt-and-pepper hair, a big jut of a nose, and intelligent deep-sunk dark eyes. He was wearing a shearling coat, a black silk turtleneck and fashionably

Oh, what the fuck does it matter what he looked like or what he was wearing? I just came back from a walk around the property. All is silent in the early-morning mists. I checked out the boathouse, the pump house, and the two-car garage, in which I have parked my rented Cadillac Escalade, a vehicle nearly large enough to contain me in the driver's seat. I can see why these behemoths are popular among the bulky Americans. Next to my rental is Mickey's Harley-Davidson Electra Glide, which he bought shortly after I got my BMW bike back in the day, to show me, I suppose, that he was a daring fellow too, although I had bought my machine because I could not afford to run a car in the city. A little breakfast and here I am back at the keyboard.

I must have looked around inquiringly because Shvanov caught the look and said, 'What, you're expecting someone else?' and I said I had always imagined that Russian gangsters traveled with an entourage. This made him laugh and show teeth that had been expensively capped in one of the industrial democracies. 'Yes, six bullet-heads in black leather and a couple of Ukrainian sluts. Would you like? I can make a call.' He spoke a nearly unaccented English, and made only infrequently the mistakes of article and pronoun omission typical of people whose native tongue is highly inflected. He wished to make small talk, as if we were old friends meeting after a brief separation. I indulged him in this, and we spoke about my sister and her fabulous career and about Rasputin's and he said he was one of the early investors and I made a crack about had he made an offer they couldn't refuse.

Here his smile grew a little tighter and he said, 'Mr Mishkin, I don't know what you think I am, so let me tell you, so we won't have any misunderstandings. I am a businessman. In past times, I worked for Soviet government, like everybody, but since fifteen years, I am in business. I have interests in Russia, in Ukraine, in Kazakhstan, in state of Israel, and also here. What kind of business, you wish to know. Primarily, I am investor. Someone has an idea, I have the money, and also the contacts. Contacts are very important in Russian community, because this is how we learn to do business in the old days. Trust, you understand? Because we don't have what you call the business norms, the court system, and so forth. In return for this investment I have a piece of the business, just like New York Stock Exchange.'

'You're a loan shark,' I said.

'And Citicorp is loan shark, J. P. Morgan Chase is loan shark – what do you think, they don't charge interest? They don't take over collateral? This is subprime lending I do, like for this place, no one else would find this money for them, so they come to Shvanov and they give me some piece of this and we are all happy.'

'And if not happy, you have people come and break their legs, which is one thing that distinguishes you from Morgan Chase.'

Again the tight smile and he waved his hands dismissively. 'Please, I have no contact with any types of collection business. This is all outsourced to completely different firms, I assure you.'

'Outsourced?'

'Exactly. You buy a pair of Nikes, how do you know who made? Maybe a kidnapped little girl chained to machine in China, they starve and beat her. It says Nike – this is all you know, a respectable firm. I think Nike don't even know who makes. If you want to be so pure as that you should be in church and not in business. You agree?'

'Not really. And speaking of kidnapped girls, since you bring the topic up, I believe one of your outsourced firms assaulted an employee of mine and kidnapped a young woman from my domicile the other night.'

Shvanov motioned to a waitress and ordered tea and blini. When she was gone, he said, 'And why should I do that, do you think?'

'Perhaps you could tell me.'

He ignored this and looked grave. 'Kidnapping is a serious offense. You have contacted the authorities, I presume?'

'About the assault on my employee, yes. But not about the kidnap. I would prefer to keep that between us businessmen.'

The waitress brought over his order, much more quickly than she had brought mine. He drank some tea, ate a bite, sighed, and said, 'Look, Mr Mishkin, we are both busy men, so let's cut to the chase, yes? Here is entire story, my end. This academic fellow Bulstrode comes to me and says, Shvanov, I have a key to a great cultural treasure and I appeal to you as a man of culture to help me find it and restore to world. I need some small monies to do this thing. And I say, of course, Professor, of course, here is some twenty grand, U.S. dollars, you ask if you need more. You understand, even a businessman such as myself has a soul, and wishes not to spend life entirely with bathhouses and piroshki shops and bars with girls, and besides I see it as perhaps a source of substantial cash flow for my firm. So I give him money to explore for this treasure. After this, he leaves country, and I hear nothing. Some weeks pass, and I receive disturbing message from reliable source. This source is saying, the professor has returned and has found this treasure but does not wish to share it with Shvanov. So, what shall I do? I call him and he denies everything: no treasure, it is a dead end. Now, in my business, many times people do not wish to share and I must take strong measures . . .'

'You had him tortured.'

'Please! I had him *nothing*. I had *nothing* to do with any torture, same as President Bush. In any event, my sources tell me that my professor has deposited the papers – which is, I believe, my property – with your firm, Mr Mishkin, and I hear from my sources that there is heiress showing up, who can dispose of this, and naturally I hope she will do the correct thing and turn these papers over to me. So she joins with you, in a legal manner, and I expect she will soon contact me and we can do business. And now you tell me she has been kidnapped. Of this I know absolutely nothing, so help me God.'

Oddly enough, I believed him, which I never would have had I not known that my Miranda was a fake. I said, 'Well, Mr Shvanov, that puts things under a completely different light. If you are not holding Miranda Kellogg, why are we meeting?'

'Why? Because you are the Bulstrode estate attorney and the estate has something belonging to me; namely, a manuscript of seventeenth century written by Richard Bracegirdle. I have seen this manuscript. I have paid to establish authenticity by scientific tests. I have papers giving me title to it. It is all quite legal and aboveboard. This is not why *you* came to this meeting?'

I said, 'Well, when I had my sister set this up, I imagined that you were trying to obtain the Bracegirdle manuscript by violence and threats.'

'What do you mean, violence and threats?'

'Sending people to steal the manuscript at my residence. Sending people to my gymnasium to menace the proprietor, so that I am expelled from membership. And, as I said, the supposed kidnap of Miranda Kellogg.'

He was shaking his head. He was waggling a finger in the

air. 'First of all, I have never sent such people to steal. As I have explained, why should I? As to gymnasium, this is some misunderstanding. I only wish to contact you in confidential manner, no threats implied. As I say, is often difficult to control subcontractors. I will have words and reinsert you as desired, with my apologies.'

'Thank you.'

'You're welcome. Now, how shall I go about to obtain my property?'

'Ah, well, there we have something of a problem. I regret having to tell you that the woman I knew as Miranda Kellogg was not Miranda Kellogg at all, and moreover this woman is missing now, and the manuscript with her. I think we have both been outsmarted by the same person.'

For an instant, Shvanov let slip the persona of a genial businessman and something truly awful flashed out of his eyes. Then it was gone. He put on a rueful smile and shrugged. 'Well, this may be true. You win some, you lose some, correct? If you manage to locate her or it I would expect you will contact me, agreed? I have all legal papers to prove this ancient document is my property.'

I said that I certainly would and requested that he do the same. 'Naturally,' he said, 'and any other papers of same type, of course.'

'What do you mean by other papers?'

'I have some information that when the Bracegirdle manuscript was found there were other historic papers that the people who sold to Bulstrode did not deliver. This is not standard business practice, I think. Tell me, Mr Mishkin, have you these papers?'

'I do not.'

'Should you come across them sometime, you will recall that they are also my property.'

'I will recall your claim, certainly,' I said, and realized that this was the real reason he had agreed to meet me, the possibility that I had the damned ciphers. I immediately discounted everything he had said.

'Thank you. I believe that concludes our business. A pleasure.'

We shook and he extracted a thick roll of currency from his pocket, dropped a twenty on the table. 'For the girl,' he said. 'For the rest there will be no charge, my treat.' Then he stared at me, his head cocked and eyes narrowed, as we do when comparing something in our sight with a mental image, and the next thing he said almost knocked me off my chair.

'You know, it is amazing how much you resemble your father.'

'You know my *father*?'

'Of course. We have done some investments together, and so forth. In state of Israel.' He stood up and added, 'The next time you see him, please offer my sincere regards.'

He walked out, leaving me gaping.

THE FOURTH CIPHERED LETTER

My Lord my best obedience to y'r lordship & hartie comendaciouns to you & all your howse. Tis now long sence I had anie letter from you my lord nor Mr Piggott neither; but you doutlesse hath greater affayres to tend. My newes is that W.S. hath the play finished, that is of Mary Quene of Scotland & hym having told me soe I begged him let me reade it most instant. First hee saith nay let me fayre-copie it mayhap there shalbe correctiones as he oft doth make but I beyng further importunate hee yieldeth. Soe I read hys foule papers. My lord I thinke we hath mistooke oure man: unlese I judge wronglie hee hath not made what wee comanded hym. But you shall see for I have heere wrote down from memorie its burthen & the matter of som speches; for hee would not lett me copie of it even a line.

First comes a prologue that saith this play treateth two grete queenes in contentioun wherein the fate not alone of kingdomes is at hazard but of sowles: with strifes of church oure Englishe state is done/Yet as you pitie her who lost so also pitie her who won. Or some thinge lyke. So has he don. We fancied he would shew Elizabeth arbitrary & tyrannous & he doth; yet sighing for her barren womb & that another woman's sonne shal have her kingdome, that verie woman that she must slay & he cryes pitie for her lonlynesse who must from policie kill the onlie human creature fit to be her friende.

We fancied he would shew Mary as a goode Christian lady to stir oure anger at her fate & he doth; yet as a lustie recklesse self-destroyer too. She goes into the plot that ruines her with open eies; for (as he tells it) she sees Babbington is a foole, she knows well her messages are reade by Walsingham yet proceeds with the matter all the same. And for why? She despaires of rescue & cares no longer if she be Quene of England or Scotland or anie where if she can but breathe free aire and ride. From her window she espies a gentlewoman a-hawking & wishes to change place with her, trade all her titles for a little breze &c. She repentes her wickedness of former tymes yet thinkes her she is forgiven it by her popish superstitiones. Though a prisoner she vauntes herselfe & despiseth Elizabeth the Quene for her shriveled womb & haveing no venerie & saith Grete Bess thy mayden-hoode a faster prison be than these my bars. Boastes too she hath hadde love where the Quene of England hath naught but the shewe of it. Further he saith of Quene Mary that the evidence brought gainst her be false in parte; for he saith Mary ne'er plotted the death of Elizabeth but onle wish'd to scape her power & be free. Soe Walsingham sheweth herein as a perjured knave.

On religion: he hath a parte for Mary's chaplain onne Du Preau who hath contention upon the right faith of Christianes with Sir Amyas & I thinke doth gain the daie if but by a little. He putteth in low clownes, one a Puritan & t' other a Papist who argue the causes in mockerie. Perhaps these alone be enough to hange W.S. but 'twould be better bolder. The scena wherein Quene

Mary goeth to her death is verie affectyng & designed to make who heareth it forget she was a vyle murthering whore. Mayhap this shall pleaze you enough my lord, but the telling I doe is as naught to the heering of it in full, for it be most artful & fulle of witte though I am a poore judge of plaies. But when I am able to sende it shal you judge if it be fit for your purpose. Until then I remayne thy faithful & obd[t] serv[t] wishing all prosperytie & long lyfe to your gracious lordship London 28th October 1611 Richard Bracegirdle

14

Being armed, Crosetti found, felt a lot like having a broken zipper on your fly, something that made you feel self-conscious and somewhat stupid, and he wondered how his dad had been able to stand it during his entire working life. Or maybe it was different for cops. Or criminals. When he arrived at work, he was torn between leaving the thing in his bag (It might get stolen! Someone might find it!) and keeping it on his person. At first he left it in the briefcase but found that having done so, he was reluctant to leave the briefcase out of his line of sight, and after an uncomfortable hour or so he removed it and clipped it to his waistband, concealed under the cotton dust-jacket he wore in his basement workspace.

Mr Glaser had gone on an extended buying trip, and so Crosetti's workload was rather light, except that he had to relieve Pamela, the non-Carolyn person, upstairs during her breaks. High-end rare books shops don't get much walk-in business, even on Madison Avenue, and so Pamela spent most of her time on the phone with her friends, who were all top-of-the-line comedians to judge from the shrieks of fun that floated down the basement stairs, or cruising Craigslist for a better job, publishing, she had volunteered, unasked. Crosetti realized he was being something of an ass with her – it wouldn't kill him to be a little friendlier – but he could not bring himself to generate an interest in a preppy girl who wanted to break into publishing.

On one of the changings of the guard that day she asked him to reach down a book from an upper shelf and he did so and heard her make a small sound of alarm. When he handed her the book she asked, eyes wide, 'Is that a gun on your belt? I saw it when you reached up . . .'

'Yeah. It's a dangerous business, books. You can't be too careful. There're people who'll do anything for a Brontë first – *anything*.'

'No, seriously!'

'Seriously? I'm an international man of mystery.' A lame line, and he thought very briefly about saying he was just glad to see her, to see if she would pick up on the line from *She Done Him Wrong* and then he could ask her if she'd actually seen the film the line came from, that it was Mae West's only Academy nomination and so on and so forth, his usual rap, but why bother? He shrugged, gave her a tight smile, handed her the book, and walked behind the counter.

When she came back from her lunch she seemed less interested in being friendly than previously, seemed a little frightened of him in fact, which suited Crosetti very well. He spent the rest of the afternoon calling people he knew about places to stay, and trolled the Web sites with the same intent. After work, he went by the likeliest place he had found, a room in a loft near the Brooklyn Navy Yard occupied by a friend from college, a freelance sound engineer, and his girlfriend, a singer. The tenant list was rich in media wannabes and the friend said the Navy Yard was destined to be the next

Williamsburg. The building stank of old toxins but was full of pale ocher light from the huge, filthy industrial windows and so reminded him painfully of Carolyn's place. As he was a sucking-on-a-bad-tooth sort of fellow, this alone was enough to make the sale, and Crosetti walked down the splintery stairs eight hundred dollars poorer and with a date to move in after Thanksgiving. He then followed a difficult multiple bus route back to the A line and the train to 104th Street, Ozone Park.

As he turned off Liberty Avenue onto 106th Street, where he lived, he passed a black SUV with tinted windows. It was not the kind of neighborhood that ran to new, shiny, $40K vehicles, and since he knew every car native to his street, and since Klim's warning of the previous night instantly sprang to mind upon observing it, Crosetti was, if not exactly ready, not completely astounded by what happened next. As he hurried past it, he heard two car doors pop open and the sound of feet on pavement. He turned and saw two men in black leather coats moving toward him. Both were larger than he was and one was a whole lot larger. They had sweatshirt hoods drawn tight around their faces and their eyes were obscured by large dark glasses, which he thought was an indication of bad intent. Without much thought, Crosetti pulled out his father's .38 and shot in the general direction of the larger man. The bullet went through this person's leather jacket and shattered the windshield of the SUV. Both men stopped. Crosetti raised the pistol and pointed it at the head of the larger man. Both men backed up slowly and reentered their vehicle, which flew from the curb with screaming tires.

Crosetti sat down on the curb and put his head down below his knees until the feeling of wanting to faint and to vomit passed. He stared at the pistol, as at an artifact of an alien civilization, and dropped it into his briefcase.

'Albert! What happened?'

Crosetti swiveled around and saw a small gray-haired woman in a pink tracksuit and a heavy pale blue cardigan standing just outside the front door of her bungalow.

'It's nothing, Mrs Conti. Some guys tried to kidnap me and I shot one of them and they went away. It's all over.'

Pause. 'You want me to call 911?'

'No, thanks, Mrs Conti. I'll call it in myself.'

'Madonna! This used to be a nice neighborhood,' said Mrs Conti and returned to her kitchen.

Crosetti picked himself up and walked on wobbly legs to his house. An elderly Cadillac hearse shone at the curb, and he regarded it sourly as he walked up the driveway to the back door. He wanted to slip through the kitchen, maybe pour himself a tumbler full of red wine and then up to his room for a nice rest, but no, Mary Peg was there twenty seconds after he had eased the door shut.

'Allie! There you are. I've been trying to get you all day. Don't you respond to messages anymore?'

'Sorry, Ma, I was on the cell a lot.' He took a breath. 'Actually, I was looking for dwellings. I think I found a place in Brooklyn, with Beck, you know, from school?'

Mary Peg blinked, nodded, and said, 'Well, it's your life, dear. But the thing I wanted to talk to you about, Bulstrode's lawyer called here.'

'Bulstrode is dead,' he replied stupidly.

'Yes, but dead people have lawyers too. It's the estate.' She gave him a closer look. 'Albert, is there something wrong with you?'

Crosetti thought briefly of trying to conceal the events just transacted a block away but realized that Agnes Conti distributed information with a velocity that telecom engineers were still struggling to match, and would shortly be phoning to supply the details, real and imagined. He said, 'Sit down, Ma.'

They sat in the kitchen, Crosetti had his glass of wine and told his story. Mary Peg heard him out and thought she took it rather well. Actually, she thought, it put her in a somewhat better position than she would have been, given what she now had to relate to her son.

'Ma! What did you do that for?' was Crosetti's wail. 'God! I hate when you pull stuff behind my back.'

'Like stealing your father's guns and turning my home into an armed camp?'

'That's not the same thing. It was an emergency,' said Crosetti without enthusiasm. He really wanted to lie down.

'Well, I too thought that some action was required, and since you were unavailable and too busy running away from home, or whatever, to answer messages . . .'

The sound of a car pulling up in front of the house stopped her short. 'Oh, I bet that's Donna,' said Mary Peg and went to the door. Crosetti poured another glass of wine. As Crosetti drained this, Radeslaw Klim came into the room, freshly shaved in a black uniform jacket and tie, and holding a shiny-peaked black cap.

'Want some wine, Klim?'

'Thank you, but no. I must drive shortly.'

'It's dark already. They don't have funerals at night.'

'No, it is not a real funeral. It is for vampires.'

'Excuse me?'

'Yes, is quite à la mode now, you know, rich young people pretend to be vampires and ride in hearses, and have a party in crypt of a former church. Ah, here is your mother. And this must be the daughter. How do you do?'

Donna Crosetti, or The Donna, as she was known in the family, was a skinny red-haired clone of her mother and an ornament of the Legal Aid Society of New York, a friend of the downtrodden, or a bleeding heart who sprung hardened criminals to run wild in the streets, depending on whether you were talking to her mother or her sister, Patsy. She was the youngest daughter, just a year older than Crosetti himself, and had a more than full measure of the middle child's sense of cosmic injury, the focus of which had been, from the earliest dawn of consciousness, the slightly younger brother, the Irish twin, the object of hatred and resentment, yet also the creature to be defended from all threats, to the last drop of blood. Crosetti felt exactly the same way and was just as inarticulate about it: a perfect stalemate of love.

Klim introduced himself, shook hands with the rather startled Donna Crosetti, kissed Mary Peg formally on both cheeks, and took his leave.

'Who was *that*?'

'That's the new live-in boyfriend,' said Crosetti.

'What?' exclaimed The Donna, who had not been consulted.

'Not,' said Mary Peg.

'Is too,' said Crosetti. 'He drives a hearse.'

'At night?'

'Yeah, he says it's for vampires. How are you, Don?'

'He's *not* my live-in boyfriend,' said Mary Peg. 'How could you say such a thing, Albert!'

'He is *too*,' Crosetti insisted, feeling the years slip away in a manner that was unpleasantly quasi-psychotic and comforting at the same time. In a minute Donna would be screaming and chasing him around the kitchen table with a cooking implement in her little fist and their mother would be yelling and trying to stop them and dishing out random smacks and threatening apocalypse when their father got home.

Donna Crosetti glared at her mother and brother. 'No, really . . .'

'Really,' said Mary Peg. 'He's a friend of Fanny's who's helping us decipher a seventeenth-century letter Allie found. He was working late on it so I offered him Patsy's room for the night.'

'Which was three nights ago,' said Crosetti. He wrapped his arms around himself and made kissing noises.

'Oh, grow up!' said his sister. Crosetti stuck his tongue out at her, she rolled her eyes at him and sat down at the kitchen table. Removing a leather portfolio from her capacious bag, she flipped it open with a businesslike snap and said, 'If this guy's coming at eight, we don't have much time. Let's have it, from the beginning.' Crosetti looked at his mother. 'I don't understand why we have to do this,' he grumped.

'Because you were cheated, and we're here to see if you have a case against the estate, to make them pay you what the original was really worth, or get it back.'

'I don't *want* it back,' said Crosetti, getting sulky as the wine fumes rose from his empty stomach to his head. 'I want none of this ever to have happened. *That's* what I want.'

'Well, my child,' said Mary Peg, 'it's a little too late for that. This has to be disentangled by a lawyer, and Donna is the lawyer in our family. And I'd think you'd appreciate her volunteering to help, especially since you just shot someone right outside our house –'

'What!' said the family lawyer. 'You *shot* someone? Did you call the –'

'No, and I'm not going to. A couple of guys tried to kidnap me –'

'What! Who?'

'Donna, calm down,' he said, 'you're sounding like an Abbott and Costello act. You want the story or not?'

Donna took a breath or two and seemed to snap her professional persona into place. It took nearly the whole hour to spin out the tale, what with her questions and the backtracking and prevarications by the little brother, so typical and so maddening, and the elaborate explanations of the ciphers and Klim's role in the household, and the peculiar case of Carolyn Rolly. By the time Donna was satisfied, the little kitchen was uncomfortably warm and the level in the gallon jug of red wine had descended two inches or more.

Donna riffled through her pages of notes and checked her watch. 'Okay, let's review a little before this guy gets here. First of all, you have no claim whatever on the Bulstrode estate for any purported swindle, because you had no right to sell that manuscript. Nor had your pal, Rolly. Both of you conspired to steal property rightly belonging to your employer. So the main thing I'm going to have to do is convince this Mishkin to forget the damn thing and go home. You really should've talked to me earlier.'

'Nobody stole anything, Donna,' said her brother. 'I explained this to you. Sidney told us to break the books and we broke the books. He got full value for the maps and plates and the rest was fully insured. It was just like a junked car. The junk man pays ten bucks for it and if he finds a CD under the front seat, he doesn't have to give it back.'

'Thank you, counselor. I see you went to a different law school than I did. Finders keepers is only on the playground. If your junk man found a diamond ring in the wrecked car, do you think he could give it to his girlfriend?'

'Why not?' asked Crosetti.

'Because he had no reasonable expectation that the car would contain a diamond ring. If the legal owner happened to see the ring on the girlfriend he could sue for replevin and he'd win. When Glaser gave you those books he had no idea that they contained a manuscript worth serious money. When you found it your duty was to inform him of the increased value of his property, not convert it to your own use.'

'So if I find a painting in a yard sale and I know it's a Rembrandt and the seller doesn't, I have to tell her? I can't just give her ten bucks and sell it for ten million?'

'A completely different situation. You'd be profiting from your superior knowledge, which is legit, and you would *own* the painting before you sold it. That, by the way, is what Bulstrode did to you. It's sneaky, but perfectly legal. On the other hand, you never owned the books from which the manuscript emerged. Glaser did and does. In fact, I would suggest you contact him right now and tell him what's going on.'

'Oh, get out of here!'

'Idiot child, focus on this! You *stole* an object worth between fifty and a hundred thousand dollars. In a few minutes, a guy is going to show up who thinks that value is part of an estate he holds in trust. What do you think he's going to do, as an officer of the court, when we have to tell him that this valuable object actually belongs to someone else, and did when you sold it to his client?'

'Listen to her, Albert,' said Mary Peg in a stern voice.

Crosetti rose from the table and stalked out of the room, seething. At some rationalizing level of his mind he had convinced himself that the whole manuscript transaction was something of a prank, on the level of swiping a stop sign from a pole, for which he had been duly punished by Andrew Bulstrode's scam. Morally, he had argued to himself, the thing was a wash. But now he was sitting with two of the three women in the world he most wished to impress (Rolly being AWOL), and they were agreed that he was a colossal jerk and a felon, and here all the family weight bore down: the disappointment, however veiled by kindness, that he was not the hero his father had been, that he was not an achiever like his sisters, that he *especially* was not a graduate of Princeton *and* Columbia Law School like Donna. He was woozy with wine besides and thought that he might as well go upstairs with his gun and shoot himself, that would save everyone a lot of trouble.

But what he did instead, since he was in fact a decent young man from a loving family and not the tortured neurotic artist he sometimes imagined himself to be (as, briefly, now) was to pull out his cell phone and call Sidney Glaser in Los Angeles. He had Glaser's cell phone number inscribed in his own device, of course, and Glaser answered on the third ring. An old-fashioned fellow, Sidney, but he made an exception for cell phones.

'Albert! Is there anything wrong?'

'No, the shop's fine, Mr G. Something's come up and I'm sorry to trouble you, but I need an answer right away.'

'Yes?'

'Well, um, it's sort of a long story. Can you talk?'

'Oh, yes. I was about to go down to dinner but I can talk for a little while. What is it?'

'Okay, this is in reference to the Churchill. The one that got ruined in the fire and you asked Carolyn to break it?'

'Oh, yes? What of it?'

'I was just wondering about the, ah, remainder. I mean the stripped books . . .'

A pause here. 'Have you had a call from GNY?'

'No, it's not really an insurance issue . . .'

'Because, ah, what they paid out wasn't nearly what we could have got at auction and so, ah . . . look, Albert, if they call, if they *ever* call, please refer them to me, understood?

Don't discuss the breaking of those books, or what Carolyn did, or anything with them. I mean the prints and maps, the decorator backs, these are really quite trivial matters and you know how these insurance people are . . .'

'I'm sorry . . . decorator backs?'

'Yes, Carolyn said she had a customer for the backs and could she burnish them up and deodorize and so forth and sell them and I conveyed them over to her. There should be a paper bill in the files. But the main thing is –'

'Excuse me, Mr G. When was this?'

'Oh, that day, the day after the fire. She came upstairs and asked me if she could play with the carcasses, the leather and so on. Did you know she was an amateur bookbinder?'

Mary Peg called out, 'Albert? Come back here and talk!' Crosetti stuck his thumb over the microphone slits and yelled, 'In a minute, Ma. I'm on the phone with Mr Glaser.'

Resuming his conversation, he said, 'Uh-huh, yes, sir, I did know that. And so you actually sold her the books?'

'Oh, yes, just the carcasses, net of the prints and so on. I think she paid thirty dollars a volume. I really don't like to bother with that aspect of the trade and Carolyn made a little business of it for some years, sprucing up fine bindings off worthless books and selling them to decorators, who would then sell them, I imagine to illiterates for concealing their liquor cabinets. Now, what was it you wanted to ask me?'

Crosetti made something up, a question about how he should handle the fire loss in their inventory accounting system, got a brief answer, and closed the conversation. He was both relieved and stunned by what he had just learned: relieved because this cleared up the legal ownership of the manuscript, stunned because Carolyn had allowed him to think there was something shady about the deal when there wasn't. So why had she allowed him to take the manuscript for his own? Why had she pretended to be semi-blackmailed into letting him have it? Why had she used this supposed crime as an emotional lever to get him to sell it to Bulstrode? None of it made sense. And how was he supposed to get all that past his sister?

He went back into the kitchen and related the gist of the conversation he had just had, and, as expected, Donna was full of the objections that he just passed through his own mind. He cut her off, however, feeling rather more aggressive, now that he had right on his side. 'Donna, for crying out loud, none of that matters. For all practical purposes I own the Bracegirdle manuscript. Carolyn isn't here, and Glaser is not going to make a fuss because I got the impression he's scamming the insurance company on the ruined volumes. He probably put in for the whole value and forgot to mention to them what he'd realized on the maps and prints, five grand or so. So that part's fixed.'

'Oh, I don't know,' said Donna. 'The insurance company might have a case that they own the thing. They paid for it.'

'Then let them sue,' snapped Crosetti. 'Meanwhile, do we have any chance of getting the manuscript back from the estate?'

'*You* could sue,' replied Donna with equal heat.

'Children,' said Mary Peg in a familiar tone, 'calm down. If no one stole anything, we have a completely different situation, thank God. Why don't we wait and see what this Mr Mishkin has to say. What I'm a lot more worried about is this attempted kidnapping business. I'm going to call Patty. I think the police should be involved.'

With that, she went to the kitchen phone, but before she could dial, the doorbell rang. Mary Peg went to the door and admitted a very large man in a black leather coat. He had a close-cropped head and a bleak, hard look on his face, and for a panicked instant, Crosetti thought he might be one of the men who had just attacked him. But as he came forward to introduce himself, Crosetti saw that, despite the hard features, the man was not a thug, that there was a sad look in his dark eyes, reminding Crosetti of his own father, also a man with a hard face and a sad look.

Mary Peg declared that they would all be more comfortable in the living room (she meant: away from the disgraceful jelly glasses on the table and the reek of red wine), and so they all trooped off to the worn upholstery, the knickknacks, and the Portrait, and she said she would make some coffee, and could she take Mr Mishkin's coat?

When they were seated, Donna lost no time showing that she was in charge. She told the big man who she was and that she was representing the family temporarily and stated what she believed were the primary facts of the case: that her brother had gone to Professor Bulstrode in good faith for an assessment of a seventeenth-century manuscript he owned; that Bulstrode had abused his professional responsibility to provide an honest assessment, had, in fact, lied about the content of the manuscript, which was a valuable addition to Shakespeare scholarship, and had purchased the document from Albert Crosetti for a fraction of its value, a transaction that any court would find unconscionable. And what did Mishkin intend to do about it?

Mishkin said, 'Well, Ms Crosetti, there's not much I *can* do about it. You see, I'm here under false pretenses, in a way. My personal involvement in this affair was prompted by the fact that Professor Bulstrode came to me shortly before his tragic death and deposited the manuscript he had bought from Mr Crosetti here with our firm. He was seeking some intellectual property advice, which I provided. The manuscript was part of his estate at death, and when a woman appeared claiming to be his heiress, we accommodated her in our trust department. I personally am not handling that aspect.'

'So why *are* you here?' asked Donna, and then, as she registered the import of his phrasing, demanded, 'And what do you mean by "*claiming* to be his heiress"?'

'Well, as to that: it seems we've been defrauded. This woman, the supposed niece to the decedent, Miranda Kellogg, made off with the manuscript. Her whereabouts are at present unknown.'

At this, astonishment. 'You must be joking!' said Donna.

'I wish I were, Ms Crosetti. And I admit it was entirely my fault. This person secured my confidence with an entirely plausible story and I gave her the document.'

Mishkin turned his sad eyes on Crosetti. 'You asked why I came to see you. Tell me, have you or has anyone associated with you been threatened in any way?'

Crosetti exchanged a brief glance with his sister, then answered: 'Yeah. As a matter of fact a couple of guys tried to snatch me a little while ago.'

'These were two men, one very large and one somewhat smaller, traveling in a black SUV?'

'Yeah, that's right. How did you know?'

'They attacked me too, last week, and tried to steal the thing. I was able to fend them off at the time, but shortly after that, they, or someone else, invaded my home, knocked out my assistant, and made off with the manuscript and the woman who was posing as Ms Kellogg. I had imagined that she was kidnapped, but it now seems that she was in league with the assailants. I can only suppose that the first attack was to establish a bond between me and the woman, to allay my suspicions. That, or we're dealing with two separate antagonists. Speaking of which, Mr Crosetti, I assume you know the person listed in Bulstrode's appointment book as Carolyn R.'

'Yes! Yes, I do. Carolyn Rolly. She's the person who found the manuscript in a set of books. Do you know where she is?'

'No, I don't, but Ms Kellogg called me after she vanished and told me there was a person named Carolyn involved. Whether she's a victim or working with the thugs I couldn't say. But clearly, she understood that you did not part with the entire manuscript, and that there were still a number of pages, apparently in ciphered form, that you retained. Whoever's behind this knows you have them and wants them.'

'But they're useless,' Crosetti protested. 'They're indecipherable. Hell, whoever it is can have them right now. You want them? You can have the goddamn things . . .'

'I don't like the idea of surrendering your property as a result of threats,' said Donna.

'No? Then why don't *you* take it?'

'Take what?' said Mary Peg, entering with a tray full of coffee cups and a plate of biscotti.

'Albert wants to give his ciphered manuscripts to the thugs,' said Donna.

'Nonsense,' said Mary Peg as she handed out the coffee mugs. 'We don't give in to violence.' She sat down on the sofa next to her son. 'Now, we all seem to be involved in this in various ways, so why don't we all share our stories from the beginning, just like they do in the mysteries, and then agree on a course of action.'

'Mother, that's insane!' cried Donna. 'We should call the police now and turn this whole mess over to them.'

'Darling, the police have other things to worry about besides secret letters and attempted kidnap. I'll let Patsy know what's going on, but I'm sure she'll agree. The cops can't possibly put a twenty-four-hour guard on everyone in this family. We have to figure this out ourselves, which we're perfectly capable of doing. Besides, my Irish is up. I don't like it when bums try to muscle my people. When that happens I muscle back.'

At this, both of Mary Peg's children stared at her, and for the first time in many years recalled certain mortifying events of their childhood. All the Crosetti children had gone to school at Holy Family down the street, and were part of the last generation of American Catholic children to be educated at least in part by nuns. Unlike the parents of all their friends, Mary Peg had taken no guff at all from the sisters and had often appeared in the chalky hallways to rail against some injustice or inattention or incompetence she had detected in their relations with her children, and continued despite all their pleas to stop. Yet at some level, they still believed that anyone who could take on a fire-breathing eleven-foot-tall Sister of Charity could handle any number of mere gangsters.

'Why don't you begin, Mr Mishkin?' she said.

'Jake,' said Mr Mishkin.

'As in *Chinatown*,' said Mary Peg.

'I certainly hope not,' said Mishkin, withdrawing a small diary from his breast pocket. 'Let's see. October eleventh, Bulstrode arrives at my office, seeking some intellectual property advice . . .' And he told the whole story, except the dirty parts, ending with his conversation with Osip Shvanov, and his denial of involvement with any rough stuff.

'And you believed him?' asked Mary Peg.

'Not at all. He actually asked me about the ciphered letters.

The people who just tried to kidnap you tried it because they want something you have, which can only be those letters, which you tell me you have not been able to decipher.'

The three Crosettis shared a quick look among them, and after a pregnant pause Crosetti said that they had not, and explained why, after which Mary Peg said, 'Albert, you understand what this means?'

Crosetti said, 'No, I don't,' a temporary lie, this, to ward off dreadful knowledge.

'Well, it's very clear to me,' said his mother. 'There were only two people still alive who knew that the ruined books contained a set of ciphered letters, you and this Carolyn person, and the only people you've told are completely reliable –'

'Oh, right! What about Klim?'

'. . . *completely* reliable, which means that this Rolly woman has been behind all of it from day one.'

'Uh-uh.'

'No, really, Albert, face facts! Who got you to sell to Bulstrode? Rolly. Who disappeared to England right after you sold to Bulstrode? Rolly. Bulstrode must have found out something in England, and they were probably together when he found it. Then he comes back and he's tortured to death to reveal whatever it was, and how could whoever did it know what he found out? Rolly!'

'Mother, that is so . . . so completely off the charts. You assume that Carolyn's the perpetrator here on zero evidence. She could just as easily be another victim. She could've been tortured too, and *that's* how whoever it is knows about the ciphers.'

'He's right, Ma,' said Donna, as her natural defender's personality emerged. 'We just don't know enough to speculate about the guilt of Carolyn Rolly, although unless the leak comes from Allie indirectly, the source of knowledge about the ciphers has to come from her. Meanwhile, this is clearly a criminal matter and –'

Bang.

The sound came from the street, and the three Crosettis knew immediately what it was, because they were not a family to ever say 'I thought it was a firecracker or a car backfiring.' In the next seconds a fusillade sounded from the street. Everyone stood up and Mary Peg made for the cordless phone sitting on an end table. Now came breaking glass, the sound of heavy feet, and three big men charged into the room, all of them carrying large 9 mm semiautomatic pistols. One of them shouted at Mary Peg to drop the phone. She ignored him and continued to punch in 911. When the operator came on she gave her address twice and said, 'Shots fired. Home invasion,' before the phone was torn from her hand and a big man grabbed her around the neck and held a gun to her temple.

The Fifth Ciphered Letter

My lord I have not had message from you these five moneths & what shal I doe? W.S. saith he will not give hys plaie of Mary to anie hand but my lord of Rochester's owne or onne of hys house. Shal I steale it of hym & sende? Mr Wales is dead this weeke, found stabbed in Mincing Lane. From London 2nd December 1611 Restyng y^{r} Lordships moste loyal & obd^{t} serv^{t} Richard Bracegirdle.

15

After Shvanov left I used the cell phone to call Miriam. She was, of course, out and with her own cell phone switched off (I have never once, in more than twenty years, connected with my sister on the first try), so I left a somewhat frantic message. Why? Because no one is supposed to know Dad but the three of us? Ridiculous, but there it was, a feeling of dread.

Around ten the next morning I received a cell phone call from a woman named Donna Crosetti, who said she was representing her brother, Albert, in the matter of certain papers fraudulently obtained by the late Bulstrode. I replied that it remained to be seen whether any fraud had taken place, but that I would be happy to meet with her, or Albert, to discuss the matter, all the while thinking that it was odd for a lawyer to be representing a family member, and odd too was the venue she proposed, a house in Queens rather than a law office. After we had arranged the meeting for that evening, I dialed the number she had called from and was surprised to find it a Legal Aid office. This is yet another indication of how nuts I was then, as in my right mind I never would have agreed to such a meeting.

Meanwhile, my diary helps not at all, as I was now cut loose from my normal office routine. My appointments were cleared indefinitely, which turned out not to be such a good thing. People in stressful jobs are often told to take a rest, but sometimes it is just that stress that has held them together, like the proverbial ancient biplane kept in the air with rubber bands and baling wire, without which it falls from the sky. So, now, in unaccustomed idleness, all the little wheels started to wobble loose or jam up. I paced. I flicked channels. I watched pigeons and traffic out my window. I had a massive coronary . . .

What it felt like for a moment, but which was only the start of panic: short breath, sweats, tingling in arms, a little dyskinesia. The cell phone buzzed its simple factory-installed tweedle and I grabbed for it like life itself and it was Omar, and would I be going out today? Actually, I would. I had the usual number of friends and acquaintances around town, but there was only one person I thought I could go to after getting fired from my job for malfeasance, which was my wife. So I cleaned myself up, dressed casually but with care, checked my image for corporal signs of depravity, found many, took a Xanax so as not to fret about these overmuch, and away we went uptown. More *dummheit*! I always forget that my wife understands me.

I believe I mentioned that Amalie runs a financial newsletter out of a small office in our town house. This is somewhat misleading, because there is also an actual office full of gnomes down on Broad Street, and in other offices scattered throughout the planet in the time zones that matter to international money. My wife visits these as infrequently as she can get away with, because it is her fancy that she is a simple wife and mother with a paying hobby, as if she were crocheting pot holders instead of running a multimillion-dollar enterprise. It is something of a joke in the financial district, I am told, but it turns out (ask Mike Bloomberg) that after a while one's financial information empire more or less runs itself, and the founder's main responsibility is to resist kibitzing.

Thus I had every reason to believe that Amalie would be free for a nice consoling chat, but when I arrived at the house and was let in by Lourdes, and asked where Amalie was, she told me (with what I thought was excessive satisfaction) that Amalie was not available, that she was having a meeting. I could wait in the living room.

So I waited and fumed and wished for more drugs and got tight in the chest for what seemed like hours, but by my oft-consulted watch was less than forty minutes, until I heard voices in the hallway and sprang up and was able to witness Amalie showing out a trio of suits, who looked at me curiously, as at an exhibit (I imagined): unemployed ex-husband, lurking. Amalie, for her part, showed no surprise, nor did she introduce me to the suits but ushered them graciously out the door.

When she came back, I said, 'Big meeting?' keeping the tone light.

'Yes,' she said. 'What's wrong, Jake?'

I related the law firm story in the most pathetic and self-deprecating manner possible, sitting on her/my leather couch while she perched primly on the chair opposite. I omitted only the horrible Russian of the previous evening.

'Poor Jake,' she said when I was finished. 'What will you do?'

'I don't know. Take some time off, think about life. Maybe I'll look for this lost play.'

'Oh, don't even joke about that!'

'Why not?' I said. 'Where's the harm?'

'The harm is that one man has been killed over this, according to you, and my children are having to be watched by Paul's gangsters. I cannot stand to live like this, Jake. I have said to Paul, thank you very much, but please no.'

'What, no one is watching the children?'

'No, and there is no reason for anyone to bother with them because you have nothing they want any longer.' She must have observed something in my face that I was not aware of, because she added, a little more forcefully, 'Or so you have led me to believe. Is there anything?'

'No,' I said quickly. 'Of course not. They have the original letter already and that was all I ever had. It's over.'

She kept looking at me as if waiting. At last I said, 'What?'

'Nothing. I have nothing to say. You are the one who came to my house.'

'I thought we could talk,' I said.

'Upon what subject? Shall we discuss your new woman?'

'There's no new woman.'

'That would amaze me. Look, we have had a terrible fight, yet *another* terrible, shameful fight about your lying and your girls, and now you have ruined yourself in your profession because of one of them, and you come back to me for . . . for what, I should like to know? Punishment? Shall I stand in the door like a cartoon wife, tapping my foot, with my arms folded, holding a rolling pin? Or take you back? On what basis? That you will act like a mutt dog in heat whenever you please, and I shall be waiting with the lamp in the window?'

I can't recall what I said in reply. I can't recall what I wanted from the wretched woman. For the past to be erased, I suppose, for a clean slate. I believe I did actually sink to the level where I appealed to her Christian charity: did she think I was beyond forgiveness? Whereupon she pointed out to me what I knew very well, that there is no forgiveness without repentance, and that I had not really repented; and then stopped herself and cried out that I was doing it again, making her feel like a damned prig and a Sunday school teacher, I am not to instruct my husband as to morals, he is supposed to know all this already.

And so on. Early in our relationship, Amalie had revealed to me that when she was thirteen her beloved dad had been discovered with an entirely separate second family on the other side of the Mont Blanc tunnel, mistress and two daughters, à la Mitterand, very high tone and civilized, of course, no question of divorce, just a continuing slow hell of silent meals and separate bedrooms and the children sent away to boarding schools. Amalie thus had a horror of infidelity, why she fled sophisticated decadent Europe for America the puritan, we are fat and stupid and lack culture but American men are perhaps not such hypocrites about their marriage vows. And married me.

Then she changed the subject, standing up, and pacing back and forth, bent over a little, her hands stuck in the pockets of the cashmere cardigan she often wears while working. She told me that the men I saw going out were from the Dow Jones organization. They had been dickering for *Mishkin's Arbitrage Letter* for some time and Amalie had agreed just now to sell it for a figure not quite sufficient to purchase a squadron of air-superiority fighter planes. She added that she was going to sell the town house as well and move to Zurich. Her mother was getting on and was lonely and depressed and it would do her good to fuss over the grandkids, and Amalie was angry at my nation, she did not wish to bring her children up in a christo-fascist empire, that was not what she had bargained for when first she flew the ocean to America the free, and she wanted to devote herself full-time to charitable works in the earth's more desperate regions. And on cue I blurted out, 'What about me?'

It certainly hurts when someone you have loved looks at you with pity, as Amalie did then. Now that I think about it, I should have known then that the love was still alive in my heart, or it would not have hurt so much, I could have remained the cool 'separated' man about town like all the others one sees in the parks and tony restaurants on Sundays in Manhattan: uncomfortable, phony-jolly, overindulging the unhappy tykes. She lowered her eyes, as if embarrassed by what she saw, and retrieved a Kleenex from the wad that always lurked in the pocket of her cardigan, wiped her eyes, blew her nose. In my wickedness I thought, Ah, she weeps, that's a good sign! I found myself begging her not to go, that I would be different, etc. She said she loved me and always would, and wished very much that she could be complaisant, but could not, and if I ever decided to return on terms of perfect honor to my marriage, she would see, and I said, Now, now, I *have* decided, and she gave me a searching look as only she can and said Oh, no, Jake, I am afraid you have not.

Which was true because just *before* that moment, when I thought she might roll, I was still thinking that somehow I could retrieve Miranda and clear up our little misunderstanding and have both the old and the new Amalie at my disposal. I can't stand to type any more of this hideous account of what was taking place in my weasel mind. It doesn't matter.

What did I do after she had, quite properly, shown me the door? I went to the gym, where Arkady welcomed me with a warm handshake, an embrace, and a false look. God knows what Shvanov had arranged to get me back in there, but it was clear that the easy gym comradeship was over. The word had apparently also spread to the other Russian lifters in the place because I was treated like a radioactive prince, no waits for the benches or machines for me! I pumped iron until I was ready to throw up, then took a painfully hot shower; Arkady's is known for the dangerous heat of his hot water (there are even cautionary signs), and I wondered if you could accidentally on purpose kill yourself in this way. When I was meat-loaf red I turned the hot faucet off entirely and suffered under the icy drench until my teeth chattered.

I was getting dressed when my cell went off and it was my sister. Without preamble I asked her if she knew that Osip Shvanov knew our father. Sure, she said. They knew each other from Israel. What about it?

What about it indeed? The fact filled me with a particularly infantile kind of fear, where you know you have to keep something hidden from the parent without quite knowing why, only that if they found out they would act out of malice, or worse, some unconscious impulse to claim a chunk of your soul, to innocently *eat you up*.

'Jake, is there something wrong?'

Honestly, I can't remember what I was saying that made her say that; I must have been babbling in an uncharacteristic fashion. And it brought me up short, because Miri is rarely interested in what is wrong with her loved ones, there is so much wrong with *her* that she prefers to talk about.

'Nothing,' I lied. 'Look, Miri, have you, like, *discussed* this whole manuscript thing I'm involved in with anyone? Shvanov? Or Dad?'

'What manuscript thing?'

'You know, I told you about it that night at Amalie's . . . Shakespeare, death by torture?'

'Oh, that. I don't think so, but you know, I don't keep a meticulous, like, *transcript* of everything I talk about. Why? Is it supposed to be some big secret? No, don't leave it there! Move it over by the piano!'

'Excuse me?'

'Oh, they're delivering something. Look I have to go, darling, these people are going to totally destroy my living room. Bye-bye.'

With that she was gone, leaving me to deal with the probability that my sister had spread the amusing story of how her brother had found the key to a fabulous treasure throughout her wide circle of friends, including quite a few in the demimonde between business and crime. Miri had never much worried about the distinction, which meant that Shvanov might possibly be telling the truth – the city was full of Russian thugs for hire, and those who had attacked me might not have had anything to do with Shvanov's outsourced violence. But perhaps they did. Perhaps it was a vast conspiracy, watching, waiting to strike, and why had I been so stupid as to come to a gym full of tough Russians? Panic does not really stick in the mind, I believe, it is as transient as smell, although it can be brought back Proust-like by a recurrence of the original stimulus. I am a little batty now, and so I can recall fairly well my irrational desperation sitting half-naked in that wintergreen-smelling locker room. I had the cell phone in my hand and almost without thinking, I dialed Mickey Haas's number. I left a message demanding that he contact me immediately and I must have sounded crazed because he rang me back about twenty minutes later, while I was waiting at the curb for Omar to bring the car around.

'Lunch?' I said when he was connected.

'This is a lunch call? You sounded like your pants were on fire.'

'It's a desperate lunch call. I'm being chased by Russian gangsters. I really need to talk to someone.'

'Okay. I had something with my publisher, but I can cancel. You'll send Omar?'

'I'll come up. We'll go someplace new.' Of course *they* would be watching my usual haunts . . .

We went to Sichuan Gardens on Ninety-sixth, somewhat to Mickey's amusement. The place is dim and on the second floor of a commercial block, and I sat with my back to the mirrored wall where I could watch the entryway. To fine my alertness to an even higher degree I had a martini.

'So, Lefty,' he said when we had ordered, 'you think Big Max got a contract out on you?'

'This is not funny, man,' I said. 'This is not supposed to be my life.'

'No, your life is supposed to be long dull days at the office doing work you don't particularly like, whose purpose is to render the creative act even more of a commodity than it already is. And chasing pussy in your off hours, looking for the romantic fix that will stay fixed, even though you already found it years ago, and if you did once again convince yourself you found Miss Perfecto, you'd go off chasing pussy again as soon after the wedding as you possibly could, a dreary cycle that will end only when you locate someone sturdy, reliable, and mercenary who will stick around to nurse you through your final illness and collect all the chips.'

'Thank you for your support, Mickey,' I said as icily as I could. 'And fuck you very much.'

'Whereas now,' he continued, undismayed, 'you're living the life of a man, every moment rich with import, with danger and excitement. A Shakespearian life, you could say, a life worthy of Richard Bracegirdle. Would you want Hamlet to go back to college and join a frat? Get drunk and party and get a B minus in Scholasticism 101?'

'Doesn't he get killed at the end of the play?'

'He does, but don't we all? The choice is only how we live in the previous five acts. Have you come any closer to finding the Bracegirdle original, speaking of spine-tingling excitement?'

'No, and I don't intend to,' I snarled, since I was being frank with Mickey and did not require any sympathy from him, did not care if he thought I might be in danger, which is why I had mendaciously suggested this possibility to my wife. 'I want to have nothing to do with Bracegirdle apart from insuring that Russian gangsters or whoever is after the ciphers leaves me the fuck alone. What about you? Have you penetrated the mysterious manuscript any since I saw you last?'

'No, and I don't intend to,' he echoed. 'Giving something like that to a scholar is like giving a glossy photo of a roast beef dinner to a starving man. It'll make his mouth water but is devoid of nourishment. Without the original, as I think I've said, the text itself is a nullity. Never mind a putative letter from a guy who spied on the man, I could whip up a convincing facsimile of Shakespeare's personal diary in a spare afternoon, answering questions that have plagued scholars for years. What Russian gangsters?'

Now the whole thing emerged in a rush – Miranda, Amalie, Russians, the law firm, and all. Mickey chopsticked up his spicy beef with buckwheat noodles and listened quietly, as for years I have depended on him to do, as he has on me. When I ran out of words, I asked him for his opinion and suggested that he not just tell me I was fucked up, because I already knew that.

He said, 'You're going to see this Crosetti kid with the ciphers?'

'Yeah, but they think I'm going there to dicker about returning the original that Bulstrode screwed him out of. I have absolutely no leverage on him, except money.'

'That's always seemed to be a decent enough lever to me. Meanwhile, what do you intend to do with your life? Do you think it's likely you'll really be disbarred?'

'Maybe, if there's a complaint from the heir. I'd have to make restitution, obviously . . .'

'You ought to go see him.'

'The heir? I can't do that!'

'Why not? Have a chat, tell him what happened, beat your breast and cry mercy. You know the trouble with you lawyers is that sometimes, in your efforts to be absolutely legal, you forget ordinary human intercourse. What can he do to you? Call you an asshole? You already know that. And maybe you'll find out something about you-know-what. Maybe Andrew confided in his longtime companion. Anyway, you'll have a nice talk. You were probably one of the last people to see his boyfriend alive – he'll probably be grateful for the meeting. And you can return the personal effects. It'd be a nice gesture after your various peccadilloes.'

Yes, it was definitely Mickey who first put it into my head to go to England and talk with Oliver March. Whether I would have gone or not was still in doubt when I left Mickey at the campus, but later events changed that. I felt somewhat better after my lunch. For some reason, virtually every Chinese restaurant in New York has a full bar, even joints that look like they don't sell a martini a month. I had three, something I had never done at lunchtime before in my life.

The remainder of the afternoon is somewhat blurry. Perhaps there was a discussion of marriage with Omar, me quizzing him on Muslim practices in this area. Was fidelity easier if you had two or three? I can't recall his answer exactly. We went back to my loft and I had another drink, a scotch, and then a nap. From which I was awakened by the merry dinging of my cell phone, upon which I was sleeping. I punched the green button and it said 'You jerk!' in my ear, by which I knew it was my brother.

Clearly, he'd been talking to Amalie and Miri while I was eating and sleeping and had the whole story from both those angles and he let me know what he thought of my recent behavior. 'Was that it?' I said after the blast had dissipated. 'Because I have an appointment at a child brothel in twenty minutes.'

This he ignored as it deserved, and said

What does it matter what he said, exactly? I was blurred with drink and unpleasant sottish dreams and so I can't really recall. I think we talked about Amalie and about her asking him to pull his thugs off the case and her plans to leave the country. I was probably rude to him as I so often am, for I have never quite forgiven him for turning out a better man than me, and also I was sick of being lectured by my family about my many defects. I may have asked him about our father, about whether he was connected in some way with Shvanov and his doings. He told me he didn't know, but it was possible, if any scams were going down. What kind of scams?

He said, this Shakespeare business, dummy. It has all the earmarks of a big con: the secret document, never authenticated and now lost, the priceless treasure, the dupe Bulstrode, the false heiress. It stank of fraud, and since it was a bunch of extremely dangerous gangsters who had been defrauded, it would be a wise move not to get involved any more and to get the word out that I was no longer a player. Something like that. Did I beg him to intercede with Amalie not to leave the country? I may have. As I said, it's vague.

Hideously clear, in contrast, is what happened during the remainder of my evening. My stomach was acting up, as it always does when I drink to excess during the day, so I made myself some poached eggs, toast, and tea, and around six or so had Omar drive me out to godforsaken Queens, to Ozone Park. It was dark when we arrived at a street of depressing little bungalows, all with vest pocket front yards protected by chain-link fencing and decorated with Madonnas and mirror balls on pedestals. It reminded me forcefully of my Brooklyn roots and my unhappy childhood. I was prepared not to like the inhabitants.

My ring was answered by a thin woman with an Irish kisser and a head full of russet ringlets, wearing a black cotton crewneck and worn blue jeans. A nice freckled face but supplied with the kind of sharp blue eyes it would be hard to lie to. I introduced, we shook. This was Mary Crosetti, mother of. Into the living room: furnishings old, worn, reasonably well cleaned, a middle-class home such as I had been reared in, cared for, but not kept like my own mother kept house, no odor of furniture polish or bleach. A powerful odor of wine, though. Albert Crosetti was a well-fed medium-size fellow with a frank, open face and large dark eyes that seemed to want to be wary if only they knew how. The lawyer-sister, in contrast, was one of *us* – bright, cool, something of a killer. Pretty and slim, though, another redhead, brighter hair, worn in a schoolgirlish ponytail, fewer freckles than Mom: the sort of woman upon whom my charm does not work. The father of the family had been a cop, apparently, and he stared down at us from one of those awful portraits made from photographs, in which everyone looks stuffed and sprayed with vinyl.

After the preliminaries I told my story, made my confession. Learned they had the ciphers but had made no progress in interpreting them. We then talked about Carolyn Rolly, the woman with whom Crosetti had gone to sell the manuscript to Bulstrode. Rolly seemed like an interesting woman and perhaps a key figure in the affair, and I was about to ask whether anyone had made a serious effort to locate her, when the gangsters came in.

I believe I have already stated that I am not a violent man and that my military experience consists largely in caring for the stricken; my deeds in the events that followed should therefore not suggest that I am anything other than a quite ordinary coward. There was a shot from the street, which I did not identify as such, and then many more ditto. I thought firecrackers, but the Crosettis all rose to their feet and young Crosetti looked out the window. Mrs Crosetti picked up a cordless phone and dialed 911. I said, inanely, 'What's happening?' No one answered and then some glass broke and three men came running into the living room; to comprehend what happened next you have to understand that we were all in a space about ten feet across.

I recognized them as the men from the street outside my loft, the very big guy, the human-club guy, and the third man. They all had pistols. There were shouts, although neither of the women screamed. I think the thugs were trying to get us to lie down or something, but none of the Crosettis were moving. What I do recall is that the human-club guy came toward me and raised his pistol, as if to hit me on the head, in revenge, I suppose, for my prior ill treatment, and I recall feeling something like relief, because this meant that they were amateurs.

I caught the descending gun in my hand, grabbed his wrist, and wrenched it away from him. He had a surprised expression on his face as I did this, because the movies he had seen, in which pistol-whipping was a common feature, had not prepared him for this obvious maneuver. As my brother has pointed out to me, if you wish to hurt someone and you have a handgun, the thing to do is to shoot them. This is why there are bullets in it, he says, and besides, a semiauto handgun is a fairly delicate piece of gear and not designed for hard contact with a human skull.

Meanwhile, the very large one had rushed over and knocked the phone out of Mrs Crosetti's hand. He grabbed her around the neck, with his pistol pointed at her temple. He was shouting something, but his accent was so thick and he was so agitated that I, at least, could make nothing of it. The third man was just inside the living room door pointing his gun around and also shouting. When he saw that I had his pal's gun he fired a shot at me, but his angle was blocked by the body of that same fellow. I now shifted this weapon into firing position, took a backward step, and turned to face the man who held Mrs Crosetti.

He was making a good deal of noise, desiring me to drop my gun or he would shoot her, and to make this threat more obvious, he pressed the barrel of his pistol hard against her head. This was another movie watcher repeating what he had learned on the screen, thus ignoring the obvious advantage of any firearm, which is that one can stand off from one's victim and do damage while the unarmed victim cannot get at you. Mrs Crosetti knew reality from fiction, however, and so shoved the man's gun away from her head. It fired harmlessly into the ceiling, whereupon I shot him through the bridge of his nose at a range that could not have exceeded four feet.

Then I was seized from behind by the human-club guy, but at that moment another shot sounded and the man let out a cry and slumped against me, for the third man had inadvertently shot his comrade, who had heroically attempted to grab me from behind and had thus moved into the line of fire. The wounded man screamed in a foreign language (probably Russian) and sat down on the coffee table, collapsing it, and as he opened the target I shot the third man twice in the chest. He dropped to the floor and poured blood.

I would say that about forty-five seconds had elapsed since we heard that first shot. I have an image of myself standing there with the pistol in my hand while the thug from whom I had taken it slowly rose from the splinters of the coffee table. He was holding himself crooked, as if he had aged forty years in that short time. He looked me in the eye and backed away from me, shuffling. My ears were ringing from the shots, but it seemed that there was still gunfire coming from the street, and I wondered, rather abstractly, what was going on. I made no move to stop the man and when he saw my indifference he turned and dragged himself slowly from the room. No one attempted to stop him.

All of that is remarkably clear and burned into my memory, and has formed the theme of many nightmares since: I awake sweating, imagining that I have killed two men, and then it hits me that it is not a dream, that I really have killed them. A uniquely unpleasant experience. It is actually quite difficult to kill someone with a handgun unless the bullet strikes and destroys the heart or the brain, or creates internal bleeding, for pistol bullets are not terribly powerful. A standard 9 mm round generates about 350 foot-pounds of energy at the muzzle, which is no fun if it hits you, but not absolutely devastating, which is why you get those situations where the cops shoot someone forty times. Cops are trained to keep shooting until the target is down, and occasionally it takes that much lead to do it. Rifle bullets are vastly more powerful, and this is why soldiers carry rifles. A 30.06 round hits with nearly three *thousand* foot-pounds, and yes I am avoiding the next part with this bumf, which I got from my brother during his glorious military career, because the memory is both horrible and vague in that bad-dream way where you imagine that it might even have been worse than you recall, a supposition supported in the aftermath when, from time to time, a mercifully forgotten detail will bob up out of the dark to appall you anew.

So here I am standing amid the gun stink and the Crosetti children are gathered around their mother lifting her to her feet and placing her on the couch and she is absolutely covered in blood and tissue bits from the wounds of the guy whose brains I just blew out. I am looking down at the dead face of the third man: I only shot him twice but obviously I got lucky because he's clearly dead, the eyes half-open, the face white and slack, the blood pool is huge, the size of a small trampoline. A good-looking guy, late twenties. Well, I don't care to study him, nor the fellow with his brains spattered over Mrs Crosetti's end table, so I stroll over to the window and shift the blinds, and I see a gun battle going on, whose participants are a guy from the black SUV, a man shooting over the hood of a Cadillac hearse, whom I've never seen before, and Omar, shooting from behind the Lincoln. Somehow, I can't get interested in this, it all seems so far away, and now I notice that my knees are shaking so badly that I literally can no longer stand up. I therefore fall into an easy chair. I hear sirens, although at first it is hard to distinguish these from the ringing in my ears. Now there is a transition that I can't quite recall, although perhaps Mrs Crosetti asked me how I was doing.

Then, somehow, the room was full of shouting cops, the kind with submachine guns, helmets, and black uniforms, rather like the ones my granddaddy wore. (And how did

American police come to dress like the SS, and how come no one objected to it? Or to the Nazi-style helmets our troops now wear? Where are the semioticians when we need them? All bitching about Shakespeare, probably.) Many of these submachine guns were pointed at me and I realized I was still holding the handgun on my lap, like a lady holds a purse at the opera.

I was made to lie prone and I was cuffed, but I did not get arrested, since the person directing the invasion had been a colleague of the late Lieutenant Crosetti and was, therefore, inclined to listen to sense from Mrs Crosetti, or Mary Peg, as she has since asked me to call her. We are all buddies now, it seems. Ms Crosetti – Donna – has appointed herself defense lawyer for both me and Omar, and for a hearse driver named Klim, who is also a Polish cryptographer working on our ciphers, as I later learned. Paramedics arrived too and declared my victims dead and carried them off, leaving a truly remarkable amount of gelling blood behind. The police took statements at the scene. Each of the participants went singly into the kitchen and spoke to a pair of detectives, whose names I have forgotten, as I have forgotten the burden of what I told them. They seemed satisfied that I acted in self-defense; I got the impression that Mary Peg disposed of a good deal of authority in the NYPD. The only people arrested were the driver of the SUV and the wounded thug, who had been picked up wandering through the neighborhood some blocks away.

Eventually the police left. They had two fall guys to blame all the gunfire on, and they could not see a way to arrest anyone else without involving the widow and son of a heroic cop. Mary Peg looked at the wreckage of her living room and began to wail and I joined her, quite disgracefully. Klim threw his arms around her and spoke softly in her ear, and

Omar did the same for me. In retrospect, the story of the gunfight on the street is obvious. Omar was waiting in the Lincoln when the SUV zoomed up and the three armed men jumped out and ran into the house. Omar grabbed his gun and took off after them, but the driver shot at him, and Omar dived behind our car and returned fire. Then the hearse arrived and Klim joined the fray. Remarkably, none of the three was injured, which shows again how paltry is the handgun for any serious slaughter, except by accident or at extremely close range against the unarmed.

Later, pizzas were ordered and we all sat around the kitchen table and ate them and drank red wine and congratulated ourselves on our survival. Donna Crosetti left, after advising her clients not to talk to the police, and Mary Peg and Albert Crosetti seemed to relax a little, and become somewhat more free in their conversation and their drinking. We had coffee made with generous slugs of Jameson whiskey. The events of the evening retreated a little, and I only burst into tears one additional time, although I was able to slip out to the bathroom before the spasm arrived. Post-traumatic stress is the current term for what you feel when you have killed another human, and it doesn't really matter if it was justified or not, although murder is the national sport of many of the world's nations, and thousands upon thousands of people seem to be able to do it without concern or remorse. I will probably never recover from it myself.

Actually, that's not true. You *think* you'll never recover, but you do, or I did. Perhaps there is more of Grandfather in me than I thought. Paul has apparently recovered from a much more extensive career as a killer, although he says he prays daily for the souls of the people he dispatched over in Asia. I don't really know what this means, 'pray for the souls.'

At any rate I emerged from the john, and none of the party adverted to my red eyes. Klim was engaged in an argument with young Crosetti that I found intriguing, in which the Pole made the case that the only thing that would stop what now seemed to be escalating violence was to retrace the footsteps of Bulstrode and to find what he had found, if anything, and if anything, get hold of it. Once the Thing was in hand, of course, and public, there would be no question of anyone needing to commit further acts of violence. If there was Nothing, on the other hand, then we would need to convince the bad guys of this, a somewhat more difficult, but not impossible, task. The important thing was to up the tempo, so that we were not reacting defensively but in control of the game. As in chess.

Crosetti was saying that no, the point was *not* to get any deeper into it, to stay close to home. If someone wanted the papers they could have them, he wanted nothing more to do with the whole thing. I felt sorry for the kid. I sympathized – I also wanted all of it not to have happened. But I also thought that Klim was right. As long as someone with no morals and access to armed men thought we had a lead on an Item that might be worth a hundred million bucks, then not one of us was safe. Klim thought he could watch over Mary Peg well enough for a short time, and the cops would keep an eye on the rest of the Crosettis, at least for a while, as well as turning up the heat on various Russian mobsters. But that was only a temporary solution, as he pointed out. The tale of the treasure would spread in the underworld, and before long, some other fiend would take a crack at it.

Crosetti at last said, 'Okay, let's say I agree. What am I supposed to do? Wander around England indefinitely? With what for money?'

'You have savings, don't you?' asked Mary Peg.

'Oh, right! I worked like a dog for that money. It's for school and I'm damned if I'm going to blow it on some crazy idea.'

'I could cash in some of the IRA,' she suggested.

'What, and live on the pension? That's nuts! You barely get by as it is.'

'Money is not a problem,' I said, and they all looked at me as if I had declared the Earth flat. 'No, seriously,' I said. 'I'm loaded. And I would be glad to take Albert to England as my guest.'

The Sixth Ciphered Letter (Fragment 1)

wherefore I should have anie favour of you? For I have gone against my Kinge but I sweare my Lord on anie thinge you shall name that I knew it not and was betrayed and made traitour by the wiles of my Lord Dunbarton as I have told.

Now shall I relate how came it I was myself betrayed and so to throw myselfe upon yr. Lordship's mercie. Twas in the winter now passed some days after Candelmas I thinke when I did spie Mr Piggott walking on Fenchurch Street. I made to greet him but he signed me privilie that I should not and he walketh on. Yet I was not to be uzed so for I had been many weekes without word from my Lord D. or indeed Mr Piggott and it vexed me sore that they should slight me thus as I had been to much trouble for theyre plottinges. I followed him and he turned him toward the river at St Clements Lane and he enters a publicke house called The Lamb, a low dirty dark place and I found me a sweeper lad and gave him a tester and bade him go in and buy him ale and mete with it and sit him as near as he could by Mr Piggott, who I described as well as I could and come out & tell what he had heard and who the man met with if any & if he did well he should have another 6d.

Soe wait I in shadowes under eaves & after a time out cometh the lad and he tells me my man met with Harry Crabbe and John Simpson & they spake low but he heard money passed in a purse. We wait in shadowes & soone out comes Mr Piggott & in a litel comes two ill-favoured men, one with his nose cut off & wore a leather one in its playce & the other a verie beare, black of face but trumperie dressed with a longe yellow plume to his hat. The lad pointeth now privilie, telling these be the men he met with. And what manner of men are these, I asked him, and he replies, Crabbe (he of the false nose) is well-named for he loveth the crabs so much he feedes them on men & this Simpson is called John the Baptist heerabouts, for he baptises in Thames water & better than a bischop too, for those he baptiseth sin no more in this world; by which he meant he drowneth them. Quoth I: did you then heere nothynge of theyre plots? He saith: yea, I heard that the playere must die & Simpson saith ten angels maketh but one angel & must give ten more if you want yon lad Richard in the river bye him & your man agreeth but with bad grace and giveth over more & may you my master, be generous as he. Soe I payde him and left that street much afeared & knowing not where to turn for aide.

With my harte thus confuzed I got me over river to the Globe & set to my taskes there, but verie melancholie & otheres of that company saw & sence there be no company lyke a company of plaieres for gossip I was butt of verie much bayting that day, one saith hee is in love, another nay, he hath learnt he hath the pox, yet another nay, he hath lost all at cartes & shall pawn his cloake & hanger at the Jewes: til I threw a stool at Saml. Gilbourne, and soon thereafter Thos. Pope & I were at daggeres nearlie, when Mr Burbadge and some otheres bade us stop upon feare of ducking, yet we would not & were thrown in the river for oure owen goode.

Then we had the tragedie of Hamlet that after-noone & I was set to plaie a lord attendant on the King & come out with them alle in Actus Primus, scena ii, but when I look out at the groundlings in the penny-places my harte near stopps in my breast for there at the fore stood those two villains from the Lamb & I sware I could not move more than a painted man on a board & missed my cue til Harry Cordell cloutes me in the short ribs to move me on.

16

Crosetti's doubts about the rationality of the present voyage were somewhat assuaged by the thrill of traveling on a private jet. He had, of course, never ridden one before, nor had anyone he knew ever done so. He thought he could get used to it. Mishkin apparently never traveled any other way. He had a card from his firm entitling him to a certain number of hours of private jet flight and if you loaded enough people onto it, as now, it was only a little more expensive than first class, if you considered a couple of grand each a little, which Mishkin did. He had explained this to Crosetti on the ride out to Teterboro. He seemed to want Crosetti to believe he was just an ordinary guy and not an incredibly rich person. Yes, he was an income millionaire, but just barely. It was mainly that he did not really fit, physically, on commercial airliners. Otherwise, he'd be happy to line up and take off his shoes with his fellow citizens. Crosetti didn't know why Mishkin was trying to sell him this line, but he'd noticed the same impulse in a couple of people he'd met through his film contacts, guys who'd sold scripts for six, seven figures and were bending over backward to demonstrate that they were still just regular fellas like everyone else: I only bought the Carrera for my bad back, it's got the most orthopedically correct seating . . .

The aircraft was a Gulfstream 100 and it was configured for eight passengers, and, somewhat to Crosetti's surprise, they were carrying six: besides him and Mishkin, there was Mrs Mishkin and the two Mishkin Munchkins (a phrase that popped into Crosetti's mind when they arrived at the terminal and stuck there like a bit of bubble gum beneath a theater seat) and a guy who looked so much like Rutger Hauer that it was a little scary, and who turned out to be Paul, the brother of the host. Apparently, the wife and kids were going to be taken to Zurich after the stop in London, but the brother was going to come along on the Bulstrode mission.

Crosetti thought this a little peculiar, but then he was getting the impression that Jake Mishkin was not all that tightly wrapped. For example, while they waited in the lounge provided at Teterboro for private jet passengers a man arrived who was apparently one of those people upon whom business empires utterly depended, for it seemed he could not be out of touch for one instant. That his underlings were a lazy and recalcitrant lot was evidenced by his management style, which was loud – screaming nearly – and laced with obscenity. His interlocutors were told repeatedly to shut the fuck up and listen, and advised to tell other stupid motherfuckers to fuck themselves. Mrs Mishkin was clearly upset by this person, as were the other inhabitants of the lounge. At last the churl finished his conversation with the command, 'Tell that fuckhead to call me right away! This second!' He stared at the little instrument for almost a minute, mumbling curses, and then the thing rang again, with Wagner's Valkyrie theme, and he resumed his tirade at the new fuckhead, whereupon Mishkin rose, walked over to the man, looming above him like the Jungfrau over Stechelberg. He said something in a low voice and was answered with a 'Fuck off!' at which Mishkin plucked the cell phone from the man's hand, snapped it in two, and tossed it in the trash. There was a pattering of applause from the other waiting passengers, Mishkin walked back to their group, and, after a stunned interval, Mr Obnoxio dashed out of the lounge, perhaps to obtain another phone or a cop, but which it was they never discovered, because at that moment a trim young woman in a tan uniform came out of a door and informed Mishkin that they could board now.

Crosetti was the last one to enter the airplane and took the remaining seat, which was leather smooth as girls and comfortable enough to qualify as a mortal sin all by itself. The uniformed woman asked him if he wanted something to drink and of course he asked for champagne and got it, a split of Krug, perfectly chilled, and a crystal flute to drink it from and a basket of little crackers and a ceramic tub of soft cheese. The man across the aisle was having a beer, but he had a little basket too. This was the brother. Crosetti examined him peripherally as the plane rolled across the taxiways. He was wearing a dark sweater and blue jeans and wore cheap sneakers on his feet. The poor relation? He was reading the morning's *New York Times*, scanning it really, as if the news bored him, or he knew what it was going to say already. Crosetti appreciated the feeling; this was how he himself read the paper, except for the movie reviews. He wondered if the man were an actor, a terrific-looking guy really, and wondered too at the genetics that had cranked out this one and Mishkin from the same batch.

Suddenly the man snapped the paper shut, folded it, and jammed it into a seat pocket. He turned to Crosetti and said, 'I've lost the ability to distinguish truth from fiction in the news, with the exception of the scores in sports. I don't know why I bother. It just makes me angry without a reasonable outlet.'

'You could tear the paper into shreds and stamp on the scraps.'

The man smiled. 'I could, but that sounds like something my brother might do.'

'He has a temper. That cell phone business?'

'Yes, and killing two people. But the strange fact is he *doesn't* have a temper. He's the mildest, longest-suffering guy in the world. *I'm* the one in the family with a temper.'

'Could've fooled me.'

'Yeah, but he's not himself,' said the brother. 'Violence sometimes does that. I saw it in the army a lot. People construct a persona, a mask, and they come to believe that it's really them, down to the core, and then events happen that they never expected and the whole thing just cracks off, leaving their tender pulpy insides exposed to the harsh elements.'

'Like post-traumatic stress?'

The man made a dismissive gesture. 'If you buy psychobabble. It suits the culture to dump a whole set of unrelated symptoms suffered by completely different kinds of people as a result of completely different kinds of events into a box with that phrase on the label. It's about as useful and as intellectually valid as stamp collecting. My brother lived a tightly controlled existence that, while enormously successful, was cut off from the wellsprings of life by addiction. He was living a lie, as the saying goes, and such lives are in fact fairly fragile. There is no real resilience in them.'

'What's he addicted to?'

'My, you're a nosy fellow.' This was said not unkindly, and Crosetti grinned.

'Guilty. It's a bad habit. I excuse it by saying it's because

I want to plumb the depth of the human condition for my work.'

'Oh, right, you're the screenwriter. Jake mentioned something about that. Plumb your own depths then. What do you think of Tarantino?'

'Not a plumber of depths,' said Crosetti and imitated the other man's dismissive gesture. 'What're you doing in Europe?'

'Family business.'

'Connected to all this? I mean the paper chase, the secret manuscript . . . ?'

'Indirectly.'

'Uh-huh. You're a lawyer too?'

'I'm not.'

'You know, if you want to keep stuff mysterious, the way to do it is not to make cryptic comments but to adopt a fictitious and boring persona. James Bond always said he was a retired civil servant and that usually closed out the conversation. Just a tip from the world of movies.'

'Okay. I'm a Jesuit priest.'

'That works for me. I think we're departing. We didn't even get a safety demonstration. Is that because they don't care or because no one can conceive of any misfortune befalling the ruling classes?'

'The latter, I think,' said Paul. 'It's hard to remain rich without developing a defect in the sympathetic imagination.'

Crosetti had never experienced a quicker takeoff. The engines strained briefly, the cabin tilted back like a La-Z-Boy, and they were above the clouds in what seemed like a few seconds.

When the plane was flying level again, Crosetti said, 'I assume you know the whole story thus far. I mean about the Bracegirdle letters and the cipher and all that.'

'Well, I've read the letter and Jake told me a little of what you've learned about the nature of the cipher.'

'What do you think?'

'About our chances of interpreting it and finding this supposed lost play? Negligible. I mean we'd need the actual grille according to you, and what are the chances of a piece of perforated paper surviving for nearly four hundred years? And how would we even recognize it? And no cipher, no play – that seems fairly clear.'

'So why are you here?'

'I'm here because since this letter emerged, my brother has asked me for help for the first time in our entire lives. Twice. I want to encourage this. Jake needs a lot of help. And I owe him. He was very good to me when I was in prison and for a period afterward, although he utterly despised me. It was an act of real charity, and I want to pay him back if I can.'

'Why were you in prison?' asked Crosetti. But the other man smiled, gave a short, low laugh, shook his head, took a thick paperback out of his flight bag, and slipped on reading glasses. Curious Crosetti glommed the title: Hans Küng's *Does God Exist?*, which struck Crosetti as an odd choice for an airplane book, but what did he know about the man? He slid his laptop out of his briefcase, placed it on the solid table provided, and turned it on. To his surprise, the little icon that announced the availability of an Internet connection lit up, but of course the sort of people who flew in private jets could not bear to be cut off from the Internet while airborne. Cell phones probably worked too. He put the headphones on and slid a copy of *Electric Shadows* into the drive. Oh, of course, the seat had an A/C plug in it too, God forbid the rich would ever have to depend on laptop batteries! He watched the movie with the usual critical discontent he felt when watching debut features by someone of his generation. And a woman, too. And a *Chinese* woman. Xiao Jiang was pretty good, and he tried to give her credit for it and not think bad thoughts about what she had done to get the chance. It was *Cinema Paradiso* against the background of the Cultural Revolution and the point seemed to be that no amount of bad art and state control could keep movies from being glamorous. The thirty-year time shifts were handled well, and the film had the typical aesthetic grace of all Chinese films, but the plot and the emotions generated by the cast seemed soap opera-ish, he thought, writing the review, a good debut from a talented director, not to be compared with Albert Crosetti, of course, who would *never* get a chance to write and direct a feature . . .

When the film ended he brought up the Final Cut scriptwriting word-processor and started a fresh script. It wanted a title. He typed in *Carolyn Rolly*, and thought about films named after women: *Stella Dallas. Mildred Pierce. Erin Brockovich. Annie Hall.* Yes, but . . . He deleted it and typed *The Bookbinder*, an original screenplay by A. P. Crosetti. A. Patrick Crosetti. Albert P. Crosetti.

Crosetti was a slow writer ordinarily, a big deleter, a pacer, a procrastinator, but now it wrote, as the silly expression went, itself. He had nearly the whole first act done, from the bookshop fire through the first night in the bookbinder's loft, and the discovery of the manuscript, including the first flashback, a short scene from Carolyn's childhood and its horrors. He read it over and found it good, suspiciously good, better than anything he'd done before, deep and dark and European, but with a higher tempo than the general run of serious Eurofilms. He checked his watch: nearly two hours had passed. Outside the window it was growing dark; the plane flew over a clotted field of Arctic clouds. He stretched, yawned, saved his work, and got up to visit the toilet. When he returned he found Mishkin in his seat in what seemed like urgent conversation with his brother.

'Could you give us a moment?' asked Mishkin.

'It's your plane, boss,' said Crosetti. He retrieved his laptop and walked forward to occupy the seat vacated by Mishkin, across the narrow aisle from Mrs M. Or ex-Mrs, he hadn't figured out the relationship there yet. He had to pass the two children and could not help noticing that they were both supplied with the latest Apple PowerBooks. Crosetti had never known a really rich kid and wondered what their lives were like, whether they were spoiled rotten and whether they pretended to be less rich than they were, like their daddy, or whether they were so embedded in the life that they no longer gave a damn. The girl was watching a music video, rappers living out a dream of sex and violence. The boy was shooting monsters in Warcraft. Crosetti sat down in the seat vacated by Mishkin, across the aisle from the wife-or-ex, who seemed to be sleeping, with her face pressed against the window, nothing showing but the curve of a blond head and a white neck emerging from a gray sweater. He set up his machine and plunged back into the fictive universe.

The attendant came by and delivered another glass of icy champagne and dropped a menu on his table. Apparently you could have a filet mignon cordon bleu or cold Scottish salmon or a chili dog. Crosetti went for the filet and was typing again when he became aware of a peculiar sound, like a small dog barking, no, coughing – a kind of suppressed high-pitched squeak. At first he thought it was sound leakage from one of the kids' machines, but when he looked over at Mrs Mishkin, he observed that the sounds were coordinated with the spasmodic jerking of her shoulder and head. She was weeping.

He said, 'Excuse me, are you all right?'

She made a hand gesture that could have been 'give me a moment' or 'mind your own business' and then blew her nose, a surprisingly hearty honk, into a wad of tissues. She turned to face him, and his first thought was 'foreigner'; Crosetti had always thought there was something vague about American faces compared with those he saw in the films of other lands, and this was an example of the difference. Mishkin's wife had the sort of interestingly constructed northern European face that seemed designed to glow in black-and-white cinematography. The tip of her nose and her eye rims were red, which rather spoiled the effect, but he could not help an entranced stare. It was one more indication that he had departed his real life and was now in a shooting script. She caught his stare and her hand flew to her face and hair in the eternal gesture of the woman caught out of toilette.

'Oh, my God, I must look frightful!' she said.

'No, you look fine. Is there anything I can do? I mean I don't want to get nosy . . .'

'No, it is fine. Just the normal stupidity of life in which sometimes it is necessary to cry.'

She had the right accent too. In a couple of seconds Bergman or Fassbinder was going to come out of the cockpit and adjust the lighting. What was his next line? He groped for something suitably world-weary and existential.

'Or to drink champagne,' he said, raising his glass. 'We could drown our sorrows.'

She rewarded this small sally with a smile, which was one of the great smiles he had seen so far in his life, either on-screen or off. 'Yes,' she said, 'let us have champagne. Thus the sad problems of the rich can be made to dissolve.'

The flight attendant was happy to bring a chilled bottle, and they drank some.

'You are the writer,' she said after the first glass went down, 'who discovered this terrible manuscript that has disrupted all our lives. And yet you still write away despite this. In my misery I hear you click-click-clicking. I'm sorry, I have forgotten your name . . .'

Crosetti supplied this and in return was directed to call her Amalie. 'What are you writing?'

'A screenplay.'

'Yes? And what is this screenplay about?'

The champagne made him bold. 'I'll tell you if you tell me why you were crying.'

She gave him a long look, so long that he was starting to think she had taken offense, but then she said, 'Do you think that is a fair exchange? Truth for fiction?'

'Fiction *is* truth. If it's any good.'

She paused again and then gave a quick nod of the head. 'Yes, I see how that could be so. All right. Why do I weep? Because I love my husband and he loves me, but he is afflicted in such a way that he must sleep with other women. And there are many women who would put up with this, would have affairs of their own and keep the marriage as a social arrangement. This is called civilized in some places. Half of Italy and Latin America must do like this. But I cannot. I am a prig. I believe marriage is a sacrament. I wish to be the only one and have him be the only one, and otherwise I cannot live. Tell me, are you a religious person?'

'Well, I was raised Catholic . . .'

'That is not what I ask.'

'You mean *really* religious? I'd have to say no. My *mother* is religious and I can see the difference.'

'But you believe in . . . in what? Movies?'

'I guess. I believe in art. I think that if there is such a thing as the Holy Spirit it works through great works of art, and yeah, some of them are movies. I believe in love too. I'm probably closer to you than to your husband.'

'I think so. My husband cannot believe in anything. No, that is incorrect. He believes I am a saint and that his father is the very devil. But I am not, and his father is not, but he believes this because it saves him from thinking he is hurting me – she is a saint, so of course she is above such jealousies, yes? And he need not forgive his father for whatever his father has done to him, he has never said what it is. He is a good, kind man, Jake, but he wishes the world to be other than what it is. So this is why I cry. Now, what is your movie?'

Crosetti told her, and not just about the script proper but about its basis in real life, Carolyn and their pathetically brief encounter, and about his own life and where he wanted it to go. She listened attentively, and in near silence, unlike his mother, who was full of lame ideas and not shy about sharing them. When he'd finished, Amalie said, in a tone of frank admiration, 'And you have thought all of this up in your head. I am amazed by this, as I have not one creative bone in my body, except to produce children and small things, like decorations and cooking. And to make great heaps of money. Is that creative? I don't think it is.'

'It's certainly useful,' said Crosetti, who had nothing of that talent.

'I suppose. But in the end it is a low art, like plumbing. And one has always the nagging feeling that it is undeserved. As it is. This is why the rich find it so difficult to enter heaven.'

At this point the attendant emerged from behind her curtain and began the dinner service. Amalie made her children take off their earphones and have what she called a civilized dinner. The seats swiveled around so that Crosetti found himself facing the little boy across a wide wood-grained table, which had been laid with a cloth and real china and silverware and a little vase with a baby white rose in it. Apparently Mishkin had decided to eat with his brother instead of with his family. After a few minutes, Crosetti could appreciate why. Neither of the kids shut up for a second during the meal, which for the boy was, remarkably, a bowl of Cheerios. The girl's conversation consisted largely of wheedling – things to buy, places to go, what she might be allowed to do in Switzerland, what she refused to submit to. Amalie was firm with her, but in an exhausted way that, in Crosetti's opinion, presaged tears and screaming fights amid the lofty Alps. The boy responded to a polite question about the computer game he was playing with a continuous stream of information about his entire history in the Warcraft universe, every feature of his game persona, every treasure he had won, every monster fought. The spiel was uninterruptable by any of the conventional sociolinguistic dodges and the boredom was so intense it nearly sucked the flavor out of the excellent filet and the Chambertin. Crosetti wanted to stab the child with his steak knife.

His mother must have picked up the vibrations, because she said, 'Niko, remember we agreed that after you talk you have to let the other person talk too.' The boy stopped in the middle of his sentence like a switched-off radio and said to Crosetti, 'Now you have to say something.'

'Could we talk about stuff besides Warcraft?' said Crosetti.

'Yes. How many pennies are there in a cubic foot of pennies?'

'I have no idea.'

'Forty-nine thousand, one hundred and fifty-two. How many are there in a cubic meter?'

'No, now it's my turn. What's your favorite movie?'

It took a while to figure this out, especially as Niko felt it necessary to review the plotlines of his choices, but eventually they settled on the original *Jurassic Park*. Of course the boy had it on his hard disk (he had watched it forty-six times, he announced), and Crosetti made him run it with the promise that he would tell him how they did all the effects, and he brought out the special little plug that enabled two people to use their headsets at once off a single computer. After that it was dweeb vs. dweeb, and Crosetti felt that he had not disgraced himself as a purveyor of tedious facts.

The pilot announced their descent into Biggin Hill airport, and they reversed their seats and buckled in. The attendant distributed hot towels. Amalie smiled at Crosetti and said, 'Thank you for bearing with Niko. That was very good of you.'

'No problem.'

'It is for most people. Niko is unlovable, but even unlovable people need love. It is a wretched fate to love them, but I think perhaps you are one of us who shares that fate.'

Crosetti couldn't think of anything to say to this, but found himself thinking about Rolly. Certainly unlovable, but did he love her? And did it matter if he did, as it was unlikely that he would ever meet her again?

The plane landed gently and taxied briefly through the small airport to the terminal. A blowing rain beat against the windows of the jet. Crosetti and the Mishkin brothers gathered up their carry-ons and outer garments. Crosetti got a handshake and an unexpected kiss on the cheek from Amalie Mishkin, who said, 'Thank you for talking with me, and with Niko. And now you will go off to whatever insane adventure Jake will take you to and we will not see you again. I hope you will make your movie, Crosetti.'

Then Jake Mishkin stopped in the aisle, looming behind

him; Crosetti got a strong third-wheel feeling and quickly left the plane. The terminal was small, clean, efficient, and a small staff of uniformed ladies carried him through customs and immigration with the sort of service now available only to the very rich, and which Crosetti had never before experienced. A Mercedes limo waited outside along with a fellow carrying a vast umbrella. Crosetti entered the vehicle and within ten minutes was joined by Paul and Jake Mishkin. The car drove off.

'Where are we going?' asked Crosetti.

'Into town,' said Jake. 'I have some legal business to attend to, trivial really, but enough to write off this trip and keep my firm happy, or at least less unhappy with me than they are. It should take no more than a day, if that. I'm sure you'll find a lot to do in London. Paul can show you the sights. Paul is quite the world traveler.'

'Sounds like fun,' said Crosetti. 'And after that?'

'We'll go up to Oxford and see Oliver March. We'll return Bulstrode's personal effects and see whether we can get a line on what he was doing here last summer. Beyond that we'll just have to play it by ear.'

They stayed in a small, elegant hotel in Knightsbridge. Mishkin had stayed there before, and the staff made noises indicating they were glad to see him and that Crosetti was included in the welcome. Paul did not stay in the hotel.

'My brother dislikes the trappings of luxury,' Mishkin explained later in the hotel's tiny bar. He had drunk several Scotches to Crosetti's single pint. 'I believe he's gone to stay with his fellow Jesuits. And also to arrange for our security.'

'He's a security guy?'

'No, he's a Jesuit priest.'

'Really? He said that, but I thought he was putting me on. What does a priest know about security?'

'Well, Paul has a range of talents and interests, as I'm sure you'll learn. I often think he's one of the elite corps of papal assassins we read so much about nowadays. What did you think of my lovely family?'

'They seemed very nice,' said Crosetti warily.

'They are nice. Nice as pie. Far too nice for me. My wife is Swiss, did you know that? The Swiss are *very* nice. It's their national specialty along with chocolates and money. Did you know that Switzerland was a very poor country before the Second World War? Then it was suddenly very rich. That's because they supplied the Nazis with all kinds of technical goodies from factories that couldn't be bombed because they were oh so neutral. Then there's the matter of the hundred and fifty million reichsmarks the Nazis stole from exterminated Jews. That's nearly three-quarters of a billion bucks in current dollars. I wonder what became of that? Not to mention the art. My father-in-law has a superb collection of Impressionist and Post-Impressionist paintings – Renoir, Degas, Kandinsky, Braque, you name it.'

'Really.'

'Really. He was a bank clerk before and during the war. How did he manage to accumulate such a collection? By being *nice*? My children are half Swiss, and that means they're only half nice, as you probably observed. You're probably a good observer, Crosetti, being a creative type, a writer like yourself, always lurking and taking things down. You probably have Amalie and me and the kids all figured out by now. You got a screenplay working in there? The Family Mishkin, now a major motion picture. The other half is half Jewish and half Nazi, which is definitely *not* nice. Have another drink, Crosetti! Have a Cosmopolitan. The drink of your generation.'

'I think I'll stick with beer. As a matter of fact, I'm feeling a little lagged out so –'

'Nonsense! Have a Cosmopolitan on me. Best thing for jet lag, everyone knows that. Bartender, give this man a Cosmo! And have one yourself. And give me another, a double.'

The bartender, a swarthy fellow a little older than Crosetti, made eye contact before he started fixing the drinks, the kind of glance that asks whether this moose is going to go batshit in my tiny bar and are you in a position to get him out of here before he does? Crosetti let his eyes slip downward in a cowardly way.

'You think I'm drunk, don't you?' asked Mishkin, as if reading the vibes. 'You think I'm going to be out of control. Well, you're wrong there. I'm *never* out of control. Except sometimes. But this isn't going to be one of those times. Jews don't get drunk, according to my mother-in-law. That's the only advantage she admitted in reference to my wife's generally disgraceful marriage. They were not fooled by my membership in the one, holy, Catholic, and apostolic Church. That, and they're good providers, Jews. Money, sobriety . . . oh, yeah, plus they don't beat you. She actually said that, lounging on her silk settee under her stolen dead-Jew Renoir. The Catholics of southern Europe are extremely anti-Semitic, did you know that, Crosetti? Most of the major Nazis were Catholic – Hitler, Himmler, Heydrich, Goebbels. How about you, Crosetti? You're a Catholic. You anti-Semitic? You ever get pissed at the Jewish mafia controlling the media?'

'I'm half Irish,' said Crosetti.

'Oh, well, that lets you off the hook, then, the Irish being notably free of all taint of racism whatsoever. I myself am half anti-Semitic on my mother's side. Isn't it funny that all the big Nazis sort of looked Jewish. Goebbels? Himmler? Heydrich was constantly getting pounded in the school yard because the kids thought he was a Yid. Aryan features but a big fat soft Jewish ass. My grandfather, by contrast, was a real Aryan, as so of course was my mother, his daughter. And my wife. Do you think my wife is attractive, Crosetti? Desirable?'

'Yeah, she's very nice,' said Crosetti, and checked the distance to the exit. The place was so small and Mishkin was so huge that it would be a damned close-run thing if he had to make a dash for it. It was like being trapped in a bathroom with an orang-utan.

'Oh, she's more than *nice*, Crosetti. There are deep wells of heat in my Amalie. I noticed how you leaned toward each other across the aisle. You got a little kiss there too at the end. Did you arrange to meet somewhere? I mean, it wouldn't surprise me in the least – it cries out for redress. I must've fucked forty or fifty women since we got married, so what could I say, right? You should go for it, man! Forget this Shakespearian horseshit and fly out to Zurich. They're at Kreuzbuhlstrasse 114. You can fuck her in her little yellow girlhood bed. I'll even give you some tips on how she likes it: for example –'

'I'm going to bed,' said Crosetti and slid off his bar stool.

'Not so fast!' cried Mishkin; Crosetti felt his arm gripped; it was like being caught in a car door. Before he knew what he was doing he'd grabbed his untouched Cosmo off the bar and flung it into Mishkin's face. Mishkin grimaced and wiped at his face with his free hand but did not let go. The bartender came around the bar and told Mishkin he'd have to leave. Mishkin shook Crosetti hard enough to rattle his teeth together and said to the bartender. 'It's all right. I was just explaining to this gentleman how to fuck my wife and he threw a drink at me. Does that seem right to you?'

The bartender now made the mistake of grabbing Mishkin's arm, perhaps hoping to establish a come-along grip, but instead the big man let go of Crosetti and threw the bartender over the bar and into his brightly lit shelves of bottles. Crosetti was out of there on a run, nor did he wait for the elevator but ran up three flights of stairs and into his room.

The next morning, Crosetti left the hotel very early and went to the British Film Institute on the South Bank, where he watched Jean Renoir's *Boudu Saved from Drowning* and *The Rules of the Game*. He would have stayed for *The Grand Illusion*, but while he was in the lobby seeking a drink of water, someone tugged at his sleeve, and when he turned around it was Paul Mishkin in a leather coat and clericals. Crosetti thought he looked like an actor playing a priest.

'How did you know I was here?'

'Where else would you be? Not Madame Tussaud's. Come on, there's been a slight change of plans.'

'Such as?'

'We're leaving for Oxford immediately. The car's outside.'

'What about our stuff at the hotel?'

'It's been collected, packed, and loaded. Just come, Crosetti. You can ask questions later.'

The Mercedes waited in the street and Jake sat slumped in the back seat, wrapped in a lined Burberry and muffler with a tweed cap pulled low on his head. Paul got into the shotgun seat (startlingly on the wrong side!) and Crosetti sat in the back as far as he could from Mishkin, who said not a word. The small area of skin visible above his collar looked gray and reptilian.

They drove out of the city through miles of wet brick suburbs, growing increasingly like country as they passed Richmond, and soon they were on a freeway. Crosetti noticed that Paul was checking the side mirror and inspecting passing vehicles with more interest than the average car passenger ordinarily showed.

'So, why the change of plans?' Crosetti asked when it became apparent after many miles that no one was going to volunteer an explanation.

'Two reasons. One is that there's a couple of teams of people following us. They're good at it, serious professionals, not like those jerks you were fooling with in New York. The second reason is that after Jake's performance in the bar last night, he was asked to leave, and rather than find another hotel in London we decided to go to Oxford now, stay the night, and see our guy tomorrow morning.'

'I want to hear more about the professionals,' said Crosetti. 'If they're so hot, how did you find out they were there?'

'Because we've retained a firm of even more highly skilled professionals. Right, Mr Brown?'

This was addressed to the chauffeur, who replied, 'Yes, sir. They were on Mr Crosetti from the minute he left the hotel this morning, and of course, they followed you from the Jesuit hostel to St Olave's. They're in a blue BMW three cars behind us and a maroon Ford Mondeo in front of that white lorry in the outside lane just ahead.'

'Brown is a member of a highly respected and extremely expensive security firm,' said Paul. 'It's a good thing we're made out of money.'

'Is there going to be a car chase?'

'Probably. And at least one substantial orange gassy explosion. Do you want to know what I found at St Olave's?'

'Clues to the location of the Holy Grail?'

'Almost. You'll recall Bracegirdle wrote that the key to the ciphers was 'where my mother lieth,' and that his mother was buried in St Katherine Colemanchurch. Unfortunately, St Katherine's, which survived the Great Fire, succumbed to the depopulation of the old City of London and the sad tide of unbelief and was demolished in 1926. The parish was united with St Olave Hart Street in 1921, and so I went there.'

'Why you're wearing your priest costume.'

'Right. Father Paul doing a little genealogical research. Apparently, when St K.'s bit the dust the graves were moved to Ilford Cemetery, but there were also crypts beneath the church. In medieval times, you know, people were buried in graveyards until they decayed to bones, and then the bones were dug up and put in ossuaries, because obviously a small urban graveyard couldn't possibly hold the dead of a parish for more than a few generations. And this crypt had a door, in which was a sort of window covered by a small rectangular brass plate, perforated to let in some light. The perforations were in the shape of a weeping willow tree. When St K.'s was demolished, this plate came to St Olave's along with the other church valuables and memorabilia and was displayed in a glass case in the vestry.'

'Did you see it?' asked Crosetti.

'No. According to the curate I spoke to, someone broke into the church last summer and swiped it. Didn't take anything else, just the plate. I suppose we have to refer to it as the grille now. One other interesting thing. Shortly before it got ripped off, a young woman visited the church. She was taking rubbings of church brasses and asked if there was any furniture or brasses from St Katherine Colemanchurch on hand. The curate showed her the various things and she took a number of photos and a rubbing of the crypt window plate. A few days later the thing was gone.'

Jake Mishkin stirred, cleared his throat. 'Miranda,' he said, at nearly the same time that Crosetti said, 'Carolyn!'

The Sixth Ciphered Letter (Fragment 2)

yet the two held me & struggle as I might I could not get free: & there was the box empty & the accusing coines strewn about. Then Mr W.S. held up a candle to my face sayinge Dick what's this? Dost steal from thy friends? From me? With such a look on his face that I burst forth in unmanly teares. Then he sits me kindly upon a chayre & sending my captor to wait without he sits him too & saies Dick you are no thief, an you are in need cannot you come to your owen cosen, will Will not help thee? More teares upon this til I thought my harte would breke & say I Nay, thou art too goode for I am a foule traytour & no friend to thee for I have werked to thy destruction these manie moneths & now I am so tangled in complots I cannot see my waye clare, o woe &c. He saith, now Dick thou must confesse alle I shalbe thy priest & no man shall know what may be said between us.

Soe, my Lord Earle, I tolde him all, which I have related to you before in this letter, the Lord Dunbarton, Mr Piggott, the playe of Mary & all the plottinges. And further what I had learned that morn at the Lamb, St Clements, & the two murtherers who tread close upon us both. Here he looketh most grave & stroakes his beard som tyme & saith: Dick thou foolishe boy we must twist harde to scape these netts. O cosen saies I dost forgive me, & he answereth yea thou art a childe in these thynges and were compelled to advaunce the plotts of these rogues to save thee from the Tyburn daunce. Yet all is not lost, for I am no childe.

Then he strides crost the room & back manie tymes, at last he saies know you the Lord Verey is clapped in the Tower, the same as carreyed you the supposed letter from my Lord of Rochester that began these merrie games; & I say nay, I did not & what's this news to us? Why, he saies, Vesey is my lord Rochester's man & if he be taken up, it telleth that he hath been discouvered plottinge in some way gainst the Spainish match, it matteres not howe & may soone be put to the queastion & thus all will be revealed & this affayre of oure play will oute withal. Therefore must they covere the trayle they have laid: you & I must be cut off & the play burnt, so my lord Dunbarton may saye if asked nay my lord tis but a phantasma of a racked man wherein I had no hand & no one left to give him the lye.

I asked how we may escape this troubel what shal I do & he answereth canst use a sword lad & I saie passing onlie for I am a gonner & never learned fenceing & he saies no matter we shal have Spade & Mr Wyatt & Mr Johnson shal be of oure partie he hath killed his man, or soe he often saith & I too. What you, quoth I? Aye, saies he, have I not fought more duellos than half the dons in Flanders? Yea, but with false swords onlie, say I. Think you, so? saies he. This sword at my belt is no trumperie boy and have I not walked a thousand nights through Shoreditch with a sack of silver from the box & fought cut-purse rogues for't with my steel? Ask Spade can I wield a blade for he taught me & I ween he'll call me not his least pupil: ho now Shakespear shall shake sword to-night. Tremble thou murtherers!

Soe did we gather oure forces Spade & Wyatt, Mr W.S. & Mr Johnson & mee at the George Inn at South-Wark & that night did set out Mr W.S. & I alone with the otheres at a distanse & lo we are set upon by these rogues three or foure of them I think. I drew but some man knocked me on the head & down & I saw naught but dark shapes & smale lights & when I could rise agen I saw Mr W.S. playing his blade & heard one cry oute in payne o I am slain you bugger & then did oure partie come to oure aide & fought, but I did but knele & spew. Yet we gayned the field those two murtherers dead & Mr Spade gets hym a hande-cart & lades the corpses upon it they will feed fishes saies he & Mr W.S. saies no mete but jointes for us Dick for fortnight at least lest we be called canibbals at one remove & no crabs til Michaelmas.

17

In the days following the Evening of Death I arranged our trip, which included my family as well as Crosetti. Amalie likes to spend the holidays in Zurich, and while she could have chartered a plane by herself, she took my offer of a lift, and I only had to cry a little and make her feel sorry for the trauma I had just been through, besides which it was a considerable saving, and like most rich people, Amalie prides herself on small economies.

Cops – no problems there, but no information either. The captured thugs just laughed at them when asked who they worked for. The firm – happy to see me off for a nice rest and delighted to let me use the flight card for some minor legal work in London. I did not tell them I was going to visit the heir of Bulstrode.

Went to see Paul, nice conversation about killing, wanted to weep but resisted with help of 2 mg Xanax. He volunteered to come along, to, in his phrase, watch my back. I'd never heard this used literally before and I laughed, then reconsidered. I inquired after his sacred mission. No problem, God would watch over, and besides he wanted to spend

Xmas with Amalie and kids, he deserved a vacation from the fields of the Lord. So I agreed. From time to time, as then, I acquire the notion that my brother actually loves me, that I am not merely a contemptible nuisance. This always inspires a kind of nervous fear, I don't know why. Omar wanted to come too, but he is on all the terror watch lists and this makes it inconvenient for him to cross borders. But he said he would pray for me.

Next morning early we picked up Crosetti at his hut, made sure he had copies of the ciphers, just in case. He said the originals were with a reliable pal of his at NYPL, behind bronze doors, good move. Met the others at Teterboro, was wound up tight, unpleasantness with little asshole cursing into cell phone, approval from waiting room but Amalie stared in dismay. What? I snarled. We had words. On plane: the usual fine service and, as luck would have it, the flight attendant is Karen 'Legs' McAllister, and both of us are acting cool as sherbet in the circumstances, although we have been several times to the Eight Mile High Club on past flights. Amalie naturally sniffed this out. How? Do I leave spoor on women? Does my face betray me all unknowing? Anyway, we had a crying jag, silent heaving, the worst, she shrugged me off, couldn't bear it, I went aft, tossed Crosetti out of his seat, and talked to Paul.

I recall complaining about the wife, a tedious stanza I shall not relate and him listening and then somehow we were talking about Dad and Mutti, and who was the least and most favored son, a familiar trope of ours on the few occasions when we talk about our mutual past, and we merrily recalled an incident in which Paul, aged around seven, had broken a precious Meissen figurine, and Mutti took after him with the hairbrush, our usual instrument of discipline. This was, by the way, not one of your cheapo drugstore plastic models, but a solid chunk of Deutsche maple stuck with boar bristles from the Schwarzwald, a weapon suitable for seizing Jerusalem from the Saracens. On this occasion Paul was attempting to escape by running around the oval dining room table, shrieking hysterically, Mutti in pursuit, uttering threats in German, with we smaller kids watching in fascination. After we had milked this one of its warmth, I happened to remark that, unlike him and Miriam, I had hardly ever felt the hairbrush, me being the good son. He looked at me strangely and said, 'Yeah, she used to beat you with her hand. In the bedroom.'

'What're you talking about? She never touched me.'

'You really don't remember this? Almost every time Dad punched her out, she'd pick a fight with you and take you into the bedroom and lay you across her knee and pound your bare butt with her hand, and you'd wail like a lost soul, and then she'd hold you on the bed and rock you and murmur endearments until you stopped. Miri and I used to watch it through the keyhole. She used to call you *mein kleines Judchen*.'

'Oh, bullshit! You're making this up.'

He shrugged. 'Hey, don't believe me – ask Miri. We thought it was weird even then, even compared to the normal freak show that was our home.'

'You think I *suppressed* this abuse? God, how unbelievably trite! And this explains all my current problems on the love and family front?'

'No, the explanation is that God has given you free will and you have decided to use it to sin, rather than abandoning your monstrous pride and submitting yourself to God's will. Since you asked.'

Or something to that effect, a style of discourse that goes right past me. The other interesting thing from that conversation is that somewhat later I musingly asked Paul why our parents had ever hooked up in the first place, and he looked at me strangely again and said, 'You really don't know?'

'A wartime passion, I always thought. They never talked about the feeling part, though.'

'No kidding. You never thought it was strange that a Nazi princess would choose to marry a Jew? And a very Jewish Jew at that.'

'The mysteries of exogamy?'

'No, she was just being a good Nazi.'

I must have shown puzzlement because he said, 'Look, they took this master race business seriously. The *Herrenvolk* have the right to conquer everyone else because they're strong, yes? And who is the chief rival for world domination?'

'The Russians?'

'No, the Russians are cattle. The Jews are the only rival race. They control Russia and they control the western powers, especially including the United States. The war was fought against the Jews. And the Jews won.'

'What? The Jews were destroyed.'

'They won. They lost six million, sure, but they got back to Jerusalem, and the Germans lost *seven* million. And the armies that beat Germany into the ground were controlled by the secret machinations of the Jewish race. You never got this from her?'

'Never.'

'Lucky me, then. It follows that since the Jews conquered, it was the Jewish race that was superior – sorry about the camps – and it further follows that it behooves an Aryan maiden to join her loins to those of the superior breed. It all makes perfect sense, if you happen to be crazy.'

I have to say that this had never occurred to me, and neither Paul nor my sister had ever brought it up. My parents fought like fiends, of course, but I had woven a romance around this, which I got from the movies. People fell in love, they had children, the man was unfaithful and the wife threw plates, at which point the man reformed and realized that home was where the heart was, or else he left, and the mom found a new and better husband (Robert Young) and turned the bad old husband away when he came crawling back, or (even better) he died.

After what seemed like a very long interval, nor did the plane drop from the sky, I said, creakily, 'So what're you saying, Paul? That we're phase two in the plan to breed the master race? I thought that mongrelization was what they were trying to avoid.'

'Yes, but they were fascinated by mutts and the idea of breeding. They even saved Aryan-looking Jewish kids from the ovens and gave them to good Nazi families to raise, which they shouldn't have done at all if they really believed their racial purity line. And all that skull measuring they did and the Mengele experiments with twins . . .'

I recalled something he'd just said and interrupted. 'What did you mean by "lucky me" just now?'

'Oh, just that Mutti gave me and Miri the blood lecture, which apparently you didn't get. I mean, did you think I figured all this out myself?'

'She *told* you she married Dad to advance the racial theories of the Third Reich?'

'Not in so many words, but we were often told that the Nazis lost because they were too pure and noble and so she was sacrificing herself to inject some sneaky-smart Jew genes into the mix. I mean, didn't you think that the peculiar assortment of physical characteristics in our family had something to do with the way she treated the three of us? Oh, right, you kind of forgot some of that. In any case, we were disappointments in the *Übermensch* department:

although of unimpeachable Aryan appearance, I was a thug and Miri was a whore, but you were, so to speak, the golden mutt who would make all of it worthwhile. That's why she killed herself. The two of us were out of reach and she didn't want to distract you from your studies with having to care for an old lady. *Ritterkreuz mit Eichenlaub, Schwertern und Brillianten* for heroic Mutti. You look surprised, Jake. You never figured this out?'

'No, and I want to thank you for bringing it to my attention. We should have more of these brotherly talks – I feel so terrifically *up* now. Gosh, and what a shame Mutti didn't stick around to see the prodigal return in glory to judge the living and the dead. She would've been so proud!'

Paul ignored my sarcasm as he almost always does and replied mildly, 'Yes, I've always regretted it. Are we finished with this, by the way? Because I have some thoughts about your present situation.'

After that, we talked strategy, and he developed his idea that the whole thing was a con and what that meant for our actions while in the U.K., and I thought he made sense. Of course it was a con. Wasn't everything?

The plane landed. We drove to London, in a limo supplied by Osborne Security Service, the security firm Paul had engaged. The driver, one Brown, was an agent of said firm and according to Paul an ex-SAS piano wire artist. He did not impress me, being rather slight and weaselly in appearance. At the hotel I had rather too much to drink – understandable under the circumstances, I believe – and went to bed. In the morning, far too early, I awoke to a crushing headache, a foul, dry tongue, and my brother, dressed in his clericals, with the information that we were moving immediately. Apparently, his security team had spotted some bad guys and we needed to shake them. I allowed him to get me together and in short order we had picked up Crosetti, who seemed to have turned into a hostile little twerp overnight. He was barely civil on the ride to Oxford.

I may have dozed but awoke to Paul's voice describing something he had found at some church in the old City. He thought it was the grille Bracegirdle had used to encipher the letters, which I suppose was a major find, but, frankly, I could not work up much interest at the time. I am a man of settled habits, as I believe I have indicated, and zooming around in cars in foreign parts holds no attraction. I noticed young Crosetti's eyes were shining, though, and I might have drifted back to sleep were it not for Paul's mentioning that this grille had been swiped by a young woman. Who else could it have been? I dismissed out of hand Crosetti's opinion that it could also have been Carolyn Rolly. The crime had Miranda's prints all over it: the innocent come-on, the inveigling into the confidence of the perhaps lonely curate, the swift, violent denouement . . . Miranda! I didn't even bother to argue with him. I recall thinking that we have the ciphers so she had to come to us with her grille, and I recall a sense of anticipation such as I have rarely known, like a kid on the way to a carnival.

We approached the outskirts of Oxford as it was getting on toward noon, and I was growing hungry. I mentioned this to Paul and he told me that we were to meet Oliver March in a country pub. Shortly after this information passed, Brown started to drive like a lunatic, swerving across four lanes of the M40 at the last moment to shoot onto the A40 and then quickly leaving that for a local road, just west of Oxford.

Crosetti asked him if he were trying to lose our pursuers

and Brown replied, 'No, just one of them.' After this we roared down smaller roads, throwing up rooster tails of water and mud and tossing us all around unmercifully. I caught a look at my companions, who seemed to be enjoying the ride, and perhaps also enjoying my increasing discomfort. Then, after a particularly jarring turn down what looked like a farm track, Brown halted the car, leaped out, popped the trunk, and dragged from it a long black nylon bag. I left the car too, staggered over to a low fence, and was sick for a good long time. When I recovered, I heard the sound of an approaching vehicle and looking in that direction saw our Brown under a bare roadside willow, with a huge exotic-looking rifle propped in a crotch of that tree and pointing down the road. A blue BMW drove toward him at speed and when it was about a hundred yards away he shot it. Its engine made expensive breaking noises and the car rolled to a stop, with steam rising from its hood. Brown put his rifle back in its bag and noticed me standing there goggling and dabbing at my mouth with a handkerchief.

'Are you all right, sir?' he asked.

'I'm fine. Did you just shoot somebody?'

'No, sir, just the vehicle. This is a Barrett rifle, sir, nothing like it for stopping a car. Father Paul wanted some privacy for this meeting.'

I stared at him and he took my elbow. 'We should get back in our car now, sir.'

We did and drove off down some more little roads until we came to a perfect little English village, whose name I have quite forgotten: Dorking Smedley? Inching Tweedle? Something like that; and pulled up in the yard of what looked like a coaching inn off the cover of a fancy biscuit package: thatched roof, black Tudor beams, heavy, purplish, leaded glass, the kind of place Dick Bracegirdle used to frequent for a pint of malmsey. We all trooped inside except for Brown, who waited with the car, talking into a crackling radio.

Inside it was dim and cozy, with a fire in the grate. A large man with unfashionable red sideburns was behind the bar, and when he saw us he nodded and gestured to one side, where there was a door. Through the door was a small room with a gas fire and a battered round table in it, at which sat a slight, handsome man in his late fifties wearing a tweed jacket, a tattersall shirt, and a black wool tie. He stood when we came in, and Paul made the introductions and we all shook and sat. This was Oliver March, the companion. Another evidence that Paul has taken charge of this expedition. I didn't mind. I felt like one of those great black bladders of industrial chemicals one sees in barges in the harbor, inert and massive, pushed about by little tugs.

After some small talk, March said, 'Well, secret meetings. It all seems so odd: when did you last see your father and all that . . .'

At this I started and looked wildly at Paul, who explained that it was a famous painting of a Cavalier boy being questioned by Roundhead soldiers, a figure of speech. The professor continued. 'Yes, quite: and I would not have agreed to meet you in such an inconvenient place were it not for your suggestion, Father Mishkin, that the police explanation of Andrew's death was not accurate.'

This was the first I had heard of Paul's involvement in the Bulstrode case and I listened with interest as he explained. 'No it's not. They found a doped-up rent boy named Chico Garza using your friend's credit card and muscled a confession out of him. The boy had nothing to do with Andrew's death.'

'On what evidence?'

'Well, first, I visited the boy in jail. He was sleeping in a squat at the time of the murder and he woke up with Andrew's wallet in his bag. He never met Andrew Bulstrode, but he was carefully framed for the killing. The police found forensic traces of Garza in Andrew's apartment, so it was well prepared. The other, and more compelling, reason is that no one outside of my brother and his secretary knew that Andrew had deposited the Bracegirdle papers with the law firm, yet within days of the murder, Russian thugs were shadowing him. How did they know? They must have extracted that information from your friend.'

The word 'extracted' hung in the air, and March briefly shut his eyes. What I was thinking at that moment was this: Shvanov had mentioned 'sources' when he told me how he had come to take an interest in me and I hadn't pressed him on it. Of course, gangsters have 'sources.' People tell them things, or they have people followed. Or maybe Shvanov was lying, maybe he was the torturer . . .

(Again, in hindsight, at an emotionless remove, things are marvelously clear, but in the instant of occurrence they are covered in layers of fog. And we are so good at denying what is before our eyes, as for example, the vignettes of Mutti and me that Paul had provided on the plane, and which I have, from that moment to this, thought about on a daily basis. So you must not blame me for not coming up with what became so obvious later.)

A barmaid came in at this point, not the sort of barmaid such an inn should have had, a jolly pink blonde in a peasant blouse and a canvas apron, but a thin, dark, dour girl in an olive pantsuit, a Maltese or Corsican perhaps, who took our drink and food orders and departed without any Falstaffian badinage at all. March now said, 'I fail to see how Andrew could have got himself mixed up with Russian gangsters. I mean it just boggles the mind.'

'He needed money to finance the validation of the manuscript,' I said, 'and if found valid, for locating the manuscript play Bracegirdle mentioned.'

'Excuse me . . . Bracegirdle?' said March, and the three of us gaped at him in surprise. Crosetti blurted out, 'Didn't Andrew tell you *anything* about why he came to England last summer?'

'Only that he was doing some research. But he was always on to some research or other. Who is Bracegirdle?'

I gave him the short version, and while I was doing this the barmaid came in with our food and drink. I had ordered a pint of bitter and finished it in time to flag the girl for another. March listened carefully, asking few questions. When I was done, he shook his head ruefully. 'Andrew and I have been together more or less continuously for nearly thirty years,' he said, 'and we've always been reasonably open about what's going on in our lives – open for dons, I mean, not actual gushing or anything like that – but I must say that I had not the slightest clue about any of this. Andrew could keep things dark, of course, especially after the bloody catastrophe he went through, but still . . . and this doesn't answer the original question at all. Why, if he needed funding, did he not come to me?'

'Are you particularly wealthy?' I asked.

'Oh, not at all, but I do have some assets, some property, some inherited things. I suppose at a pinch I could have raised a hundred or so without descending into absolute beggary. Would you say he would have needed much more than that?'

'If you're talking about a hundred thousand pounds, then no. We have no indication that what he got was more than about twenty thousand dollars from the Russians.'

'Good Lord! Then it makes even less sense. Why didn't he come to me?'

I said, 'Perhaps he was embarrassed because of the scandal,' and mentioned that Mickey Haas had asked the same question. As soon as the name was out I was surprised to see a sour expression appear on March's refined face.

'Well, of course he wouldn't have approached Haas,' he said. 'Haas hated him.'

'What! How can you say that?' I objected. 'They were friends. Mickey was one of the few people in academia who stuck up for him when the fake quarto scandal broke. He gave him a place to work at Columbia when no one else would look at him.'

'I take it Haas is a particular friend of yours,' said March.

'Yes, he is. He's my oldest friend and one of the most decent and generous people I know. Why did Andrew imagine that Mickey hated him?'

'It had nothing to do with imagination,' snapped March. 'Look here, twenty odd years ago, Haas produced a book on Shakespeare's women, female characters in the plays, that is, the point of which was that thinking about Shakespeare as an original genius simply reinforced the toxic individualism of bourgeois culture. I believe he said that *Macbeth* was really all about the three witches, and a load of similar twaddle. Andrew was asked to review it for the *Times Literary Supplement* and gave it the mighty bollocking it deserved, not only poking holes in its logic and scholarship, but also implying that Haas knew better, on the evidence of his own earlier writing, and that he had produced this farrago merely to curry favor with the Marxists and feminists and whatnot who control, I am informed, all hiring at American universities. Not that I know a thing about it myself, barely passed my A-levels in the damned stuff, just a simple biologist really. Amazing that Andrew and I got on so well together; absence of rivalry perhaps, two halves making a whole. He used to read me bits in the evenings. Well, it was a great scandal, outraged letters back and forth to the *TLS*, screeds in the little journals, and I recall thinking at the time how happy I was to be in a business where you have actual data. It blew over, as these things always do, and when Andrew lost his reputation because of that awful little man, Haas was there with a stout defense, and later a job offer. As I recall, neither of us mentioned the earlier dogfight. We assumed that it had been forgotten, simply part of the usual give-and-take of academic debate. But it hadn't been. Almost as soon as Andrew arrived in New York, Haas began to torment him. At first it was just sly digs, little things that could have been confused with some kind of bumptious American humor, but then it grew worse, petty acts of tyranny . . .'

'Such as?'

'Oh, he was promised a Shakespeare seminar, and some graduate courses, but instead he was given freshman composition sections, rather like a brain surgeon being asked to tidy up the wards, mop up the blood, and empty the pans. When he complained of this outrageous treatment, Haas told him he was lucky to have anything at all, he was lucky not to be on the dole, or selling watches on the street. Andrew called and told me about this gruesome business, and of course I demanded that he tell Haas what he could do with his bloody appointment and come straight home. But that he would not do. I think he felt it was a kind of expiation for his scholarly sin. And . . . you know I see that this will sound odd, as if Andrew were descending into some hell of paranoia, but he told me that he believed Haas was tormenting him in more underhanded ways as well. His salary cheques would go missing. Little items would vanish from his briefcase, from his room. Someone changed the lock on his office door. One day he came to work and found all his things in the hall. He'd had his office moved without notice. Classes he was meant to meet in one room were mysteriously scheduled for another room on the other side of the campus, and he had to rush to meet them in the heat of the summer. Those terrible New York summers, and he suffered so from the heat. Not used to it, you see, being from here. And his air-conditioning was always breaking down . . .'

'Did he blame Mickey for that too?' I asked unkindly.

'Yes, I see where you're going and I confess I thought that as well. Is he running mad? But it was the weight of evidence, you see, I mean the accumulation of horrible details – could he possibly have made them up? Unlikely, in my opinion: poor Andrew wasn't a fantasist, not in the least. We used to joke that he had no imagination at all, and then there's what I saw when he returned last August.'

He paused here and drank some of his beer. His eyes looked wet to me, and I fervently wished for him not to break down about poor Andrew. I took on some of my own pint, my third.

'It's difficult to describe. Manic and frightened at the same time. He had a young woman with him and insisted she had to stay in our house, although there are some perfectly adequate hotels nearby.'

'Carolyn Rolly,' said Crosetti.

'Yes, I believe that was her name. She was helping him in some research . . .'

'Did he say what the research was?' Paul asked.

'Not really, no. But he said it was the most important find in the whole history of Shakespeare scholarship, and dreadfully hush-hush. As if I would blab. In any case they were out and about. He seemed to have plenty of ready money, renting a car, staying away for days, returning in a mood of exhilaration. One thing he did say, that he was authenticating the antiquity of a manuscript and couldn't be seen to be doing so. That was the main reason for Miss Rolly tagging along. From what I could gather, they did authenticate it by technical means and then they were off to Warwickshire.'

'Where in Warwickshire, do you know?' I asked.

'Yes, I happened upon some papers Miss Rolly left behind that suggested they had visited Darden Hall. Andrew returned alone, and he seemed much deflated and more frightened. I asked him about Miss Rolly, but he put me off. She was 'away' doing research. I didn't believe him for a moment – I thought perhaps they'd had some sort of fallingout. In any case, as I say, he was a changed man. He insisted on having all the curtains drawn and he would stalk the house at night, holding a poker and shining a torch in dark corners. I begged him to tell me what the problem was, but he said I was better off not knowing.'

Crosetti pressed March on what had become of Rolly. Did he think she had gone back to the States when Bulstrode had? He didn't know, and that was more or less the end of our interview. After assuring the don that we would have all of Bulstrode's personal items delivered to him and that Ms Ping would handle the decedent's will (and of course avoiding the issue of the lost manuscript), we took our leave.

Back in the car, we had a small disagreement about what to do next. Paul thought that we should continue with our original plan of following Bulstrode's tracks, which meant going to Warwickshire and visiting Darden Hall. Crosetti objected that Bulstrode did not seem to have found anything there and why did we think we'd do any better than an expert? He was for staying and investigating at March and Bulstrode's home and looking at these 'papers' March had mentioned. I observed that he seemed far more interested in finding Ms Rolly than in locating the Item. He replied that Rolly was the source, key, and engine of the entire affair. Find Rolly and you had all currently available information about the Item, including in all probability the purloined grille. We tossed this bone back and forth for some minutes, with increasing irritation on my part (for, naturally, I knew it was *Miranda* who had stolen the grille!) until Brown reminded us that other agents would be cruising these roads and asking the locals whether anyone had seen a Mercedes SEL, of which there were probably not many on the lanes of rural Oxfordshire, and by such means arriving back on our heels.

Paul suggested that Crosetti return to the inn and ask if March would consent to an inspection of these papers; he could stay at one of the perfectly adequate hotels. March was not averse to this plan, and we left Crosetti there with him. I was relieved, for I'd been finding the man ever more annoying. I mentioned this to Paul as Brown drove us away from the pub and he asked me why that was, since Crosetti struck him as mild enough. He'd hardly said a word in the car during the journey north.

'I don't like him,' I said. 'A typical poseur from the outer boroughs. A *screenwriter*, for God's sake! Completely untrustworthy. I can't imagine what I was thinking when I invited him along.'

'You should pay attention to the people who irritate you,' said Paul.

'What's that supposed to mean?'

'Oh, I think you know,' he said in that irritatingly confident tone he sometimes has, like a voice from the clouds.

'I *don't* know. I would have said if I knew, or have you been vouchsafed the power to read minds?'

'Hm. Can you think of another poseur from the outer

boroughs, this one an actor rather than a screenwriter? But this one didn't have a family as happy as Crosetti's, didn't have a loving mom, didn't have a heroic dad –'

'What, you think I'm *jealous* of him? That I'm *like* him?'

'– who decided to play it safe and go to law school instead of taking a shot at what he really wanted to do, and he sees a kid with a warm and loving family who has the guts to follow his dreams –'

'That is such horseshit . . .'

'Not. Plus, you practically accused him of trying to seduce your wife, in fact, you encouraged him to do so. Just before you wrecked the bar in your hotel and put the bartender in the hospital.'

'I did no such thing,' I said spontaneously.

'I know you think you didn't, but you really did. Have you ever had blackouts like that before?'

'Oh, thank you! I'm sure you have an AA group in your church basement that I'd fit right into.'

'No, I don't think you're a drunk, or not yet, although three pints of strong English beer is a lot to drink in the middle of the day.'

'I'm a big guy,' I said, a little lamely, for it was all starting to come back, little fragments of horrid memory. I am *not* a drinker ordinarily.

The hell with this.

We got to Darden Hall about four, under sodden skies. The surprisingly short autumn day of these latitudes was nearly gone and our headlights illuminated dark drifts of leaves on the long drive up from the road. The place had recently come into the National Trust, on the demise of the final Baron Reith in 1999, and had not yet been renovated for public view. We had called ahead to arrange a conversation with the resident conservator, a Miss Randolph.

The place was the usual crumbling pile familiar to us all from horror films and *Masterpiece Theatre* Anglophiliac fantasias, although the hour and the weather gave it the look more of the former's sort of prop. It had a Jacobean core, a couple of Georgian wings, and some Victorian gewgaws despoiling the facade. We chanced to meet a workman on a tiny tractor in front of the house and he directed us around to what was once the servants' entrance. Our knock was answered by a solid fortyish woman of the English Rose type who wore half glasses, a tweed skirt, and two cardigans, wisely in the case of these last, for the room she showed us into was almost cold enough to show breath. A tiny electric fire hummed valiantly, but clearly to little avail. It was the old steward's office, she explained, the only habitable room in the house, and her headquarters.

She asked what she could do for us and I said, 'We're here to see Count Dracula.' She grinned and replied in an appropriately *Masterpiece Theatre*-ish accent, 'Yes, everyone says that, or else something about the peasants coming for Frankenstein. Too many Gothic novels and films, but I think there's something in all that nonsense, you know. I think that even then, in the nineteenth century, when it seemed as if the life that produced these houses would go on forever, writers knew there was something wrong with them, that they rested ultimately on the most dreadful suffering, and it bubbled up in the Gothic tale.'

'What sort of suffering is this one built on?'

'Oh, take your pick. The original Lord Dunbarton stole it courtesy of Henry VIII from some Benedictine nuns who ran a charity hospital here. None of that for the baron, of course, and afterward the Dunbartons made their pile in sugar and slaves. That funded the Georgian buildings and afterward they had coal and gas and urban property in Nottingham and Coventry. None of them ever did an honest day's work in their lives and they lived like emperors. But . . .'

'What?' Paul asked.

'It's difficult to explain. Come with me, I'll show you something.'

We followed her out of the office and down a dim corridor lit by wall sconces holding fifteen-watt bulbs. The chill in that room was coziness itself compared with the damp cold of the corridors, cold as the grave I recall thinking, slipping easily into Gothic mode. We went through a door and she pressed a light switch. I gasped.

'This was the Jacobean dining hall and later the breakfast room. It's considered the finest example of linenfold walnut paneling in the Midlands, not to mention the carving on the sideboards and the inlaid parquet flooring. Look at the detail! This was done by English craftsmen for thugs who couldn't tell a dado from sheep dip, so why did they put their souls into this walnut? Love is why, and I honor them for it, which is why I'm in the business of preserving it. Come, there's more.'

The next room was a ballroom. 'Look at the ceiling. Giacomo Quarenghi, circa 1775, Britannia ruling the waves. There she is in her amphibious chariot drawn by dolphins and all the darkies paying homage around the border. The room itself is by Adam. Look at the proportions! The windows! The parquet! No one will ever build a house like this again, ever, even though we have people in this country who could buy any of the Lords Dunbarton with the change in their pockets, and that means that something wonderful has gone out of the world, and I'd love to know why.'

'So would I,' said Paul. 'I know the feeling. It's one I often have in Rome. Corruption and vice of every sort, the ruin of real religion, and yet . . . what gorgeous stuff they made!'

After that, they chatted animatedly about Rome and aesthetics while I stared up at Britannia and tried to ID the subject peoples. Then we went back to the half-warm office and the business of the day. Paul did the talking, he having already established a relationship, and besides he had the collar – who cannot trust a priest? After he'd finished she said, 'So you've come all this way because of a miscarriage of justice? You're following the track of this Bulstrode fellow in the hope of pulling a thread that will lead you to his real killer?'

'You have it,' said Paul. 'Do you recall his visit at all?'

'Oh, yes, of course I do. I don't get many visitors with whom I can discuss anything more than the football and the price of petrol, so I'm afraid I rather seized on them and simply chatted their heads off. As I did with you, shame upon me. Yes, Professor Bulstrode, ex Brasenose, seconded to some university in the States, and he had a young woman with him, Carol Raleigh? Is that right?'

'Close enough. Do you happen to recall what they were looking for?'

The woman considered the question for a moment, staring at the coils of the electric fire. 'They said they were researching the family history of the Dunbartons, but there was something else going on, I think. They were exchanging looks, if you follow me, and they were rather short on details. Scholars, I've found, are typically expansive on their subjects, and Professor Bulstrode and his assistant were distinctly not. But it was none of my affair after all, he had the proper scholarly credentials, and so I gave them the key to the muniment room and went on with my own affairs. They were up there for the entire day, remarkable really, because the place is a mare's nest, never really been properly cataloged, and they descended covered in the dust of ages. I asked them if they'd found what they'd been looking for and they said yes, and thanked me and the professor made a contribution to the trust to help with the restoration, a hundred pounds, actually, very generous, and they left.'

'Did they take anything?'

'You mean make off with a document? I shouldn't think so, but they might have taken rafts of them. I wasn't looking, and I certainly didn't search them before they left.'

At that point the telephone rang, and Miss Randolph picked up the heavy antique instrument and listened, and said she had to take this call, it was the builder, and they thanked her and left.

Back in the warmth of the car I asked Paul what he thought.

'My guess,' he replied, 'is that they did find something and Rolly ran off with it. She seems to be quite a piece of work.'

'I suppose. Well, brother, what now? We seem to have exhausted our possibilities.'

'Yes, on this line anyway.' He looked at his watch. 'Today is shot, obviously. I suggest we return to Oxford, spend the night in a perfectly adequate hotel, pick up Crosetti in the morning, and go over to Aylesbury.'

'What for? What's in Aylesbury?'

'Springhill House, one of Her Majesty's prisons. I want to have a talk with Leonard Pascoe, the internationally famous forger of old documents. Mr Brown, do you think we could arrange to be followed there?'

'Yes, sir. I'm sure some wicked person might tip someone off about our destination.'

'Yes, there's a great deal of wickedness in the world,' said Paul, with such a look of sly satisfaction on his face that I wanted to punch him.

'Oh, and Mr Brown?' said Paul.

'Sir.'

'Would you try to locate a farm along the way? One that raises geese.'

'Geese,' said the driver. 'Yes, sir.'

'What's going on, Paul?' I asked him.

'Oh, we're just going to meet Richard Bracegirdle,' he said, and would yield no more information, that smug bastard.

The Sixth Ciphered Letter (Fragment 3)

we to the George & conversed late: Mr W.S. saies as to hym-selfe I have killed a man I must be shriven & where shal I fynde a priest in these tymes. Then saies hee, Dick, now have we sent your two rogues to Hell but Hell hath yet a greater store, the devil hath 'em in barrels lyke haringes, soe when yon Piggott shal heere of this afray he shal send more & yet more til we are o'er-come at last, nay we must strike at the roote & that is my lord Dunbarton. Now we must crye out to greater than wee, for great lords are ne'er toppled but by greater ones. Now I am well with the Montagues & the Montagues are well with the Howards, being both friends of the old religioun & Frances Howard hath the harte of my lord of Rochester, as all the court knoweth & she shal carrie the letter & sware it be true, for true it is & thus shall my lord Dunbarton be disconfited & you saved. What letter is that, sir, saies I. Nay, saies he, I ought to have sayde two letters, the first being the one gave thee by the false Verey, that pretended issue of my lord Rochester his hande & the other one that thou shalt write to-night, wherein thou shalt tell all youre tale. And soe I wrote My Lord what you read now & when done hee readeth it & makes markes where I shall change it mayhap but I say nay for tis my letter do not make me one of your creatoures because this be all earnest & no play. He laughs & cries mercie sayinge lad, thou hast the right of it for like some butcher I must poke anie calf I pass be it mine own or no.

Then I ask hym, Sir art certayn this will sauve us or must we doe else & saies he I think twil sauve thee but as for mee that I know not. But why, an you are freyndes with the great as you have sayde & hee answereth mee thus: thynges change ever & the tyde floweth not in my favour. Royal Henry of France lately slain, and by a monk too, turnes royal James's minde onece again to Papist plots. He appointeth a fanatick Puritan to be Archbishop of Canterbury & his partie presses ever harsher upon us plaiers. I myself am attacked in publick print & none dare rise to my holpe. The power of my friends in the house of Montague & others of worship wanes, theyre houses, formerly secure, are now searched like common dwellinges. I saie: yet still you wrote the playe. Aye, saies he, I did, as a prisoner long hobbled may sport & click heeles when the fetters drop. O lad did you imagine that I thought such a playe could e'er be heard? Nay, but it flowed from mee upon the smale excuse you gave it & would not stop; a grete foolishenesse I know but here it is still-borne & what shall be done with it? It must be burnt, saies I. Yes, burnt it must be, saies he, my paper heretic.

18

Tap.

Crosetti stirred in his sleep and tried to return to a rather nice dream in which he was sitting around a movie set with Jodie Foster and Clark Gable, just having a comfortable conversation about the movies, and he was giving Jodie the eye because they were in on the secret about Gable not really being dead and waiting for him to explain about how he'd fooled the world but there was this rattling sound behind them and he said he'd go find out what it was . . .

Tap tap tap taptaptaptap

He was up, in the unfamiliar room of the Linton Lodge Hotel, on the outskirts of Oxford, a very nice room that Professor March had kindly arranged for him. It had a triple bay window giving on the garden, these windows being black with the night and also the source of the noise that had separated him from dreamland. Another rattle of pebbles hit the glass. He checked his watch: two-thirty in the morning.

Rising, he pulled on his jeans, went to the window, opened it, and got a faceful of gravel. He cursed and leaned out the window and spied a dark figure on the lawn below, stooping to retrieve another handful of pebbles from the path.

'Who the hell is that?' he demanded in the sort of loud whisper one uses when not wanting to wake a sleeping house.

The person below stood and announced in the same style, 'It's Carolyn.'

'Carolyn *Rolly*?'

'No, Crosetti, some *other* Carolyn. Get down here and let me in!'

He stared below at the white, raised, familiar face for a long moment and then shut the window, pulled on a shirt and sneakers, left the room, ran back and got his key just before the door swung shut, dashed through the short hallway, flew down the stairs and through the lounge to the garden door. He opened it, and there she was, in a long-sleeved black T-shirt and jeans, soaked through, her dark hair plastered in strings on either side of her face.

She pushed past him into the lounge.

'Christ, I'm freezing,' she said, and she seemed to be: in the dim red light of the emergency exit lamp her lips looked dark blue. She glanced at the bar. 'Can you get me a drink?'

'This is closed and locked up. But I have a bottle in my room.'

He did too, a fifth of Balvenie purchased in the duty-free for his mother. When they were in the room, he turned on the hot water in the bath, handed her his old plaid bathrobe, and told her to take her wet clothes off. He poured a couple of generous shots into the hotel water glasses while she changed in the bathroom, and when she emerged, in the robe with a towel around her hair, handed her one of them.

She gulped it down, coughed, and sighed, while he stared at her face. She met his eye. 'What?' she said.

'What? Carolyn, it's the second of December, no, the third

now, and you've been missing since, I don't know, the end of August. Bulstrode is dead, did you know that? Someone killed him. And his lawyer shot two guys in my mom's living room and gangsters tried to kidnap me and . . . oh, Christ, I can't begin to . . . Carolyn, where the hell have you been and what the *hell* have you been up to?'

'Don't yell at me!' she said in a strained voice. 'Please, can I just sit down and be quiet for a minute?'

He gestured to an armchair by the window and she sat on this and he sat on the bed facing her. She looked ridiculously small and young now, although there were smudges under her eyes and their blue seemed dulled, like tarnished metal.

She finished her whisky in silence and held out her glass for a refill.

'No,' said Crosetti. 'The story first.'

'From what point? My birth?'

'No, you can start with your marriage to H. Olerud of 161 Tower Road, Braddock, Pee-Ay.'

A sharp intake of breath and he saw those familiar bars of rose bloom on her cheekbones. Rolly had less control of the blush than he would have supposed necessary for such an accomplished liar.

'You know about that?' she asked.

'Yeah. I actually went out there, to the house. I had a nice conversation with Emmett.'

At this her eyes widened and she clutched her mouth. 'Oh, God, you *saw* him? How is he?'

'Reasonably healthy, a little skinny maybe. He seems like a bright kid. I saw the girl too, also healthy, the bit I saw of her. Their father seems like a pretty violent guy.'

'You could say that. Harlan is fairly free with his hands.'

'I saw. How did you come to hook up with him? He seems a lot older than you.'

'He was my brother-in-law. My mom died when I was thirteen, and my sister Emily took me in. She was four years older than me and he was six years older than her.'

'What about your father?'

She uttered a short derisive laugh. 'Whoever he was. Mom was a small-town waitress and barmaid and she supplemented her income by cultivating guys. Pay the rent this month and you get all the ass you can handle. She was what they call a trucker's friend. One of them shot her and the guy she was with at the time. I guess he thought it was true romance. I came home from middle school one day and the cops were there and I called Emily and she picked me up. This was in Mechanicsburg, and I started to live with them. Do you need to hear this?'

'Yes. So there was no Uncle Lloyd.'

'No, I lied about that. There was Harlan, though. He started messing with me when I turned fourteen and Emily didn't do anything to stop it, he had her beat down so bad. I got pregnant with Emmett when I was sixteen and with Molly four years later and what can I say about it but that was the way I thought things were. Harlan had a job at the battery plant, there was food on the table, and that's how we lived. I had Emily and she had me and we both had the kids. You'd be surprised how many people there are in places like Braddock who live like that. Then Harlan lost his job and had to take a shit job in a Wal-Mart warehouse and Emily died and –'

'How did Emily die?'

'She got electrocuted by the washing machine. It was always kind of sparky, and Harlan was always promising to fix it but he never did, and we had to be careful around it. I sort of think she accidentally on purpose killed herself. He was beating her pretty regular by then.'

'Uh-huh. And how does the bookbinding come into this?'

Suddenly her face turned rigid. 'You want to know my whole life story? Why do you? Because we had a fuck? That entitles you to the whole fucking five-CD collection of the life of Carolyn Rolly?'

'No, Carolyn,' said Crosetti. 'I'm not entitled to anything. But you came to me, in the middle of the night. Why? A warm bath? A drink of Scotch? A chat about old times in the bookstore?'

'No, but . . . look I need your help. I ran away from them. I didn't know where else to go. And we don't have the time to get into every detail. When they wake up and find I'm gone they'll come here.'

'Who's "they," Carolyn?'

'Shvanov's people. There are four of them, in a hotel about two miles from here. They know where you are. That's how I knew to come here.'

'And now. . . what? We're on the same side again? Why should I believe anything you say?'

'Oh, God! I told you before, I don't know how to behave with . . . *real* people like you. I lie, I get into desperate panics and I run and . . . Christ, can't you give me another drink? Please?'

He did. She drank. 'Okay, look we don't have time for the long version. Bookbinding – I took the kids to a doctor one day, for shots for school, and while I was waiting in the office . . . I saw this book. It was part of the decorations, you know? How some people have fancy bookcases with old hardcover books in them? Well, this doctor had one of those and Emmett and Molly were playing with them, taking the books down and using them like blocks and the receptionist told them they had to stop and I replaced them on the shelf and there was one of them that was called *The*

Bookbinder's Art and I swiped it. It was bound in half-calf with gold tooling. I don't know why I took it. Maybe it was, it felt so rich, the feel of the leather and the paper, it was so *not* Braddock, like a piece of a different world that fell there by accident, right there in my hand, like a jewel. And when I got home I hid it and read it at night, every night, for months, and the idea that people could just make books by hand and they would be beautiful things . . . I don't know why but it just got under my skin. And then Emily died and he started beating on *me* and I knew if I didn't get out I'd be as dead as Emily, either he'd do it or I would, or I'd kill him. So I left. The first time, he caught me and locked me in the cellar and beat me so bad I could hardly walk. The next time I waited for his payday and I took five hundred in cash while he was sleeping and walked away and hitched a ride and ended up in New York and stayed in a shelter. I got a job cleaning buildings at night. I found my loft through that job. It was illegal and toxic, like I told you, but it was dirt cheap because the owner wanted someone on the property so scavenger gangs wouldn't rip out the copper. That was the first time I heard Shvanov's name.'

'Why?'

'Because he owned the building, or part of it. Able Real Estate Management. Okay, so I had a place to stay and I was a cleaner for over two years, working nights, spending all my spare time in the library reading about bookbinding and about the book business and learning what I had to know to fake a résumé. Then I quit the cleaners and got a job in a midtown restaurant waiting tables because I needed to look at regular people, see how they dressed, how they talked, the gestures. I converted myself to a middle-class person. That took the better part of another year. And then

I got the job with Glaser. My sad story. Now, do you want to hear about the manuscript?'

'I do.'

'I knew Bulstrode from before – I think I told you that in New York. Sidney introduced us, and I took a course he gave on manuscripts at Columbia General Studies. As soon as I saw the pages I took out of the Churchill I knew it was a big find.' She sipped at her drink and looked out the window at the black night. 'And you want to know why I lied about owning the carcasses, why I pretended it was nothing much, and why I lied about being a fugitive so that you'd sell the pages to Bulstrode for spare change.'

'I'm all ears.'

'Okay, I'm a bookstore clerk who found a manuscript in what's supposedly a back I bought for pennies from my employer. I have no resources and it's going to take significant resources to get the thing authenticated and sold at auction and as soon as I go public with it Sidney is going to come out swinging and –'

'What do you mean, swinging?'

'Oh, I see you don't know Sidney. He's going to say that I opened the covers and found this manuscript and then swindled him into selling me the books as backs. So there's immediately a cloud on the title and no auction house will touch it. Sidney's a big gun in that world and I'm nobody. So I needed a front man and I thought of Bulstrode. I called him while you were waiting in the street that morning, told him what we'd found, and set up what went down in his office. He said that if it was genuine he'd give me five grand for it over and above what he gave you. So then it was Bulstrode's manuscript. Even if he'd been fooled once, he's still a major scholar and paleographer with access to tons of manuscript sources. There wouldn't ever have to be a connection with me or Glaser.'

'Right, but Carolyn, I still don't get why you didn't tell me this off the bat.'

'Oh, for God's sake – I didn't *know* you. You could have mentioned it to Glaser the next day – hey, Carolyn found a priceless Jacobean manuscript in those books you sold her for junk, ha-ha. So I had to pretend to involve you in the scam without at the same time letting you know what the manuscript really was.'

'I see. And what happened afterward, that night – that was part of the scam too?'

For almost the first time that evening she looked him right in the face. Crosetti's father had once told him that pathological liars always looked the interrogator right in the eye and kept the stare for longer than was natural, and he was happy to see that Carolyn did not do this. Her look was tentative and, he imagined, a little ashamed.

'No,' she said, 'that wasn't part of the plan. I knew you were pissed off at me, and I'd told you that porker about Uncle Lloyd and I thought you'd just walk away, and when you didn't and you did all those nice things . . . look, in my whole life I *never* had a single other day like that, someone taking me places, that beautiful music, and buying me things, just because they cared about me as a person and not just because they wanted to paw me . . .'

'I *did* want to paw you.'

'I meant someone I wanted to get pawed by, someone my age, someone sweet. I was never a kid, never a teenager. I never hung out at the drive-in with boys. I mean, it was like drugs.'

'So, you like me?'

'Oh, I adore you,' she said, in a tone so matter-of-fact that it was more convincing than any sighing avowal. His heart actually gave a little thump. 'But so what? You're so much too good for me that it's ridiculous, and that doesn't even count my kids, you really need to get saddled with that mess, and so I figured, okay, just one night of . . . I don't know, what you said, one night of *youth*, the kind of things regular people do when they're our age and after that it was like the end of Cinderella, except there was no glass slipper and no prince. The next day I got together with Bulstrode to plan out what to do next, and he said he had a source for the money he needed and we went to meet Shvanov. Did you ever see Osip Shvanov?'

'No. Only people who work for him.'

'Oh, he's something rare. Very smooth, except around the eyes. He reminded me of Earl Ray Bridger.'

'I'm sorry . . . ?'

'A felon my mom once went out with for a while, who I don't want to talk about right now. Anyway, I spotted him for a bad guy right away, but poor Bulstrode didn't have a clue, and for sure *I* wasn't going to tip him off. He did his little pitch about the Shakespeare play to Shvanov. He said the Bracegirdle document itself was worth fifty to a hundred grand, but if we found the Shakespeare manuscript, there was no way to calculate how high the price would go. A hundred million? A hundred fifty? And Shvanov would risk nothing because even if we came up empty on that, he'd still have the Bracegirdle to sell. Anyway, Shvanov gave him twenty large and told him to take off for England immediately to research Bracegirdle and Lord Dunbarton and get on the trail of the play. Which he did. And I went with him –'

'Without a good-bye. Don't you think that was a little harsh?'

'That was the best thing about it, knowing you weren't ever going to be involved with that son of a bitch.'

'You were *protecting* me?'

'I thought I was,' she admitted, and then added defensively, 'and don't think you didn't need it. You don't know this guy.'

'Speaking of whom – how did a Brit scholar happen to know a thug like Shvanov anyway?'

'I have no idea. A mutual friend hooked them up. I thought it was some loan shark deal – Bulstrode was stony broke and maybe he tried to raise money on the street for this thing and it led him up the chain. God, I'm so tired! Where was I?'

'Leaving on a jet plane, don't know when you'll be back again. And no good-byes.'

'Right. Okay, we get to England and go straight to Oxford and we stay with Ollie March. Bulstrode said I had to stay with them, which March didn't much like, but he said it was for security. I had to get the manuscript dated, so no one would know Bulstrode was involved, and when the dating came back positive, that's when he really got squirrelly. I wasn't allowed to make phone calls, and the only reason I got to write that letter to Sidney was I convinced him that it would be more suspicious not to write and make up a story about the plates and send him a check. He was insanely suspicious of me, that I was, like, working for Shvanov and telling him what we were up to, our research and all.'

'But you weren't.'

'But I was. Of *course* I was working for Shvanov. I'm *still* working for Shvanov, as far as Shvanov knows. He gave me a cell phone before I left New York and told me to keep in touch. What was I supposed to say to a man like that? No?'

Crosetti was silent under her defiant look. She snatched the towel from her head and dried her hair so violently that he winced. After a moment, he asked her, 'What did Bulstrode say when you told him about the ciphered letters?'

Here she blushed again. 'I didn't tell him. Shvanov did.'

'But you told Shvanov.'

'I confirmed his suspicions,' she admitted quickly. 'He knows things, Crosetti. He has people everywhere. Obviously he knew about you from Bulstrode, and he must have checked around. You don't think he can find out what's happening at the New York Public Library? He can find out what's happening in the CIA, for Christ's sake!'

'So much for keeping me out of it,' he said.

'I'm sorry. I'm a coward and he scares me. I can't lie to him. Anyway, when Bulstrode got the news about the ciphers, he went ballistic. I had to practically sit on him to calm him down. He realized that the ciphers were the key to finding the play manuscript and if Shvanov got hold of them from you, then he wouldn't need *us* anymore, which was probably not that good for our health. I said we should try to see if the fair copies of the ciphers Bracegirdle sent to Dunbarton were still in existence at the receiving end.'

'That's why you went to Darden Hall.'

'Right. But they weren't there, or anyway we didn't find them. We did find a Breeches Bible, though. Do you know what that is?'

'Yeah,' said Crosetti, 'a small Tudor Bible, 1560, nine by seven. We think it was the basis of the Bracegirdle cipher. But how did you know that? You didn't have the ciphertext.'

'No, but we found a Breeches Bible with pinholes in it, in Dunbarton's library, pinholes through random letters. Bulstrode figured out that the selected letters were the cipher key and that a grille must have been part of the cipher. He knew a hell of a lot about antique ciphers.'

'That's why you stole the grille from that church.'

'You know about that?' This with some alarm.

'I know everything. Why didn't you just steal the Bible?'

'Bulstrode *did* steal it. And then he got me to swipe the

grille. Man, by that time he was so paranoid he thought there were gangs of scholars on the same search and he wanted to slow them down, if they happened to have just the ciphertext. He assumed that you'd give the ciphered pages to someone, your pal at the library for instance, and a general hunt would be on. That's why he came back to New York. He wanted to get to you and get the cipher pages from you. He had the grille and –'

'Shvanov grabbed him up and tortured him. Why was that?'

'He thought Bulstrode was double-crossing him. Someone, I never found out who, called Shvanov and told him that Bulstrode was dealing with another group hunting for the play manuscript. Shvanov went crazy and –'

'Another group? You mean us? Mishkin?'

She considered this for a moment, chewing her lip. 'No, I don't think it's you they meant. Someone else, some other gangsters. A guy named Harel, also Russian. They're all Russian Jews, all related in some way, rivals or former partners. They mainly talk in Russian, so I don't get much information . . .'

'And what about this Miranda Kellogg that Mishkin is always going on about? What's her story?'

'I only met her once,' she said. 'I have no idea who she really was, some kind of actress or model Shvanov hired to get the Bracegirdle original away from Mishkin. They sent the real heiress away on a freebie vacation and presented the actress as Kellogg.'

'What happened to her?'

'I think she held up Shvanov for more money after she had the thing and he got rid of her.'

'Killed her?'

'Oh, yeah. She's dead. Gone.' She shivered. 'Dead as Bulstrode. Shvanov doesn't like people screwing him.'

'*Was* Bulstrode double-crossing Shvanov?'

'Oh, yeah. Not with any other gangsters, though, as far as I know. But he never had any intention of handing over the play if we found it. Are you kidding? March told me he was planning to give it to the nation, with of course the proviso that he have sole access to it and the right to do a first edition. They'd lock him and it up in the Tower and Shvanov could just go suck a frog. I mean the man was a Shakespeare scholar down to the bones. He used to talk about it, with fucking stars in his eyes, the poor jerk!'

'Well, no perforated Bible has turned up as far as I'm aware, so we have to assume that Shvanov has it. What happened to the actual grille?'

'Shvanov has that too, obviously, because Bulstrode took it with him when he left England. And when they put the boots to him Bulstrode must have told him about Mishkin having the original letter and he already knew you must have kept the originals of the ciphered letters. Didn't anyone try to get them from you?'

'Oh, yeah, they tried,' said Crosetti, and briefly related the events lately transpired in Queens. He added, 'So the basic situation is, we have only the ciphers, he has only the grille: the classic Mexican standoff. Or am I missing something *again*, Carolyn?'

This last was in response to a peculiar expression that swiftly crossed her face. She said, 'Do you have the ciphers here? I mean right here in this room.'

'Well, the originals are safe in a vault at the New York Public Library. But I have a digitized version on my laptop here. Encrypted, of course. I have a Breeches Bible too. Mishkin bought two of them. And I have a digitized text of the 1560 edition I put in there back in the city before we –'

'I have the grille,' she said.

'You do? Where?'

In answer, she stood and pulled the robe aside and propped her foot up on the arm of the chair, exposing her inner thigh. 'Here,' she said, pointing to a constellation of tiny blue dots on the smooth white skin. He knelt and peered, his face just inches away. The scent of rose soap and Carolyn made his knees tremble. At first the dots looked random, but then he saw the pattern: a stylized weeping willow tree, symbol of mourning. He cleared his throat, but his voice still croaked. 'Carolyn, is that a jailhouse tattoo?'

'Yeah. I made it in my room at Ollie's after I swiped the grille. I used a pin and ballpoint ink. There are eighty-nine holes.'

'Jesus Christ! Is it accurate?'

'Yeah. I transferred it to tracing paper and compared it with the Bible from Darden Hall. The holes match up.'

'But why?'

'Because I figured I might run into you someday, and you might still have the ciphers. And paper gets lost, or stolen, as we well know, not to mention the bastards searched me about fifty times. But of course the bitch who searched me wasn't told any details about what she was looking for, only that I wasn't supposed to have anything up my various holes. And lots of people have tattoos. Do you have any tracing paper?'

'No. But I have a fine-point marking pen. We can use the glass from that little picture frame. It's about the right size.'

She lay on the edge of the bed, on her back, with her left thigh flat and at a right angle to her body, while Crosetti knelt on the floor between her spread legs. All the lights in the room were on. He held the glass against her skin and used the marking pen to place a red dot carefully over each blue dot on her skin. He had to keep his left hand against the warm flesh and his face quite close as he did this. It was the most erotic experience of his life, save one, and he was almost giggling with it. They didn't speak. Rolly was as still as a corpse.

When it was done, Rolly adjusted her robe and said, 'Bulstrode figured out from the pattern of the pinholes in the Darden Hall Bible that they started with the second page of Genesis and worked forward in order. You place the outermost grille holes on the lower left and the lower right over the first and last letters of the bottom line on each page – those're the index markers – and you read the letters under each of the holes off in the usual reading order, left to right, top to bottom.'

Crosetti was already at the desk with the old Bible opened. His laptop was plugged in and running Word. He placed the glass plate over Genesis and lined up the index dots over the proper letters. The marker ink was semitransparent, and he could easily read the letters beneath.

'I'll call the letters and you type them in,' he said. 'D . . . a . . . v . . . o . . . v . . .'

It was unbelievably tedious work. Crosetti had, of course, done a character count of the ciphered letters, and there were over thirty-five thousand of them, not counting spaces, and there was a nonrepeating Biblical letter key for each one. He did a quick calculation in his head. Dictating at the rate of, say, one character a second, thirty-five thousand characters would require almost ten hours, not counting breaks and checking. This was far too long, if the people Rolly had skipped from were looking for her, and he was sure they were. So they could leave now, and hole up – and as soon as Crosetti thought about this he hit on just the right place to do that – but he was perishing just then to read the secret ciphers immediately. He stopped dictating.

'What's the matter?' Rolly asked.

'This sucks, is what. There has to be an easier way. We're

not Jacobean spies. Shit! I'm looking at a computer and it never occurred to me . . .'

'What're you babbling about, Crosetti?'

'This. Look at the grille. The first letter of the key is the third letter of the first line, then the fifteenth letter, then the twenty-second. Next line: letter two, then seven, then fourteen. The grille generates the same pattern for every page they used. They didn't use title pages, did they?'

'No, the only pages marked were ones with solid text. And of course every other page so they wouldn't confuse the pinholes that came through the paper.'

'Of course. They'd only use the right-hand nontitle pages. So all we have to do is bring up the digitized version of the 1560, strip out the chapter title pages, and the left-hand pages, and then write a simple search to count and list just the characters the grille indicates. We can generate the key automatically. I have a Vigenère solver in there too. If this works, we could be reading Bracegirdle's secrets by morning.'

'Could I take a nap while you do that?'

'Be my guest,' he said and turned back to the desk.

As with all projects involving computers, it took a lot longer than expected. The first of the dawn had appeared in the bay windows by the time Crosetti mashed the Return key and sent the long string of letters comprising what he hoped was the key into the virtual maw of the Vigenère solver, which had already been charged with the entire string of characters from the Bracegirdle ciphers. The program screen showed 'SOLVING. . .' and in a long blank slit below that word a string of little rectangles appeared one after another like a line of boxcars on a track. Crosetti had been drinking the hotel's do-it-yourself coffee all night and he was dry-mouthed and twitching with it.

'Crosetti. . . Christ, what time is it?'

This in a mumble from under the quilt.

'Almost seven. I think I'm done. Want to see?'

'I smell coffee.'

'There's some left, but it's awful. Come and see this. This could be the solution.'

She rolled out of bed and stood next to him, smelling of bed. The last little rectangle appeared and was replaced by a screen showing a single file title:

Bracegirdle cipher plaintext.txt

Crosetti placed the cursor on it and said, 'You should have the honor. Hit the Return key.'

She did. The screen changed to a solid block of single-spaced text, the first line of which read:

mylfrdithdsnowpascedtwowereksandsomedaitssincgilefmyouphowsa

'Oh, no!' she cried, 'it didn't work.'

'Yes, it did. Remember they were working out of two different Bibles, Bracegirdle's and Dunbarton's, and the average print quality was pretty bad, especially with a mass market item like the Breeches Bible, so no two copies were exactly alike. And they must have had the same problem back in the day. The grille on Bracegirdle's copy would give a slightly different key letter set than Dunbarton's but it's close enough. Here, let me copy this to a new document – so – and put in spacing and punctuation and correct the obvious errors – so – and . . . here's the first line.'

My Lord: It has now passed two weekes and some daies since I left your howse

'Oh, God! Crosetti, you're amazing.'

There was a smile of delight on her face, the same that had penetrated his dream life for these many months, and he felt a similar grin break out upon his own face. 'Not really,' he said. 'It was obvious to any really transcendent genius. Are you going to kiss me now?'

She did. Soon afterward, he was naked under the quilt and so was she. Crosetti pulled away from her and looked into her eyes.

He said, 'I guess we're not going to read the ciphers right now.'

She kissed him again. 'They've kept four hundred years. Another hour won't hurt. And you're probably too tired.'

'Tired of looking at text on a screen, yeah, not too tired for *this*.' Some more of *this* followed and then he pulled away from her abruptly and met her eyes.

'You're going to stay now, right?' he said. 'I mean you're going to be here tomorrow and the next day . . .'

'I think I can commit to those particular days.'

'But not *additional* days? Or is this going to be a continuing daily negotiation?'

'Crosetti, please don't . . .'

'Ah, Carolyn, you're going to kill me.' He sighed. 'I'm going to be a dead person if you keep this up.'

And he would have gone on longer in this vein, but she stopped his mouth with her tongue and pressed Richard Bracegirdle's long-lost cipher grille against his groin.

'**That was fast**,' he said.

'It was. It was fast and furious.'

'I like the way your eyes pop open when you get your rocks off.'

'An unfailing sign,' she agreed, 'so I'll remember who.'

'Wise. Now, although I would like to extend this more or less indefinitely . . .'

'You want to read the ciphers. Oh, so do I but I didn't want to say.'

'Lest it be misinterpreted. I understand. So since we're agreed, let us visit the bathroom in turn and then make it happen.'

She kissed him briefly and slid out of the bed and he thought, There can't be many things more lovely than watching a woman you've just made love to walk across the room, that way her back and her ass look in the dawn's early light, and he was thinking about how to make that shot on film look like what it actually looked like in real life when Carolyn gave a yelp and dropped to the floor.

'What?'

'They're here!'

Carolyn's face had the fox-in-the-headlights look he recalled from New York, the animal fear in her eyes. In an instant it broke his heart all over again. 'Who?' Although it was an easy guess.

'One of them's standing in the garden, Semya. The others must be in the front. Oh, Christ, what're we going to do!'

'Get dressed! And keep away from the window!' She slid into the bathroom like a lizard and Crosetti got up and went to the window naked, stretching and scratching his belly like a man who'd just slept the sleep of the just and had nothing to fear. There was indeed a man in the garden, a broad-shouldered fellow in a knee-length black leather coat and a knitted cap. He looked up, saw Crosetti, stared briefly, and then turned his attention elsewhere. So even if they knew his location, and that Carolyn might come to him, they still didn't know *him*. Which was strange, because they had spotted him easily enough on the street in Queens. Unless that was a different group of people entirely. Carolyn had mentioned two rival organizations . . .

But he couldn't think about that now. He pulled clothes on, yanked the phone cord out of the wall, plugged in a phone adapter for U.K. systems, connected it to his computer, compressed and encrypted the Bracegirdle material and dialed up his Earthlink mailbox. He hadn't used a dial-up connection to the Internet in years, but it still worked of course. It seemed to take eons for the thing to go through – perhaps five minutes – and after that was done he used a disk-scrubbing program to strip the cipher, the key, the Bible, and the plaintext version from his hard drive. He looked up and saw Carolyn in the bathroom doorway.

'What are you *doing*?' she stage-whispered.

'Protecting our secrets. It's funny, I've seen so many movies about this situation that it's like I'm following a script. The guy and the girl have to escape from the bad guys . . .'

'Oh, fuck you, Crosetti, this isn't a fucking *movie*! If they catch us they'll torture us until we fucking *give* them the secrets. They use *blowtorches* . . .'

'That's not in the script, Carolyn. Put it out of your mind.'

He sat at the computer again, worked for another few minutes, then switched off the machine and packed it in its case. 'Now we have to pack you,' he said and dumped the contents of his duffel bag onto the floor. 'I hope you're limber enough to do this.'

She was, but barely. When this trick is done in movie land, Crosetti knew, the hero doesn't really carry the girl in the bag, but a styrofoam simulacrum. In real life, he now found, hauling a 125-pound woman down a flight of stairs in a duffel bag was a lot harder than he had imagined. He was sweating heavily and breathing hard when he reached the lobby.

There were two of them standing there as he checked out.

He was careful not to examine them, but he absorbed peripherally an impression of leather, largeness, and quiet determination. At the front desk, he handed the clerk the note he had prepared:

Please don't say my name out loud. I am trying to avoid the people who asked for me. Thank you.

There was a twenty-pound banknote folded into this message. The clerk, a young Asian, met his eye, nodded, and did the checking-out process in silence, with a simple 'Goodbye, sir, hurry back,' at the end.

Crosetti now opened the duffel bag and removed the rain jacket, muffler, and hat he had squashed down on top of Rolly and put them on in full view of the thugs, who regarded him without interest, their eyes on the main stairway and the emergency stairwell at the lobby's other end. He picked up the duffel and walked right by them out to the street. The E-class Mercedes he had arranged over the Internet was waiting, as was a Daimler V8 just behind it, with yet another leather thug leaning against the fender, smoking. The limo driver, a Sikh with a white turban, helped him load the duffel bag into the trunk, and when he was seated, he told the driver to take him to the nearest department store. The man suggested Templar Square, which was fine with Crosetti. He thought the place looked like any small-town American mall, with less energy; it made him obscurely sad.

Back at the car with his purchases, he had the driver pop the trunk. Rolly crawled out, groaning, and he helped her into the back seat. She smelled of dampness, canvas, and unwashed clothing. With the car again under way, he handed her a shopping bag. She looked through the clothing it contained.

'You're always buying me clothes, Crosetti. Should I be worried about that? Undies too. That must've been a thrill.'

'Just being tidy. It's a vice of mine. How do you like them?'

'I hate them. I'm going to look like a starlet or an amateur whore. And what's with the Dolly Parton wig? I thought the point was to avoid notice.'

'That's how you avoid notice, if you're someone who always dresses in black and has brown hair. You should put them on.'

She grumbled but did as he asked, donning a lilac sweater, tight yellow jeans, an oversize white parka with a fake fur collar, and fleece-lined boots.

'This all fits,' she said. 'I'm amazed. What've you got there?'

'Makeup. Turn this way and hold still.'

As the car sped down the motorway, he painted on foundation, blusher, a heavy plum-colored eye treatment, and dark scarlet lip gloss. He showed her what she looked like in the little mirror of the compact he'd bought.

'Hey, sailor, lookin' for some action?' she asked the mirror. 'Crosetti, how the hell did you learn to do this?'

'I have three older sisters and I worked on lots of very, very low-budget movies,' said Crosetti. 'And don't thank me. Mishkin gave me an American Express card before we left.'

'And where are we going on Mishkin's American Express card?'

Crosetti's eyes flicked to the driver.

'Casablanca. We're going to Casablanca – for the waters. I have a standing invitation. We should be safe there until things settle down. We can study the Bracegirdle ciphers and figure out where they lead us, if anywhere.'

'What if they have people at the airport?'

'That's extremely unlikely. We're not running from the government or Goldfinger. This is a bunch of local gangsters. Right now they're probably breaking into our room, noticing the pile of clothes and books and realizing how they were scammed. They'll know we're going to the airport because they saw me get into an airport limo. They'll chase us, but we should be okay.'

She exhaled and leaned back on the soft leather, closing her eyes. He took her hand, which was warm and damp, like a child's, and he too closed his eyes as they drove south.

The Sixth Ciphered Letter (Fragment 4)

drawes out from his presse the fayre copy, saying you shal burn this & I goe to do it drawing neare the flames but at last could not, I know not why, it was to me neare to killing a babe; for I loved him & saw he loved it much. But this I had not in my harte to say in wordes; instead I sayde upon second thought perhaps we should keep it safe as evidence of this vile plot. Now he looketh longe at the fyre, in scilence, drinkinge: then saies he, there is a thought my Dick, a happy thought. We will not burn her, nore uze her to stop draughts or start fyres, but she shal drowne; as who knowes what may rise from water in a comeing tyme when men may see these thynges with a new eie. Then he laughs & saies I trow that this poor unheard play will be all of Will that's heard of an age from nowe & that a mere mocke. Nay, saies I, for the mob doth flock to thy plaies & it is oute of question thou'rt best for comedies. At this he doth pull a face as if he bit upon a rotten fish & he saies, Codso, how thou dost prattle, Dick. What's a play! New a' Tuesday & sen-night later they cry have you not some-thynge else, we have hearde this before. Tis a penny-tuppence businesse withal, emplaced curiouslie betwixt the bawds and the bears, of no consequence, a thynge of ayre and shadowes. Nay, if a man would live after his bones are in the earth he must make weightier stuff out of his braines, epic poesie or histories, or from his loines make sonnes. I have no histories & of epics onlie two, and those slight ones.

Had I landes & wealth or learning I might have been another Sydney, a better Spenser, but from my youth I must earne, earne, & a pen can draw readie money only out of yon wooden O. And my son is dead.

We spake no more to our purpose that night. Later, wee left for Warwickeshire & a hard going we hadde, it being winter & all myres, but arrived in Stratford 18th Febry & took us to a certayne place & hid safe the booke of that playe. Where it is have I writ down in a cypher knowne but to me and Mr W.S. It is not this cipher my lord, but a new one I have devized with Mr W.S. for he sayde hide what I have writ with my writing and wrote me out the key on the instant & this direction is kept by me all ways, and anie man who hath it & hath the key & hath the scille to uze my distance rule may find that place where it resteth.

My Lord, if you have need of this playe of Mary of Scotland but send word, as I aime to submit to youre desyres in everie thynge. I am yr. Lordship's most humble & obdt. servt.
Richard Bracegirdle
London, 22nd Februarie 1611

19

We were expected at the prison, welcomed even, by the deputy warden herself, Mrs (not Ms) Caldwell, a dame of Thatcher-esque dimension, polish, and accent. I wondered at the time how long prior to this visit Paul had arranged things. Did he foresee the need to visit prisoner Pascoe as soon as he learned about my involvement with Bulstrode and the various secreted manuscripts? Unlikely, but it would not entirely surprise me. As I noted, Paul is very smart, and subtle with it. His predecessors in the Society of Jesus used to run whole nations, so that outsmarting a bunch of Russian thugs, even Jewish ones, might not be a major challenge. Is that a logical statement? Perhaps not and perhaps also a little reverse anti-Semitism in there: Jews are smart, therefore tricky, got to watch yourself around them, *jew* still a verb in many parts of my nation, nor am I immune to the cozy embrace of casual anti-Semitism. Rather the opposite, in fact, as Paul has often pointed out.

The prison was a class D facility, which is what Her Majesty calls her minimum-security facilities or, as we might say, her country club joints. Springhill House had actually been a private home at one time and all in residence were, according to Mrs Caldwell-Thatcher, rehabilitating themselves fit to be tied. And of course we could see Mr Pascoe, a model prisoner. Take as long as you like.

Pascoe was an unattractive little man, carefully dressed in a blue silk shirt, a fawn lamb's-wool sweater, tweed slacks, and polished slip-ons. His small monkey eyes shifted behind thick clear-rimmed eyeglasses and he wore his thin hair (dyed a deplorable shade of yellow) swept back to his collar. He spoke in what Brits call a posh accent and suffered from the sin of pride. It was Paul's religious duty to point this out and offer the opportunity for repentance; I'm sorry to say he did not, but exploited it, for our advantage. Or for the greater good, depending on one's point of view. As I say, a subtle fellow, my brother.

We met in Pascoe's room, a comfortable nest that could have been in one of those cozy-shabby hotels the English seem to like. The furniture was dorm-room institutional, but Pascoe had tarted it up with framed pictures and manuscript reproductions, an Art-Deco bedspread, colorful throw pillows on his bed, and a worn Oriental carpet, perhaps genuine. He reclined on a pile of these pillows while we sat upon straight chairs. He made tea for us, fussing.

We began by discussing old Bulstrode. Pascoe had heard of his death and was avid for more information, which we supplied, although we did not deny the police theory that he had fallen prey to rough sex. Then there was some business I didn't then understand about 'was the payment through' and Paul said it was and handed him a slip of paper, which he examined, folded, and put away. After this he leaned back in his cushions like a pasha, folded his long delicate hands, and looked dreamily up at the acoustic tiles.

And proceeded to tell us exactly how he brought off the

scam: that is, he told us that the Bracegirdle manuscript was a forgery (here he included copious detail about the source of the paper, the recipe for the ink, how to fake or subvert dating technology, etc.) and that someone, who he did not name, had contacted him, given him the text, and provided him with the appropriate materials. In prison? I asked. A piece of cake, Father. I could run ten-pound notes off in this rest home and no one would be the wiser. He'd done the job and smuggled the pages out and payment had been received. He'd also advised his mystery client about how to run the scam. The important thing was to string it out, make the mark work a bit, so that he thought he'd found it himself. So your first hint had to be produced into evidence as coming from an old book or books before a naive witness through legerdemain; and afterward bring in Bulstrode, the expert.

Why Bulstrode? Pascoe laughed nastily at this: once bitten twice shy is a load of bollocks, my son. Your best mark is a man who wants to recoup his loss – the poor bastards never learn. Prompted by Paul's questions, he described just how he generated the supposed ciphered letters (nothing more intriguing than a cipher, gentlemen, as I said, you want to give the marks something to do), including the 'discovery' of the indispensable grille, and then, almost smacking his lips, he laid out how to arrange the finding of the long-hidden treasure. He went into a lot of detail, which I will not repeat here, but it was highly convincing, and amazingly intricate. The forger's agent within the camp of the mark – for this too was vital, and it had better be a bird, a little crumpet never hurts if the mark gets iffy – this girl would contrive to deliver the Shakespeare manuscript into the hands of the mark. Who would then sell it to the real mark, the moron with the money. Because, needless to say, you could only pull off something like this with illiterates. You couldn't *actually* forge a Shakespeare play – the merest junior don would catch you out – so you had to find someone with more gelt than sense, d'you see, and then there had to be a secret transfer, the manuscript for cash, and goodbye. The final act was the girl swiping the cash from the original patsy – a trivial operation – and there you have it.

And we did have it, on my little machine. Paul had been insistent about that, even going so far as insuring that the batteries were freshly bought ones. After Pascoe wound down, Paul said, 'Well, let's see what you can do,' and brought from his briefcase some folio sheets of what appeared to be old paper, a small glass bottle of sepia-colored ink, and three goose quills. Pascoe's face lit when he saw them, as a mom's might at the sight of her baby, and he quickly rose, took the material, and sat at his little desk. He examined the paper carefully, holding it to the light of his desk lamp, and made sounds of appreciation. Then he opened the ink bottle, smelled it, tasted it, rubbed a drop between his thumb and forefinger.

'Marvelous stuff,' he said at last. 'The paper is genuine seventeenth century and the ink's tallow soot and oxgall. I assume the ink's extracted from old documents?'

'Of course,' said Paul.

'Brilliant! Wherever did you get it?'

'The Vatican Library,' said Paul. 'A deaccession.'

Pascoe grinned. 'Well, that's one word for it,' he said, and without further speech set about trimming the goose quills, using an X-Acto knife Paul provided. While he was doing that, Paul brought out what I recognized as a page photocopied from our Bracegirdle ms. Pascoe readied his quill and, after testing it on some scrap paper, set to work. We sat. Paul took out his breviary and mumbled. It was like an afternoon at a Benedictine scriptorium, without the bells.

'There!' said Pascoe, handing over the page. 'What d'you think of that?'

We looked. He had copied the first ten lines of the Bracegirdle ms. three times in all, the first one rather crude, the second one much better, and the third indistinguishable, to my eye at least, from Bracegirdle's own hand.

It seemed to satisfy Paul as well, because he began to put all the things we had brought, including the forgery practice page, back into his portfolio. Pascoe watched the paper and ink vanish with an expression of longing.

I waited until we were back in the Merc before I spoke. 'Would you mind telling me what that was all about?'

'It's a forgery. I told you before, the whole thing is an elaborate scam.'

'So it seems. What was that at the beginning about a payment?'

'Pascoe has a boyfriend and wants to keep him provided for. That's why he did the forgery and that's why he spoke to us. I arranged for the boyfriend to receive a nice check.'

'You're abetting unnatural acts?'

'Not at all. Mr Pascoe is safe in prison and incapable of doing any but solitary unnatural acts. He shows a laudable concern that his honey not be forced to go out on the streets as a rent boy, and wishes to support him. I believe it's simple charity to help him out.'

'You really are a perfect hypocrite, aren't you?'

Paul laughed. 'Far, far from perfect, Jake. The interesting thing is that this young fellow our Pascoe is supporting in luxury is the same one whose testimony landed him in jail after that *Hamlet* thing.'

'And how did you figure all this out?'

'Oh, I have contacts. The Society of Jesus is a worldwide organization. I had someone go talk with Pascoe and out came the story, perfect confidentiality of course, and I approached Pascoe by phone before we left.'

'So what do we do now?'

'The same thing we would have done if the thing were genuine,' said Paul. 'Go through all the hoops, get the fake play, and deliver it to the bad guys. That gets you and yours off the hook.'

'And what *about* the bad guys? What about Bulstrode and whoever sent the people I shot? They get a free pass?'

'That's up to you, Jake. You're an officer of the court, I'm not. My only interest is in making sure this whole mess goes away.'

The car was now moving in the direction of Oxford, and Mr Brown informed us that we had been followed to the prison and were still being followed. Paul was pleased at this, as it would confirm to the bad guys that we had actually been to see Pascoe and would add an important detail to our forgery story. What was I thinking of after these revelations? I was plotting about how to use them to secure another meeting with Miranda Kellogg or whoever she was. I have described my Niko as an obsessive-compulsive, and he is, poor little guy, but, you know, the apple does not fall far from the tree.

I pulled out my cell phone and dialed, not because I particularly wanted to speak with Crosetti, but as what psychologists call a displacement activity. Animals, for example, lick their genitals when placed in anxious situations, but higher animals reach for a ciggie or, latterly, their cell phones. I was annoyed to receive a recorded message that the cell phone customer I was trying to reach was unavailable. Was the man really so stupid as to have turned off his phone? I disconnected and made another call, booking a suite at the Dorchester: for people like me spending lots of money is another sort of displacement activity. During this ride, we managed to transfer the recording of the conversation we'd had with Pascoe to my laptop and thence to a CD, which Paul took. I forbore to ask.

They dropped me off at the hotel some hours afterward. The atmosphere in the car had been fairly chilly and unrelieved by any dramatic confrontations. We discussed security. Mr Brown assured us that his people would be watching over me in the city as well.

'This must be costing a fortune,' I observed.

'It is,' said Paul, 'but you're not paying for it.'

'What? Surely not the law firm?'

'No. Amalie is.'

'Whose idea was that?'

'Hers. She insisted. She wants us to be safe.'

'And to get a report on all my doings too, no doubt,' I replied, with an uncharacteristic nastiness. Paul ignored this as he so often does my remarks in this tone. We shook hands, or I tried to shake hands, but he embraced me, something I don't much care for. 'It's all going to work out fine,' he said, smiling with such a good humor that I was forced to allow my own face to break. I hate that about him. Mr Brown, at least, was content with a brief shake, and then they were gone into the confusing British traffic.

My room was blue, elaborately upholstered the way the Dorchester does, tufts upon tufts, no swaggable space unswagged. I called Crosetti again, with the same result, had a Scotch, and another, and made some business calls setting up appointments for the next several days. Our firm was representing a large multinational publisher and the meetings were about European Union handling of digitized text and the royalties pertaining thereto. It was exactly the sort of grindingly dull legal work I have specialized in, and I was looking forward to being as grinding and dull as I could manage with a group of colleagues compared with whom I am Mercutio.

Every so often during the next day I called Crosetti, with no luck. The first evening, after a dull supper with several international copyright lawyers, I briefly considered hiring one of the elegant prostitutes for which that part of London is justly famous, a leggy blonde, perhaps, or a Charlotte Rampling type with a sly smile and lying blue eyes. But I declined the tempt; I might have enjoyed the in-your-face defiance of Amalie's unseen watchers (and their employer, of course), but against that I knew that it would not be particularly pleasurable and that I would be suicidally depressed afterward. This was a demonstration that I was not doomed always to take the most self-destructive option and it made me feel ridiculously pleased with myself. I slept like the just and the next morning at breakfast received a call from Crosetti.

When he said he was at Amalie's place in Zurich I experienced a stab of rage and jealousy so intense that I almost upset my orange juice glass and at that same instant I recalled in detail my conversation with him at the bar of my former hotel. In the vile sexual phantasmagoria that my domestic life has become, I have never crossed a particular line, which I know is one that many philandering husbands flit by without a thought, and by this I mean projecting one's sins upon the injured wife, either accusing her of infidelity or subtly encouraging a self-justifying affair. 'Everyone does it' gets you off the moral hook, and then we can all be sophisticatedly depraved. Had I really encouraged Crosetti? Had he really taken me up on it? Had Amalie . . . ?

Here I felt the moral universe tremble; my face broke out in sweat and I had to loosen my collar button to drag enough air into my lungs. In the sickening moment I understood that my excesses were made possible only because my mate was the gold standard of emotional honesty and chastity. If *she* were proved corrupt then all virtue would drain from the world, all pleasure become dross. It is hard to express now the real violence of this perception. (And, of course, like many such, it soon faded; this is the power of what the Church calls concupiscence, the force born of habit – and the Fall of Man, if you want to get theological – that drags us back into sin. An hour later I was both mooning about Miranda and giving the eye to a fresh young assistant at my first meeting.)

After some long seconds, I rasped into the instrument, 'Are you fucking my wife, you guinea son of a bitch?' quite loud enough to turn heads at nearby tables in the Dorchester's elegant breakfast room.

To which he answered, in a shocked tone, 'What? Of course not. I'm with Carolyn Rolly.'

'Rolly? When did she turn up?'

'In Oxford. She's on the lam from Shvanov's people.'

'And you decided to shelter her with my wife and *children*, you asshole!'

'Calm down, Jake. I thought it was a good move. Why should they look for her in Zurich? Or me, for that matter? Meanwhile, there've been some developments . . .'

'I hate this! Get out of there and go someplace else!' Incredibly stupid, I know, but the idea of Crosetti sharing a house with Amalie got under my skin.

'Fine, we'll stay at a hotel. Look, do you want to hear this . . . it's important.'

Grumpily, I told him to spit it out. It was quite a story. The long and short was that Rolly had smuggled a copy of the grille away from the bad guys and they had been able to decipher the spy letters. I am trying to recall what I felt when I heard this and I suppose the answer is, not that much, because I knew the whole thing was a fraud. I told him to e-mail me a copy of the decipher and asked, 'So, does it locate the play?'

'It says he buried his copy, and waits for an answer from Rochester. He was double-crossing Dunbarton and wanted to use the play as proof of the plot. He may have gotten his answer and dug up the play and then who knows what happened to it?'

'Wait a second – one of the ciphered letters was to someone else?'

'Yeah, the Earl of Rochester, the man Dunbarton was conspiring against. Dunbarton apparently got caught plotting and decided to cover his tracks by whacking both Bracegirdle and the Bard. Bracegirdle panicked and tried to rifle the playhouse strongbox to fund his getaway, got caught, confessed all to Shakespeare, and they decided to blow the whistle. There're some pages missing from this letter but it's still pretty clear. Shakespeare knew some high-level people who could vouch for the whole thing and they wrote the letter in the same cipher.'

'And they weren't afraid that Dunbarton might get hold of it and read it?'

'No, that's the beauty of his cipher: all you needed was a grille, which is easy to copy, and a reference to a page in the Breeches Bible and you're all set, but unless you have the page to start on you're out of luck. He must've hand-delivered the grille, the ciphered letter, and the page reference to one of Rochester's people and . . .'

I didn't care about the details and said so, adding, 'So we still don't have the whereabouts of the play?'

'No. He wrote that he has the directions where they'll be

safe, whatever that means. Apparently you also need that range finder he invented.'

'Oh, good. I'll check out Portobello Road. So that's it? A dead end.'

'It looks like it, boss, unless someone has retained a trove of Bracegirdliana. On the other hand, this is still the biggest find for Shakespeare scholarship since forever. It should be worth a bundle to the Folger.'

'Yes. And what are your plans now?'

'Back to New York, I guess. Carolyn owns the ciphers, so she'll want to sell them. Amalie said you knew a big-time Shakespeare scholar . . .'

'I do. Mickey Haas – what about him?'

'Well, maybe you could ask him to handle the sale – in exchange for first look and all that.'

'I'd be glad to. And if you want to return with me, we'll be leaving late on Thursday, day after tomorrow, from Biggin Hill. And, Crosetti? Forget about what I said about Amalie and about leaving the house. I'm a little nuts nowadays.'

Why didn't I tell him at that moment that it was a fraud? I can't recall, but it must have been the fear that if I short-circuited the denouement of the scam I would not get to see Miranda again. Perhaps more than a little nuts.

I went to my meetings, had my flirt, as I've said, and a charming dinner with Miss Whoever-Someone, but I put her in a cab with a mere handshake, unmauled. The next day I met Paul for breakfast in the Dorchester and handed him the printouts of the e-mail Crosetti had sent. He sat and read them while I sipped coffee. When he was done I asked him what he thought.

'Brilliant,' he said, 'I almost wish it were real.'

After that we talked about Mickey and the dead Bulstrode and the scholarly life, and about Mary, Queen of Scots, and how no one was able to really pin down what she'd actually done. Had she really conspired to kill her husband, Lord Darnley? What had possessed her to marry a maniac like Bothwell? Did she write the incriminating letters that plotted the assassination of Elizabeth? Why did she never, in the entire course of her life, stop to think?

I said I didn't know – it was all *Masterpiece Theatre* to me. It wouldn't be the first time, however, that the fate of nations swung on someone wanting a piece of ass to which they were not strictly entitled.

'Yes, but what would *Shakespeare* have made of her? I mean he had absolutely nothing to work with on Cleopatra and Lady Macbeth and the women in the history plays and here he had loads of material, and it was all about something that happened in his grandparents' time. He must have heard people talking about it when he was a kid, especially in a Catholic part of the country like Warwickshire.'

'Well, we'll never know, will we? Speaking of conspirators, have you heard from the Russians?'

'Not a peep. I can't believe you're not interested in this. You're supposed to be the romantic one in the family.'

'Me? I'm the prosaic one. Intellectual property law? You're the war hero. And priest.'

'The most antiromantic profession.'

'Please! There's nothing more romantic than a priest. The unobtainable is the *essence* of romance. That's half of what brings the suckers in, the fascination with celibacy. Plus you guys get to dress up as women without looking ridiculous.'

'Or not very ridiculous,' said Paul, grinning. 'Although as I recall, *you* were the one who used to dress up in Mutti's clothes.'

'Oh, now you're definitely trying to drive me crazy. I never dressed up in –'

'Yeah, you did, you and Miriam were always going through her bureau. Ask her if you don't believe me. She sends her love, by the way.'

'Where is she?'

'In transit. She called last night. She wanted to know what we were up to, but didn't want to *seem* prying – you know how she tries to weasel stuff out of you when you'd be perfectly willing to tell her if she'd just ask up front?'

'Yeah, and getting anything out of her is like picking crab-meat. Does "in transit" mean she's in Europe?'

'So I gathered,' said Paul vaguely. 'My impression was that she's on her way to see Dad.'

'How about you? Going to join them?'

'I might, as long as I'm here,' he said, with his annoying smile.

'All forgiven, is he?'

'It comes with the job.'

'And he's all apologetic for what he did?'

'Not in the least. He's never said a word to me or Miri about that time, or about Mother. He thinks I'm a jerk and a clown and treats Miri like a servant. As far as I can see he hasn't changed one bit since Brooklyn, except he's older, richer, more corrupt, and boinking successively younger women. Oh, and of course, politically he's a total fascist, way to the right of Kach. Death to the Arabs, Sharon a sellout, the usual.'

'Charming. Paul, why the *hell* do you waste your time with him?'

His turn to shrug. 'Filial duty. Or so Miri doesn't have to carry the whole load by herself. Or maybe I have hope that he'll put himself in a position where I can give him what he needs.'

'What would that be?'

'I'm not sure. Penitence and reconciliation? My prayer is that I'll know it when it happens. In the meantime, he's my father, and although he's a nasty bastard he's still part of me, and it does me good to see him every once in a while. You should try it sometime.'

I said I'd pass on that and he didn't press me. He never does. I can't recall the rest of the conversation and I had left my little machine in my room, but I vividly recall the next time I saw my brother, which was when he burst into my room at about ten that evening with the news that my children were missing.

Of course, Amalie had called me first on my cell, but as you have probably gathered by now, I dislike them intensely and always turn mine off during meetings and this evening I had forgotten to turn it back on, and I also recall that I had neglected to inform her I was staying at the Dorchester instead of my usual Knightsbridge place. Therefore, she could not get ahold of me and called Paul instead.

I immediately called her, of course. In a curiously dead voice she told me the story. Amalie had taken the children ice-skating near her house. Ice-skating is Niko's sole athletic activity, so his mother is always ready to take him to the rink. He typically skates in tight obsessive circles, staring down at the ice. Imogen is a fair figure skater and loves any sort of showing off. They went out with Crosetti and his girlfriend and afterward had their hot chocolate at Zic-Zac. The kids finished and ran outside to wait, the way kids will, especially if their mother thinks they are rude American barbarians not fit to be served in even a low-end Zurich joint. The adults finished their coffee and pastries, and when they emerged the kids were gone. A bystander told her that a sedan had pulled up to the curb, a blond woman had stuck her head out the window, engaged them in conversation, and they had both jumped into the car willingly. She assumed that they knew the woman in the car, or she would have given the alarm. Of course, my first thought was that it was Miranda, and I have to confess that for a brief moment I felt a kind of joy – even though she was a criminal who had kidnapped my children, she was in a way back in my life, I might see her again!

'I'll come right over,' I said to my wife, 'I can be there by seven.'

But she said she didn't want me. She said I should have been there already, that it had happened because I wasn't there, because I had broken up the family and let nastiness into what should have been the safe refuge of our home, and do you now pretend to offer me comfort? I don't want your comfort. You have no comfort to give. And now that your children have been taken by gangsters you will be even more free to do whatever it is you want, and do you want to know what I feel? I feel I was so foolish as to want to raise children with a man like you, I thought yes, I could fix it all with love, I could spread a blanket of love around all of us so that in this frightful world there would be one corner that would be for us alone but no, you didn't want this, you tore it to pieces my poor little blanket and now what will you do, Jake, on what basis will you mourn for your children? Will you even miss them very much? I don't even know that and so how can you come and sit with me and give me comfort?

And a good deal more in this vein, with me making excuses and defense and for God's sake Amalie what are you doing? Have the police been notified? And all sorts of operational stuff that I wanted her to focus on, not to mention the thought (which I was not ready to share with her) that the only reason anyone would have snatched my kids was to trade them for the Item. Which I had not got, and had not much hope of getting if Crosetti was right, and on and on talking past each other like people in a postmodernist play, and eventually she said she didn't want to talk with me at all anymore and asked to speak with Paul. I gave him the phone and sat on the bed, dull and paralyzed, staring at the desk, which happened to be in my direct line of sight. The desk was covered with neat stacks of paper and folders in various colors into which I was arranging the results of my recent legal work, my laptop computer glowed invitingly and the demons put into my mind the thought that oh, well, I still had my work; no family, shame about that, but still . . . and then followed the realization of what my work actually *was*, at which point I went *matagalp*, as I believe they call it in the Philippines.

I let out a howl like King Kong and began to tear the room apart. I overturned the desk, the chair crashed into the mirror, the laptop went clattering into the bathroom. I threw a fairly heavy Regency armchair through the window and was trying to toss all the papers and my briefcase after it when Paul tackled me. I am, of course, much stronger than he is, but he managed to get me in a painful hold of the type used to disable sentries and after a few seconds of painful, futile struggle my rage collapsed into sobbing. I believe I screamed and cried for some time and then the police came because of the broken window, but Paul was able to deal with that, since priests are nearly always given the benefit of the doubt.

Some hours later, having Xanaxed myself into dull apathy, the expected call came through. Paul took it on the hotel phone and handed it to me. The voice was accented, Russian maybe, but not Shvanov's. This person was not threatening in any way, explained that he was not a barbarian, that my children were safe and comfortable, not taped to chairs in abandoned factories or anything, and neither you nor your wife was going to be so foolish as to involve the police. I assured him we would not. He said that all this could be handled in a civilized way, since I surely knew what they wanted, and that as soon as I had obtained it I should place an ad on such and such a Web site and they would contact me, and when I said I had no idea where the goddamn thing was he said, we're patient and we have confidence in you and broke the connection. Nearly as soon as I hung up, my cell phone made the noise it makes when there's a message waiting and I went into my mailbox and there was a photo of both kids smiling and a message from Imogen: 'Hi, Dad, we're okay and healthy and not getting tortured like in the movies. Don't worry, okay?' Proof of life, they call it, very professional. And she really did sound okay.

Okay, fast-forward a little. Paul's gone. He wanted to stay and talk but I kicked him out, mainly because he was taking the kidnapping worse than I was and I had no taste for his empathy. I'm alone in the wrecked suite. The management has placed heavy plastic over the window, but I told them I would pick up the place myself, to gather my important confidential papers. Money has been liberally schmeared among the staff. I am actually gathering up the papers and stuffing them any which way into my briefcase, when my eye falls on a thick pack of printouts that I don't immediately recognize. On closer inspection I see it is the genealogy of the Bracegirdles that Niko prepared for me. I am about to toss it in the can when I notice that it's the female branch, the one I never looked at. I sit on the edge of the bed and leaf through the stack and learn that Richard Bracegirdle has one surviving female relative in the direct line, a Mary

Evans, born 1921, in Newton, Maryland, and still there residing.

It's 9:30 p.m. here, afternoon on the East Coast. I get the number and make the call. A woman's voice. No, she's sorry to say Miss Evans is deceased. Recently deceased. My speaker is Sheila McCorkle, and she's a church lady from Miss Evans's church, a Catholic church, of which the late Mary had been a pillar. Mrs McCorkle is helping to clean out the place, and my! Isn't there a lot of old stuff! I say I'm calling from London, England, which impresses her, and I ask her if she has disposed of any of Miss Evans's possessions. No, not yet. Why? I tell her that I am the lawyer for the Bracegirdle family and would like to inspect Miss Evans's home to see if there are any important memorabilia extant, would that be possible? It would, she supposes. I get her home number and make an appointment for the following day.

Well, I was crazy, I suppose, to believe in such a long shot, but did not the great La Rochefoucauld say that there were situations so dire that one had to be half-crazy to get out of them alive? I called Crosetti and told him to get ready to move to London on my call, because I had a lead I was following up over in the States, and if it paid out I would need someone in England. A brief pause on the line. Shouldn't he stay with Amalie? I said that this might be our only chance to get our hands on the Item, and that this was perhaps more critical to getting my kids back than any comfort he could give my wife. We made the arrangements and then I hung up on him and called our pilot.

By six the next morning I was in the air flying back across the Atlantic. We had a tailwind and made it to Baltimore-Washington Airport in slightly over seven hours. Three hours after that I was pulling my rental Lincoln up to the front of a modest frame house sitting white and weathered under leafless oaks and dogwoods, in Newton, Maryland. Mrs McCorkle proved to be a stout fiftyish lady with a homely open face, dressed in country work clothes, an apron, and gloves. Inside, the place had the burdened atmosphere of a long life eviscerated by death. The cartons were out and Mrs Mc. was valiantly trying to separate the salable from the junk. Miss Evans had been, she told me, a spinster (she used that now very unfamilar antique word), a sad case, had a fiancé once who didn't come back from the war, had a father who lived too long, she took care of him, never married, poor thing, and yes, she was a Bracegirdle on her mother's side, Catholic of course, from an old family she said, they came to America in 1679, one of Lord Baltimore's Catholic shiploads, well, she could believe the *old* part, look at all this stuff, it looked like they hadn't got rid of anything since *1680*! Feel free to look around. Over there near the fireplace is the stuff I thought would sell. Her will left everything to St Thomas's, which is why I'm here.

I looked at the box of books first. An old Douay Bible, crumbling leather, inside it a family tree going back to Margaret Bracegirdle, the original emigrant. Margaret had obviously married in America, and her sons and daughters had married, and the name was lost to the record books but not to memory, for there were numerous among the family tree who bore the ancestral name: Richard Bracegirdle Clement, Anne Bracegirdle Kerr . . .

Putting the old Bible aside I dug deeper in the carton.

It was a quarto, of course, its red full-calf binding leather nearly black with age and the covers and the endpapers foxed and swollen with damp, but the pages were all there, the binding was intact, and the name on the flyleaf in faded sepia ink was 'Richard Bracegirdle' in the familiar hand. An edition of 1598, I noted, as I flipped through the front matter.

Genesis was marked with tiny pinholes. On the back flyleaf was inscribed in that same hand a string of letters in fourteen uneven rows.

I closed the book with a snap. Mrs McCorkle looked up from her sorting and asked if I had found something I liked.

'Yes, I have. Do you know what this is?'

'A Bible, it looks like.'

'It is. It's a Geneva Bible, from 1598. It belonged to Richard Bracegirdle, an ancestor of your friend.'

'Really? Is it valuable?'

'Well, yes. I suppose that it might fetch twenty-five hundred dollars at retail, because of the damage. It's not a perfect copy, and, of course, this particular translation was used by practically every literate person in England for eighty or so years, so there are a lot of them.'

'Lord! Twenty-five hundred dollars! This is like *Antiques Road Show*.'

'Almost. I'm prepared to write you a check for twenty-five hundred right now, which is a good deal more than you'd get from a dealer.'

'That's very generous of you, Mr Mishkin. Could I interest you in some nice Fiesta ware?' We were all smiles now.

'Not really, but there is another item I'm looking for, mentioned in some old family papers, a kind of old surveying instrument, made of brass . . . ?'

'Surveying instrument? No, I don't think so. You mean one of those things with a tripod and a little telescope?'

'Not necessarily. This would have been portable, maybe a yard or so long, and a few inches across, like a big ruler . . .'

'You don't mean *that*?' She pointed. Dick Bracegirdle's invention was hanging above the mantelpiece, softly gleaming, kept and polished by generations of his female descendants, ready for use.

Or a concoction of the scam artists, I should say. Once again, I was impressed with the intricacy of the plot. Had Miss Evans been involved in some way? Had they actually found a real descendant of Richard Bracegirdle, or had they begun with this old lady and built up the whole fraud around this antique instrument and an old Bible, and invented an ancestor to suit? Even a master of the involved lie such as myself could not help admiring the clockwork detail.

At Baltimore-Washington Airport, I went into one of those lounges they reserve for the prosperous traveler and called Crosetti in Zurich. I told him what I had just bought and then I used the computer facilities to scan and send off to him via e-mail the cipher from the flyleaf of Bracegirdle's Bible. He said he would run it through his solution program and get back to me. I had a coffee and some snacks and killed an hour or so, and then he called me back, and not with good news either. The cipher did not work with the Bible and grille key that had been used for the letters.

'Why would he have done that?' I asked Crosetti. 'He had an unbreakable cipher. Why the change?'

'I don't know. Paranoia, maybe? He was dealing with two hostile parties, Dunbarton and Rochester, and both wanted something he had, and both of them had the Bible cipher. Maybe he wanted to hold something back, or maybe he wasn't thinking too clearly by then.'

Oh, yes, I sympathized there. 'So it's another grille?'

'Not necessarily. I think it's a regular book cipher. I mean it's a running key based on a text.'

'What text? The Bible?'

'I don't think so. Do you recall all that business in the last ciphered letter when he's talking with Shakespeare about where to hide the play and he explains how a key works and he says something to the effect that Shakespeare said to use his own words to hide his play?'

I did, but vaguely. I said, 'So we'd have to run through all of Shakespeare's work to find it? That'll take forever.'

'Not really. Remember that Shakespeare's plays weren't published in a complete edition until 1623. Bracegirdle wouldn't have wanted to use a play that might be out in different editions, some of them corrupt. I mean he was in the business – he knew that.'

'So what then?'

'Well, fourteen rows of ciphertext. Maybe it's a sonnet. The sonnets were published in 1609.'

'So try them.'

'Yes, boss. By the way, if this is a bust too, you'll have to go and see Klim at my mom's.'

'Because . . . ?'

'Because he's the only serious cryptographer I know. If it is a running key and not from a text we already know, then you'll need to do a much more sophisticated analysis. Not impossible, not with the kind of computer power that he can put together, but not trivial either, maybe a keyspace of two to the fortieth or so. But I can't do it, and he can. And you'd have my mom there too.'

'And she's also a cryptographer?'

'No, just a real smart woman who does the Sunday *Times* crossword in twenty minutes or so. I'll call her and tell her you're coming.'

So then up to LaGuardia by plane, alerting Omar en route. He met me and was devastated when I told him about the children, real tears sprang from his eyes, the match of which the dad had not himself shed. Even my servants conspire to abash me, was my ignoble thought as we drove out on the ever-clogged Van Wyck. It was a short drive from the airport, perhaps the only advantage of a residence in Queens. At the little house I immediately saw that all was not as it should be. There was a filthy pickup truck parked in front with one wheel up on the curb, and the front door of the house hung open, although it was a chilly day. I told Omar to drive up the street a bit and to stay in our car with his cell phone at the ready while I took a look around the house. Omar objected, saying that we should both go and him armed, but I refused the offer. I didn't say it, but it occurred to me that I had risked his life several times in this miserable affair and could not bear to risk it again, if risk there was. If risk there was, I reasoned, it were better that the lesser man should bear it, nor would I have minded the worst happening. And I rather looked forward to the opportunity of handing out some pain.

Thus I crept down the alley at the side of the house, keeping low and peering into each window in turn. In the living room, nothing. The bathroom window was obscure glass. Ahead lay the tiny backyard, two fig trees wrapped in burlap, a little patch of brown lawn, a dormant flower bed with a concrete statue of the Blessed Virgin in its center. From this yard I could see into the kitchen: and here was a tableau. Mrs Crosetti and Klim were sitting in chairs at the table and their mouths were covered with tape. There was a large, crop-haired man in the room with them with his back to the window. He seemed to be haranguing them, and in his hand was a large nickel-plated revolver.

Without thinking I plucked the statue from the earth – it weighed perhaps fifty pounds – raised it over my head and took a little run at the house. The man must have heard something, or perhaps it was Mrs Crosetti's eyes widening in shock, because he turned and faced the window and so took the full force of the flying Mary (plus glass fragments) right in the kisser.

After that the familiar ritual of the police and the slow extraction of information. Mrs Crosetti was gracious under the circumstances, although she did question my propensity for doing violence in her home, which I thought a little unfair. The man was not dead, I was happy to learn, but would certainly miss the senior prom. His name was Harlan P. Olerud, and he was a security guard from somewhere in Pennsylvania and he was under the impression that Albert Crosetti had absconded with his wife, Carolyn, and he wanted her back. Apparently he had been led to the Queens dwelling via a computer map that young Crosetti had carelessly left on the road near his home while searching for the mysterious Carolyn Rolly. The police found the map in Olerud's pickup truck, which also held two frightened children. In the ordinary course of events, these would have been handed over to the bureaucracy that cares for parentless kids in New York, but since Mary Peg was involved, events took a different course. She wanted to take care of the tykes until we all figured out what was what with the mysterious C.R., and also I think because of an empty-nest syndrome the size of Montana. I believe I made up a little for my use of force in her home by getting dear Father Paul on the line from London. There is nothing Paul does not know about the child-care bureaucracy in New York; he made some calls, vouched for Mary Peg, made noises – unusual circumstances, police investigation, potential danger, best interests of the child, etc. – and the thing was done, at least temporarily. Board games emerged from the attic, pizza was generated out of basic ingredients, a jolly time was had by all, except that Klim beat me by fifty points at Scrabble, which I thought was a bit much, English being my first language.

Mary Peg came into the living room from putting the children to bed looking remarkably happy (here a pang at memories of Amalie in the same situation, my lost home . . .) and sat down next to Klim on her sofa. With all the police and kid business this was actually the first time we had been able to manage a quiet talk. I brought them up to date on what I had been doing and showed them the Bible and the Bracegirdle range finder I had purchased in Maryland. Not a word about the whole thing being a scam, of course. I also distributed printouts of the deciphered letters, and while they were reading through them I woke up Crosetti in Zurich and asked him if there were any developments. He said that Paul had told him yesterday that someone had e-mailed Amalie a picture of the kids holding that day's copy of the *New York Times*. They were both smiling and seemed perfectly all right, no threatening guys in black masks. I said that seemed odd, and he agreed. 'It's like they're on a class trip. That doesn't sound like the Shvanov we know.'

I admitted it was peculiar, but good news at any rate. Then I told him about Harlan P. Olerud and the two children. He said he'd let Rolly know and I said I'd arrange for a call from the kids and that I'd let him know if we had any luck with the new cipher. He wanted to speak to his mother, and so I turned the phone over to her.

Klim was fooling with the range finder. 'An ingenious device, quite ahead of its time. It will require a new little mirror – here – and then I believe it will work as designed. May I see the cipher from the Bible?'

I gave it to him and he examined it for a while and then said he would enter the ciphertext into Crosetti's desktop PC and see what could be made of it. 'All Shakespeare's works are available in digital form, of course, so if the key is from his known work we should get a good hit.'

'Unless he used lines from the lost play,' said Mary Peg. 'That would be a Bracegirdlian thing to do.'

'In that case,' said Klim, 'we will have to use more strenuous methods.' He hefted the Bible, smiled, and walked off.

Mary Peg bid her son good-bye and said, 'That's awful about your kids. Your wife must be in agony. Shouldn't you be over there with her?'

'I should, but she doesn't want me. She blames me for the whole affair and she's right. And I have a sense that the kidnapping is not what it seems.'

'What do you mean?'

'I'd rather not say just yet. But I've been putting some things together and I don't think that they're in any immediate danger. In the future, who knows, but not now, provided we can locate this thing.'

'Oh, it's perfectly clear where it is.'

I expressed astonishment. 'Yes,' she said, 'they tossed it down that well he mentioned, you know the one where Bracegirdle followed Shakespeare and his goon into the forest and they saw the recusant service. That ruined priory . . .' She shuffled through the printouts and found the page: 'Saint Bosa's Well. Where else would it be? He says they went up to Stratford and the well is just half a day's ride away.'

'Maybe,' I said, 'but where is the well? Bracegirdle said it was a secret even in Shakespeare's time. It could be under a factory or a housing development.'

'True. And in that case we'll have to announce it publicly and turn the whole mess over to the authorities. Which I sometimes think we should have done from day one. But' – here an uncharacteristically wolfish expression appeared on the Map of Ireland – 'I sure would like to find that play. So we can only hope that the well is still bubbling away, forgotten for centuries.'

After that she made more coffee and we drank it with Jameson whiskey in it. We talked about family, I recall, and children, and their joys and discontents. I rather regretted not liking her son and decided that it was an aspect of my craziness and resolved to be more agreeable to him in future. After some time had passed in this desultory fashion, Klim emerged with a glum look.

'I am sad to say that this ciphertext does not generate plaintext from any writing of William Shakespeare that is recorded by history. This is not deadly for us, because as I believe I have said earlier, we can run guessed probable plaintexts along the ciphertext and see if we get something intelligible and this I have started to do, but I desired to have some of your Irish coffee at this time.'

This was provided, and I asked him if he had found something intelligible yet.

'Yes, of course, we start with the commonest words in English and see if the ciphertext gives us, let us say, a *the* in either direction using a standard tabula recta. Of course Bracegirdle could have used a nonstandard tabula, but he has not before this, so let us suppose he is hurried and wished to stay simple. So we use the computer to query if any three letters of the ciphertext will generate a *t-h-e* trigram as part of our key, and you see here that we do: both *TKM* and *WLK* give us *the*, and when we run that key back against this ciphertext it gives us *ADI* and *DEG*, which fortunately are both trigrams common in English. Similarly running *and* gives us one hit and the plaintext *FAD*, which is also a good English trigram. Running *be* gives two hits, and we get *ENDF* for the plaintext and also a little bonus, because the first *be* comes right before that *the* we have already discovered, and so we know that *be the* is part of the key text. And so we go on from here. Each little advance gives us more of the plaintext and more of the key text and the two decipherings reinforce each other, which is why the running key based on a book is so weak. For this reason the KGB only used almanacs and trade reports with many tables of numbers, so the entropy is higher. Now the next word we try should be *is* or *of*, I believe . . .'

'No,' said Mary Peg, 'try *Jesus*.'

'This is religious advice, my dear?'

'No, the word. You said you ran the key against the complete works and came up empty?'

'Yes. Aside from some purely random runs of pseudosense.'

'But he wrote one thing that's not in his published works. His epitaph.'

She ran to a shelf and pulled out Schoenbaum's *Shakespeare's Lives*, and there it was on the first page:

Good friend for Jesus' sake forbear
To dig the dust enclosed here.
Blessed be the man that spares these stones
And cursed be he that moves my bones.

'On second thought,' she said, 'it should be with the archaic spelling. I think it's in Wood's book.'

It was. Klim entered the old spelling into the Vigenère solver and it worked, giving us:

fromguystowrheadingeduesout
hseteightysevendegreeseachsyd
esheliethfourfadomsandfoot
belowcopyngeintheeastwall

'This seems plain enough. One stands upon a place called Guy's Tower and sets Bracegirdle's instrument so that the zero point in the center is pointing due south by the compass set in it. Then the arms are placed at eighty-seven degrees, and then I suppose one must have a man with a flag walk out, and one looks in the eyepiece until the two images of the flag join and there is your distance and direction. Then when you find this well, one lowers oneself down on a rope with a candle stuck to one's head with hot grease and there at a depth of . . . what is a *fadom*?'

'A fathom,' said Mary Peg. 'Six feet.'

'Yes,' said Klim, 'so at a depth of let us say seven point six meters in the east wall of this supposed well we shall find your play. Or an empty hole. If we knew where this 'Guys Towr' was.'

'It has to be Warwick Castle,' she said confidently. 'Bracegirdle wrote that you could see the castle from the ruins of St Bosa.'

A moment on the Internet confirmed that there was indeed a Guy's Tower on Warwick Castle, and on the south side too. I said, 'That'll be an interesting experience. Trying to sight off the top of a major tourist attraction while a man with a flag walks through the suburbs.'

But Klim's fingers were already flying on the keys, and in a few minutes the screen showed a view from above the tower battlements of a castle. It appeared to have been taken from about twenty feet up.

'Very impressive,' I said. 'This is a commercial satellite picture?'

'No, it is U.S. military. I have accessed it through an anonymous link but still we cannot stay on it very long.'

'How did you do that?' I asked.

'He's a spy,' said Mary Peg with something like pride.

'I am a retired Polish spy, perfectly harmless. But I retain some knowledge of this sort of thing. America has the worst security of any nation, it is well known in those circles, a kind of joke in fact. Now we shall use some tools to drop a smart bomb on Mr Shakespeare's play.' More clicking and a red grid appeared over the picture and a palette of drawing tools sprang up along one edge of the screen. He said to Mary Peg, 'My dear, if you could just measure that device?'

'Three feet exactly,' she replied after some manipulation of a tape measure.

'So . . . let us see, ninety-one point forty-four centimeters, which we center on the north-south diameter of this tower . . . so . . . and we then draw a line from either end at eighty-seven degrees from that base and we generate two lines which intersect . . . so. As you say, X marks the spot. We need not go up on the tower and bother the tourists. Thank you, United States Air Force satellite-based tactical program.' He pressed a key and the printer growled. I looked at the printout. Due south of the castle and veering off to the west was what looked like a plowed field bordered by copses of trees. The red lines from the tower converged in one of the dark little woods.

'How accurate do you think this is?' I asked Klim.

He shrugged. 'As accurate as it was in 1611 at any rate. There does not seem to be a car park and lemonade kiosk there, so perhaps your well is still lost.'

I called Crosetti again and told him what I wanted him to do. It took quite a while. What a lot of cleverness and effort expended on a fraud, how many nice people would be disappointed! A perfect symbol of my life.

20

Carolyn Rolly wept for what seemed like a long time after Crosetti told her what had happened to her kids and to Harlan P. Olerud at Crosetti's mother's house in Queens, and then she insisted on calling there to talk to them until Crosetti managed to convince her that it was late at night in New York instead of the early morning it was in Zurich. Then his cell phone delivered a call from a man from Osborne Security Services who said that a plane was waiting at a local airport and they said good-bye to Amalie, with whom Carolyn had struck up a surprisingly warm relationship, surprising given the differences in their backgrounds and general approach to life. Perhaps, he thought, it was the commonality of motherhood and the peculiar situation of both sets of children bearing a similar horrible stress. With his usual curious eye, Crosetti watched the two women exchanging embraces. They did not really resemble each other physically, but both presented to the world the same air of solid particularity. He couldn't imagine anything really changing either of them: Carolyn and Amalie, what you saw was what you got, although Amalie was honesty incarnate and Carolyn lied like a snake. Had Carolyn been blond, he concluded, they might have been two sisters, the good one and the bad.

A short flight on a tiny powerful Learjet, the pilot uncommunicative, efficient, moving his craft through angles eschewed by mild commercial aviators. Midflight, Rolly got through to her children, or so Crosetti imagined: she did not share but sat damp-eyed, staring out at bright whiteness. But she let him take her hand.

Landing at some Midlands airport whose name Crosetti never caught, they were met by Mr Brown of Osborne, dressed in yellow coveralls and work boots. Mr Brown conducted them to a white Land Rover painted with the insignia of the Severn Trent Water Board. On the motorway he explained the plan: go right in, bold as brass, find the thing, if it were there to find, drive off. Another plane waited near London to take them back to New York. Crosetti asked him if he knew what they were after.

'Not me,' said Brown, 'no need to know, I'm just the help. There's a rental van behind us with all the equipment and a couple of lads to run it, ground-penetrating radar, resistivity gear, the lot. If there's a well there they'll find it. We'll all do the digging, I expect.'

'This is pretty expensive, all this,' Crosetti observed.

'Oh, yes. Money no object.'

'And you're not curious?'

'If I was the curious type, sir, I'd be long dead,' said Brown. 'That'll be Warwick up ahead. We'll be able to see the castle in a bit.'

It rose white above a line of trees, hung there for a while, and then vanished when the road dipped, like a vision in a fairy story. After some driving through anonymous suburbs it appeared again on their left, huge, looming over the river.

'Not like Disneyland, is it?'

'No, that's the real thing,' said Brown, 'although Tussaud's have tarted it up like mad. Still, there's real blood soaked into the stones. A horrible time, of course, when that was the last word in military technology, but still . . .'

'You would've liked to live back then?'

'On occasion. A simpler time: someone got on your nerves, say, you put on your tin suit and chopped away at 'em. Half a sec, I think we're just on our mark.' He pulled over to the side of the narrow road they were on and consulted a large-scale Ordnance Survey map, then folded it and turned the Land Rover into the ditch on the right and down a track through a grove of oak and beech.

'There's gear for you in the van,' he said as he got out. 'It's important to look authentic and official.'

Crosetti and Rolly went to the rear door of the van, which opened to reveal an interior that included a steel table, tool racks, long steel pipes, ladders, rigging gear, electronic equipment, and two men, who introduced themselves as Nigel and Rob, Nigel owlish and bespectacled, Rob broad-shouldered and gap-toothed with a tan buzz cut. They handed out yellow coveralls and boots and yellow hard hats with lamps in them. Crosetti was not surprised to find that the boots and the coveralls fit him perfectly. Carolyn reported that hers did too.

'Osborne seems like a very efficient outfit. Does it make you nervous to learn that they have both our shoe sizes?'

'Nothing surprises me anymore,' she said. 'What are they doing?'

'I have no idea,' said Crosetti.

They watched the two men roll a four-wheeled cart made of steel pipe out of the van, and Crosetti was conscripted into off-loading various pieces of heavy electronics and car batteries from the van and lifting them onto the cart.

'By the way, what *is* all this?' he asked Rob.

'It's a ground-penetrating radar set, absolutely top drawer. It produces a picture of the subsurface from a few feet to a hundred feet down, depending on the soil. We should get good penetration here. It's Triassic sandstone.'

Nigel said, 'Unless there's a clay intrusion.'

'What if there's a clay intrusion?' asked Crosetti.

'Then we're fucked, mate,' Rob answered. 'We'll have to go to resistivity, and we'll be all week.'

'You both work for Osborne?'

'Not us,' said Nigel. 'University of Hull geology. We've been corrupted by corporate gold, haven't we, Robbie?'

'Utterly. What're you lot after anyway? A Viking hoard?'

'Something like that,' said Crosetti. 'We'll have to kill you if we find it though.' They both laughed, but nervously, and both looked around for Brown, who seemed to have wandered off.

Rolly was poking at the ground some distance away and Crosetti walked over to see what she was doing.

'You don't have to claw at the earth with your fingers,' he said. 'We have all this high-tech equipment.'

'Look what I found,' she said and held out her hand. In it was a flat, roughly triangular white stone upon which had been incised a perfectly straight double line and below it what appeared to be the petal of a rose.

'It's the priory,' she said. 'This is the place. I'm getting chills.'

'So am I. You look terrific in coveralls and a hard hat. Would you whistle at me as I walk by?'

One of her stern looks followed this sally, and then Nigel and Rob called him over to help draw the cart. They heaved the thing through the wood, over ruts and roots, with Nigel leading the way, staring at a Global Positioning Receiver and

Rolly trailing behind carrying several picks and spades across her shoulders.

'Let's stop here and light up the radar, people. If that satellite view we had from you is correct, Mr GPR says this is the place.' They were in a shallow dip of land thickly littered with golden beech leaves between three old gray trees, whose reaching limbs crisscrossed against the milky sky above. Nigel made some adjustments and switched on his set. It hummed, and a broad paper tape emerged from a slit in one of the metal boxes. Nigel shoved his glasses back up his nose and studied the colors printed on the paper. He hooted and cried out, 'Well, I'll be blowed. Got it in one. There's the void and it's full of what looks like chunks of cut stone. Clear as a bell. Take a look, Robbie.'

Rob did and confirmed the find. They cleared away the leaves and surface soil and began to dig, and before too long had uncovered the remains of what looked like the coping stones of a well, in the center of which was a mass of irregular pale stones.

'It's dry,' said Crosetti.

'Well, yes,' said Rob, 'the hydrology's changed a good deal in the last four hundred years, what with digging canals and ornamental ponds for the gentry and public water schemes. Still, bit of a job, here,' he said, frowning down at the opening. 'Some bastards have stuffed the thing with rocks. How deep did you need to go?'

Crosetti said, 'Something like eight meters.'

'Oh fuck,' cried Rob. 'We'll be all fucking day.'

It was nasty, heavy work of the type that all their ancestors had done every day of their lives in the not too distant past, the movement by human hands of massy bits of the planet's fabric from one place to another. Only one person could fit down in the hole at a time, and this man had either to lift a rock onto a canvas sling attached to chains that led to the steel pipe tripod and pulley that the two geologists had rigged above, or else, if the stone were too heavy to lift, he had to drill a hole, anchor an eyebolt into it, and secure it to a hook. An hour into the work it started to rain, a steady chilling drench from the greasy low clouds, just enough to cause slips and frequent painful injuries and the dull stupidity that comes from cold. Crosetti's mind went dim as he worked. He forgot Shakespeare and his fucking play. The world shrank to the problem of the next stone. Each of the three men worked half an hour and then clambered up an aluminum ladder to collapse exhausted on the bed of the van. Rolly had found a Primus stove and kept the kettle going and fed them all pints of thick, sweet tea. When she wasn't doing that she stood at the head of the well with a steel tape measure and dropped it down after each layer of stone had been raised and called out the depth: five meters, twenty: six and eighteen; and made jokes and encouraging cheerful noises and laughed at the snarls and curses she got in return.

At half past noon they broke for lunch. Ever-efficient Mr Brown had packed the Land Rover with plenty of groceries and Rolly had made soup and sandwiches and more tea, this time with rum in it. They ate in the van to be out of the rain and from this vantage could see Mr Brown out in the distance, by the road, talking with a man in a Barbour jacket and tweed cap. The man was gesturing with a stick and seemed upset. After a few minutes he returned to his own Land Rover and drove off. Brown walked back across the squelching field to the van.

'That was the National Trust man,' said Brown. 'He is much vexed. This field is a registered site and we are absolutely forbidden to disturb it. He's gone off to fetch the authorities, who will call the water board and find out we are not who we say we are. How close are we?'

'Six point eighty-two,' said Rolly.

'Then we're going to have to move a little over a meter and get the Item, if it's there, and clear out in something like half an hour. Break's over, gentlemen.'

They returned to the well and delved like demons for ten minutes, and here they finally caught a break, because the next layer of rubble consisted of small regular stones the size of cobbles that could be readily flung into the sling. Crosetti was at the bottom when the tape descended past his face and struck the rubble and Rolly called out, 'Eight point sixteen.'

He crouched and directed his miner's lamp at the east wall. At first he saw nothing, only the roughly rectangular stonework of the well shaft. He grabbed a short wrecking bar and pounded on each stone in turn, and on the fifth try one of the stones seemed to move. He forced the straight blade of the bar between that stone and its sister and heaved and the stone slid a little farther out of alignment. In two minutes of violent exertion he had pried it from its place and was looking into a void from which issued an odor of ancient damp earth. His lamp shone on a round shape, about the size of a number ten can.

Hardly breathing now, Crosetti inserted the curved end of the wrecking bar into the hole as far as it would go and wiggled it around until he felt it catch, and slowly pulled out what appeared to be a lead pipe a little over a foot in length and a hand-span in diameter, closed at both ends by soldered sheets of lead. Crosetti carried it up the ladder, cradling it tenderly, like a rescued infant.

'That's it?' asked Rob.

'It shows how much you know, Rob,' said Nigel. 'That's

King Arthur's willie, preserved in brandy. Now England can be great again.'

Crosetti ignored them and went into the van, with Carolyn following close behind. Rob was about to follow but Brown put a hand on his arm. 'Time to go, gents,' he said in a tone that did not encourage objection. 'I suggest you take down your gear and drive off before the police arrive.'

'We're not going to get a look?' asked Rob.

'Afraid not. Best you don't know.' Brown extracted a thick envelope from the inside pocket of his anorak. 'A pleasure doing business,' he said, handing it to Nigel. The two geologists went meekly off to gather their equipment.

Inside the van, Crosetti found a heavy clamp, a hammer, and a cold chisel. He fixed the cylinder to the steel table and cut through the lead at one end. Inside he found a roll of heavy paper tied with a dark ribbon. The paper was nearly white and seemed almost fresh, not brown and crumbly as he had imagined four-hundred-year-old paper would be. He realized with something of a shock that the last person to have touched this paper was Richard Bracegirdle and before that, William Shakespeare. He voiced this thought to Carolyn.

'Yes, now you're one with the great. Open the ribbon, for Christ's sake!' He untied the knot and spread the sheets on the table. The ink was black, barely oxidized, he saw, and not in Bracegirdle's hand. The pages were all neatly ruled and written on in three vertical columns, for character name, dialogue, and stage directions: the thrifty Swan of Avon had used both sides of each sheet. Automatically he counted them: twenty-one folio sheets in all. Across the top of the first sheet in letters large enough for even his trifling familiarity with Jacobean secretary hand to read was written *The Tragedie of Mary Quene of Scotland*.

His hand was shaking as he held the page. What had

Fanny called it? The most valuable portable object on the planet. He rolled the pages up again and placed them back in the cylinder with the ribbon, and stuck the lead seal in his slicker pocket. Then he grabbed Rolly in a mighty hug and swung her around and yelled like a maniac and ended by planting a kiss on her mouth.

On the road again in the Land Rover, Brown said, 'I assume all was satisfactory? That noise you made was the crow of victory and not the sob of defeat?'

'Yeah, all our dreams are fulfilled. I assume you're going to ditch this car.'

'Yes, just up ahead,' said Brown. 'We have a few more vehicles as escort just in case security has been breached.'

They pulled into a lane, and there was the familiar Mercedes, or one just like it, and an anonymous black Ford van with two men in the front seat. Security had apparently not been breached because they drove to Biggin Hill without incident. It was cozy in the van and Crosetti, in the shotgun seat, kept drifting off. He had the lead cylinder on his lap. Brown hadn't asked about it, or asked to see what was in it, but simply placed them both in the hands of a sweet-faced motherly woman in a blue uniform, Ms Parr, their handling agent, and departed into his efficient anonymity.

Ms Parr directed them to the passenger lounge, and after looking Crosetti over, asked if he would like an opportunity to freshen up, to which he responded that he would like a shower and a change of clothes if it could be arranged, and it needless to say could be arranged, as what could not be arranged for the fliers in private jets? And how about two large padded envelopes and some packing tape? These appeared, and Crosetti went into the men's room with them and his carry-on bag and the most valuable portable object on the planet in its lead casing. Alone in the blue-tiled room, he removed the play and sealed it in one of the envelopes and taped this under the lining of the back of his corduroy sports jacket. This he hung on one of the shower hooks, outside the plastic curtain, then stripped and took a shower, and was amazed at the almost Mississippian quantities of silt that flowed off his body and down the drain. While he showered he considered why he didn't just leave the damned thing with Carolyn and why he was, in effect, concealing it from her.

Because you don't trust her, came the answer from Rational Albert. But I love her and she loves me, replied Amorous Al. She said so. But Crosetti realized that part of the woman's appeal was her utter weirdness, the proven fact that she might do anything. Even at this moment he had no guarantee that when he emerged from this bathroom she might not be gone and that he might never see her again. This thought prompted an acceleration in his toilette. Five minutes later, still damp but neatly dressed in the jacket, black jeans, and a flannel shirt, he emerged into the lounge, holding his carry-on (containing Bracegirdle's lead pipe) and a padded envelope, which he had stuffed with flyers for tourist spots and sealed with tape. Carolyn was seated in the lounge. She had taken a shower and changed her clothes too, and her damp hair seemed darker than it had been.

He sat down next to her. 'One more flight,' he said, 'and this adventure is over.'

'I hope so,' she said. 'I hate adventure. I want to be in a place where I can get up in the morning and see the same people and do pretty much the same thing every day.'

'Bookbinding.'

'Yes. I know you think it's boring. I know you think that

making movies is serious art and making books is like . . . I don't know, knitting afghans. I don't care. That's going to be my life. I'm going to get my children and go to Germany, where I can study bookbinding, and I'm going to do nothing else but study bookbinding, and make books. That'll be my life.'

'And what, I'll come visit in the summer?'

She turned her head and made that pushing gesture with her hands. 'Not now, Crosetti. I can't hold any more *stuff* in me. Could we just, like, *be* together for the next couple of hours without devising contractual long-range plans?'

'Sure, Carolyn. Whatever you say,' he said, and thought, That's what'd be printed on the outside of the package if our relationship was a product, like CONTENTS POISONOUS OR HIGHLY INFLAMMABLE. Whatever you say.

He walked a little distance away and called Mishkin in New York. Mishkin took the news in and said congratulations and that he'd have a car meet them at the airport.

Their plane was a Citation X this time, smaller and sleeker even than the Gulfstream, configured for six, with a closed-off partition in the rear where there were two bedlike lounges. Seeing these, Crosetti was about to suggest that here was an unusually comfortable way for the two of them to join the Eight Mile High Club but did not. The vibrations were wrong, as they so often were around Carolyn Rolly. He sighed, belted himself in, drank his champagne. The aircraft screamed, slammed him back in his seat, shot into the air at an aggressive angle. He felt the Most Valuable Portable Object crinkle against his spine. The envelope with the decoy ms. was lying on the seat next to him. He read a magazine for a while and then pulled his blanket around him and over his head. It was not the skimpy towel the commercial airlines gave you but a thick, fullsize thing as used by the best hotels. He adjusted his seat to near horizontal and fell into exhausted sleep.

And awoke to the sound of clinking dinnerware and a delightful odor of cookery. The flight attendant was about to serve a meal. Crosetti sat up, adjusted his seat, and looked across the aisle. Carolyn was in the lavatory. He examined the padded envelope he had left on the seat. The tape was untouched, but careful inspection showed that one of the bottom corners of the envelope had been carefully pried apart and skillfully resealed by someone for whom neither paper nor glue held any secrets. He sniffed the edge and detected a faint acetone pong. She'd used nail-polish remover to relax the glue and then resealed it after, obviously, finding that the envelope was a decoy. He wondered what she would have done with the real thing, and what she thought when she discovered that he had created a decoy and left it out in plain view. Who could he have been trying to decoy but her? Oh, Carolyn!

But he kept his mien agreeable when she returned, and they had a stiff little heartbreaking meal together, after which she went back to her seat. He watched *The Maltese Falcon*, memorizing yet more of the script, and as he watched he very much wished that she would ask him what he was watching, and he could invite her to watch it with him, and he would see if the character of Brigid O'Shaughnessy caught her conscience. But he feared another rejection more than he wanted to find out; in fact, he decided that he didn't want to find out at all.

At JFK they passed together through customs and immigration and when they left the terminal proper there was a dark-skinned man with a sign that read CROSETTI standing in the exit lobby; and as soon as she saw it, Carolyn touched his arm and said, 'Oh, gosh, I forgot something back in the customs shed.'

'What did you forget, Carolyn? You just have that little bag.'

'No, something I bought. I'll be right back.'

She whipped back through the doors and was gone. Crosetti went up to the man with the sign and introduced himself and the man said that he was Omar and worked for Mr Mishkin, and had been instructed to drive Mr Crosetti and Ms Rolly to Mr Mishkin's residence. They waited there, with people rushing and brushing by them for half an hour and then Crosetti went back into the terminal and looked around, quite hopelessly, and returned and drove with the man Omar into Manhattan, slowly through the clotted traffic of the morning rush. Crosetti was not thinking at all clearly, the combination of jet lag and exhaustion both physical and emotional having reduced his brain to a barely sentient sludge, and so it was a good forty-five minutes (the limo then a quarter mile from the Midtown Tunnel) before he remembered to call his mother.

'Albert, you found it!'

'Mom, how did you . . . ?'

'Your friend was just here and told us the whole story.'

'Just here?'

'Yes. She came in a cab, hugged her kids for about ten minutes, and left in the same cab.'

'What? She didn't take the kids?'

'No, she said she had some business to do first and promised that she'd send for them in a couple of days. Really, Albert, I mean they're perfectly nice kids but I hope you don't make a habit of –'

'Did you get the cab number?' Crosetti asked.

'I certainly did not. Why, were you thinking of asking Patsy to run a trace on the ride?'

'No,' Crosetti lied weakly.

'Yes, you were, and you should be ashamed of yourself. That's dangerously near stalking, darling, and I mean she's a charming enough woman but it's also clear that she wants to pursue her own life and that it doesn't include you.'

Perfectly true, but not something a man needs to hear from his mother. Crosetti broke off the conversation with unnecessary gruffness and tried not to think of Carolyn Rolly for the remainder of the trip to Mishkin's place and failed.

Crosetti had one friend who had made it big directing commercials, and this friend had a classy SoHo loft, although nothing like the loft that Jake Mishkin had. He commented on this and observed, 'I guess I should've gone to law school.'

'Perhaps,' said his host, 'but I don't think you have the proper parasitic mouth parts. I believe you're unfortunately a creator and doomed to support a great pyramid of people like me. Speaking of creators, where is it?'

Crosetti took off his jacket and pulled out the envelope. Mishkin went to a long refectory table and carefully laid out each page, making two rows of eleven.

They both stared at the pages for a while in silence, which Mishkin broke with, 'That's really remarkable. It looks like it was written last week.'

'They were sealed in this,' said Crosetti and took the cylinder from his bag. 'It was air- and watertight, so hardly any decay or oxidation. Bracegirdle did a good job.'

'Yes. Who knows that you found the play?'

'Well, there are three people over in England who know we found something, but not necessarily what, then there's me and Carolyn and my mom and I guess Klim.'

'And where is Carolyn?'

'I don't know. She bolted at the airport, dropped by my mother's house to see her kids, and left.'

'Good Lord! Why would she do a thing like that?'

Crosetti drew a deep breath. Now that he had to actually say it he felt his throat constrict around the words. 'I think she's going to Shvanov, to let him know what we found.'

'Shvanov? What the hell does she have to do with Shvanov?'

Crosetti gave him a short version of what Carolyn had told him in the Oxford hotel room the night she had come tapping upon his window. Mishkin seemed stunned by this revelation. 'You mean she's been Shvanov's agent all this time?'

'In a way, although I think Carolyn is pretty much always working for Carolyn. But my sense is they have a relationship too.'

'As do you, I presume.'

'Yeah. I thought we were pretty close, but who knows? Have you heard anything about your kids?'

'No. I have a number to call when I have what they want.'

'Which you now have. Are you going to call them? Obviously, Shvanov is going to find out pretty soon if he hasn't already.'

'Yes, but I'm not sure it's Shvanov who has the children.'

'Who else could it be?'

'As I said, I'm not sure, but I've thought for some time that there are other players involved.' Mishkin picked up the title page and stared at it, as if the ability to read the strange handwriting might thereby flow into his head.

Crosetti said, 'You don't seem very concerned.'

'Oh, I'm concerned. I'm just not frantic.' He turned and faced Crosetti. 'You probably don't think I'm a very good father. I would agree: I'm not. I wasn't trained by my own father, which I understand is required. How about you, Crosetti? Did you have a good father?'

'Yeah, I did. I thought he was the greatest man on the planet.'

'Lucky you. Deceased, I understand.'

'Yeah. He was driving down the street, coming home from the office, when he spotted a couple of cops chasing a mutt. He got out of the car and joined in and he popped an artery. DOA. I was twelve.'

'Yes. Well, this seems to conclude our business. We didn't discuss payment for your time. What would you consider fair?'

Crosetti suddenly wanted to get far away from this man and far from the tangled plot he represented. He couldn't help thinking that Carolyn had a point about the exciting life. The right movie line would have been 'You don't owe me anything,' followed by a slamming exit, but what Crosetti said in real life was, 'How about a round ten grand now, and another forty if it proves out?'

Mishkin nodded. 'I'll send you a check.'

21

It's snowing now, a heavy wet snow such as they get in the Northeast when the temperature is just cold enough for snow to form. I am back at the keyboard after a bracing trip in the chill. I visited the boathouse again and checked out the old mahogany speedboat. It is a seventeen-foot 1947 Chris-Craft Deluxe Runabout, with a ninety-five horsepower six, and it looks in mint condition. I filled its tank from a fifty-five-gallon gasoline drum with a hand pump on it. The key was in the ignition and I started it up. After a little coughing it roared nicely and filled the boathouse with a pungent cloud of blue smoke. The other thing I did was to stow my pistol under the cushion of the driver's seat. Do I have a plan? Not really. I am preparing for various contingencies. If you are expecting a visit from a number of armed men and you have a weapon yourself, you can either start shooting as soon as they arrive, since if you don't they will come in and take it away from you, or you can hide the thing and hope you can get to it at need. I was not prepared for a firefight with an unknown number of bad guys and so that is what I did. I wonder whether the snow will interfere with my visitors.

To return to this account (and I expect it will be closing soon, as time past rushes toward its rendezvous with time present): after I spoke with Crosetti in Zurich there passed some days of waiting, a dead period, as I had nothing to occupy my time. I really can't recall what I did except I called Amalie several times a day, to reassure her that things were actually going quite well and to inquire whether she had heard from the kidnappers. Yes, she had. Each morning a video would arrive by e-mail showing an apparently unstressed Niko and Imogen, the latter smiling as at a secret joke, with a copy of that day's paper, and the message spoken by both of them, always the same: 'Hi, Mommy, we're fine, don't worry, see you soon.' Fade to black. No warnings, no threats, no clue as to where they were being held or by whom. Beyond that there was nothing for us to talk about, and I believe both of us were happy to break the connection.

Then the call from Crosetti that they actually had the thing and a further day of waiting, during which I left at least six messages with my brother and with my sister. My sister never replied, but late that night my brother called me.

I asked him where he was and he said he was in Zurich with Amalie and updated me on the status of his plan. He said a package would arrive at my house by air express the following morning which would give me what I needed, and I asked him again if he had identified the other players in this game, the ones besides Shvanov, and he said he had not, but his sense was that they were heavily connected to the people who did big-time art heists in Europe, not the kind who stole to sell or to ransom but the ones who supplied very rich immoral people with the odd Titian or Rembrandt for private contemplation. I said that I thought that those people were concocted by writers of cheap fictions and he assured me that they were not, that sinister forces were definitely involved in the affair and that his plan was the only way he could think of to extricate us all from their grip. I sensed that he was hiding something from me but I had no leverage on him then to make him come clean, or perhaps it was my native paranoia with respect to my family.

The next day I received an international FedEx package from Paul, and somewhat later Omar called from the airport saying that Crosetti was off the plane. An hour later Crosetti walked into my loft and handed it over. Of course, I had given Omar, who was armed, instructions to watch the man like a hawk from the second he left the customs shed, but still . . . I'm not sure I could have done it myself, turning over something he believed was worth tens of millions at least, of uncertain ownership, to rescue two kids he barely knew. A decent man, clearly, and a reproach to all my kind, and I think it speaks badly of me that I could not like him. Like many of his type, he was also something of a schmuck – this Carolyn Rolly apparently had put him through the wringer, and I was not entirely surprised to learn that she was and had always been an agent of Shvanov. I suppose I should have asked him if he had heard anything of Miranda, but I decided that the fewer people who knew about my continuing interest in her the better. In any case, we were not best buddies. He made his feelings about me quite clear as well, and we completed our business quickly.

Shortly after Crosetti left, my phone rang and it was Shvanov. He congratulated me on having recovered a great cultural treasure and told me he would be by shortly to pick it up. I inquired about my missing children. A considerable pause on the line and then he said, 'Jake, you are always accusing me of kidnapping people from your life and I have told you sincerely that I do not do such things. This is now becoming boring, you know?'

'Nevertheless, Osip, you see that I can't release the manuscript to you, as that is what the kidnappers demand for the return of my children. If you don't have them.'

He said, 'Jake, believe me, you have my greatest sympathy and I would be happy to help you in any way, but that does not affect our business relationship. That manuscript was located through means of Professor Bulstrode's information, which is my property, and so the manuscript is also my property.'

'I think you would have a hard time with that argument in a court of law.'

Another longish pause and then in a voice some decibels quieter he said, 'And are you going to take me to court, Jake?' Here a mirthless chuckle. 'Maybe I should take *you* to court.'

'Well, we do have the rule of law in this country, or did. Unlike your own homeland. In any case I will not –'

'But, Jake, listen to me: you will do this. You will give it.'

'Or what? You'll outsource some persuasion?'

'No,' said Shvanov, so quietly that I had to strain to hear him. 'I believe I will handle this in-house.'

After this unsatisfactory conversation I was rather at a loss as to what to do next. I suppose I had regressed in a way to the period just after my mother's suicide, when I was entirely alone, the main difference being that now I had plenty of money. They say that love will get you through times of no money better than money will get you through times of no love, but this is only partially true, I have found. I had Omar come over with his little machine pistol and I set him to guard the manuscript. He loves this kind of stuff and is full of little ploys to determine how different players in a conspiracy have been compromised and how to communicate that fact by unobtrusive signals. After that I went out for a walk and maybe a drink and lunch at a place I frequent on West Broadway. Walking alone always helps to clear my head.

Although lower Manhattan has of late become a bustling collection of boutiques, it is still possible, particularly on a weekday and in cold weather, to be quite alone on many of its streets. I was walking east on Franklin when one of those awful white Cadillac stretch limos with smoked windows glided past me, pulled to the curb in front of me, and stopped. The curbside door popped open and a large man emerged and opened the rear door. He gestured to the opening. I made to walk around him but he moved lightly into my path and drew a long-barreled .22 semiautomatic from the side pocket of his leather car coat and used that to gesture more forcefully. My brother says you should always pay attention to people carrying pistols of this type because the little gun is an advertisement for the ability of the person holding it to shoot you very accurately, through the eye, for example, if need be, and he can also blow your toe off if you don't do what he says. The man's face was intelligent and its expression was the slightly bored but efficient look of the professional doorman. He had the large, merciless brown eyes of a seal. I immediately sensed that I was dealing with a higher order of thug than I had heretofore. I got into the car.

These vehicles can be variously configured, but this one had a typical layout. There was the driver's seat of course, and behind it two regular bench seats for the lesser entourage, here occupied by a couple of well-tanned fellows with good haircuts and the typical wiseguy expression of confident viciousness on their faces. In the rear, where there are doors only on the curb side, there was a kind of semicircular banquette, with the bar and stereo and TV positioned so that the big shot, who sits in the rearmost part of this sofa, has them at his or her disposal. I slid in, the gunman slid in beside me, and I sat down across from the big shot.

'Where are they?' I said.

'That's a fine way to greet your father,' he replied. '"Where are they?" No, "How are you, Dad, glad to see you?"'

'You kidnapped my children, your own grandchildren, and you expect filial affection?'

He made a sour face and his hand flapped a familiar go-away gesture. 'What're you talking "kidnap"? I'm their *zaideh*, can't I take them on a little trip?'

'Without telling their parents where they are?'

'I sent her a nice video every day. You saw them? Did they look fucking kidnapped to you? Believe me, they're both having the time of their life.'

Oh, it all came back in a rush and I sat there gaping in frustration, as I had gaped as a boy at the ingenious rationalizations he spun out so easily to his wife and children. The very structures of reality had shimmered and dissolved under the flow of his words, and we'd always ended up thinking that somehow *we* were in the wrong. Decent people who have read this document thus far would be justified in thinking me a conscienceless, selfish piece of shit, but here sat my master. In that miserable department I couldn't tie his shoes. A life of perfect egoism had done him good, however, and at eighty years old he looked ten years younger. He'd had implants and maybe a little work around the eyes, and his face had that leathery tan you see on rich old guys. He seemed strong enough for at least another decade of corruption.

'So where are they having this super time?' I asked, in a voice I hardly recognized as my own, my throat constricted, my head pounding, my vision going red around the edges. I heard in my ears the sound of gritting teeth. Had I not feared a bullet through the elbow I would have ripped his head off right there.

'They're here, in an apartment belongs to a friend of mine up on the East Side. Miriam's with them.'

Of course. That's why a savvy city kid like Imogen had walked without a fuss into a strange car in Zurich: the occupant had been no stranger, but her beloved Aunt Miri.

'Then I'd like to see them,' I said.

'Not a problem. You'll go get the manuscript, we'll take a drive, we'll see the kids, everything'll be fine.'

'And if not, what? They'll stop having the time of their life? You'll cut off pieces?'

He sighed dramatically and said a brief something in a language I didn't know, but which I supposed was Hebrew. The thugs laughed. To me he said, 'Don't be stupid. I'm not going to hurt anyone. But you are going to get me that manuscript, and you know it, so why fuck around?'

'What about Shvanov? He thinks it belongs to him.'

Again the hand waggle. 'Shvanov is a putz. He's a small-time loan shark with fucking delusions of grandeur.' He raised his voice and called out to the driver, 'Misha, let's go.'

The car moved smoothly away from the curb.

'Where're we going?' I asked.

'To your place, to get the thing, where'd you think?'

'No,' I said.

'No? What do you mean, no?'

'Just what I said. Why should I give it to you? And how the hell did you get involved in this at all?'

He rolled his eyes and sat back in the cushioned seat, with his hands laced across his belly and his dark eyes (mine!) regarding me with the amused contempt I recalled as being their almost perpetual expression during my childhood. 'Jake, your problem is you got my kisser and your mother's brains. That wasn't the good combo.'

'Fuck you!'

'An example – you're sitting in a car with three guys who'd rip your eyeballs out with their thumbs as easy as they'd pick their nose and you're using language? To me? But since you're family I'm not going to get mad, I'm going to explain to you the situation here. Okay, I'm in Tel Aviv, I'm semiretired but I still keep an interest, a nice deal comes along I might go in on it. I have a lot of connections. So Shvanov – he's in Israel three, four months ago and he's talking big, he's got a line on the treasure of the ages but he won't say what it is, and people are thinking he's on to some gold, some art, because he's talking to people who handle that kind of thing. I'm curious, and the next time I see Miriam I ask her what her pal Osip is up to and she tells me about Shvanov and this Bulstrode character and the Shakespeare manuscript. Of course, by that time Bulstrode's dead – why, I never figured out . . .'

'Shvanov thought he brought it back from England and was holding out.'

'Okay, that's the problem with Shvanov right there,' said Izzy, 'he's too quick with his hands, he doesn't think it through, and so he goes and kills the one guy with the best line on this thing. Anyway, after that, Miriam tells me you're involved, you have these papers that point the way to the thing, so I talk to some people and we set up a little syndicate, start an operation to keep an eye on you and Shvanov and see if we can get our hands on this. And then it starts to look like you and this guinea, what's-his-face . . .'

'Crosetti.'

'Yeah, him: it looks like you've got the best leads on it, so we start to follow you . . .'

'So it was you and not Shvanov's, who mugged me in front of my apartment and broke into Crosetti's house and made me kill two people?'

He shrugged. 'Someone associated with the syndicate set that up, and I have to say, you buy cheap, you get cheap. The fuckin city's full of Russian patzers don't know their ass from a hole in the ground. These boys here, on the other hand, are a whole different proposition, in case you get any ideas.'

'But before that you sent someone to pretend to be Bulstrode's niece and she stole the manuscript I got from Bulstrode.'

'I don't know what the fuck you're talking about.'

I studied his face; no liar more skillful than Izzy, but the look of confusion appeared genuine.

'Never mind,' I said, 'so that was your gang following us in Europe?'

'I don't have a gang, Jake. Izzy Numbers, remember? I got nothing to do with any rough shit, never had, never will.'

'So who are these eyeball-tweezer guys in this car?'

'They work for people you don't need to know their names. People in Israel, people in Europe – I told you, it's a syndicate. Shvanov proposed a simple deal. If he gets hold of this thing, we make sure it's authenticated up the ass, total legit, Shvanov has the guy to do it, and we agree to buy it off him. He's asking ten million, the thing's worth maybe a hundred, hundred fifty mill, but who knows?'

'But you're trying to grab it without Shvanov, aren't you?'

'Oh, the lightbulb goes off. Of course, we're trying to grab it if it's up for grabs. Ten million is ten million, and why should we give it to that cocksucker?'

'So why did they send you? I thought you were above all this kind of work.'

'Because if there's an item in play might be worth a hundred fifty mill, they want someone honest on the scene.'

'You? Honest?'

Another dramatic sigh, a specialty of his. 'Yeah, me. Tell me, counselor, did it ever fucking occur to you how come I'm still alive? I'll tell you why. Because I been in this business nearly sixty years, handling fucking *billions* of dollars, almost all of it in untraceable cash, and I never skimmed a nickel. If Izzy the Book says the numbers add up, they add up. If he says they don't, guys get whacked. This is in a business full of *momsers* who'd cut your throat for your shoes. So don't you look down your nose at me!'

'Oh, excuse me, I beg your pardon: you have a sterling rep with the scum of humanity. You walked out on us, you piece of shit.'

'Oh, and you didn't? The difference is you did it because you couldn't stop chasing strange pussy and I did it so I wouldn't do twenty in Sing Sing. You would've been happy to see me in the joint? How the hell would I have supported you?'

'You didn't support us.'

'No? Did you ever miss a meal, ever not have a roof over your head or a warm bed to sleep in, ever not have toys and clothes? You think she supported three kids on her salary, pushing a mop in a hospital?'

'She didn't push a mop. She was an administrator.'

'My sweet ass, she was! Schmuck! She could barely read the *Daily News*. How the fuck could you believe she was handling medical paper? Listen, I sent each of you a card with money in it every birthday and every Christmas, and every year they came back with "not at this address" written on it in her writing. And no money in them either. She steamed them open, took the cash, and sent them back to me. "Fuck you, Izzy!"

'I don't believe you,' I said, with my stomach roiling and a splash of bile high in my throat.

'Then go to hell, you want to hold a grudge your whole life. Meanwhile, here we are. People live in factories now, I can't believe it. Go up and get this fucking thing and then, *alivai*, you'll never have to see my face again. Eli, go with him, make sure he doesn't trip on the stairs.'

When I got out of the limo, my knees were so weak with fury that I staggered. I had to lean on my front door for a few moments and my hand shook when I used my key. I entered and Mr .22 followed me at a discreet distance, enough, that is, to put a few rounds in me if I tried anything. When I reached my door I had a spasm of coughing.

'I'm sorry,' I said to Eli, 'I have a little asthma and it acts up when I'm upset.' He gave an uninterested nod and pointed to the lock. I opened the door and stepped in and the man followed at his usual careful distance and received a heavy blow on the head from a barbell rod wielded by Omar, lying in wait next to the door. The coughing fit I staged had been one of Omar's little signals.

'Who is he?' he asked.

'An Israeli,' I said sadistically, and then had to stop Omar from breaking more than a few of the man's ribs with his foot.

I went to my filing cabinet while Omar taped the man up and I retrieved the Shakespeare manuscript, my laptop, the FedEx envelope from Paul, and my German pistol.

'What are we doing, boss?' Omar asked.

I had no idea, but defying Izzy, even over a fake, seemed essential to me now, and after the revelations of the last few minutes I had come up with a plan of my own, one that had nothing to do with any member of my family. 'The roof,' I said.

One of the peculiarities of this part of town is that once on the roof of any building one can pass along the whole street by climbing over low parapets and then descend via one of the fire escapes with which these old loft buildings are generously supplied. Since burglars know this too, the roof doors are alarmed; since this is New York, no one pays any attention to the alarms.

We raced across the rooftops and climbed down onto Varick Street, out of sight of my father's limo. From there it was an easy matter to go to the garage and get the Lincoln. In the car I called Mickey Haas.

'You're joking,' he exclaimed when I told him what I had. I assured him I was not and told him a little of the recent cryptanalysis and the adventures of Carolyn and Albert in Warwickshire.

'Good Christ! You say you've recovered all the spy letters?'

'Yes, and it's quite a tale.'

'Oh, Jesus, I'm nauseated. Jake, you have to come to my office this very second. I can't believe this – you have the *actual manuscript of an unknown Shakespeare play in your fucking hands!*'

'On my lap, actually. But, Mickey? I'm in a bit of a jam here. You remember those gangsters we discussed? Well, they're after me, and one of the gangs is being run by my father.'

'Just get up here, Jake. I mean it, just drive to my office –'

'Mickey, you're not listening. These people are on my tail and it won't take them long to figure out that I might want to show this thing to you and then they'll come up to where you are and kill the two of us and take it.'

'But this is Hamilton Hall in broad daylight. We can just walk over and deposit it in the –'

'No, you're not getting this, man. Listen to me! These are

completely ruthless people with almost unlimited resources and they would be happy to wipe out everyone in Hamilton Hall to get their hands on this thing.'

'You have to be kidding –'

'You keep saying that but it happens to be true. Between this minute and the time when you announce the existence and authenticity of this item in public we are totally vulnerable to these people.'

Or words to that effect. I recall that Mickey made a lot of noise over the phone, cursing and shrieking because he couldn't see this pile of paper right away. It was quite an act, better than I would have given him credit for. Between the two of us I always considered myself the actor. I told him my plan: I would get a four-wheel-drive vehicle and go up to his place on Lake Henry. I had been there many times and knew how to get there and where he stashed the keys. In a while, a couple of days maybe, he would come up and join me and look over the material, both the spy letters on my laptop and the manuscript and render an opinion and also take a sample of the ink and paper to be tested in a lab. That done and should the thing prove real, we would drive to some neutral city, Boston perhaps, and call a press conference. And he agreed to this, as I knew he would. Before ending the call I made him swear on the Bard that he would tell absolutely no one where I was or what our plans were, and as soon as I was off the line with him I rang an exotic car rental place on Broadway at Waverly and arranged for the Escalade I've already mentioned. In less than an hour I was on the Henry Hudson, heading north in my comfy domestic tank.

And here I am. Perhaps it's time for a summing-up, but what should it be? Unlike Dick Bracegirdle, I am a modern man and thus further than he was from moral truth. My mind is still reeling from my interview with my father. Could what he said possibly have been true? Who could I ask? Not my siblings. Miriam would not know the truth if it bit her on her liposuctioned ass and Paul . . . I suppose Paul thinks he has a professional commitment with the truth but he is also in service to a Higher Truth, and people in such service are often inclined to lie like bastards when defending same. What if everything I thought about my past was wrong? What if I am a kind of fictional character, fed with lies for the purposes of others, or maybe for no purpose at all, or for sadistic amusement? Being alone, having no social function just now, aggravates this feeling of unreality, or incipient madness. Perhaps I will start to hallucinate, whatever hallucinations are. Although feeling one is going mad is supposedly a sign one is not. If you really go crazy, everything makes perfect sense.

What is the ground of reality then, once you admit mnemonic forgery? When I consider this question I have to think of Amalie. As far as I know, Amalie has never told a serious lie in her life. I mean, I believe she would lie to save someone, like to the Gestapo about a hidden fugitive, otherwise not. But it turns out that if you consistently lie to someone like that, they sort of have to *withdraw* their function as the foundation of your reality, like a little snail pulling in its horns, leaving you adrift in a dense and opaque gas of fiction. It's not intentional on their part, it's an aspect of the underlying physics of the moral universe. And so, thus adrift, I naturally produce nothing but more fiction. I am a lawyer and what is a lawyer but someone hired to produce a work of fiction, which, in court, will be compared with opposing counsel's work of fiction by a judge or jury, and they will decide which fiction most closely resembles the fictional picture of the world in their respective brains and decide for one or another side and thus is justice done. And in private life, I will continue to dream up people to play in the continuing tedious novel of my existence, Miranda, for example, as the Ultimately Satisfying Mate (and by God I am still thinking about her, wanting her, that phantasm) and Mickey Haas as the Best Friend.

Well, in the midst of this sorry maundering, my sister just called. Reception is quite good here, for there is a tower right on the property, artfully painted to resemble the trunk of a pine. Here is how plans break down. My father had stashed her and my children in an apartment known only to himself, and what did she do but journey from that apartment to her own apartment on Sutton Place to get some clothes and other things, her Botox perhaps, and she took the kids along with her because they were getting so bored with being cooped up and needless to say some of Shvanov's people were waiting for her there and they took the kids. So the quasi-fictional kidnapping is now a real one. This occurred early this morning and they tied her up, and it was only the cleaning person's arrival that released her. My sister is not really that stupid, but she does like to look her best.

I did not expect this part of it. But I did and do expect the imminent arrival of various parties to *l'affaire* Bracegirdle. Mickey will come, because he wants to complete the last part of his marvelous scam, but he will not come alone. I am trying, for the record, to recall when I first understood that Mickey was himself the tertium quid we had discussed, the link between Bulstrode and Shvanov. The mind assembles bits of information in its own time and then the revelation. I can't imagine why I did not immediately see this. Who else could it be? Maybe it was when Oliver March told us the story about how Mickey had treated poor Bulstrode or maybe it was when I learned that Shvanov was a loan shark who had done well out of the market crash, lending money to rich assholes suddenly illiquid. And is not Mickey a rich asshole with money problems? And did I imagine that his wives, in the midst of the sort of arguments Mickey always got into with his wives, would not have, as a sort of marital nuclear strike, confronted him with the fact that I had screwed them all, and would that not make him hate me and plan some terrible revenge? Why didn't I think of all this? Because I had dreamed him up as the Best Friend, of course. The Confidant.

I also must have known at some deep level after our meeting with the forger Pascoe that there was only one person in my ambit who could have come up with the scam he was hired to assist, the world's premier Shakespeare expert, the only person who had connections with Shvanov, with Bulstrode, with Jake 'The Schmuck' Mishkin. He is about to take a bunch of Jewish gangsters for many millions of dollars, and I rather doubt that I can do anything to stop him. In a strange way, he's like my father: When Izzy says the numbers add up, no one can doubt him. When Mickey says it's Shakespeare, ditto.

The question remains why I came up to his place in the country rather than really hiding out in one of the zillion anonymous and untraceable places available to a man with a supply of ready cash. Because I am tired of this. I want to be real. I don't care very much if they kill me but I do want to emerge into the realm of truth before that. Very noble sentiment, Mishkin, but there is one other reason. I realized quite recently that the picture that Miranda presented to me – her hairstyle, her dress, her whole aspect – was designed to be as much like my wife when I first met her as it was possible to contrive. That was what knocked me off my admittedly not very secure perch, that was the inside curveball. And who knew what that distant girl was like, who had seen her innumerable times back then, who had heard from my very lips just what turned me on about her? Why the Best Friend, of course. God, this is banal. Any halfway intelligent future reader of this will have seen it coming long before I did, but isn't that true to nature, don't we see everyone else's secrets but our own, the mote in our brother's eye? Yes, good old Mickey set me up, and God help me, I hope that as part of his revenge he brings her along. I would like to see her one more time.

22

On the subway, Crosetti could hardly stop laughing to himself, and not entirely to himself, which drew looks from the others in the car. A woman with two small kids in tow changed her seat. Laughing because there he was back on the subway after some weeks of living the high life, private jets and five-star hotels and everything paid for, and having just dropped off what was essentially the budget of *Titanic*. The ten grand, or maybe even the fifty, would help, though, if he ever got it. No, Mishkin would pay. He was a sleazebag, but not *that* kind of sleazebag. The money would mean that he could take some time off, work on his screenplay, and, with his savings, just about get through NYU film school.

So he was actually feeling fairly good when he walked into his mother's house and was unpleasantly surprised by the reception he got. Mary Peg, it turned out, had wanted to see the thing and was outraged that her gormless son had *again* parted with a treasure, and beyond that, she had told Fanny Doubrowicz that it had been found and *she* of course was vibrating with anticipation. Fruitlessly did Crosetti explain that at least two independent criminal gangs were searching for it too, and that it was at present about as comfortable an object as an armed nuclear bomb, and in any case Mishkin had paid all the expenses for its recovery and provided protection, in the absence of which he might not have found it at all or, if he had, might at this moment be dead in a shallow English grave.

This had a sobering effect on Mary Peg, but only for a while, and it took all of Crosetti's jollying skills and Klim's as well, to bring her back into countenance. The children helped here. Crosetti stayed for supper, which was spaghetti and meatballs (and had been Spg & MB many, many times in the past week, confided Klim), and he marveled at the way a grandparentish milieu had been created from scratch out of what amounted to happenstance. It was the sort of thing that happened all the time in Dickens, Crosetti knew, but he had not looked for it in modern New York. Or perhaps, he thought later, all times were the same, the urge to form families always bubbling up from beneath the surface crud of selfishness. Mary Peg apparently had vast reserves of grandmaternal energies untapped as yet by her natural progeny, all still childless; and Klim had transformed himself into a granddad out of fairy tales: what stories he told, with funny faces, what clever carving of whistles and little toys, what horsey rides, what silly songs he knew, all with pokes and tickles involved! The children, especially the little girl, Molly, had blossomed under this treatment, as children do. They all believe implicitly in magic and think nothing of being carried away from the ogre's castle to the land of the good fairies.

And Crosetti was happy for them all, but he did feel somewhat extra now, as if this development had confirmed his instinct that his time in his mother's home was quite over. Besides, there was no room. Besides, it made him uncomfortable to see Rolly staring out at him from her children's faces. He packed his things, hired a U-Haul trailer for the family car to pull, and was out by the following evening with, however, a check for ten grand from Mishkin that had arrived that morning in a FedEx envelope. No one insisted that he stay.

He was unpacking cartons to music in his new shared loft when he felt his phone vibrating in his pocket. He unplugged his earbuds and put the phone to his cheek.

'Write this down. I have thirty seconds.'

'Carolyn?'

'Write this down. Oh, Christ, you have to help me!' And there followed an address and directions to a lakeside house in the Adirondacks. Crosetti pulled out a ballpoint and scribbled the information on the underside of his left forearm.

'Carolyn, where are you? What the hell is going on?'

'Just come and don't dial this number. They're going to kill –' with the rest of the sentence lost in static.

Not good, Crosetti thought, a cliché in fact, especially that business with the call cutting out. The film was going to end on a downer note, bittersweet, tracking the hero returning to his work, maybe the hint of a relationship with the kids, life goes on, or maybe even a hint that Rolly is still alive, a teaser: but not this banal . . . and he actually kept thinking this way for minutes, stacking books on raw pine shelving, before the reality of the call sank in. Sweat popped out on his face and he had to sit down on the dusty, sprung easy chair he'd scavenged off the street. She really is going to drive me crazy, he thought; no, make that past tense. Okay, I'm game, he thought, I'm an international man of mystery too. What do I need? The Smith & Wesson was back at his mother's house, and no way was he going back there and explain why he needed it, and now that he thought about actually handling the thing again . . . no, thanks. But he had hiking boots, check. Richard Widmark black seaman's sweater, check. Ball cap? No, the watch cap, much better, and the Swiss Army knife, and the grenade launcher . . . no, just kidding, and the trusty black slicker, still with the mud of Old England on it, wallet, keys, oh, binoculars, can't forget those, and boy, I'm about as ready as I'll ever be to face God knows how many heavily armed Russian mobsters . . .

'Come again?'

It was Beck, one of the roommates, looking at him from the doorway with a peculiar expression. Beck was a cadaverous being who worked as a sound engineer and wrote reviews of films no one but him had ever seen, or perhaps did not yet exist.

'I didn't say anything,' said Crosetti.

'Yeah, you were talking, loud, like you were pissed off. I thought you had someone in there with you and then I remembered you came in alone.'

'Oh, then I was talking to myself. I'm having a psychotic break is all.'

'Fuck, man, join the club. If you need a lobotomy I could start sharpening the screwdriver.'

'It's a girl,' Crosetti admitted. 'A girl has driven me crazy. She dumped me and now she wants me to rescue her. This is the second time for the dump 'n' rescue motif.'

'Whatever. I tend to stick to the gospel according to St Nelson Algren: never fuck anyone with more problems than you have yourself. Of course, *he* fucked Simone de Beauvoir . . .'

'Thank you. I'll remember that in my next life. Meanwhile, a man's gotta do what a man's gotta do. Can I borrow your computer? I need some maps.'

*

It took him the usual forty-five minutes to clear the city but on the thruway past the Tappan Zee he made up for lost time. The old Fury had been maintained in perfect trim: inside was a 440-cubic-inch V-8 engine and outside was waxed midnight blue lacquer, plus the various shields and decals that police officers use to identify themselves to other police officers so as to render their cars virtually immune to any ticketing, whether rolling or parked. Crosetti cranked it up to ninety and made it to Albany in a little over two hours. Another ninety miles and seventy minutes got him to Pottersville, where he filled his tank and ate a horrible gas station microwave meal, by which time it was dark and snowing, fat floaters that seemed the size of golf balls when they hit the glass, although it was still too warm for the snow to stick to the asphalt of the highway and he did not slow down. Crosetti was deep in the blankness of the freeway dream, on autopilot, his brain running with plots of movies, odd facts, straining for coherent memories of trivial life occurrences, including especially his pathetically brief skein of days in the company of Carolyn Rolly.

State Route 2, which he turned onto fifteen minutes later, was a narrow tunnel of headlight through a shake-up snow-globe toy; after the zoom of the thruway, Crosetti felt like he was parked. He drove for what seemed like an impossibly long interval and at last a few lights shone ahead, which was New Weimar, two gas stations, some tourist traps, a scatter of houses, and then the search for the sign that marked the gravel road to Lake Henry. He missed it once and had to slew the car around on the snowy road and backtrack until he found the thing, bent over at an angle and full of bullet holes. Thus did the armed locals take out their class rage on the rich people who owned the lake.

An even narrower tunnel now and here the snow was

sticking well, making the car fishtail on the hills. Time slowed; he lost track of its passage. The Fury boasted only an old-fashioned AM radio, which, for the last dozen miles or so, had produced only static-filled country music. He switched it off. Now only the hiss of the wipers, the competent purr of the great engine. A flash of yellow ahead a double arrow, the road ending in a T. He switched on the dome light and read his maps. A right turn then, and shortly there appeared a cluster of mailboxes, thick with the wet snow, and a white-clotted driveway. He pulled the car forward a dozen yards, took a four-cell flashlight from the glove compartment, and started down the drive. It was a little after three in the morning.

And here was the house, a substantial country lodge made of stripped logs, with a sharply peaked roof and a wide veranda running along three sides. A thin light spread from the front windows and made a yellowish patch on the new snow. As Crosetti walked around the house he felt, rather than saw, the presence of the lake, absolute blackness where the snow ended, with a thin white finger pointing into it, the dock.

He carefully mounted the steps to the veranda, pressed his face against the lighted window, saw a large room, rustic furniture made of polished cedar logs and upholstered in red plaid, a huge stone fireplace with a fire blazing away in it, Indian rugs on the floor, a moosehead over the fireplace. On another wall was a large built-in bookcase and an elaborate and expensive-looking sound system. No movement visible, no sounds. He tried the door, which swung open when he turned the brass knob, and he entered and closed the door behind him. Once inside he could hear over the whisper of the fire some domestic sounds from another room, clink of crockery, and a man's humming. The place smelled of cedar, and the fire, and, faintly, fresh coffee. There was a round pine table near the side windows with a glowing laptop computer on it. Next to it was a familiar thick padded envelope. Crosetti was about to take a peek at the screen when Jake Mishkin entered the room carrying a steaming mug.

He stopped short and stared. 'Crosetti? What're you doing here?'

'I was in the neighborhood. I thought I'd drop by.'

Mishkin smiled faintly. 'That's a good line. Would you like some coffee? I'm having mine with Irish whiskey in it.'

'Thank you. That'd be great.'

Mishkin started to go back to the kitchen, then stopped and went to the laptop and snapped the screen down. Crosetti sat on the sofa that faced the fire and gave way a little to his exhaustion, feeling now that strange sensation one has after a marathon drive, of still traveling fast behind the wheel of a car. In a few minutes Mishkin returned with another mug and set it on the pickled pine coffee table in front of the couch.

'I trust this is not about your check,' said Mishkin after they had both drunk a little.

'No, I got that all right, thanks.'

'Then, to what do I owe . . . ?'

'Carolyn Rolly. I got a panicky call from her giving me the address of this place and so I came up.'

'You drove – what? Eight hours through a snowstorm because Carolyn Rolly beckoned?'

'Yeah, it's kind of hard to explain.'

'True love.'

'Not really, but . . . it's *something*. Basically, I'm just being a schmuck.'

'I can relate to that,' said Mishkin, 'as it happens, she's not here, and I should point out that I'm expecting other visitors. There might be unpleasantness.'

'You mean Shvanov.'

'And others.'

'For instance?'

'For instance, Mickey Haas, the famous Shakespearean scholar and a dear friend of mine. This is his place we're in. He's coming up to authenticate our manuscript.'

'I thought you needed a lot of technical equipment for that, carbon dating, ink analysis . . .'

'Yes, but clever forgers can fake the ink and paper. What can't be faked is Shakespeare's actual writing, and Mickey is the man for that.'

'And he's with Shvanov?'

'That's a long story I'm afraid.'

Crosetti shrugged. 'I got plenty of time, unless you're going to force me at gunpoint out into a raging blizzard.'

Mishkin stared at him for a while and Crosetti held the stare for an unnatural interval. At last, Mishkin sighed and said, 'We'll need more coffee.'

Another pot, then, also with whiskey, and toward the end of it they dispensed with the coffee. They talked in the manner of strangers who have survived a shipwreck or some historic disaster which, while it leaves similar marks, does nothing to provide elective affinity. The two men were not friends, nor ever would be, but the thing that had brought them together, to this house on this snowy night, that lay now in its envelope on the round table, allowed them to speak to each other more openly than either of them normally would; and the whiskey helped.

Mishkin supplied the fuller version of his involvement with Bulstrode, and his sad life, not stinting on a description of his own sins, and when he came to his connection with the supposed Miranda Kellogg and his hopes regarding her, Crosetti said, 'According to Carolyn she was an actress Shvanov hired to get the manuscript away from you.'

'Yes, I thought it was something like that. Do you . . . did she say what happened to her?'

'She didn't know,' said Crosetti shortly and then began to speak about his own family and about movies, ones he loved and ones he wanted to make, and Mishkin seemed remarkably interested, fascinated in fact, with both of these subjects, about what it was like to grow up in a boisterous and happy family, and whether movies really determined our sense of how to behave, and more than that, our sense of what was real.

'Surely not,' Mishkin objected. 'Surely it's the other way around – filmmakers take popular ideas and embody them in films.'

'No, the movies come first. For example, no one ever had a fast-draw face-to-face shoot-out on the dusty Main Street in a Western town. It never happened, ever. A screenwriter invented it for dramatic effect. It's the classic American trope, redemption through violence, and it comes through the movies. There were very few handguns in the real Old West. They were expensive and heavy and no one but an idiot would wear them in a side holster. On a horse? When you wanted to kill someone in the Old West, you waited for your chance and shot him in the back, usually with a shotgun. Now we have a zillion handguns because the movies taught us that a handgun is something a real man has to have, and people *really* kill each other like fictional Western gunslingers. And it's not just thugs. Movies shape *everyone's* reality, to the extent that it's shaped by human action – foreign policy, business, sexual relationships, family dynamics, the whole nine yards. It used to be the Bible but now it's movies. Why is there stalking? Because we know that the guy should persist and make a fool of himself until the girl admits that she loves him. We've all seen it. Why is there date rape? Because the asshole is waiting for the moment when resistance turns to passion. He's seen Nicole and Reese do it fifty times. We make these little decisions, day by day, and we end up with a world. This one, like it or not.'

'So screenwriters are the unacknowledged legislators of mankind.'

'You got it,' said Crosetti. 'I mean we're in a movie *now*. Why in hell are the two of us waiting in an isolated cabin for a bunch of gangsters? It's nuts. Why is a hundred-million-dollar manuscript sitting on a table in that isolated cabin? Totally wack. I'll tell you why. Because we both made a chain of decisions, and each of those decisions was conditioned by a movie theme. When the mysterious girl calls John Cusack and tells him to rescue her, he doesn't say, "Get real, bitch!" He moves heaven and earth to rescue her, because he knows that's the script, and here I am, and right next to me is William Hurt, the slightly corrupt, guilty guy, still clinging to decency, but not sure if he wants to live or not and he's put himself in this dangerous situation for . . . for what? Oh, there's *his* mysterious girl, of course, but mainly it's self-punishment, a need to have some major explosion to either wipe him out or blow him the hell out of his expensive unsatisfactory life. Stay tuned.'

'William Hurt. That's not bad.'

'No, and when the gangsters get here, they'll act like gangsters in the movies, or, and here's a subtlety that's not often used, they'll act the *opposite* of movie gangsters. That's the great thing about *The Sopranos* – movie gangsters pretending to be real gangsters watching movie gangsters and changing their style to be more like the fake ones, but the fact is, it really happens. The one thing you can be sure of is they're not going to be authentic. There's no authentic left.'

'Amalie is authentic,' said Mishkin, after a moment.

'Yeah, she is,' Crosetti agreed. 'But Amalie's unplugged from the culture, or maybe she's plugged into something else, God maybe. But it's the exception that proves the rule, and notice, she's not in this movie.'

'No, she's not. But I'll tell you one thing: you're wrong about me. I don't mean about my character, the William Hurt business, but about what I'm doing here. It's not just a vague despair. It's part of a plot.'

'Yeah, but that's just what I've been say –'

'No, not a movie-type plot. A scheme, a device, a manipulation, so that the bad guys get theirs.'

'What is it? The plot, I mean.'

'I'm not going to tell you,' said Mishkin. 'I'm going to reveal it when everyone gets here.'

'Jake, that's the oldest dodge in the book. Will there be redemption by violence after?'

'I certainly hope so. Are you worried?'

'Not in the least. The John Cusack character has to escape and get the girl. You, on the other hand, might not make it.' He yawned vastly and added, 'Shit, man, I mean this is fascinating but I'm falling over. It'll be daylight in a couple of hours and I have to get some sleep. You look pretty beat yourself as a matter of fact.'

'I'll be fine,' said Mishkin. 'There are bedrooms galore upstairs, beds all made, rafts of cozy quilts: make yourself at home.'

He picked a bedroom with a view over the water, kicked off his boots, slipped under the quilt, went out in an instant; and awakened to the coughing roar of a large powerboat engine. He rolled out, scrubbed at his eyes, and went to the window. On the lake someone was inexpertly trying to dock a twenty-eight-foot Bayliner cruiser. They had the canvas top on and the plastic windshields rigged, but Crosetti figured it must still be fairly cold in a trailerable boat like that, designed for summer cruises. The snow had stopped, the sky was pearly bright, and a wind from the east whipped up small whitecaps. The unskilled pilot was trying to bring the boat into the west side of the dock, so of course the wind was blowing him away from it, the craft's high profile acting as a sail, and he wasn't giving the boat time to answer the helm, was also gunning the throttle, banging the prow against the dock and bouncing away. He should have just pulled back and gone around to the other side, where the wind would have bedded him up against the rubber fenders with no trouble. So thought Crosetti, who had spent every summer of his boyhood out on Sheepshead Bay with his parents and sisters and assorted cousins, packed dangerously into a twenty-two-foot rental.

Now a man dressed in a leather car coat and city shoes came out of the cabin and went forward, slipping on the wet fiberglass, and he went down sprawling when the boat slammed the dock for the sixth time. Crosetti figured this clown show would take a while, so he used the bathroom, pulled on his boots, made a short cell phone call, and descended to the kitchen. Mishkin was there, drinking coffee.

'They're here,' said Crosetti, pouring himself a cup. 'Pop-Tarts?'

'Yes, my daughter corrupted me when she was small. Have a couple.'

'Thank you,' said Crosetti, putting a pair into the toaster. 'Have they managed to dock yet?'

The kitchen window was on the wrong side of the house, but by moving close to it one could just make out the foot of the dock. Mishkin peered past the chintz café curtains and said, 'Just about. They've secured the pointy end and now they're trying to maneuver the stern into place.'

'I guess they're probably better gangsters than they are pilots.'

'Oh, yes. There were some fairly mediocre gangsters sent for me in New York, although not by Shvanov. I bet he's brought his first team on this venture. So . . . still think it's a movie?'

'No, I'm starting to get scared, since you ask.'

'You could leave. No one expects you to be here.'

'There's Rolly, though.'

'True. Any final advice from the movies?'

'Yeah,' said Crosetti, 'whatever your plan is, it'll have a flaw.'

'Because . . . ?'

'You can't think of everything, one; and two, you need a reversal in the last six minutes to keep the tension up.'

'Well, at least we won't have a fistfight in the abandoned factory. Let me go greet our guests.'

Mishkin walked out of the kitchen and Crosetti went to the window. As he did so, he heard the engine of the boat cut off and observed that they now had it tied up and people were getting off: the tall man in the leather coat, who had gone out on the deck, then a medium-size man in a camel hair overcoat and a fur hat (the Boss), then a linebacker-size fellow, also coated in black leather, leading two children, a boy and a girl, then a woman in a white parka, with the hood up over her head, then a man wearing a Burberry and a tweed cap, with the lower part of his face swathed in a striped woolen muffler, and finally another black-leather guy, only this one's coat came down to his shins. Crosetti went into the living room. Mishkin was poking the huge fire he'd just started and it was ablaze, filling the room with the scent of burning resin. The fatal envelope still sat on the table, but the laptop was gone.

The front door slammed open and two of the thugs tromped in – the big one and the long-coated one, who had a pale ill-formed face like the monster Pillsbury Doughboy from *Ghostbusters*. Then came the man Crosetti knew must be the famous Shvanov. He said something in Russian to his boys and they immediately grabbed Mishkin, beat him to the ground, and started stomping him. As this proceeded, the rest of the boat party entered, pushed along by the Deckhand. Crosetti noticed a number of things at once. First, Mishkin was taking the beating without resistance, although in London Crosetti had watched him toss a big guy through the air like a Frisbee. Next, the children: Imogen very angry, started to go to her father's aid, and would have, had the Deckhand not grabbed her; there was something wrong with Niko, his head held at an unnatural downward angle, and his hands moving in meaningless little patterns. He seemed to be humming or talking to himself and he smelled of vomit, traces of which smeared the front of his parka. Finally, the woman. She had pushed back her hood on entering the room, revealing neck-length dark hair, not too clean, and her face, upon which was a look of horror at what was being done to Mishkin. The man in the Burberry was also staring at the beating, but not with horror – morbid fascination maybe, or even satisfaction.

This all in a quite short time, which seemed longer, an interval, Crosetti knew, that would be drawn out for well over a minute on the screen. The woman shouted at Shvanov to stop it and Shvanov shouted back at her, but he told his men to stop. They dragged Mishkin to his feet, holding him by his arms. He blinked, he wiped at the blood and saliva issuing from his mouth, he said to his children, 'I'm sorry, kids, this wasn't supposed to happen. Did they hurt you?'

The girl said, 'Not really. But Niko was sick on the boat and he's acting weird.'

Shvanov strode forward and slapped Mishkin hard on the face.

'This is entirely your fault, Mishkin,' he said. 'I try to act in a civilized manner to obtain property that is rightfully mine, and what do I get? Respect? No, I have to chase you here, which is a colossal inconvenience, and you require me to also kidnap children. This is unconscionable. Osip Shvanov does not kidnap children, as I have told you before, but you don't listen. And now we have come to this. So, now, at last, hand me over my property, namely one manuscript of William Shakespeare.'

But Mishkin was staring at the woman. He said, 'Hello, Miranda. Why did you change your hair? And your eyes.'

The woman was silent. Shvanov slapped Mishkin on the face again, spraying blood in a wide pattern against the wall above the fireplace. 'No, don't look at her, look at me, you stupid pig lawyer! Where is my property?'

'It's in the envelope on that table,' said Crosetti.

Everyone in the room turned and stared at him.

'Who is this man?' Shvanov demanded.

'This is Albert Crosetti,' said Mishkin, 'the man who found the original Bracegirdle manuscript and sold it to Professor Bulstrode. Or so he claims.'

Shvanov went to the table and removed the contents of the envelope. He gestured to the man in the Burberry, who hurried to his side.

Mishkin said, 'While we're making introductions, Crosetti, that is Professor Mickey Haas, the world's foremost Shakespeare expert. Or so he claims.'

Haas took the stack of papers from Shvanov, sat at the table, stuck reading glasses on his face, and began to peruse the first sheet. Crosetti could see that his hands were shaking. For almost half an hour, the only sounds in the room were the crackling of the flames, the muttering of the boy, and the rustle of the stiff old paper.

'So? What do you say, Professor?' said Shvanov.

'It's astounding! Obviously, there are technical tests to go through, but I've seen a lot of seventeenth-century manuscripts, and as far as I can see this is genuine. The paper is right, the ink is right, the handwriting is . . . well, we don't actually have any examples of Shakespeare's hand aside from some signatures and of course there's the so-called Hand D from the partial manuscript of the Thomas More play, but there certainly, I mean most probably –'

'Bottom line, Professor, is it a salable property?'

Haas replied in an odd strained voice, speaking with unnatural precision, 'I think, yes, the language, the style, my God, yes, I believe that subject to various tests as I've mentioned, that this is a manuscript of an unknown play by William Shakespeare.'

Shvanov clapped Haas on the back hard enough to loosen his glasses. 'Good! Excellent!' he crowed, and all the thugs smiled.

Then Mishkin said, 'Osip, what did you expect him to say? The thing is a fraud. He set the whole thing up with the forger, Leonard Pascoe. I have proof.'

Haas leaped up from his chair and snarled at Mishkin, 'You son of a bitch! What the hell do you know about it? This is real! And if you think you can –'

Shvanov poked Haas hard in the arm and he stopped talking. Then Shvanov stepped closer to Mishkin until he was staring up into the bigger man's face. 'What kind of proof?'

'I'll show you. Make them let go of me.'

A nod and Mishkin was released. He went to a magazine rack by the fireside couch and took out a FedEx envelope, from which he removed some papers and a compact disk. He said, 'First the documentary evidence. This' – handing a sheet to Shvanov – 'is a copy of the original Bracegirdle manuscript. This is a sheet on which Leonard Pascoe forged Bracegirdle's hand. Even a novice such as yourself, Osip, can see that they are identical. Your pal over there found a seventeenth-century letter from a dying man and interpolated a sheet or two in a forged hand and then concocted the whole cipher business out of whole cloth and then arranged for this so-called play to be found in just the place called for in the ciphers.'

'That's insane!' shouted Haas. 'Pascoe's in prison.'

'A country club,' said Mishkin, 'which we visited, as the people Osip had following us have no doubt informed him. Osip, didn't you wonder why we stopped by there?'

Crosetti saw Shvanov exchange a quick glance with the Deckhand.

'We stopped by for this,' said Mishkin. He held up the compact disk. 'Leonard Pascoe is quite proud of his trade, and this was his biggest coup. He'll have a nice little nest egg waiting for him when he gets out, courtesy of Mickey, or I should say courtesy of Osip Shvanov, because the money he used was the money he got from you, or part of it. It was a perfect fix for him. How much is he into you for by the way?'

'Osip, this is crazy! How could I –?'

'Shut up, Haas! Play this disk, please, Mishkin, and I very much hope that this is not some foolish trick.'

Mishkin turned on the sound system and inserted the CD into the player. The voice of Leonard Pascoe filled the room and they all listened in silence as he explained how to use a phony letter and a phony cipher and various agents to pull off a massive con. When it was over, Mishkin said, 'The bird in this case is, of course, the mysterious Carolyn Rolly, who was perfectly positioned to carry it off – well connected to Shvanov, desperate to get out from under him, needing money to rescue her children and leave the country. She supposedly discovered the doctored manuscript in an old book, inveigled our friend Crosetti into fronting it, because we need an innocent mark, don't we? And she has, throughout this adventure, been somehow always in the right position to advance the plot, although there's a little variation on Pascoe's original plan. Carolyn doesn't have to steal the money because she's already been paid, and the main purpose of the plot is in any case to get rid of Osip Shvanov. So, now you have the manuscript, and the people from Israel who are ready to buy it are in New York right now. You'll sell it to them, get your ten million dollars – on the strength of the excellent Professor Haas's recommendation – whose debt is thereby canceled, and everyone is happy, until your buyers try to present it in public for the big score, and suddenly it turns out that the play is not quite what we have come to expect from the Bard, is in fact the work of a lesser literary figure, Mickey Haas for example, a pastiche. Because you're a fucking illiterate, Osip, and a foreigner, and therefore a perfect mark, as our friend Pascoe just told us. Shakespeare can't be forged, but you'd never be able to tell that. And what do you suppose will happen to you when your buyers find out they've been had?'

Crosetti saw that Shvanov had gone white around the lips and that a vein in his temple was pulsing. He said, 'How do you know the price is ten million?'

'Because my father told me. He's the syndicate's man in

New York, and his principals are going to be very, very unhappy with you.'

'You have told him this?'

'Of course. And now I'm telling you, which is why I arranged for everyone involved to be here so we could get it all thrashed out. Oh, except for Carolyn Rolly. She seems to be in the wind just now, but I'm sure you can put your hands on her.'

Crosetti observed a puzzled expression appear on Shvanov's face. He pointed to the woman in the white parka. 'What do you mean? *That* is Carolyn Rolly.'

'Oh, Carolyn,' said Crosetti, half to himself. No one seemed to hear him. Everyone was looking at Mishkin, who had staggered as from a blow. His face had taken on a crushed look that the beating had not been able to put there. Shvanov saw it and it appeared to delight him.

'Yes, I can put my hands on her as you say, Jake,' he said and put his arm around Rolly's shoulder. 'And should I believe him, Carolyn? That you have conspired to cheat me with this professor? Osip, who took you in off the streets, gave you where to live, and showed you what is to be with a man.' In falsetto: 'Oh, fuck me more in the ass, darling, it is so good.'

He took her jaw between his thumb and fingers and twisted. 'Heh? Have you done this to me, you whore? Yes, maybe: it is something you would do, if maybe you don't like your children anymore, or you forget I know where they live in Pennsylvania? But who knows what a whore will do?'

He walked to the table where Haas was standing, gaping at him, a rabbit to the cobra, and picked up the packet of manuscript. He evened the edges and weighed them in his hand. 'But you, Professor, you are not a whore. We have a business relationship, we are dealing with each other for all this time, I have confidence in you, man-to-man, how could you do this? I am very disappointed.'

'He's lying,' said Haas, speaking rapidly, stuttering over the words. From where he stood, Crosetti could see the man's knees actually trembling. 'He made all that up to . . . confuse you. He's very clever, he thinks he can get away with anything, the great Jake Mishkin, but he's lying here, this is a genuine play, the greatest manuscript discovery of all time. I'm the fucking expert, Osip, for Christ's sake, and anyway how could I have "conspired" as you say with this woman, I never set eyes on her before in my life, and going to Pascoe and arranging all this . . . it's ridiculous . . . you can't believe. These pages in your hand, and the ciphers, and everything, they're precious, precious, I never dreamed I would ever have my hands on something like this . . .'

Mishkin said, 'He *did* know Carolyn Rolly. She was a student at Columbia. Bulstrode introduced them. Ask Crosetti.'

Crosetti cleared his throat, which felt like it was full of white library paste, and said, 'Well, yeah. She definitely knew Bulstrode. And Bulstrode knew Haas.'

'You see, Professor?' said Shvanov. 'It will not add up. And so I think he is right, I think this is all a cheat, and this paper is garbage.' With that, he took two quick steps and tossed the stack of pages into the fireplace.

Haas uttered a cry that seemed to come up from his descending colon, a brute scream of desperate loss, and immediately dashed across the room and threw himself into the heart of the fire. He grabbed handfuls of paper off the coals, pinching out any fire that had bit into them with his bare hands and tossing the pages back into the room, like a dog tossing earth out of a hole. Some of the pages, Crosetti saw, had caught in the updraft and had been plastered against the back of the deep fireplace, but Haas heaved his whole body across the blazing logs and pulled them free. As he did this he never stopped screaming, nor did he stop when he pulled himself out of the fire, ablaze all down the front of his clothes, his scarf a necklace of fire. He trotted in little circles slapping at the flames, his face a hideous black-red mask, his glasses warped and partially melted.

Mishkin now snatched up the flaming professor as if he had been a hollow man and made for the door, carrying him on his shoulder. The Deckhand tried to stop him and was stiff-armed out of the way, falling on a side table with a crash. Once outside, Mishkin dived into a hollow where the snow was relatively deep and used handfuls of it to douse the flames and after these had hissed out, used more snow to cool the red and tortured flesh showing through the charred clothing and on the face.

Crosetti observed this through the open door and watched as the Deckhand got up and tromped over to the kneeling Mishkin and kicked him hard in the ribs. He would have continued to kick had Shvanov not called him off.

'You know this gives me an idea,' said Shvanov. With a start, Crosetti realized that the gangster was addressing him. He immediately understood that the man was going to give him an explanation, because this is what movie gangsters always do for their victims, and he wondered if gangsters behaved so in earlier times. Probably yes, he thought, because you saw that in Shakespeare, the self-justifying villain, the delight in describing the prospect of death to the helpless victim. But did Shakespeare *invent* that, like screenwriters invented the quick-draw gunfight? Probably. He invented most of what passes for human behavior. Crosetti made himself concentrate on what Shvanov was saying.

'. . . so don't you agree? Everyone will sacrifice for something, but not that kind of sacrifice, not the body, not even for money. For children maybe.' Here he looked coldly at the two Mishkin kids. 'Or as we have just seen, for this manuscript. So, of course it is real.'

'You took a risk,' said Crosetti.

'Yes, but a man such as myself must take risks, it is entrepreneurial spirit. Now I have payoff.' He looked over to where his two men were gathering the sheets of scorched paper. 'And I don't think that some little burnt places will reduce the value too much if any. It gives a look of more authenticity, I believe, for so old a piece. But, as I say, this burning gives an idea. The professor Haas invites his good friend Mishkin to his cabin with his two children, and also his friend Crosetti with his girlfriend Carolyn, and they go out in the Haas speedboat on this beautiful lake, even though it is cold, because it is so beautiful in the snow and there is a tragic explosion, a gasoline leak, or whatever, and they are all burned and sunk in the water.'

'I don't understand. I didn't have anything to do with this scam and neither did Carolyn.'

'Yes, but you are witnesses. This is a Russian thing, I believe. Stalin taught this to us and we remember. In doubt, get rid of everyone except those who are . . . what is this word? Com . . . ?'

'Complicit.'

'Exactly. Complicit. So now, you will all go into the boat.' He reached under his coat, brought out a pistol, and shouted something in Russian to his troops. Soon they were in a sad procession down to the lake's edge. In the front, Mishkin carrying the moaning Haas in his arms, then the Mishkin children, then Crosetti and Carolyn. The Russians now had their weapons out, the Deckhand with his submachine gun, and the others with semiautomatic pistols. It was the Deckhand who escorted the prisoners into the boathouse and made them enter the speedboat. The Doughboy was filling a five-gallon jerrican with gas from the pump. Shvanov and the third murderer had gone to start up the cruiser.

Mishkin placed Haas in a corner of the rear seat and then helped the others into the craft. As Crosetti climbed in Mishkin said in a whisper, 'Can you drive this thing?'

'Sure.'

'Then get behind the wheel.' Crosetti did and Mishkin sat beside him in the front.

The Doughboy finished filling the can and climbed into the boat with it, resting it on the rear seat. He said something to his companion, and they both laughed, and then said something to Imogen, grabbing her arm and his own crotch, and laughed again. The Deckhand said something back, threw off the stern line, and went forward to untie the line that held the prow of the speedboat to a cleat. From outside, they heard the roar of the Bayliner's engine starting.

The Doughboy was still talking to Imogen, with his face close to hers. She screamed and tried to push him away. He grabbed her hair, forced her head down, and yanked open his fly, at which point Mishkin, to Crosetti's immense surprise, reached under the seat cushion, pulled out a Luger, and shot the man in the face. Then, as the Doughboy collapsed and fell overboard, Mishkin turned and put five rounds into the kneeling, and even more surprised, Deckhand. 'Crank it up!' he ordered Crosetti. 'Go!'

Crosetti turned the ignition, the engine coughed, roared; he threw the gearshift forward and the speedboat shot out of the boathouse.

He felt an absurd giggle rise in his chest as they flew through the water. Of course there would be a chase at the end and here it was. It took a moment or two for Shvanov and his guy to understand what was happening, but when they saw that no black-coated figures were on guard in the speedboat, they took off in pursuit. Crosetti knew that there was no way that a Chris-Craft woodie with an ancient V-6 was going to outrun a modern Bayliner, with maybe three times the horsepower, but he jammed the throttle to the stop and awaited the denouement.

The white boat steadily gained on them, and when they were less than twenty yards astern one of the men started to shoot at them. A bullet snapped overhead and left a long pink scar on the mahogany deck of the runabout. From behind, over the roar of the engine, Crosetti could hear the boy howling in fear.

Ahead and closing fast a line of small wooded islands extended from the eastern shore, to the left of which line stood a pole with a green light fixed to its top. Mishkin was pulling at his sleeve and pointing.

'Go between the marker and the last island!' he shouted. Crosetti twitched the wheel. The runabout whipped past the marker, struck a hidden rock with a jarring crash, ran another fifty feet, and then settled deep into the chilly waters. Crosetti struggled out from behind the wheel, grabbed a floating cushion, and went into the lake. Looking around, he saw the inverted stern of the runabout bobbing just above the surface, and beyond it an object that at first he did not recognize, but in a moment it came into focus as the front three-quarters of the Bayliner, floating on its side. With its deeper draft the pursuing craft must have hit the rocks even harder.

He saw a smaller white object, which he identified as Carolyn Rolly's parka. She was floating face downward. He went underwater, undid the laces of his boots, pushed them off his feet, and, using the cushion as a float, kicked his way toward her. As he reached her, he saw the head of Jake

Mishkin moving toward them with powerful strokes. Together, they got her turned around with her head and shoulders out of the water on the cushion.

'I got her,' cried Crosetti. '*Where are your kids?*'

At this a shocked look appeared on the other man's face. He swiveled his head wildly and shouted. Some twenty-five yards away they saw a dark little shape appear amid splashing, the boy. Then it vanished. Jake pushed away toward the spot, but it was clear to Crosetti that the big man would never reach the child before he sank beyond reach. And then, from around the stern of the speedboat came a flash of water and a fast-moving shape – Imogen Mishkin doing a perfect crawl. She dived and reemerged with her brother, locked him against her chest in the approved Red Cross manner, and backstroked with him quickly to the nearest island.

Soon the five of them were all on the island, a hump of land not much bigger than a good-sized kitchen. Crosetti got Rolly on her back and blew into her mouth until she coughed and vomited up a quantity of water.

'Are you okay, Carolyn?' he asked.

'Cold.'

He put his arm around her. 'We could pool our warmth, like this.'

She held herself stiffly. 'I don't see how you can bear to touch me.'

'Why? Because you screwed other men? I kind of knew that already. Only I would so appreciate it if you didn't run away again. That's the only thing about you that really annoys me. And the lying. I could do with less of that.'

'Besides that I'm perfect.'

'Pretty much. Oh, here's the second climax.'

She looked and saw Shvanov and his henchman wading

out of the water. Neither seemed any longer to be armed. The henchman was staggering and bleeding badly from a head wound, and Shvanov was holding his left arm at the elbow and grimacing in pain. Mishkin waited until they were knee-deep and then he waded up to Shvanov, batted away a feeble blow, grabbed him by belt and collar, lifted the man over his head and flung him at his henchman. Both men went down. He did it twice more until they got the idea and waded and swam to the next tiny island in the chain.

'You wouldn't have done it that way, unless this was a comedy,' observed Crosetti. 'The villain and the supporting lead would have a fight to the death and both of them would perish, or the villain would kill the supporting lead and then the hero would knock him off. But maybe this *is* a comedy. I was thinking it was a thriller. Here comes the cavalry, too late as usual.'

A helicopter thumped into view and hovered over the wreck. In the distance they could make out a pair of gray hulls approaching over the water, each with a bone in its mouth.

'State police,' Crosetti explained to Carolyn's wondering look. 'I called my sister the cop this morning, and she obviously arranged this rescue.'

'You could have called her last night, and the cops could have been waiting when we arrived.'

'No, I had to see that they were really coming. If I'd've brought the cops in earlier, Shvanov might've killed the kids. Or you. But, as you see, it all worked out.'

'Where's Haas?' asked Carolyn.

'Shit!' said Crosetti, standing up and looking out over the water. 'He's gone. He couldn't have survived, hurt the way he was. And the manuscript is gone too.'

'No,' said Carolyn, 'linen paper survives for a long time

in water, and gall ink is pretty tough. This lake probably isn't that deep – if it was still in that mailer it should be okay until they send divers for it.'

'Maybe. But if Haas died it can't be a comedy.'

'You know, you would be perfect too if you didn't have that habit of making everything into a movie. If I stop lying and running away will you stop doing that?'

'Deal,' he said and kissed her cold lips, thinking: fade to black, music up, roll credits.

23

I found this document while I was transferring files to my new laptop and have decided to add this coda. Clearly, the public end of this affair – the lost play, the miraculous Bracegirdle-Shakespeare mss., the involvement of Shvanov, the scene at the cabin, the fate of Mickey Haas – has been too heavily reported to bear repeating here, but I do want to tie up my own loose ends, so that, if some digital explorer of the future comes across this file, as we did poor Bracegirdle's last letter, there will be some closure.

Sorry to say, Amalie and I are not, as of the current date, which is June 10, back together, although I still have hopes. She is often in the city, and when she is we are much together and fairly amicable. We attended Easter services this year at St Patrick's and it affected me deeply, and she noted this, and she gave me a smile such as I have not had from her for a good while. And I suppose it was also because I am entering the eighth month of the longest period of celibacy I have experienced since Miss Polansky had me in the staff room of the Farragut Branch library. Amalie can no longer smell (or sense in some more mystic way) the taint of adultery on me, and it is, I think, bringing her around. I believe that my curse began lifting at the very moment, in the cold water of Lake Henry, that Crosetti drew my attention to the fact that I was trying to save a mythical woman rather than my children. And the sight of my daughter risking her own life to save her brother, whom I thought she despised. This event put into my mind that I might be wrong about every single emotional relationship in my purview, and that I should, instead of trying to be clever, simply pump out as much love from my tiny store as I could, whether or not it is reciprocated. This I have tried to do.

I am also happy to say that I attended my daughter's performance in *A Midsummer Night's Dream* (a smash, by the way, she stole the show) without nausea, and while I will perhaps never be a theater aficionado, that particular neurotic tic seems to be over. I spend a good deal of time with Niko, mainly sitting quietly with him, but a few months ago he asked if I would teach him to swim, and also to lift weights. He will still not look directly at me, but sometimes, when I touch him, he does not shrink away.

Paul is back in his mission, properly humbled and terribly affected by the death of Mickey Haas, although I have told him repeatedly that this was my fault and not his. All I had to do was call the police and tell them the whole story, and they would have investigated, and Pascoe's lies would have surfaced immediately and everything would have worked out fine, the letters and play authenticated, etc. That Pascoe! A Yank priest shows up and asks if he knows anything about a forged unknown play by Shakespeare and *of course* he says, Oh, yes, Father, done it myself, didn't I, and for fifty grand I'll tell you the whole thing. And Paul fell for it; I suppose there is such a thing as being too clever, too suspicious.

Miri has left her business, which I have to say here for the record was a high-class call girl ring. Shvanov was deeply involved in it, of course, and his arrest has done her a world of good. She is much with Paul now, doing good works. She still looks fabulous and wears a jeweled crucifix at all times and with all her outfits.

Dad was able to slip away in his characteristic fashion, and I find that, after seeing him again, he is not the cancer on my spirit that he once was. Do I believe the version of my past he conveyed to me in that limo? Perhaps. It hardly matters at this point. I suppose I have forgiven him.

I miss Mickey Haas. Even a dreamed-up best pal is better than no best pal at all. All three of the wives showed up at the funeral and all of us were as phony and civilized as could be. In the end he was true to his profession and to his artistic judgment, literally going through fire to save his Precious. How many members of the Modern Language Association could say the same?

Crosetti seems to be doing well. I ran into him and Carolyn Rolly with the two children a week or so ago on Canal just east of Lafayette. It was a Saturday, and I had just finished a dim sum lunch with a couple of guys I went to law school with who were visiting town, and I was on the street looking for Omar and the Lincoln when they hove into view. We chatted briefly and a little awkwardly. Carolyn has washed the camouflaging dark out of her hair, for the blond she showed me as Miranda is her natural color and her eyes are bright blue, not the grape green she had assumed via tinted contacts in homage to Amalie's. There is not the slightest residual attraction. They live together in darkest arty Brooklyn, in a very nice loft bought by the sale of the Bracegirdle mss., and he has sold his script about the Bracegirdle affair, helped, I imagine, by the immense publicity surrounding the case. He thinks John Cusack will actually play him in the movie, although William Hurt is unfortunately not available for me.

I told him what I was doing at work and will now tell this record, which was and is working on the immense IP case occasioned by *Mary Queen of Scotland* by William S. The actual ms. is part of the evidence in *People v. Shvanov* (murder and kidnap) and has been temporarily sequestered in a municipal vault, but as soon as I'd received it from Crosetti I had taken the liberty of securing the thing digitally, transmuting the pages into pure intellectual property, a string of words. I am naturally not the lawyer of record, since I am a principal claimant to the IP; Ed Geller is my man on it, and we are all pals again. We are mainly fighting the British crown for the rights, and so I am now one with G. Washington and the other Founding Fathers. Should the case be decided in my favor I will perhaps for the first time be wealthier than my wife, and as I mentioned this possibility on that busy street, I felt a pang of guilt. This is my new moral sense, and I fear it will sharply limit my professional practice. I proposed to Crosetti that he and Carolyn deserved a big chunk of any value accruing from the sale or rights to the play, and that they should stop by the office and discuss this matter, and then Omar swooped across three lanes and pulled neatly to the curb. I asked if I could give them a lift and they said it was Brooklyn and I said no matter, and I could see in the flash of a look that passed between them that they did not care to spend that much social time with me. So I insisted, just for form's sake, and Crosetti said, 'Forget it, Jake, it's Chinatown,' and I said, 'I bet you've waited ten years to say that in real life,' and he laughed and we all of us laughed at that.

The Righteous Men

Sam Bourne

Someone is killing good people ... why?

A series of murders as far apart as the backstreets of New York, the crowded slums of India and the pristine beaches of Cape Town can't be connected. Can they?

Rookie *New York Times* reporter Will Monroe thinks not – until his beautiful wife Beth is kidnapped. The men holding her seem ready to kill without hesitation.

Desperate, Will follows a sinister trail that leads to a mysterious cult, fanatical followers of one of the world's oldest religions – right on his own doorstep. Now he must unravel ancient prophecies and riddles buried deep in the Bible to find a secret worth killing for, a secret on which the fate of humanity may depend. But with more victims dying every hour and each clue wrapped in layers of code, time is running out ...

'Compulsive reading ... successfully blends ancient teachings with the highly charged ways of the 21st century ... bears all the hallmarks of a blockbuster' *Daily Express*

'More readable than The Da Vinci Code – the sense of menace is darker and the characters more believable' *Esquire*

ISBN 978 0 00 720330 7

The Straw Men

Michael Marshall

Fourteen-year-old Sarah Becker has been abducted, snatched from a busy shopping precinct in downtown LA. Judging from the state of the girls whose bodies have already been found, her long hair will be hacked off and she will be tortured. She has about a week to live.

Fromer LA homicide detective John Zandt has an inside track on the perpetrator – his own daughter was one of the victims two years ago. But the key to Sarah's whereabouts lies with Ward Hopkins, a man with a past so secret not even he knows about it. His parents have just died in a car accident, but they leave Ward a bizarre message that leads him to question everything he once believed to be true.

As he begins to investigate his own past, Ward finds himself drawn into the shadowy, sinister world of the Straw Men – and into the desperate race to find Sarah, before her time runs out.

'Brilliantly written and scary as hell. A masterpiece'

STEPHEN KING

'Instantly moves him into the Thomas Harris division'

Guardian

ISBN 978-0-00-649998-5